Dragon's Ridge

Brian T.N. Gunney

A Russian Hill Press Book
United States · United Kingdom · Australia

R̶H̶P̶ Russian Hill Press

ISBN: 978-1-7351763-9-0 (softcover)
ISBN: 978-1-7378246-0-2 (ebook)

Library of Congress Control Number: 2021917087

Cover art by Cheryl Magellen and Scott Woodruff

For Lynn

CONTENTS

Dragon's Ridge

From Whence the Dragons Came

Some believed dragons descended from the creature slain by Saint George, then came to the Pyrénées with the Moors. Some claimed they were demons that escaped with the ash spewed from Mount Vesuvius in long-gone days when Rome ruled the world. Some swore dragons originated from a band of evil sorcerers who changed themselves into beasts to escape God's justice.

The archbishop declared that dragons were divine retribution for the sins of men.

1

A Perilous Act

The small frontier village of Savelle nestled among orchards, bathed in summer afternoon sunlight. Two rows of thatch-roofed cottages flanked the dirt road running by the lord's bailey on the east end. Halfway through the village, on the north side, the road passed the churchyard and sanctuary. Across the road, two cottages down, a child picked thyme sprigs in the orphanage croft. At the west end, between the last cottage and the first row of peach trees, was a clearing big enough for turning large ox-drawn wagons.

Seven orphans in bare feet and ragged clothing followed a train of laborers along a worn path through the orchard toward the clearing, finishing a long day of climbing trees and picking peaches. One boy guided a donkey hitched to a cart laden with peach baskets. Two lugged a ladder. Others carried baskets and harvesting tools. The youngest, in an oversized tunic made from an old sack, trailed far behind, twisting his forearm to study a fresh scrape oozing blood.

"Xabi, hurry up," called the oldest.

Xabi let his arm drop and trotted forth along the path.

The black dragon left the sun's glare, dove beyond the surrounding hills, and hugged the forest contours toward Savelle. It skimmed the treetops of the orchard, foregoing wing strokes for

3

stealth. The trees hid it from the villagers and muffled the sound of leathery wings cutting through the air. The size of a yearling horse, it appeared much larger because of its slim, elongated body and wings spanning three rows of peach trees. Approaching the clearing, it rose for a view of the open ground, then pitched into a shallow dive toward Xabi. Hearing the wings at last, the boy turned to look. The dark shape came at him like a hole to swallow him up. He tripped.

Black claws reached down but hooked only threadbare cloth as Xabi fell. The claws yanked him into the air, but the sack ripped. Xabi fell again, tumbling across the dirt, screaming. Unexpectedly light, the dragon swooped sharply upward. A wide shadow passed over the children. They looked up, terror washing over their faces.

"Dragon! Dragon!"

Overlapping shouts and screams carried the alarm down the road. "Dragon to the west! God save us." People outside ran for their homes, crossing themselves and murmuring prayers. Some barged through the nearest door they could open. Mothers called for their children. A crowd converged on the sanctuary's door, pushing through. Outside the lord's home, a pig temporarily escaped slaughter as the butcher brought it back in. Wagons, baskets, planks of wood, heads of cabbage, and bundles of clothing were abandoned in the road. The donkey brayed and ran away with the peach cart.

A young peasant woman ran out of the orphanage. Her eyes went to the sky, then to the returning children. "Quick, quick," she shouted. "Leave everything. Just drop them!"

Tools clanged, baskets bounced, and peaches scattered on the ground. She dashed toward the panicked Xabi.

"Isodore!" he cried, his face sand-scraped and contorted with terror. Isodore passed four cottages racing to the clearing. She took his hand, eyeing the spinous blot turning overhead.

Still ascending, the dragon bent its neck down, sorting through prey scrambling below.

Isodore crossed herself with one hand and pulled Xabi along with the other. "Hurry!"

Atop its arc, the creature banked then dove along a sickle-blade trajectory, swinging back to the cottages for a run at the stragglers.

"It's coming!" Xabi cried again, twisting to look at the approaching monster.

"Don't look. Just run!" Isodore pulled him forward to shield him. She fumbled to untie her dirty apron. Ahead of her, the children dashed through the yard and into their orphanage.

"Faster!" she screamed at Xabi, then brought the crumpled apron up to her mouth, whispering desperately into it. She glanced back and flung it into the air.

The apron sailed toward the dragon, unfurled, and drifted down. The beast rose to pass above the cloth, and reset its aim for Isodore. Its claws opened. Its eyes already had her.

A second later, the apron blew into the dragon's face. The beast whipped its neck backward, shaking its head to let the wind strip the cloth away. But the flimsy cloth had caught fast on a bristling crown of horns.

Blinded, distracted, and facing backward, the dragon dropped too low. Its right wing clipped and shattered an abandoned wagon. Its elongated body cranked to one side, and crashed, bounced, then tumbled on the dirt road. Wings folded, it passed Isodore. Its spinning tail swept her legs out and she too went down.

The beast spread its limbs to stop. It pushed itself upright. Still blinded by the apron, it roared and snapped its neck side to side.

Isodore's dark hair had fallen out of its bun and whipped across her face. She shook it off, took one look at the black-scaled creature next to her, and choked. She scrambled away, gathering the long tunic in her hands, and ran.

The maddened beast hooked a wing claw on the apron to pull it off. The fabric tore but held. The dragon roared again, pointed its muzzle at the ground, and sent a burst of fire through the apron. The flame deflected off the ground and incinerated the middle of the cloth. The creature flung off the burning hem and looked for Isodore.

She ran for the orphanage, into which Xabi had dashed. Another boy was holding the door ajar for her, fear on his face and courage draining away.

The dragon vaulted into the air, driving hard to catch up, but it had lost too much time. It cocked back its neck, chin to its shoulders, then threw the head forward and spat. A barrage of fireballs whirred over Isodore. The boy slammed the door shut an instant before burning dragon mucus splattered across it. Flames licked at the thatch overhang.

Isodore angled toward the church on the other side of the road. If she could make the dragon overshoot it, she could escape. By the time it circled around to look for her, Father Serafin would have let her in. Even if the dragon burned down the sanctuary, she would be safe, for beneath the structure, the villagers had dug an underground chamber to shelter from dragons.

To trick the beast, she swerved right before turning sharply left, aiming for the alley between the church and parsonage. The beast took her feint, then corrected, throwing one leg out to catch her. A hooked claw whipped down her shoulder, plunged into her chest, and yanked her backward. Long, thick toes wrapped under both of her arms. The dragon pitched up. She swung under it, dragging her feet across the dirt, and was lifted into the air, while her shadow continued down the road, attached to the dragon's.

A sharp pain wrenched her above the right breast. A talon longer than her hand had stabbed her below the collarbone. The toe's grip pressed the entire length of its hook into her. She screamed and grasped the beast's ankle with both hands to take some of her weight off the claw. The creature's other foot reached down and hastily wrapped around the first to secure the tenuous hold. Broad, leathery wings swept down, striking her flailing legs, dragging her into the sky. The dragon ascended fast, flapping with such power that wind swirled and ripped each time the wings came down. The beast turned from the village as it rose, escaping to the south with Isodore dangling below, her tunic fluttering in the wind.

She struggled to keep her weight off the claw in her chest. The beast struggled as well, trying to secure the grip of its first foot, but that foot was trapped under the more secure second grip. Each time it shifted, she felt the claw move deeper inside her, and she screamed.

Finally, the dragon swooped upward and lurched to a midair stop. It swung her forward and released her. She gasped as her body came free and spun in the air before the beast. For an instant, she came face to face with it—two searing, crimson eyes and a breeze of warm air from a mouthful of sharp teeth. Then she dropped.

But she wasn't free.

It caught her again as she fell, one foot around her thighs and the other around her chest. The dragon pitched into a steep dive. Its long neck stretched earthward. The wind rose again past them, and giant wings opened, swinging the beast back into level flight with such a pull that she thought she would slip out of its hold. Blood leaked from the wound below her collarbone and seeped into her muddy, soot-smeared tunic.

Behind them, the village of Savelle shrank away. The dragon climbed out of range of archers' arrows. But there were neither archers nor dragonslayers in the area. The attack had been a complete surprise, leaving the village littered with the stuff of daily life but devoid of people. The only signs of the dragon's attack were a shattered wagon and the burning thatch of the orphanage.

A whimper came up through Isodore's chest as she watched her village shrink away. "No."

When the rhythm of the dragon's wings steadied, she turned her head forward, shaking windblown hair out of her eyes. Ahead, to her horror, was a ragged horizon: the Pyrénées range, known for centuries as Dragon's Ridge.

2

Marauders

The dragon carried Isodore south, up the river from Savelle, one of many rivers that kept the Independent Duchy of Gascony fertile and green. Savelle was a frontier village. No living settlements stood between it and Dragon's Ridge.

Centuries before, Gascony had faced enemies in three directions. Muslims invaded from the east, Carolingian Franks ruled from the north, and Asturians attacked from the west. The Duchy survived, at times through tenuous alliances with one enemy against another. Seeking security, Lupus, the Duke of Gascony, expanded southward, up to the Pyrénéan foothills. His armies drove the pagan woodlanders from the most bountiful lands by the rivers and brought the Duchy's southern frontier under his rule. Peasants moved in and cleared virgin woods to cultivate farmland, vineyards, and orchards. Generations lived in relative stability.

Then came the dragons.

Villages, rivers, and roads lay exposed and vulnerable, unlike the dense forest canopy, under which the woodland clans lived safely. Dragons inhabited the mountains and terrorized southern Gascony. The infestation grew over the years.

Freeholders abandoned their lands and serfs begged their lords to let them go. But the labor of cutting trees and pulling roots was too great to give up. The noblemen united their armies to counter their common enemy.

Not a single dragon fell.

The marauders soared overhead with impunity, watching troops by day, raining fire on their camps at night, ambushing them from fog banks. Pastoral fields provided no cover. No armor held against dragon teeth, no arrows could slow them, no lance could come close. Warriors, blinded by flames, were snatched and torn like rag dolls. Knights, the supreme new warriors of men's battlefields, died by the dozens. Infantries scattered, leaving the beasts to feast on the dead in the hellish aftermath.

People suffered and prayed and wondered where their God was.

Airardus, the Archbishop of Auch, responded, pointing his finger and pounding his fist. "God is indeed watching, and He sees everything we do. Every sin, whether it be in the fields or in your cottages, in the light of day or the dead of night. The dragons are divine retribution for all our sins. For your sins! We must all renounce sin in every form and root out evil from Gascony. Else, He will send more of the beasts."

People jailed their thieves and burglars, hanged their bandits and murderers, burned their witches and heretics, stoned their prostitutes and adulterers, and converted pagans at knife point.

But the dragons kept coming.

Settlements closest to Dragon's Ridge suffered the most. Close to the mountains, the marauders killed the most prized animals, horses and cows. Farther away, they took smaller prey that they could carry—goats, lambs, foals, men, women, and children. Fearing their dragon lords more than their noble lords, villagers fled north, risking capture by men to escape beasts. The southern lords abandoned their estates, turning land back to the duke to rule. In truth, no one ruled there but dragons.

The land lay fallow for generations. Trees and meadows reclaimed what the woodlanders once inhabited. Woodlander clans returned and, because they dwelled in forest cover, lived successfully with the dragon threat. Marauders searching for prey often found deer, boars, wolves, bears, and the occasional woodlander before reaching Gascony's villages. But frontier settlements like Savelle remained easy prey for any dragon that made the long flight over the forests.

THE ARCHBISHOP CALLED for an army of dragonslayers to protect Christendom. The noblemen, still nursing their humiliating defeats, balked.

The Duchy had other threats at hand—real threats—Duke Seguin II argued in quarrelsome meetings with Archbishop Airardus. Upon the death of King Louis the Pious, his sons rushed the Frankish kingdom into civil war, sowing turmoil and deepening the duke's suspicion of them and their endless greed. Danish raiders demolished Paris. Closer to Gascony, they killed the Duke of Bordeaux. The Danish longboats cruised unchallenged up the Loire, Seine, and Garonne Rivers, and the duke was convinced that only the fear of dragons kept them off his waterways.

The mission of saving Gascony's Christians from the dragon scourge fell to the Church. Airardus demanded a portion of the Duchy's taxes and fighting men for dragonslaying. Seguin assented, eager to avoid extending his record of losses against dragons and a conflict with the Church, which could weaken his authority. The archbishop levied taxes to train and equip his fledgling corps. After suffering terrible losses, the corps learned and, in time, systematically refined the art of subduing and killing dragons. They began to beat back the marauders. For a time, the future brightened. Regard for the Church rose. Droves of pagans converted, uncoerced. The corps' popularity and the archbishop's influence grew as the displays of Gascony's churches and cathedrals were filled with the skulls of dragons.

3

World's End

The land beyond the frontier was a carpet of forest canopy, cut through by meandering waterways and punctuated with the remains of long-abandoned settlements. The black dragon carried Isodore's limp body deep into this territory. It flew over a boat resting on one side, decomposing in the shallow bend of a river. Miles later, it passed the ruins of a village: rows of apple trees choked by brush, the charred husk of a church occupied by grass, and the broken dome of a brick oven. The mountain range, once crowning a distant horizon, now loomed ahead like palisades at the end of the world.

The dragon was breathing hard, grunting, and often peering down at Isodore. It slowed and dropped, skimming the treetops, flying so low at times that Isodore's dangling arms brushed the branches.

The rivers narrowed, then disappeared under a continuous canopy. The plain, too, narrowed as foothills rose on either side, channeling the dragon toward a valley that penetrated the mountain range. Isodore's captor flew along the valley, into the shadows of a towering landscape.

After a half hour in the air, she was cold from the wind and stiff from being claw-bound. Her chest had swelled from the deep wound. Tips of the dragon's claws dug through her skin. A gust rolled over a hill crest, tossing the broad wings. Startled by the motion, she looked around but, surrounded by mountains, saw only an alien world.

The dragon turned up a smaller, steeper valley. Forced to ascend more sharply, it strained to hold her above the treetops. As it climbed, it became noisier and angrier. It must be very hungry by now, thought Isodore. The end was near.

Grunting, the dragon veered into a slanted, boulder-strewn meadow. It dropped her on the grass just before hitting the ground itself. She rolled to a stop and struggled to her elbows. From behind, she saw the beast's ridged back rise and fall, undulating under deep rasping breaths. It arched its neck and let out a hollow, angry roar that echoed like replies from a line of dragons strung out along the valley.

The dragon's head swung toward Isodore, startling her with menacing red eyes. Turning on all fours, in a posture neither upright like a man nor level like a beast, its body followed. Its chest was a thick knot of muscles anchoring two triangular pectorals that coiled around the bases of impossibly long forelimbs. The limbs reached upward then turned at the elbows to bring its knuckles to ground, where spiny wing fingers swept up along the radius bones, past the high elbows. Thus the enormous wings became its arms and front legs. It rested on its knuckles, leaning forward like a gargoyle, tall as a man at the shoulders.

For an instant, she felt a pulse of hope. A small dragon, perhaps not as fierce, not as quick to anger, not as . . . malevolent. She tried to muster a plea, but it died inside as the beast crouched toward her, full of claws, teeth, and sinew. A big dragon could kill her with a single crushing bite. This one might tear her limb from limb in the effort.

It half walked, half crawled, grotesque in its human likeness. Its neck arched down, holding forth the skeletal, horse-shaped head ringed with horns. A demon in black scales, with eyes of hellfire, black pupils in a crimson sea.

Isodore tried to scoot away, but her body failed her. The beast closed in. Behind heavy breaths, a deep growl rumbled across two rows of sharp, discolored teeth. It circled with its head inches from hers.

She buried her head in her arms, shaking. The dragon radiated heat. Hot breaths struck her back, carrying a strange smell—like a warm tavern. She squeezed shut her eyes, hastily crossing herself. The dragon completed its circle and stopped. She suppressed a scream, waiting for the bite.

Suddenly, the seething breaths stopped. The radiant heat faded, leaving her face cool again. The air went still.

When she opened her eyes, the dragon had withdrawn. It retreated to settle at a mass of boulders twenty paces away. Its neck stretched toward her, watching, breathing. She turned away, feeling strangely violated by the stare, as though it could reach into her mind.

Foreboding mountains loomed over the valley, unlike anything she had ever seen in a life in the lowland. They were majestic and frightening, compounding her despair with their grim presence.

She thought of her betrothed. Surely he would come searching for her once he learned of her abduction. He was brave, and it was his bravery that moved her to action when the dragon attacked, his bravery that she felt when she ran out to help her children.

But she knew he would never come. It wasn't a question of his courage but of futility. Even dragonslayers do not venture into the mountains the beasts made their home. Anyone taken is presumed dead and devoured.

She would be dead by morning. She should be dead already.

The sun went down. Everything before her dimmed: the meadow, the mountainsides, the sky, hope. Bats fluttered. Wolves howled. Owls crossed overhead. Harbingers of death, they seemed to come for her this night.

She worried about her children and felt their distress weighing down on her own. The puncture in her chest had stopped bleeding and her arm still functioned, but the sharp, pulsing pain was there to stay.

Cold descended. It bit at her fingers and toes, touched her through her clothes, and worked into her bones. She pulled her legs into her tunic and wrapped her arms around them to keep warm. Her body shivered. Her teeth chattered.

A shadow stirred by the boulders. A broad, dark shape rose from the ground and approached her, crouching on tall spidery forelimbs. The dragon stopped face to face with her. She closed her eyes, crossed herself again, and prayed. Ironically, its heat momentarily dampened the cold.

A sudden gust hit her, tossing her hair and tunic. Another blew down from above. She opened her eyes to find the beast had taken flight. It hadn't gone far before she lost it against the dark mountainside. She didn't wonder long about why it had left her but looked for an escape. There was no moon, but she could see enough to go, step by step. She rose halfway to her feet, then paused. Could it be so easy?

The dragon had flown, which meant it could see. Many animals were at home in the dark. Dragons could see through fog and mist; that was well known. Could the creature be watching her still?

Out of the darkness came a creaking sound, pulsing louder and louder. A tree was bending. Pops and cracks preceded the crescendo of a large branch breaking under unrelenting force. It wasn't far. The sound of those enormous wings returned, beating closer and closer, fast and hard.

A whistle ended with a crack, as a stiff branch crashed down from the night sky. Dead and brittle, it shattered against a boulder. The dragon landed, facing her, watching her. It pinned the branch under its hind legs and tore limbs off with its jaws. It swung thick branches into the boulder, breaking them. Sharp cracks echoed in the night.

The creature gathered some of the wood into a big pile. It drew a deep breath, worked its muzzle down to the bottom of the pile and exhaled. A yellow glow shone through the lacework of branches, growing brighter as the dragon breathed. Orange sparks flitted through the air. A fireball engulfed the wood. The beast drew up slowly, lingering as if it enjoyed the flames against its scales. It moved its head aside and turned its fearsome eyes to hers. Flames curled up around its jaw while remnants of the fiery breath glowed behind silhouettes of pointed teeth.

The dragon retreated to the mass of boulders. In time, Isodore moved to the flames for warmth. She fed the fire with the remains of the shattered branch. The dragon's head rose each time she stood, discouraging any hope of escape.

She couldn't sleep or lie down, because the grass was wet and cold. But she survived to dawn, while the owls and their premonitions were nowhere to be seen. In their place, birds twittered gaily. When the sun peered over the mountains into the meadow, Isodore was hungry, thirsty, and anxious. The dragon's eyes were on her while she stood by the bed of embers to let the sun warm her.

Scanning her surroundings in the fresh light, her eyes fell on a line of brush cutting through the meadow. There was a stream. She looked to the dragon, to the stream, back to the dragon.

"I'm thirsty," she said. "I just need . . . some water."

It made no move, and she felt foolish. She made her way to the stream, looking back every few steps to ensure it wasn't coming after her.

On a flat rock by the bank, she dropped to her knees and scooped handfuls of cold water to drink, then dried her hands on her tunic. She lifted the blood-stained neckline of the tunic to examine the wound on her chest, a swollen, purple mound around a dark, glistening hole. The beast had had its claw in there—the entire claw, pressing into her chest.

She shuddered and looked back at the dragon. Why had it not killed her? Mercy? Or was it saving her for something else? A clutch of baby dragons? Was she to be offered to a mate? A greater dragon? Its own dragon lord?

Wincing at the pain, she took her right arm out over the top of her tunic to expose the wound. She bent over and splashed cool, soothing water on it, rinsing away dried blood and washing off what was encrusted on her tunic. Blood-stained water ran down her arm, carrying bits of dirt that the claw had left in the wound.

At the lower end of the slanted meadow was the edge of the thin forest. She stared longingly at it, knowing the dragon couldn't see her face. The woods were too sparse to hide her, but dense enough to help her. If she could get there first, she could dash through it while the beast would have to weave around the trees.

The dragon could burn her with its fire. It could snatch her before she reached the woods. But to stay captive would mean certain death. She put her arm back into its sleeve, her eyes still on the woods.

"No."

The voice came from behind—almost too deep to be human. She whirled around to find the beast staring at her. Silently, it had come within fifty paces of her. She looked around, but no one else was in sight. She turned back to the dragon, in disbelief.

"Did you . . . ? You can speak?"

The dragon's eyes fixed on her, as if it understood.

The beast could speak? Never in any story or song had there been a dragon that spoke. Dragonslayers never talked of such things. Could she beg for her life?

"What . . . What do you want with me?"

The dragon lowered its head. Could she reason with it? Would it agree to ransom her? Perhaps the Church, or her betrothed's family, would agree to the ransom. Tax collectors often reported dragons stealing riches from their caravans. Dragons valued riches.

Didn't they?

She glanced toward the woods, trying to decide whether to plead or to run. Before she could gauge the dragon's receptiveness to reason, she saw it move in her peripheral vision, the dark creature taking slow steps toward her.

A vague instinct convinced her that, despite the stories she'd heard, this creature cared nothing for riches. Despite her hope, she didn't want to know just how little silver her life was worth. Her best chance might be now, while there was still some distance between her and the beast.

She grabbed two fistfuls of her skirt and ran. Her feet splashed through the ankle-deep stream and her shoes filled with cold water. She immediately slipped on algae-covered rocks and threw down her hands to break her fall. The left hand landed on more slippery rocks, and her weight pounded down on the twisted joint.

She grunted and stumbled to her feet, ignoring the injury. On the other side of the stream, she ran for her life, bursting through the stream-side brush without a thought, without looking back, knowing the dragon was coming for her. She had a straight path, but the wet skirt hobbled her. She gathered it back in her hands while running as fast as the task allowed. Her footsteps wobbled on the uneven ground.

The woods came within reach. She saw her entry point between two trees, her path into denser forest.

But it had taken too long. The dragon's shadow fell on her. Clawed toes closed around her chest and thighs. Instead of running into the woods, she sailed over them.

4

Nest of Bones

Quiet and strong after its rest, the dragon headed up the narrow, steep valley with Isodore in its grip. Wind chilled her through her soaked tunic, except where the dragon held her.

Its toes had a warmth, the same that she felt yesterday when she was too much in despair for contemplation. The creature radiated heat and was warm to the touch. Curious, she brought her hand to the toe that came across her chest and felt the beast's warmth. She rubbed the crinkly dry skin under her fingertips. Realizing what she had done, she recoiled in horror.

Trees, grass, and rocks slipped away below her, as Savelle had, into forever. Carried through the folds of the mountains, she saw that Dragon's Ridge wasn't the single crest it appeared to be from afar. It was a convoluted landscape of mountains after mountains after mountains, whose ends she couldn't see, linked together to form a gigantic maze.

At higher elevations, meadow-lined valleys cradled lakes and streams. Creeks ran down the flanks of mountains in dark crevices and spilled over cliffs. A pressure deep in her head felt like her soul was being drawn out of her ears, but she moved her jaw and it disappeared.

The dragon took her up the narrow valley, into the barren, rocky heights. It passed through a three-sided chasm with blue lakes and rocky shores, then toward the notch of a rocky spine. The lakes they had passed, now far below, turned indigo, and boulders around them looked like pebbles.

Valleys lay in indifferent stillness, devoid of woods and life, while dizzying heights formed a world of their own, stark and foreboding. Mountain peaks towered like keeps across a desolate realm.

The dragon passed through the notch, turned right, and followed the spine for a short distance, its wingtip almost brushing the mountain. It ascended an escarpment and up a precipice, where a ledge protruded like a balcony from the steep mountainside. There, her captor deposited her with more grace than it had done the previous day. Without pausing, it continued, to a perch on the ridge above the ledge. Its wings sent blasts of wind, scattering a murder of crows pecking at the rotting remains of some dead creature.

As Isodore sat facing the sun, shivering in her wet clothing, her eyes registered, one by one, remnants of human belongings scattered around. Tattered clothing, ropes, broken spears, stiff shells of leather armor, and a Norman casque with a bent nose guard. The clothing was frayed and faded, but retained pale shades of their former colors. Further away, a pile of rocks turned out to be bones slowly giving up their colors to the intense sun.

She looked around. The ledge was some twenty paces from north to south along the mountainside and three paces deep at its widest. It tapered at each end, like half an ash leaf. It canted slightly downward, toward the morning sun. On her left was dirt, sand, then bare granite toward the northern end. The southern ground, to her right, was grass-lined. Dragon footprints crisscrossed the muddy grass.

The bone pile occupied the northern end. Skulls of calves, colts, deer, boars, wolves or dogs, and three humans stared in all directions. Atop the pile lay the dirty remains of recent kills in varying stages of decay. The scattered crows reassembled to pick over bits of meat in the crevices of a foal skeleton swarming with flies. Below the cliff, more bones lay piled in a second graveyard.

She found the remains of a surcoat among the bones. Dragon teeth had perforated it, creating a line of holes, each inked by dull blood stains. The chest bore a gold insignia, not yet faded from sun exposure—a cross above the arched neck of a suffering dragon. This beast had recently killed a dragonslayer. She dropped the surcoat, wrapped her arms around herself, and tried, in vain, not to despair.

Like a giant gargoyle king on his high perch, the dragon watched her from the ridge, thirty feet up the mountain. The ridge line ran north, curved to the east, and dropped, so she could see over it. Beyond, there was a narrow section of Gascony, but nothing else of the world she knew. She looked at the blood-stained surcoat and the bones around her and began to cry.

THE DRAGON LEFT before afternoon, to hunt or abduct and torment more helpless people, or because it grew bored watching her—Isodore didn't know. She wrung out her tunic and undergarment as much as her swollen wrist and shoulder would let her. Her skin was punctured in the chest, abdomen, and thighs from the dragon claws, but none as deep or painful as the hole below her collarbone. Her clothes dried fast in the arid mountain air and intense sunlight. But evening was much colder on the mountain than in the low lands. She gathered tattered bits of clothing and tucked them inside her tunic for insulation. With the surcoat wrapped around her shoulders, she huddled, shivering in a rock crevice still warm from the day's sun.

The dragon returned and swept up to the ledge from below. Its wings spanned the breadth of the ledge, enclosing Isodore between the mountain and a black-leather curtain. It stood for a second while the wings drew into spidery forelimbs and turned the knuckles toward the ground. Long, bony wing fingers held the membranes like leather drapery along the seven-foot-long radius bones. It approached on all fours, not angry like it had been yesterday, but its silence was every bit as menacing. Its neck extended the horn-crowned head toward her, and she shrank into the crevasse.

"There are no trees for fire," it said in a rumbling voice.

Isodore nodded.

"The cave is warm." Its head turned to guide her eyes to a long vertical shadow of a crack in the granite. She scanned the granite up and down, side to side. The crack was deeper than it first appeared, an opening hidden so well within its own shadow that it had escaped her notice all day.

The skeletal head turned back to her. "Go."

She swallowed. "My friends will pay for my safe return."

The dragon snorted, baring sharp teeth. Hot breath struck her face. She sprang to her feet and ran. She scrambled over rocks piled at the entrance and stumbled inside with a glance backward to see whether the monster was behind her.

The narrow, triangular entrance was three times her height and slanted like the mountainside. One of the cave's steep walls was, in fact, the sheer mountainside. The opposite wall was a slab of rock, leaning against the mountain like a book on a shelf. The space between formed the chamber, tall and narrow at the entrance, tapering to almost nothing at the far end. It was not so much a cave as a nook that children at play might hide in. A horse could fit inside, though it would have no room to turn around.

The cave was bare. Without a fire, she thought she might still die overnight, despite the roof over her. She sat, curled up against one wall, hungry, cold and lonely, though a bit less afraid than she had been the night before. At least she was away from the hideous beast.

Light suddenly dimmed inside the chamber. To her horror, a ragged silhouette filled the entrance. The dragon squeezed into the cave.

5

Child of the Woods

Hunger, cold, and loneliness were things that Isodore knew well. At age ten, or thereabouts, she lived in the forest after having escaped an orphanage. She stayed near the roads for fear of wild beasts in the deep woods. At night, she slept, curled up, under dense thickets.

She begged for food from travelers and learned to tell whom to trust and whom not to. Pilgrims were the kindest, for they keenly felt the eyes of God. But they were rare. Servants accompanying noblemen weren't particularly kind, but they often had leftovers to discard. Woodland heathens kept to themselves, except when trading with travelers. She had nothing to trade. When she begged, they told her to beg from her own kind. She feared the bandits, but indigent waifs had nothing of value, so they rarely bothered her. Some of them offered her food for information about the travelers on the road.

She tried to protect the people who were kind to her by pointing the bandits toward armed parties instead. Knights and their men were mean, arrogant, and reckless in their deadly squabbles. Unlike the bandits, they didn't waste their time on those who didn't challenge them. She gave them no reason to notice her. Their strength kept the bandits away, so she camped near them when she could. But she kept hidden, never trusting them to be kind. Some knights, however, were very chivalrous, even to little girls. She felt safest around these gentle knights.

She learned that begging was more effective after performing some chores, however unsolicited, and the work alleviated some of her shame. "Le' me help ye," she'd say. "I won' ask fer nothin' but yer trash." Some travelers would claim to have no leftovers, but they usually found some bit to give her, if she persisted.

One afternoon, a knight let her fetch water for him and his men while they rested. He sat apart, tearing into a loaf of bread as he watched her fill all the buckets from a trickling stream. After the ache-inducing task, she started gathering firewood for his camp.

"We don't need firewood," the knight called. "It's the middle of the day."

"But ye mus' be prepared," she replied. "By evenin', 'twill be too dark te find anythin'. The woods by the road 'ave been picked clean. Ye'd 'ave te search far, and good, dry wood's 'ard te find. And 'tis goin' te rain. Yeh." She glanced at the pitiful clouds above, then quickly returned to her work, hoping to have a good bundle to fill him with guilt, should he prove stingy. He watched her flit about, as he chewed his bread and cheese and sipped from a wine skin.

"Done." She dropped the last bundle as close to him as she dared. "I even got kindlin' for ye. Driest in these parts. Awfully 'ard te find." She nodded at the pile and wiped sweat from her brow. "I'll say, ye should 'ave no want of firewood t'night. Oh, no. Ye can jus' rest an' enjoy yerself, ye an' yer men."

"We're not staying here tonight. We have farther to go." He broke off a piece of his bread, reached toward her, and placed it on the ground, then added a chunk of cheese. "That's yours, if you want it." He continued eating.

She never had to put on her sad, hungry face. She didn't have to beg. She approached, no closer than absolutely necessary, and snatched up the food.

He held out the skin. "Wine?"

She took a hasty gulp before he could change his mind, then spat it back out, trying to rid her tongue of the sour, bitter taste. Wine dribbled down her chin, adding more color to her filthy tunic.

The knight gave a hearty laugh. "Can you believe people pay for such things? The bread should wipe away that taste, if you don't care for it."

She eyed him, then bit off a piece of bread. Her teeth sank in. It wasn't the rock-hard leftovers she typically received.

He sniffed the skin's spout. "Wine is perhaps better appreciated by the grown. Where are your parents? I shall give to them what you've earned but can't enjoy."

She looked over her shoulder, as she always did when asked about her parents. "They're restin'. They don' like bein' disturbed."

He nodded. "Of course. They must be tired, if they're as hardworking as you are. What shall I call you?"

She forgot how to answer, because for two years no one had asked for her name.

The knight lifted his brows expectantly, and his sparkling brown eyes caught hers. A dark mane of hair rested on his shoulders, and a thick mustache bent down to his jawline, framing a mouth that held a constant little smile. He was neither young nor old, but at an age where a playful countenance could disguise a skilled warrior.

"Do you have a name?" he asked again.

"Uh, no," she replied, then realized she had answered a slightly different question: Whether anyone still called her by name.

"Oh. Well, I suppose you don't need one out here, do you? Who's going to call on you after I leave, eh? The wild animals have no names, and they seem happier than most people with names." He laughed.

She didn't know what to make of the knight. The attention was a break from her lonely existence, but she had learned to be wary of unexpected things.

"So, this is your home, yes?" he asked.

"Yeh." She looked around at the trees and brush, an odd place to call home, yet so familiar to her that she felt less afraid in the woods than near villages full of mean, stingy folk. She hadn't called anything home for a long time, and it was comforting to have a home. Whenever someone gave chase, it was the trees that protected her and the brush that hid her.

"We're a lot alike," the knight said. "I've spent a lot of time in the woods, too. You might say it was my home. For nearly a year. But that was in England. Beautiful forests, England. Very cold though. Enough to make me long for home."

"What did ye do there?"

"Mostly hid from the Normans." He laughed again, as though hiding from the Normans was a fun game. "Much like you'd have to hide, too, from knights and bandits, eh?"

She shrugged. "Why'd ye go t'England?"

"To make war, of course. I was a young man, there to fight for Harold, the rightful king of England, against that Norman bastard William. Alas, our campaign failed. Most of my band was killed and I was captured."

She took a bite of the cheese, and her cheeks pinched out a coat of saliva as the smooth, salty taste spread through her mouth. Heavenly cheese.

"I survived, but William's men pursued me for nearly a year. Would you like to hear how I escaped?"

She nodded. No one had ever offered to tell her a story like this before.

"Listen carefully. I think you can learn a few things to help you survive in these woods." He winked.

He said he had killed dozens of men hunting him in the forest, angering his pursuers. He escaped captivity by disarming one of his guards. He escaped with the guard's spear, but nothing else. He threw the spear at one of his pursuers and took the man's sword, his weapon of choice, with which he defeated and chased off the rest. He survived by poaching livestock and stealing clothes, which helped to disguise him. Eventually, he came to Plymouth, where he obtained passage across the channel by offering up his modest plunder and making threats against the captain's family, should the man inform the authorities of his suspicious passenger. "The worst part was having to trust that captain. Hard to trust someone you've just met. But I had no choice. I had no armor and no idea how many Normans would stand in my way. It was frightening." He glanced at her. "Aren't you afraid, living out here? With bandits and drunk men about?"

She had been afraid at first but felt capable now, after two years without serious harm. Besides, she had ways of protecting herself, which she would never tell him. "The woodlanders aren't afraid, so why should I be?"

The knight laughed. "You're more brazen than William's men."

She shrugged and put the last bites of the bread and cheese into her mouth. She liked showing him she wasn't afraid.

"Are you still hungry?" he asked.

Her mouth watered at the prospect of more of his good food.

"You're a diligent worker, little one. You shouldn't have to beg out here. There's an orphanage run by a friend of mine. You would be well fed there, and safe."

She leaned away from him, her hopes deflated.

"He's a good man, very kind. Children love him. Children just like you."

"No." She broke eye contact, pretending to look on the ground while checking her escape route and listening for footsteps from behind. This was what she did when bandits stopped to talk with her, so they couldn't surround her. She didn't like where the knight was taking this conversation, but she was still very hungry and thought she could get him to give her more food.

"You know, you may think you have nothing of value, but you have something men will eventually want. And when—"

"Yer a very kind man yourself. What's yer name, that I might remember ye?" She tried to sound like a noble lass but didn't know why. To show him he had the wrong idea about her, she supposed.

"I am Sir Rowan of Bazas, a Knight of the Cross, at your service." He rose to one knee, spread his arms and bowed deeply to her. It made her giggle. When he glanced up, she was taken by the way he looked at her, the twinkle in his eyes and a mischievous smile.

This was the first time she had ever conversed with a knight with the title of "Sir." These knights were held in high regard in the Duchy, though she wasn't sure why. Sir Rowan explained that they were sworn to conduct themselves by Auch's chivalric code. They were entirely different from common knights, for whom might made right. Isodore knew to stay away from that kind of knights.

"Are ye a dragonslayer?" Dragonslayers were renowned, not only for bravery in the face of seemingly invincible beasts. They were the most popular knights in the kingdom.

"No. But I once squired for one," said Sir Rowan.

She slumped under the disappointment. "Why didn't ye become a dragonslayer?"

"I, ah, like my sword too much." He tapped the hilt of his weapon, winked, and sat back down.

"Dragonslayers aren't allowed their swords?"

"Certainly they are. But swords against dragons?" He laughed, "That's like daggers against bears. Have you ever tried that?"

She shook her head. "Why are ye a Knight of the Cross if yer not a dragonslayer?"

"Would you have me be a common knight?"

Isodore drew back and shook her head.

Her acquaintance laughed. "In the old days, all Knights of the Cross were dragonslayers. Now, there aren't so many dragonslayers anymore and most Knights of the Cross, like me, are retained by northern counts, to keep the Franks from feeling too bold."

Isodore nodded.

"But," Sir Rowan held up a finger, "not all dubbed knights are the same. Knights of the Crown are more chivalrous than the norm, but they don't do so well adhering to their vows, I'm afraid."

"Knights o' t' Crown?"

"They receive their titles from the duke. Instead of a golden cross, like this," he motioned to the insignia emblazoned across his surcoat, "they carry the Duchy's emblem. They aren't many, but they are also addressed by 'Sir.'"

Isodore stored that away, anticipating its usefulness. She saw Sir Rowan studying her, waiting patiently for her to finish her mental notes.

"There is another difference. Do you know what that is?" She didn't. "Knights of the Cross serve all, including you, dear lass."

"Me?" She knew they served all, but she didn't think that included her.

"Yes! It was a promise by Archbishop Airardus, who created the dragonslayer corps. It was the only way he could convince people to accept his new tax, but that's beside the point. Dragonslayers were chivalrous from their inception two centuries ago. That is why Knights of the Cross are the greatest knights in the land."

"Century?"

"That's a hundred years, ragamuffin."

It sounded like an eternity to her.

"My, my," said Sir Rowan. "This is a very pleasant conversation, but my men and I do have a ways to travel today."

Isodore was disappointed. She hadn't expected him to talk with her for so long, or even care about her curiosity. No one had ever treated her so kindly, and she wanted him to stay longer.

He peered through the trees, back at the men milling around. "I shall have my men prepare for departure. I'll give you some salt pork, if you brush down my horses and pack that firewood into the donkey's bags so we can take it with us."

She agreed. He went to talk with his men while she worked. When he returned, he lounged at the foot of a tree. He dozed off while she worked. She whispered his name and he woke, complimented her on her work and proceeded to saddle the horse. She helped him tie the wood bundle onto the donkey. When his saddle was cinched in place, he glanced at his men, who were standing by their horses, chatting. "They're enjoying their rest far too much, don't you think? I should go help them, but . . . Have you ever ridden a horse?"

She shook her head.

"How would you like to learn while we wait for them?" he whispered.

She gasped and nodded, speechless.

He helped her onto the saddle. Her feet didn't reach the stirrups. "It's all right," he said, "I'll keep you from falling off." He mounted behind her. As they rode by his men, he said, "We'll be right back." They watched him with mild interest. Sir Rowan slowly sped up, asking each time, "Would you like to go faster?" Isodore said yes each time. She enjoyed the sheer excitement of being carried along with no effort.

After some time, she realized he had not taught her anything. He only corrected her posture, but he was controlling the horse himself.

"Give me the reins," she said. "I want te try."

"Of course, in due time. For now, try to relax. Don't be so stiff. Let yourself move with the horse, like I am doing."

She couldn't relax. They had left his camp far behind. Her suspicion grew. "I've not told me parents I'm with ye. Let's go back te see 'em."

"Of course," he said with a pleasantness that she no longer trusted. "But first, how about if we get some food for them. Hmm? They won't be angry. It's hard to be angry while receiving food."

She wished she'd not gotten on the horse with him. Panic roiled in her. She grabbed for the reins, but he was too quick. He held the reins in one hand and wrapped his other arm around her. "Ye said ye'd teach me t'ride."

"I am teaching you. This is how everyone learns. You must master the basics first."

She had been tricked. She tried to push away his arm. The more she struggled, the tighter it clamped down across her chest.

"Yer no Knight o' the Cross!" she protested.

But it was too late.

6

A View from Heaven

Isodore did fall asleep in the cave with the dragon. She was too tired to resist slumber, and it was better to die in her sleep than to watch as the dragon killed her. She didn't know if the dragon also slept, how it slept, or what it sounded like. She felt it looking at her when she fell asleep, and it was looking at her in the morning. Seeing the red eyes in its black silhouette, she sat up and pushed herself away, only to yelp from a terrible pain in her wrist. The joint was so swollen, it wouldn't bend.

The dragon growled and bent its neck toward the apex of the cave, reaching up like an enormous, barbed snake. Its underside glided over the canted surface. It put its forelimbs on the wall and crawled up, turning away from Isodore, toward the entrance. Its upper body followed, up the wall then over as it pivoted on its hind legs. Every foot of the creature passed before her until the tip of its tail trailed over the rock pile at the entrance. She placed a hand on her chest and caught her breath.

There was a faint, odd smell in the cave, like a tavern—strong ale, wine, and mix of spirits on a musty background of earth and oil. The smell of the beast.

A tongue of cold air slid down the boulder pile from the entrance, no longer blocked by the dragon. By the contrast, she realized that the cave wasn't cold. The creature had kept the chamber warm with its overpowering body heat.

She came out when the sun was high. The grass-lined, rock-walled valley lay before her. The world of her new, short life. She scanned the sky, looking for her captor, and wondered if she might see other dragons, perhaps its master. The old songs recounted how dragons once filled the skies, but she saw none. Now and then, she spotted dark wings in the distance, but she couldn't tell if it was an eagle two miles away or the dragon ten miles away. Either the bards had exaggerated or the archbishop had been right that the day of deliverance was near. Not that it mattered to her. There would be no deliverance for her unless she escaped.

She looked around. To the south, the ledge ended in a dizzying drop. On the other side of the drop, there was hope of climbing down, but the only way past the drop was flight. On the north end, smaller ledges allowed her to traverse well off the safety of the main ledge. One after another, however, they narrowed to nothing, and she turned back. Climbing down the cliff was hopeless. Merely looking down its sheer drop made her dizzy. Her last option was to go up. She climbed along the edge of the triangular slab that formed the cave, but she could get no farther than its fifteen-foot apex, halfway to the ridge above. The smooth, steep mountainside gave her little to hold on to. The dragon must have known that escape was impossible.

Further searches yielded one consolation, a gap at the small end of the cave. It was big enough for her to slip through. It only led out to the ledge, but the dragon wouldn't fit through this hole, so it was a place she could run to, should it get angry.

The dragon returned at dusk and dropped the hind quarter of a dog or a wolf, with a dangling vein and blood on the fur. If her captor meant to feed her, this was among the most unappetizing presentations she'd ever seen.

"I need fire to cook it," she said, stepping back for fear of an angry response. It had said there were no trees up here, so she didn't expect it to bring wood, but she didn't know what to do. It lowered its head and breathed its fire onto the carcass, which burned like a piece of trash and emitted a dry, nauseating odor. She half closed her eyes and nostrils to avoid the smoke and stench. On the other side of the fire, the dragon seemed to find the smoke even more unpleasant than she did. It pushed itself away and cocked its head back, narrowing its nostrils. The fire burned out. The offering looked like a burned piece of trash.

"You," said the dragon, relaxing its neck, "are hungry."

She knelt and parted the charred skin with her thumbs and held the wet pink flesh up to the dragon. It drew back again, in disgust.

"It's raw inside. It requires a sustained fire."

The dragon looked at her then reared and spread its wings. She turned her shoulder and put up an arm in a feeble defense. The beast tipped to one side, dropping one wing over the edge and kept rotating until its body went over as well. She crawled to the precipice and watched the black wings skimming dangerously close to the ramparts. It sped along, then lifted up and away without looking back.

Isodore returned to the meat, hungry, yet repulsed by the glistening pink flesh under blackened skin that smelled sweetly nauseating. The thought of tearing raw, bloody meat off the bone was too savage, even though her fast now surpassed thirty hours.

A half hour later, the dragon returned clutching three dead branches. It started a wood fire. She tried to skin the canine's hind quarters, but she had no knife and only one working hand. The dragon ripped skin apart for her with its claws. She cooked the meat, while it watched from its perch above, the same place she tried to climb to earlier but couldn't reach. She found a long bone to help hold the meat over the fire. There wasn't enough wood, so she only cooked one side. When the fire diminished, she ate the meat down to the uncooked part and left the rest surrounded by coals to cook further. Her hunger was sated by the bland but unexpectedly palatable meat.

She asked for water. The dragon brought her a chunk of white rock it broke off an expansive slab on the valley's south rim. The rock was cold, wet and slippery. It was light and miraculously turned to water where she touched it. She licked it to quench her thirst. She found it soft enough to scrape with her teeth. Using a sharp bone fragment, she chiseled off bits of the rock to put in her mouth, where they turned quickly to water.

When the sun went down, the dragon returned to the ledge. "The cave," it commanded.

She crawled in. It followed, blocking the entrance and warming the chamber with its body and breath. In the morning, she woke up hungry again, and alone. The dragon had gone. A host of vultures, crows, and flies were sharing the remains of her supper.

Pain pulsed in her chest wound, which was discolored, warm, and swollen, circled by concentric red rings. Her swollen wrist had turned purple, its throbbing pain now worse than the chest puncture. She held it against the cold water-rock to soothe and cool the pain while she sat by the edge of the precipice and gazed out.

She had never been on a mountain before. She looked down on clouds, a pure white undulating blanket covering the valleys between the mountain tops. The peaks looked peaceful, like castles in heaven.

Dark wings glided over the white expanse.

Dragons! Several of them. Against the bright clouds, they were easy to see. They flew in long, sweeping lines, disappearing into the clouds while others emerged. She wondered which was her captor. The closest one appeared dark red. The rest were too far away to tell. She watched the dragons until most of the clouds burned away and the textures of forest, rocks, and earth made it harder to see them.

Never before had she reflected on how the land she inhabited looked from above. Rivers lay like loose and aimless ribbons, glinting in the low morning sun. Cloud shadows moved quietly over the valley meadows and crawled up the mountains, a beautiful sight that, for brief moments, took her mind off her misery.

She saw her captor a few times that day when it flew past the ledge. It was patrolling the nearby ridges, gliding on wind that blew up the mountain. Its wings stretched wide and strong, even the slender fingers holding the tips. The wings' trailing edges curved gracefully backward, blending into the tail. It had the calm grace of the storks migrating through Gascony in the springs and autumns.

It felt strange to look down on dragons. The sight of one overhead was always terrifying. Having one crouch over her nearly killed her with fright. But from above, a dragon in flight looked so natural, peaceful. Even beautiful.

With a shiver, she realized that God in heaven saw dragons from above.

7

For Love of a Knight

A long road rose and fell over Gascony's gently rolling hills. It cut through woodland and connected villages, farms, fields and vineyards. Out of the woods galloped a horse bearing a knight. A skinny waif with tangled hair sat squirming in front of him, straining against the arm that clamped down across her chest.

"Let me go!" cried Isodore.

She tried to bite his arm but hurt only herself as her teeth crunched down on the links of his mail coat. She twisted left and right to throw off her captor, but his legs were braced in the stirrups while hers kicked at thin air. "Damn ye, knight! Get yer filthy hands off me! I'll have ye castrated by dogs!"

"Good heavens," said the knight. "Who taught you such manners? A pack of bandits?"

She swung a fist up to hit him but missed.

"Try that again and—"

She did, feeling her fist connect with the side of his head.

He sighed. "Please don't do that. You'll force me to be unkind to you."

"Yer already unkind t'me. Help!"

"I am not unkind to you. For the fourth time, I'm trying to help you."

"Ye tricked me!"

"I saved you the trouble of wrestling with me, didn't I? You could have been hurt."

She fought back harder, just to spite him, but it only made her angrier and more tired. It failed to annoy him in the least. She gave up, waited, then tried to reason with him.

"Where are ye takin' me?"

"To get you more food."

"I'm not 'ungry anymore, truly."

"And a bed."

The pieces of his scheme came together in her mind. "Te yer friend's orphanage?" He had mentioned this friend when he was charming her with his friendly talk. It had put her on guard. She wished she'd stayed on guard.

"Yes," he said tonelessly.

"But I'm no orphan. Me parents await me in t' woods. Truly, I'll take ye to 'em."

"You have no family, ragamuffin. If you had a family, you'd have a name."

"I do have a name! It's . . . Isodore." She hesitated because she didn't want to give anything to this trickster. She'd bet his name wasn't even Sir Rowan. But the pause only made her seem untruthful. "It's Isodore. Me name is Isodore."

He had made up his mind. "You are homeless, ragamuffin. Your clothes are too small and horry. You have no food, no shelter, no lord, no protection. You're fortunate to have survived till now."

"That's what ye think," she mouthed, knowing he couldn't see her face. The thought of an orphanage scared her sick, but she would not let him know. She wanted him off guard before trying another escape. She sat back, paying careful attention to the arm he kept around her, and watched for her opportunity. To encourage him to trust her, she asked about the orphanage, the work, its food, the children there, the headmistress. He made it sound rather pleasant. She pretended to believed him, while she planned.

At last, she felt his arm soften. She waited for the right time. They passed farm fields and reentered the woods, her element. As quickly and suddenly as she could, she threw off his arm and lurched from the horse.

The knight wasn't as inattentive as she had thought. She never cleared his arm. "Bravo! Very clever." He gathered her back in front of him, squeezing her tight, until she stopped struggling. "So, now you see why I must hold on to you the rest of the way."

"Let me go. Jus' let me go!"

"That wouldn't do, would it, after I told my men I was going to take you to the orphanage. They shall think you escaped me. What kind of a knight would I be to let a child escape like that?"

Anger poured out of her. She threw herself against his arm but he hardly budged. "Impostor! Yer no Knight of the Cross. Let me go or I'll tell the archbishop. 'E'll lop off yer pretty little head."

"Ah, that would be quite amusing. I shall take you to him, if you wish."

For the rest of the way, each time she so much as twitched, he pressed his arm into her as a warning. The road became more populated. They were approaching a town. She was so afraid, she wanted to cry, but she would not give him the satisfaction. She called to the passersby for help, but they only looked on as the knight waved to them.

"Good day, good day. No need for worry. She won't harm me." To her, he said, "You know, ragamuffin, if one of those people stops us, would he then return you to the woods, or perhaps present you to his lord?"

She swallowed and kept quiet. The town was surrounded by wheat fields and vineyards. Farming cottages ringed the exterior of the settlement. Blacksmith, carpenter, baker, tanner, and other shops clustered closer to the center. She'd never seen such a big town. On the far side, a keep watched over the surroundings from atop a motte. They rode in on the main thoroughfare and stopped in the grounds of the town's church.

"Julian?" called the knight. "Julian!"

After a moment, a portly man in a long brown robe emerged, squinting into the sky. "Rowan? Good heavens! What brings you . . . ? Oh. I see you have a companion."

"I just met her. I thought she'd enjoy a ride."

"'E abducted me!" shouted Isodore.

"Woodness." Julian shaded his eyes, looked to the knight, then back to her. "Abducted? Oh, come, child. You have to forgive Sir Rowan. I'm certain he had very good reasons. He's a Knight of the Cross, you know."

She threw off the arm restraining her and wrapped hers around the horse's neck to slide off. Julian helped her down.

"Careful, there," warned Sir Rowan, "She's threatened to have me castrated and beheaded. Wouldn't want that awful fate for you, too, would we?"

She glared back at the knight. He smiled and brushed his fingers through his hair, which was disheveled from her attacks.

"Stella!" called Julian, and a girl slightly older than Isodore answered. "Take this lass to the kitchen and let her have anything she wants. I want to talk to Sir Rowan."

In the kitchen, Stella gave her carrots, a boiled egg, a cup of water and a bowl of savory, hot soup. Isodore ate greedily and asked for seconds. She couldn't recall when she'd last had hot food. Afterward, the two men came in and sat across from her at the trestle table.

Father Julian introduced himself. "I am the priest of Dorune, this town. I understand you have been living in the woods. It can be a dangerous place for a child, even one as brave and clever as you are."

The priest somehow knew much about her life in the woods, how lonely, how frightening, especially when people came with dogs, how cold it was in the winter, the long stretches of hunger. She denied that these things bothered her, but didn't argue.

"We have food for you here. We can feed you every day, give you a warm bed and new clothes, a blanket and a hearth."

Isodore remained pointedly silent and uncooperative, knowing the knight was behind all of this.

"You'll be safe in my orphanage, well protected, and you'll no longer have to beg."

"I wasn't beggin'. I was workin'."

"See?" shrugged Sir Rowan when the two men exchanged a glance.

Father Julian cleared his throat. "There are dangers you do not know for a girl who would soon come of age. You should not be out without protection."

Though the men didn't elaborate, she knew what they spoke of. She'd seen an attack that had left several men dead and a young woman alone in the forest. The young woman was wrestled into the bushes, where she screamed and cried. Then she just cried. Isodore didn't understand what was happening at the time, but it was exactly what the two men before her were warning her of. Their reluctance to name it revealed that they didn't think her tough enough to hear the word, or capable enough to survive. They were wrong.

"Girls your age can be married," continued Father Julian. "You can have a husband to provide for you. You'll have children. You need safety, protection. Without a lord, you can be harmed with impunity."

"I'm not afraid," she said. "I'll be all right." She looked them in the eyes to show that she was strong and self-sufficient, but the instant she met Sir Rowan's eyes, she knew what he was thinking under that wily smile of his.

"You need not be frightened of us, child," Father Julian said. "We are doing God's work. That is to save people, not harm them."

The girl who ladled out her soup bowl had remained, chopping herbs and laying them out to dry. Not hard work. She didn't have the look of someone who had been mistreated, although she could be acting because the men were here. Isodore resisted the temptation to lower her guard again. She folded her arms, sat back, studied the two men for a moment then told them no.

They released her as they had promised. Sir Rowan offered her a ride back to where he had met her, but she scorned the offer. Still angry over the trick he had pulled, she didn't want to sit with him on the horse.

"How about a meeting with Archbishop Guillaume then? I am a man of my word."

He smiled. She glowered.

IN THE FOLLOWING days and weeks, hunger and the stinginess of the townfolk drove her back to the church, hopeful that Father Julian would offer her food. He welcomed her every time, much to her surprise. "Come in, child. Come in," he'd say, as if she were his to protect. He always made sure she had enough to eat and wasn't given more work than a person could finish in a day. She worked alongside some of the children in his orphanage, who had no unkind words to say about the priest. In time, she assured herself that the children weren't pretending.

She kept an eye on the strict headmistress for weeks, but saw little to fear from the woman. At last, Isodore thought a bed was better lying in the fields, kicking off rats every night. Life was easier at this orphanage, except for the strict rules. Headmistress Janine lashed her for missing Mass, sleeping late, or talking like a bandit, but no child was ever beaten without real cause.

Sir Rowan visited after two months, and she was surprised to feel her heart leap at the sight of him. He gave her a peace offering: a crystalline rock that melted sweetness in her mouth and made it difficult for her to glower.

He came every few months. He was Father Julian's long-time friend, though the two differed in many ways. While Sir Rowan had long, thick wavy hair, Father Julian had only a fringe of white curls around the back of his head. Where Sir Rowan was broad, Father Julian was narrow, and where the knight was narrow, the priest was hefty. They were of different minds also, arguing over the pope's reforms, the meaning of biblical stories, tolerance for Jews and Muslims, and a host of other subjects. It alarmed her whenever she saw the two friends in heated arguments, but Sir Rowan explained that those debates were good for their friendship and essential for Christianity. She liked Father Julian and she loved Sir Rowan.

Except when he teased her and called her ragamuffin.

"Why can't ye be chivalrous t' me, like when we met? Ye said all Knights o' the Cross had t' do it," she demanded in a way she would never do with anyone else, because she had claimed him as her own knight. She was certain that she was the only lass in his life. It didn't matter that her bare feet didn't reach the ground as she sat on a bench before him, swinging her legs.

Sir Rowan, weaving two leather straps tightly around the grip on his sword, stopped and cheerfully declared, "I shall be glad to treat you with utmost courtesy and seriousness. It is how a Knight of the Cross should treat a proper lass. But first, you must stop talking like a rough bandit and conduct yourself in the manner of a proper lass." He flicked a finger under her chin.

"How?" She couldn't think of any proper lass she could copy, except for the lord's wife and daughters, whom she hardly ever saw.

"By being gentle with the way you talk, for a start. Don't demand chivalry. Ask for it with the same courtesy you want for yourself. And learn some words of good manner and kindness. You'll find you make more friends that way, too."

The knight flashed her a smile, and turned back to repairing his sword's grip. Isodore sank behind a downcast frown. Being found discourteous made her feel unworthy. Sir Rowan didn't talk anymore about that. He went on about how he had learned this method of wrapping the sword's grip from a Moorish swordsmith who had learned it from a Persian, who had learned it from someone even farther east. She wanted to ask what was farther east and hear him tell a story, but she continued in silence, unable to escape a self-loathing mood. Sir Rowan finished with the grip and stood to put the sword belt back on.

"Sir Rowan . . ."

"Hmm?"

She took a deep breath, looking around to ensure they were still in private. "I don' know 'ow t' be a proper lass."

He finished buckling the sword belt and dropped to one knee before her, smiling. "It just takes learning, like everything."

"Please, can ye teach me?" For the first time, she was afraid he'd say no. She thought it might have been a mistake to ask and wanted to shrink away.

Sir Rowan looked at her with a sly little smile framed in his handsome mustache. He patted a big hand on her leg, then stood up and straightened his tunic. "I am going for a stroll. Would you like to accompany me, good lass?" She nodded. "Stand by me." He motioned with his head.

She pushed herself off the chair, stepped to his side, and turned around.

"Let's start like this. How to carry yourself when you're treated like a proper lass. It's the easiest part." He straightened her posture, lifted her chin, and swept the hair out of her eyes. He placed her hand in the crook of his elbow. "Shall we?"

She was fine walking in the sanctuary's quiet hall, but out in the garden, she felt awkward and exposed, constantly aware of her bare feet, tangled hair, and filthy, torn tunic. Some people smiled, some snickered, and others chuckled, but she wished they'd all just disappear. She wished he would take her back inside, but she told herself, *I will go wherever Sir Rowan takes me. I won't stop. I asked for this. A proper lass doesn't return a gift she's given. I won't be afraid as long as I'm with my knight.*

Before Sir Rowan left, he asked Father Julian to continue Isodore's training. The priest thought it a silly endeavor.

"It is essential that she learns to be a good worker instead."

"She can be both," said Sir Rowan. The two old friends argued again, and Isodore found a chair to sit in until they came to an agreement. Father Julian would give her one brief lesson each Sunday, if she worked hard during the week and helped Headmistress Janine.

The lessons were short, but Isodore's practice was diligent, so she wouldn't let Sir Rowan down. She stopped using words and phrases Father Julian forbade, whether he could hear her or not. She waited for her turn to speak and learned to use a soft, dignified tone, with proper diction. She watched and listened before speaking. She learned not to slouch, stoop, mumble, glower, rest her hands on her hips, or sit with her knees apart. She learned when and how to bow and curtsy, and she practiced until she could do it without giggling. She wiped her mouth before bringing the shared cup to her lips. And she held her farts when talking to adults. She accepted the final words of her elders. She looked at the headmistress when addressing her, and in time, grew to like Headmistress Janine just fine.

Each time Sir Rowan visited, she demonstrated what a proper lass she had become.

"Ragamuffin!" he'd greet her as she trotted up to him. "What have you to show me this day?" They'd walk together to share their stories.

He kept his word to her, even those he'd used to trick her the day he abducted her. When her legs could reach the stirrups, he taught her to ride. Riding was more difficult than he made it look. His destriers were not only strong and fast but also sensitive and jumpy, with little tolerance for the mistakes of a nervous girl. There was much more to learn than simply staying on the horse. On top of all she had to remember, he insisted that she sit proudly, like she belonged there. "That horse is trained to carry a Knight of the Cross," he told her. "If he doesn't respect you, he won't let you ride him. And neither will I." She recognized that the lessons were a precious gift that no one else would, or could, give her. She kept her spirits up, for him and for the proper lass he saw in her. She enjoyed riding with him, forgetting during those times that she was only a lowly orphan child.

She grew more fond of Sir Rowan each time he visited, each time she walked or rode with him. She grew fond of him in his absence, too, when she spent her rest time alone, daydreaming. She thought of his smile, his voice, his eyes, the way he smelled.

She found another side of him, away from his happy energetic ways. Whether he was sharpening his blade or contemplating an argument with Father Julian, admiring the church garden or sitting alone, he brightened up when she arrived. He spent long afternoons in the sanctuary, praying in silence, and when she came to pray with him, it brought a smile to his lips. When she leaned into him, he put an arm around her shoulders and kissed her hair.

As Isodore grew out of childhood, she stopped trotting up to her knight when he came to visit. She worked outside, so he could see her and stop on his way to see Father Julian. And she didn't forget the horse. The week before he came, she'd save up a stash of carrots and apples. She hid how much she wanted to run up and jump into his arms. Sometimes, she would pretend she didn't see him coming. She'd greet him with an elegant, "Sir Rowan, how wonderful to see you again," stroke the horse's neck, and retrieve a treat from her apron while she talked with her knight. The way to Sir Rowan's heart was through his horse.

Isodore loved hearing his stories, from the failed campaign in England to skirmishes with the Franks and victorious battles against murderous knights. She always asked about his journeys. After a six-month absence, he returned to regale her with tales of an angry sea that came alive, of strange and barren deserts, hospitable people, and savory food he encountered on his pilgrimage to the Holy Land. Isodore listened to all his stories, from the harrowing to the wonderfully odd. Though enraptured, she kept herself composed, basking in his attention.

But it wasn't only in Sir Rowan's jolly moods that she adored him. In his melancholy moods, whether he sat gazing out at rain in the flower garden or praying at the sanctuary's altar, she would sit with him until his spirits lifted. She wondered what was on his mind, but she thought it was the sort of thing a proper lass ought not pry into.

One cold day just before Christmas, he called her ragamuffin for the last time. She ignored the teasing.

"Sir Rowan," she said, her hands clasped. "I've been looking forward to your visit. I fought very hard with the cook for a fortnight to be allowed to make kakavia for you. I had to walk to the market three straight Saturdays before finding a merchant with saffron for the recipe. Today, I woke early and finished my day's work by noon so I could cook and have the kakavia ready for you at supper." She bowed her head and added, "I hope you enjoy it."

"Kakavia! What on earth possessed you to make kakavia?"

"You said you enjoyed it most during your pilgrimage to the Holy Land. When Father Julian went, I begged him to bring back a recipe for me."

"Oh, ho, ho! Splendid," commended the knight from his horse. "You remembered that?"

"I did, Sir Rowan." She felt proud for making her knight so happy.

"Well, then, I see now that I have no choice. With Almighty God as my witness, I promise never again to call you by that dreadful name. But only if you invite Father Julian, and also bring yourself to sup with us." He stretched out the word "dreadful" and made her snort with laughter, but she pressed her lips together and remained composed, while a tingle of joy danced in every nerve of her body.

"Father Julian has been invited, but I have not, until now. I shall be delighted to join you both."

He bought her a new tunic to wear to supper. For the first time in years, she had clothes that fit. She passed on her ragged tunic to a younger girl. Each Christmas thereafter, Sir Rowan had a present for her: a hair brush, a necklace, a manteau. She wore her necklace to keep a part of Sir Rowan with her at all times.

Since the time she learned to get along with Headmistress Janine, Isodore had helped take care of the orphanage's younger children. When she was twenty, Father Julian asked her to move to the frontier village of Savelle to be headmistress of its orphanage. The current headmistress was to move after wedding a man in another estate. She didn't want to be a headmistress, for she wasn't used to giving orders, and she felt like an orphan herself. But when she visited the orphanage and met the children, she changed her mind.

She cared for the ten children, tended the croft and small animals, repaired the cottage, cooked, sewed, mediated the children's squabbles, taught them to the best of her abilities, begged for apprenticeships for those with aptitude, and prepared them for work. She looked after the ones who weren't old enough for labor. They loved her. When she asked them why, they said that she was patient, didn't yell, and she smiled when she saw them. "Yer not like other 'eadmistresses," they said. "Yer like a mother."

As a parting gift, Sir Rowan had given her a pair of shoes, so she no longer had to go barefoot, and a fine tunic with bell sleeves and lace trim, fitted to show off the figure of the young woman wearing it. She saved it for Sundays, waking before the rooster or the orphans did, to don it for Mass. Standing between the rushlight and the wall of the cottage, she would look at the shadow of the proper lass she had become. The dress was beautiful beyond anything she thought would ever grace her thin body. She ran her hands up her abdomen then slid them around her body in an embrace, wondering in the warm glow how it would feel if they were his hands.

The men of Savelle intimated some interest in the village's new resident, no more or less than they would have shown in any unmarried young woman, but she, with the grace and diction she had learned, declined their advances without exception. They didn't understand why, for she told no one she was saving herself for a Knight of the Cross. Suspicion rested on her association with the Church, her aristocratic manners, the fine tunic she wore on Sundays, even her shoes—all marks above her proper station. She was clearly a peasant with a menial job, never received by Lord Edwin, and at times, her speech slipped back to an unrefined manner. The villagers privately derided her pretension, eyeing her sideways when they passed. Savelle's priest, the young Father Serafin, was competent but lacked the charm and influence of Father Julian. The villagers were indifferent to Father Serafin, and by extension, to her. After a time, no man in Savelle or nearby settlements would admit interest in a lass so widely mocked. No respectable man, that is—the village's part-time carpenter who lived across the road often showered affection on her when she came to him for repairs. But he was married and spoke too highly of himself.

Sir Rowan sent his greetings through Father Julian's correspondence. He promised to visit Isodore in Savelle, but he was in the north, a long way from the southern frontier. And he had fallen too ill to travel. As the months passed, she heard less and less from the man who was once filled with so much strength and vigor. After a year, she received terrible news from Father Julian. The knight had gone missing after a scuffle with the magistrate's men, killing the sheriff as he escaped. Father Julian wrote that, should Sir Rowan seek her out, she was to tell him to turn himself over to the mercy of God. Based on the confession of the man caught in his room, Sir Rowan had been convicted, in absentia, then excommunicated, for the unfathomable crime of sodomy.

8

Death's Doorway

A faint quarter moon appeared in the afternoon sky, and Isodore instinctively marked the passing of a week. She hadn't expected to live this long.

If the dragon didn't kill her soon, however, she knew what would. Pus had encrusted her chest wound, and showed no sign of healing. The area around it had gone from red to purple, with dark lines meandering outward under her skin. The wound swelled and felt hot to her fingertips. The puncture no longer stung, because the skin around it had gone dead.

Death entered through the wound to wrest her soul from its mortal home. The first time it happened, her abdomen seized up so stiffly that she thought she was turning into wood. The next time, her teeth gnashed down so hard she thought they might break.

One night, she lay soaked in sweat, racked with a fever and drooling. Her neck was stiff. She woke with her body wrenched backward, from head to toe, bending so much that her back and buttocks lifted from the ground, and she fell over. She tried to scream but yielded only a strained choking sound. She'd lost control of her tongue.

Her eyes were possessed, rolling upward, back toward her skull. She could see the dim triangle of the cave entrance against the darkness, but which way was up she couldn't tell. She hung on in paralytic horror. After a moment, Death relinquished her, retreating into the darkness to retry another time. It visited every night. The dragon could only watch the spectacle, baring its teeth at a distance, as if fearing her possessed body would attack.

Another night, she dreamed she married her knight at the door of the church in Auch, the city of dragonslayers. After the solemn ceremony, they rode to his uncle's home by the towering keep. The lord and his wife had vacated it for their wedding night. Isodore and her new husband arrived after dark. Compared with the cottage she shared with her orphans, the hall was cavernous and its darkness thick.

She had prepared for this day for months, but nothing could calm her nerves. She was a maiden; that was one reason the knight had chosen her. It would have brought scandal for someone of his status to marry an unchaste woman. Yet, she felt out of place and alone in the house of a lord.

She climbed the steps to the solar ahead of her husband, slipping through the curtains to the bedside, where servants had prepared wine, candles and a warm bed. In the great hall on the other side of the curtains, the only things visible were the hearth fire at the center of the hall and the rushlight flames by the servants' beds at the far end. She turned away from her new husband and undressed. She feared he might not like what he saw, dreaded that he would realize it had been a gross mistake to marry a lowly orphaned peasant.

She lay down in the bed and awaited him, thankful for the darkness that hid her thin body. His weight pressed down on her, his warm, strong body, his hand on her breast, finger pressing into her chest, deeper and deeper. And sharp. Her chest hurt, as though the dragon's claw still stirred in her wound. She looked up, to her horror, at a pair of bulging crimson eyes. In the dim light, she had mistakenly led the black dragon to the solar.

She woke in the cave, afraid and aghast, but relieved. The dragon was settling down. She watched its dark mass moving against the entrance's triangle of cold, moonlit granite. As the dragon retreated from her, the radiant heat diminished. She detected a now familiar smell, a soft mix of penetrating spirits, earth, and something she couldn't identify, the smell of the beast.

What was it doing up in the middle of the night, on her end of the cave? Its claw had violated her once, and she suspected that somehow the beast had just violated her again. She touched her chest, still warm, still bruised, awaiting Death's return. Helpless, she crossed her arms over her chest, as if to protect herself from further violations, and turned away.

She didn't see the dragon the next day, until it came back, empty-handed. She fed on the leftover deer leg that she kept in the cave, away from the scavenging crows and vultures, but she ate little because it had begun to emit a foul odor. The dragon failed to bring back food the next day, and the next. It spent the entire day away from the nest, presumably hunting, but had nothing to show. Perhaps it was waiting for her to finish the foul-smelling meat.

Episodes of the death struggle continued to interrupt her sleep at night. A stupefying fever kept her inside long past daybreak. An insistent hunger clawed her stomach, and she reached for the half-eaten deer leg. It had a nauseating, sour odor. It felt soft, slippery and cold where she grabbed it. Despite her desperate hunger, a small bite was all she had appetite for. It tasted awful, yet familiar, stirring foggy memories of leftovers she used to find by the roadside. A part of it stuck to her face, tickling her. She scratched it away and noticed another piece of it squirming above her lips. She spat and wiped the meat and slime off her face, but no amount of frantic wiping could remove the disgust.

She brought the piece of meat into the wedge of sunlight slashing through the cave's southern opening. Inspecting it was something she should have done before taking the bite. The scavenging birds had not gotten to the meat, but the flies had. A nest of maggots squirmed where she had bitten. Her daze snapped. She screamed and spat out everything she could feel in her mouth. Somehow she found enough strength to crawl out of the cave, spitting as she went. At the watery white rock, she scraped her tongue and lips on the cool surface to remove larval traces from her mouth. She gnawed off bits of white rock to rinse her mouth and spat out the rinse water. There was, however, little she could do to remove the growing nausea. A spasm gripped her from inside and forced its way up her chest, strangling her as it passed through her throat. She retched again and again, but disgorged nothing from the empty pit of her stomach.

When the convulsions stopped, she slumped against the white rock, out of breath, done in by her anger as much as the dry heaves. Turning her eyes to the lowland in the distance, she recalled, practically a lifetime ago, hastily biting into maggot-ridden food she had found by the roadside. Hungry and desperate she was, back then, but free and unaccompanied by the specter of death. She sobbed to find herself longing for that life, a life that even peasants looked down on.

THE DRAGON RETURNED late, after another full day away from the nest with nothing to show. Desperately hungry, Isodore pointed to a knee-high boulder and mumbled to her captor, "Start the fire here."

She scraped the maggot nest off on the granite and rinsed off the slime layer with water from the white rock. Sitting by the boulder, she rested her good arm on it and held on to the deer leg so it dangled above the fire, where she let it cook long before taking a bite. It was a trick she invented when she lived in the woods. Overcooking did not restore the putrid to its prior state, but it sufficed in desperate times when she had no asterium.

After two days of minimal appetite, she finished the deer leg, then continued her descent into starvation. The dragon brought her a brown sack and the lower leg of a child. It had raided a village or a caravan. She looked at the leg and recalled her children, one by one. It wasn't one of them. Still, the sight of it, mauled flesh, protruding bone, congealed blood, brought her to her knees, retching. Nothing came. She glared at the vile beast, despising it with all her will, even though she was so weak and ill that merely looking at it was difficult.

"Don't bother," she said when it brushed the dead wood into a pile. "I do not eat my own kind."

"Your own kind?" Its crimson eyes glared back at her. She didn't know if it was mocking or simply hadn't heard her. When she refused to answer, the beast took the leg in its mouth and flew away. She untied the sack and found it filled with peaches.

When the peaches were gone, the dragon gave her crows to eat. As the unsuspecting murder pecked at the remains of the human leg, the dragon surprised them with a sudden cone of flames. Somehow, many of them escaped, squawking and trailing smoke, but the spray of flaming mucus hit the rocks and bone pile and three unlucky birds, spreading fire over their feathers. Too panicked or injured to fly straight, they circled, squawking, until they fell as three spasmodic fireballs, joining the mess of smaller mucus fires. Horrified, she turned away.

"Are you not hungry?" asked the dragon.

"I can't eat creatures burned alive like that."

It considered that for a few seconds and commented, "You are like a dragon." Then it swept the smoking birds over the cliff.

The next morning, she pushed against the cave walls to get herself outside, determined to be in the sunlight and see the beautiful mountains and the little slice of Gascony to the north, should it be her last day alive.

The dragon came back after half a day away. It brought her an egret, unburned, and an extra-large branch for firewood. She cooked and ate, watching the dragon. It lay a few steps away, seemingly bored, looking out over the valley.

It had never rested near her before. Even lying still, it was fearsome to behold, full of sharp points. Teeth, horns, claws. A line of pointed spines extended from each of its brows and ran the length of its neck, meeting above its shoulders, continuing as a single line of bumpy ridges along its back. She wanted to lash out at it, but didn't see any soft spot to strike.

After she finished eating, the dragon reached forward with one forelimb. From the calloused knuckle, where four spiny wing fingers extended backward, one clawed finger extended forward. It was as thick as her arm, stubby, and grotesquely flexible. It uncurled, dropping the shoot of a young plant no bigger than the palm of a hand. "For your wound," said the dragon, backing away with its eyes on her.

Leaning forward, she frowned, studying the plant but refraining from reaching for it. She couldn't believe her eyes. So rare! The plant's long root stem was still attached. It hadn't been plucked but dug out of the ground with care. Realizing the dragon was observing her, she sat back, conspicuously resuming her resting position, making a disdainful face in an attempt to conceal her interest in the plant. "My wound? How did . . . ? How could this help my wound?"

The dragon turned and crouched toward the cliff, snorting.

She called out to it. "Do you . . . ? Do you know how to heal my wound?"

The head turned back toward her. "I do not. I am a dragon. But you do. Don't you . . . sorceress?"

She gaped in surprise then pressed her lips into an indignant expression. "Sorceress? I'm no sorceress. I'm no such thing. How . . . How dare you make such an accusation."

The dragon shifted toward her on its forelimbs. "You," its voice rumbled. "It was you who cast the cloth at me. Wasn't it, sorceress?"

She sat up and balled her hands into fists. "I am not a sorceress. You lie! You don't know . . . anything. You're a fool." This brief protest wore her out, and she paused to take some labored breaths. "I only threw the apron at you. You were after me. What did you—"

"The cloth was bewitched," the dragon snapped. "I have no doubt."

Argument was pointless. She knew it, and she knew the dragon knew it. She leaned back and rested her head on the tilted slab, silent—the plant between them.

"I shall bring more wood," said the beast. "You will find water from the ice to be of sufficient purity." It dropped off the cliff, pushing its knuckles against the ledge's rim. A moment later, it rose back into view, heading for the notch in the ridge. She watched until it disappeared through the notch.

She eyed the homely plant through a swirl of hope and fear. A flowerless asterium, complete with the root, the most potent part.

Some people claimed the plant sprung forth where the ghost of a sorcerer wept. Her father always said that was nonsense. Whatever the truth was, the dragon knew about asterium, not just the plant but where to find it. It knew the need for pure water and wood fire. Just as it had known about the apron.

The hope and fear the asterium instilled in her quickened, morphing into temptation. She picked up the slender olive-green stalk and turned it in her fingers.

Not long ago she had some ground asterium root in a stoppered jar on the highest shelf in the orphanage. She marked it with an X in pine pitch and soot, so no one would mistake it for herb. She had used it when a regiment of dragonslayers came to Savelle to kill a beast. It had changed everything.

9

Enter the Regiment

In the fall of the previous year, a dragonslayer regiment had encamped in the dense woods surrounding a damp meadow a short distance from Savelle. Isodore couldn't contain her curiosity about the regiment and its knights, wondering if they, being Knights of the Cross, were as chivalrous as Sir Rowan. But only those who had business at their camp could visit, so that dragons couldn't trace the villagers' movements to the ambush party. The baker, the cooks, the clothiers, and the carpenter were part-time practitioners who made their primary living as farmers, because Savelle wasn't big enough to support their trade. But the regiment's need for their services called them to the camp. When they returned, they thrilled their fellow villagers with their observations, and Isodore gave in to eavesdropping on them, even as she feigned disinterest.

The regiment had over forty men, led by four knights. Their camp bustled as they prepared weapons and equipment for battle. They had racks of heavy crossbows and large wooden panels lined with hay. They filled barrels with water from the river and soaked coils of un-tarred cords. That caused much speculation among the villagers, as it would cause the hemp to rot. Some village men wondered if these were true dragonslayers or false braggarts, but Isodore thought the villagers were only trying to sound knowledgeable. The regiment appropriated an aging cow from the village and allowed it to graze in the meadow to lure the dragon down. The animal's size ensured that the dragon couldn't simply carry it away.

Father Serafin visited the camp each morning to say Mass. Isodore asked twice whether he needed her along. He declined both times, and she gave up.

The priest warned the anxious village, "The regiment commander, Sir Dalton, said it could be a long wait. Although the dragon recently took men and animals from Savelle, we never offered the dragon sacrifices, and no one could predict the dragon's habits. But Sir Dalton commends us for not giving in to the temptation to make the sacrifices. As you all know, sacrifices encourage more dragon attacks."

After the initial excitement, the wait was indeed as long and boring as promised, broken by a brief skirmish unrelated to dragons. It had begun with urgent hoof beats coming down the road. Isodore looked out her door to see the rider turning into the church grounds so abruptly that the horse whinnied.

A message from Father Julian, perhaps. Perhaps a message about Sir Rowan. She had thought that too many times, only to be disappointed. A moment after she returned to her work, she heard a larger contingent of horsemen and came back to look. Father Serafin threw up his hands to stop the wave of riders. The dozen men, clad in chainmail, surrounded the priest in front of his door. They demanded he step aside, drowning out his protest. The second group, led by Baldard, a fearsome knight with a scraggly black beard, came to arrest Armand, the man who had arrived earlier.

"I will burn down this hall if you don't turn over that criminal. Now!"

The thin young priest tried in vain to explain over bellicose demands. "Armand has sanctuary in the house of God. You must not threaten the house of God."

"He's a criminal. He doesn't deserve sanctuary!" shouted Baldard.

"What was his crime?"

Baldard stared down and said with thin-lipped anger, "Fornication."

"Fornication?" Father Serafin frowned. "The law does not call for hanging fornicators. Fornicators should be fined, or forced to marry."

"He'll pay no fines. He has nothing but debts."

The priest turned a fatherly scowl toward Armand, who shrugged sheepishly from behind the church door he had cracked open. He slammed the door shut as a dagger flew from Baldard's hand, and slammed into the wood and fell.

Father Serafin ducked. The group of armed men laughed at his obvious fear. He recomposed himself, still shaking. Isodore thought he was in over his head with these men. "What . . . What about his horse?" he suggested to Baldard.

"His horse? That horse? Hah! That horse belongs to me! That is another thing. He's a thief! Perhaps we'll cut off his hands before hanging him." His men laughed again.

"I only *borrowed* the horse." came Armand's voice from inside the church.

Father Serafin took a moment to find his words. "Hmm. Well, perhaps he could labor to pay the fine."

"Labor," balked Armand, cracking the door open again to show an indignant face. "Never! I am noble born. I shall not toil like a common serf."

Surprised by his reappearance, Father Serafin turned to speak with him. "If you cannot pay the fine, then you will be required to marry the woman."

"Very well. I agree."

Baldard threw up his hands, one hand a fist and his sword in the other. "Stupid priest! He is playing you for a fool. He knows that cannot happen."

"Why not?" asked Father Serafin.

Armand stuck his head out the door. With a handsome, boyish face and silky brown hair, he was young enough to be Baldard's son. "Because Baldard murdered her! And raped her! He is a rapist and a murderer. Hang him, not me. Rape and murder are hanging offenses, aren't they?"

"Lies," spat Baldard, spitting as he spoke. "See how he lies, priest? That's another crime. Lies while cowering in your church, priest. What does your law say about that? She wasn't murdered. She was lawfully executed. Stoned to death for her crime."

Father Serafin looked back and forth between Armand and Baldard, not knowing whom to believe. "You raped the woman?" he asked Baldard.

"Rape? Nonsense. I can't rape her, because she was my wife. Study your laws, priest. A woman can't be raped by her husband."

"But he beat her. And tied her up," accused Armand.

Baldard made a point of rolling his eyes. "You are an imbecile for believing everything that whore told you, Armand. And you would be one too, priest, if you believe him. It was not a rape. She was my wife. And I have the right, as her husband, to take his life. I can hang him, or burn down this shack on him."

Father Serafin cleared his throat. "Your wife? Then it was not fornication, but adultery."

Whispers and giggles rose from the gathered villagers repeating the words "adultery," "wife," and "whore." Baldard's men turned their horses around and feigned a charge, dispersing the crowd. At a safer distance, the villagers stopped and resumed.

Baldard seethed. "I don't much care what you call it, priest. I will hang him."

"No," Father Serafin protested with an unconvincing show of courage. "He must have his trial. And you should not threaten this church. It is a house of God. We can perhaps take this dispute to Lord Edwin. He is away in Lovishar, but should be back on Sunday. I will ask him to hold a special court to—"

"Sunday?" shouted Baldard, his anger at a new high. "I did not ride all this way to wait. Nor to defer to you. We will take this man. Either hand him over or we will burn down the church. And if you stand in our way—"

"Please," Father Serafin held up his hands. "Let me talk with him."

Baldard snarled, fuming and ready to kill. "You have five minutes." He turned to one of his men. "Bring me fire."

"Very well," said Father Serafin. "Five minutes. Please do not do

anything. You promised. Five minutes. I heard that. God heard that."
He slipped into the church.

The villagers, laughing earlier, now stood in fear at their cottage doors. "Where is the blacksmith?" Baldard's man asked one of them.

The frightened woman backed away. "We . . . we don' have one. We're a small village."

"Then you will bring me fire. Now. Before we tear down these cottages, looking for it. And we'll start with yours."

In her days on the road, Isodore had seen many violent confrontations among knights, often at tragic cost to bystanders and weak villages. Situated on the frontier, Savelle had been spared. Nobles on the frontier tended to be better united against their common enemy, the dragons. Knights from the north, from whence Baldard had surely come, were much more willing to turn on their fellow men. Her sympathy went to Father Serafin, a lone young priest without the close backing of influential officials in the towns. Neither he nor Lord Edwin's house guards could stop this band.

Baldard's man returned with a hazy bottle of oil, an ax, and four torches they distributed to the group. While they waited for the priest's return, the sound of rolling thunder rose from the clearing at the end of the road. A mounted knight turned the corner coming into view, followed by enough armed riders to fill the road, stirring up a cloud of dust. Isodore looked at the mustached knight with bouncing black curls. The golden cross over the suffering dragon was emblazoned on his chest.

"Sir Rowan?" she whispered. It had been years since he had fallen from grace, and yet he came down the road, as proud and confident as ever. Her hero, her knight. The little girl in her wanted to run out to meet him. She readied her greeting. "Sir Rowan, how wonderful to see you again. How long have you been a dragonslayer?" He would see that she still wore the necklace he had given her.

As riders came closer, she realized her mistake. Not Sir Rowan, just a heartbreaking likeness. The little girl in her disappeared in the cloud of dust kicked up by galloping hooves.

Baldard's men spread out in a line to confront the latecomers, who stopped in a line of four in the front and the rest, perhaps twenty-five men, spread out close behind them. Some men in the back had their hands on their swords but not the front four, the ones with the suffering-dragon crest on their surcoats. Their steeds, twitching from the adrenaline of the rush, stomped in the dirt and flared their nostrils.

"I am Sir Dalton, a Knight of the Cross," said the handsome, commanding figure Isodore had mistaken for Sir Rowan. "Who is the leader of this band?"

"I am Baldard of Armagnac. We are here to arrest a criminal. The priest is . . . refusing to abide."

He didn't say, "Sir Baldard." An undubbed knight, the heedless kind.

"Children, come back!" Isodore called to the orphans who came out with her and strayed toward the confrontation for a closer look. She gathered them into a tight group by the door and told the older one to hold on to the younger ones. "If they start fighting, everyone inside, immediately."

"Yes, Isodore," came the little voices.

Baldard and Sir Dalton were about the same age, no older than forty. One held the promise of calm while the other, chaos.

"What is the man's crime?" asked Sir Dalton.

"Fornication," Baldard seethed.

Despite the situation, the crowd giggled again at Baldard's attempt to hide his cuckolded status.

"Has he been tried?" asked Sir Dalton.

Baldard spoke in a manner that brooked no argument. "He was caught red-handed."

"What does Father Serafin say?"

"The priest is illegally protecting this criminal. We have asked him to turn the man over. His obstinacy has put this village in peril."

"And his reason for refusal?"

"He chose to grant sanctuary to the criminal."

Sir Dalton looked right and left, at the line of men flanking Baldard, glancing out further at the longer line of his own men, as though noticing for the first time whom the numbers favored.

He turned back to Baldard. "All church grounds are sanctu-aries," he corrected Baldard. "His crime should be judged by the lord of this domain."

"Your lord is away," Baldard snapped, seething. "And the crime was not committed in this domain. We seek only to render justice for a crime committed in our domain. It's a very simple matter."

Sir Dalton's tone changed from cordial to defiant. "It's a simple matter that an attack on the house of God is an attack on God Himself. You should be aware that we will defend our almighty Lord."

"It is exactly the Lord's law I've come to enforce, Sir Dalton. Don't you find it an affront to the Lord that a man who has broken His commandments—fornication, theft, lust—should be granted sanctuary in this building? This man deserves no sanctuary. He should be hanged and made an example of. A deterrence. The clergy's lenient treatment of criminals will only bring more of God's wrath, more suffering, to the entire frontier."

"I will defer to the authority granted to Father Serafin regarding the fate of the hunted man. This sanctuary, and this village, however, are under our protection."

"For the time being," Baldard corrected. "Sir Dalton, we have no wish to interfere with your work here. If the priest hands over this one criminal, there will be no need for you to defend the village. We can depart as friends. Should you try to stop us, there might be . . . terrible damage done, inadvertently of course, in the battle, and . . . future animosity between Lord Edwin and my great family, long after your regiment's departure. That would be unfortunate, would it not? I am sure it would anger Lord Edwin terribly to find that this priest chose to sacrifice the village to shelter a criminal who does not even merit Lord Edwin's protection.

"Think of your duty to the village, Sir Dalton. You are here to kill a dragon, no doubt. If you lose men fighting us, how would it help your cause? In the end, your regiment shall pay—as shall this village—dearly."

Father Serafin, who had come out during the conversation and heard Baldard's threat, froze in fear.

"Don't be concerned, Father," said an older dragonslayer with a grizzled face and a menacing stare. "Any damage done to this village can be paid with the price fetched by the horses, swords and armor, after we slaughter the trespassers." All eyes fell on the new speaker who displayed supreme horsemanship as he rode half-pass up to Sir Dalton. "But if you do not wish to bother with that transaction, I propose that we settle this dispute in single combat. Sir Dalton, I will represent Father Serafin."

"Thank you, Sir Baret." Sir Dalton turned back to Baldard. "You have three choices. Respect Father Serafin's authority, be slaughtered in a fight you cannot possibly win while Armand remains free, or accept Sir Baret's honorable offer."

Baldard glowered and turned to Father Serafin. "What did the criminal say?"

"He offered to turn himself over to the magistrate in Oulan."

Baldard glanced at Sir Baret, assessing his chances against the old knight. One of Baldard's men rode up to whisper in his ear. Baldard laughed a mad laugh. The others looked on, wondering. "Do you think we are stupid, Armand? You cowardly, spoiled, philandering fool. You can take your offer back to the rat hole you crawled from." He turned to Sir Dalton. "The magistrate in Oulan is his uncle. I will accept the duel. If I win, the priest will turn him over to me."

Sir Dalton looked to Father Serafin, who accepted with a nod, then spelled out the terms of the duel for all to hear. "Those torches must be extinguished. All village structures are to be spared. Entering or damaging any structure results in a loss. If Baldard dies or yields, all you men must leave immediately. You may take his body. If Sir Baret dies or yields, then Father Serafin must turn Armand over. Raise your hands if you agree." All accepted.

Sir Baret dismounted and donned the arming shirt and cap a squire brought him. Another squire brought his hauberk and helmet. They helped him get into it.

Baldard sneered at Armand. "You are as foolish as you are spoiled, Armand, trusting your life to the sword of a dragonslayer.

Tomorrow morning, you'll hang in the whore's clothes for all to see. After we cut off your hands. Ha, ha."

"Now wait!" Armand opened the door and yelled back. "I am of noble blood. I will not be hanged like a common criminal." He pulled on Father Serafin's shoulder. "Father, Sir Dalton! I am of noble blood. I refuse to submit to this treatment."

Sir Dalton and Father Serafin exchanged irritated glances; the knight shrugged.

The priest cleared his throat.

"Baldard. As a nobleman, Armand does have the right to a beheading; that is, if he is found guilty."

"I do!" shouted Armand. "It is wholly uncivilized to treat a noble . . ."

Baldard turned to Sir Dalton. "If he had true noble blood in him, he would stand and fight for himself, not run like a coward, not let another knight fight for him. You see how he whines?"

Sir Dalton beckoned to the priest, who conferred with him, then headed back into the church. The crowd waited. Sir Baret stood in the middle of the road, the tip of his unhooked scabbard in the ground and his hands resting on the pommel, his shoulders rising with each long, deep breath.

"Why does 'e want t' be beheaded?" little Xabi asked from Isodore's side.

"He doesn't. But if a nobleman is to be executed, he has the right to a beheading."

"Don't that 'urt?"

"It does, but it is a quick death. Hanging is painfully slow and humiliating. And he fears being mocked, I'm sure."

"Do I 'ave that right, too?"

Isodore sighed. "No. Unfortunately, we have no such right. The lowborn are executed in horrible, ugly ways. You must remember to be good and follow the Lord's Commandments as Father Serafin preaches, so that you will never be accused of a crime."

The priest emerged from the church and conferred with Sir Dalton again.

"Armand has changed his mind," Sir Dalton announced. "He

wants guarantee of an impartial judgment and respect for his rights as a nobleman. In return, he will agree to turn himself over to the magistrate of Belmont."

After a brief conference, Baldard agreed. Lord Edwin's son and reeve were summoned, and they, too, agreed. Armand was to be kept as a guest in Lord Edwin's home, accompanied by one of Baldard's men, both disarmed and under the watch of Lord Edwin's house guards. Baldard departed with the rest of his men, intending to bring the magistrate of Belmont as soon as possible. The villagers were happy to see the back of the undubbed knights and buoyed by their glimpse of the dragonslayers.

Isodore had overheard neighbors speak of the regiment's four knights but had trouble picturing them. The commander, Sir Dalton, had delivered fifteen dragon heads to the duke and the archbishop. Sir Baret, whom some villagers found unfriendly, was surprisingly courteous. He was a man of few words, but he smiled and dropped to one knee to talk to her children when they ran out to greet the regiment. Before he joined the dragonslayers, he was a veteran of the northern skirmishes against the Franks, making it natural for him to volunteer to fight Baldard. Sir Rowan had claimed that dragonslayers were unremarkable swordsmen generally, as the sword wasn't their primary weapon against the beasts. Sir Wilfred, slightly younger than Sir Dalton, conversed easily with everyone and made up for the few words of Sir Baret. He lingered the longest, taking a seat on the church's front steps to chat and laugh with the villagers after the dragonslayers returned to their stations. Sir Gustav, the youngest knight, was about Isodore's age. Part Norman stock with a shock of hair that shone like the golden sun, he was a curiosity to many, particularly the girls and young women. The Danes had stopped raiding and had settled in Normandy about the same time Savelle encroached on the frontier. It was strange to see a descendant of the kingdom's enemies as a protector.

Armand fed well at Lord Edwin's house and charmed the lord's daughters and servants alike. Though not allowed to go past Lord Edwin's gate, he conversed with whomever passed by. He seduced the daughter of one of Lord Edwin's servants, so went a new rumor.

He was a sweet-talking, carefree philanderer. But when Baldard returned with Belmont's sheriff three days later, he was a different man, quiet, as if death itself had come for him.

On the surface, the village fell back into its regular routine, but the villagers, in awe of the dragonslayers, were—for once—hopeful the dragon wouldn't be long in coming.

One afternoon, after two more weeks of waiting, word came to the village that regiment sentinels posted on the hilltops had sighted a dragon in the southern sky. Father Serafin rushed to the dragonslayers' camp to give them their battle blessings, should there be time. All villagers were summoned back from the orchards, and Isodore herded her children to the church to shelter in the underground chamber. As she went, she saw dragonslayers climbing to the roofs of the church, the keep, and miller's wheel-house, carrying large crossbows and coils of rope. They were covered from head to toe in clothing lined with small straw bundles. Isodore couldn't fathom why they would wear such flammable material. When she passed them, however, she saw that the straw covering their bodies was dripping wet, and the men showed no fear.

On the church's roof, a dragonslayer stood, tying a thick rope around his waist.

"May God help you today, dragonslayer," she called to him. He nodded toward her, a confident smile on his face, then proceeded with his work, wrapping the other end of the rope around the rooftop cross.

As Isodore descended the ladder into the shelter, she heard men shouting, calling decoy villagers to their positions. Half the village was under the church, the other half under Lord Edwin's keep. The shelter was hot and crowded, but they felt safe as they crossed themselves, knowing the dragonslayers were ready. A monk led them in prayer to Saint George, asking him to bless the dragonslayers and protect them from the evil beast. He asked God to deliver Gascony from the dragon scourge for all time.

An hour after they entered the shelter, Father Serafin called them out. As he helped lift the wooden doors, Isodore hardly recognized him. He was out of breath. Sweat beaded on his forehead, his eyes were blank, and his face had the frozen, pale fear of a witness to catastrophe.

10

Cries of the Crossbowman

When Isodore emerged from the underground shelter, the dragonslayers guarding the church's roof had climbed down and were collecting their weapons, their voices urgent but firm. There were a few quick exchanges between the dragonslayers before they rushed off.

Father Serafin explained, "The dragon broke free and Sir Dalton is pursuing it. He'll take all the healthy men in the regiment. We must help the injured."

How they expected to hunt down a dragon Isodore couldn't imagine, but there was no time to ask and too much confusion. All available hands, except for the few with young children, were to rush to the field. Isodore put her oldest children in charge of the others and joined the stream of people running through the orchard.

The field where the regiment had fought the dragon was oblong, two hundred paces in length, a meadow surrounded by new woods. Clumps of dirt and grass dug up by horse hooves littered the field. Deep claw marks etched the mud. The area was littered with large panels lined with straw, dropped crossbows, snaking ropes, three broken lances, and five broken bodies.

Some dragonslayers were running, some limping, some were being carried. Other dragonslayers and villagers were dousing fires with pails brought from barrels of water hidden in the woods. Lord Edwin wasn't there, too fat these days to rush anywhere. His three sons, astride their horses, directed his servants. The priest and a group of people huddled over one body. Isodore helped to dress the wounded and provide for their comfort. The injured were brought back to Savelle to rest. Not all would live. One breathed fast, short breaths and moaned now and then. He was the one at the center of the huddle. His face, head, and hands had been severely burned.

"What of the fourth knight?" one of her neighbors asked. "Only two left with Sir Dalton."

"Over there," someone said, pointing to a lifeless body in the field, dressed not in a straw suit but as an ordinary warrior.

In their rush to pursue the dragon, the regiment had left many of its spare weapons and provisions behind. No one knew when they would return, how far they had to go to find the dragon, or even how many of them were still alive. The men who stayed behind were in pain, but those who spoke were confident that Sir Dalton would prevail.

The villagers took turns looking after the injured, particularly the burned one, who was suffering the most. He was one of Sir Baret's squires, a crossbowman. Father Serafin arranged for him to convalesce in a tiny cottage. The childless couple who lived in the cottage had temporarily moved to the lord's keep. His disfigurement and delirious screams frightened the women caring for him. Just two days after Sir Dalton's departure, Isodore overheard two women asking the priest to find someone else to care for the burned man.

"I've been with him constantly, fer 'alf a day, with no break," said one woman.

"Well, I was with 'im yesterday," said the second. "All day."

"There is no one else," Father Serafin said.

"There are. There are others who 'ave not cared for him at all. They should share in this work, too. It's only fair. We 'ave no time te tend our orchard."

"Everyone is already occupied. There are other injured men as well."

BRIAN GUNNEY

"Can't they look after this man as they rest? They're accustomed to the burns. We aren't."

Isodore listened from outside the priest's study, unable to believe the women wanted to abandon this man who was in so much pain. She marched into the study. The women were suggesting one of Lord Edwin's servants take over, when Isodore stepped in.

"Father, I will care for the burned man," she said, stepping into the room, "if someone will look after my youngest children when I am away from the orphanage."

The two women happily traded duties with her.

Isodore went to the cottage, just a few paces wide, with a stone fire ring in the middle serving as hearth and stove, and a vent for smoke at the apex of one wall. A bench and small trestle table sat in one corner. A bed occupied the opposite corner. The crossbowman lay, curled up under layers of blankets, facing the wall. He still wore his battle garments, straw bundles over swine leather.

She picked up the bench and walked quietly over to him. His head was red and raw, skin peeling. His hair was burned away and only a black wad remained of his ear. She checked her revulsion. "I will not be afraid," she whispered, just enough to feel the words on her lips. "I must not be afraid. He is the one suffering, not me. I won't let him suffer alone." Step by small step, she came to the bedside.

His burns were fleshy, surrounded by charred patches at their perimeters. Blood and pus had oozed onto the bed and caked over his peeling skin. His nose was a dead black knob. Nausea rose in Isodore as she looked upon the horror. Her knees trembled and buckled under her as she lowered herself to the bench. How could a man so weak and dying be so frightening?

"Gr . . . Greetings, good man." Her voice trembled and her eyes teared up. "My name is Isodore. I am filled with so much sorrow at what has happened to you."

"Go . . . away," he hissed laboriously.

"I will not let you suffer alone," she whispered, though it was so soft he likely did not hear.

She brought him food and water, but he only accepted water

and cool porridge. His mouth hurt too much to eat. His hands were burned, too, so she fed him. He ate little. She helped him out of his straw-covered, hide clothing, only to find the clothes beneath were still damp from the soaking that was supposed to have kept him safe from fire. The failure of the women before her to change his clothes infuriated her and made her glad that they were no longer caring for him. She cleaned the hay from his bed, brought him his clean, dry clothing, and helped him change. His skin festered with red sores spreading from the burn sites. She changed his pants while keeping a blanket over him to preserve his dignity and her modesty.

She brought him buckets of cool water to soak his burned hands and extra bed linen to keep him warm. In the morning, at midday, and in the evening, she would wait outside so he could relieve himself. She emptied the bucket and cleaned it in the stream.

She tried to talk with him, but he was often too overcome by pain. When he wasn't gritting his teeth, or sleeping, he looked at nothing in particular. When she did something for him, he whispered thank you so faintly that it was little more than a breath. He didn't talk to her otherwise. He couldn't speak correctly because his lips were burned stiff. From the look of his eyes and his ears, he probably couldn't see or hear well anymore.

His name was Galt. He seemed very pious and prayed when he wasn't too tired or reeling from pain. He reminded her of Sir Rowan, who had prayed often when his mood was low. Sir Rowan had slept soundly, however. When Galt slept, he sometimes cried, "Why, God? Why have you done this to me?" A profound sadness filled the little cottage, and Isodore.

Days went by. Sir Dalton sent a man back, and Isodore brought the news to Galt. "The regiment is closing in on the dragon! It is heavily injured. More men are joining the pursuit. They will bring blankets and extra food."

Galt didn't share her enthusiasm and had even less interest in the porridge she brought him. He grew weak and could no longer sit up. Even under layers of bedding, he shivered. He stopped praying. The festering sores spread down his neck and up his arms. His screams weakened into soft moans. She prayed for him, explaining to God that Galt would have done it himself, had he the strength. Each time he slept, she feared he would not wake.

The weather turned cold, and she convinced Father Serafin to bring men to move Galt to a thatch bed she had made by the hearth. Before leaving, the priest delivered Galt's Last Rites. Word of his condition brought the other convalescing dragonslayers limping or carried in to say their last farewell. Lord Edwin and his sons also made an appearance.

Gray autumn skies poured rain. Isodore kept the fire burning strong. Rain leaked through the roof. She moved one of the cottage's kettles to catch the leak before the dirt floor dissolved into a puddle of mud. She peered outside at a village in retreat: people hunched over, dashing down the road, disappearing into the dark interiors of their cottages. A mother duck waddled happily with a dozen ducklings on the deserted road. Heavy drops of pure, untouched water streaked down from the low sky, a chorus thrumming on the roofs. The air smelled of earth's breath.

She gazed for a long time at the cottage's second kettle.

I can save him, she thought. No one will know. She'd already completed the first step, bringing him to the hearth. They all believed the excuse that she could keep him warmer there.

She scrubbed the second kettle clean and left it in the fire to dry and burn away impurities and loitering spirits. When it had cooled, she brought it to the croft to collect rain, blocking it off with the piles of firewood so the animals wouldn't foul the precious, pure water from the sky.

She went to the church to brew tea to help Galt sleep, then to the orphanage to retrieve the jar of asterium. Back in the little cottage, she helped him drink the tea. It was painful on his burned lips, but he took it to fight the cold. Shortly after, he fell back to sleep.

She began to fear as she waited, with the risky plan before her. The sky darkened. At last light, she retrieved the kettle of rainwater. She rechecked the wet road and all around the cottage perimeter. All was clear and quiet when she reentered; her hair and tunic were more wet than dry. She watched Galt for a while, then placed a hand on the burns of his face. First, his forehead, then his cheeks. He didn't respond. He lay so still that he might already be dead.

Her fingers trembled on the jar of asterium. She'd been with Galt through six nights, undisturbed by visitors despite his screams. But an unexpected event could bring a visitor in the middle of this night—news from Sir Dalton, another dragon, another armed confrontation. Someone would demand to enter, break through the flimsy wall, and she would be hauled to the stake. Baldard's words rang a cautionary tale in her ears. "He was caught red-handed." No trial would be needed.

Time and opportunity were slipping away. She may not have another night of rain to deter visitors and drown out her voice before Galt withered away. The regiment could return tomorrow. She reached behind herself and latched the door.

She built up the fire, pulled logs out, and arranged them in an oval around Galt, leaving a small opening for herself by his side. She fed new wood to the hearth and kept the fire ring burning by swapping out the cooled logs. She poured the collected water to scrub her hands, crushed the dried asterium flakes, and mixed it with another scoop of water to make a thick paste. Kneeling down, her trembling hands holding the paste against his burned face, she began chanting the words of the healing spell.

The fire ring slowly dimmed, and she felt time pass, but there was no effect. She was nervous and distracted. Unpracticed and afraid.

Her state of mind was wrong for the task. The spell was one of depth and patience, not of will and passion. Rainfall, not thunder. She tried to calm herself while rebuilding the fire ring. For the spell to work, she must disregard her safety completely, accept the chance of being discovered. She cleared her mind and knelt back down by Galt's side.

She breathed deeply until she stopped shaking. The chants came off her lips like rainfall, soothing and gradual. They shifted to their true origin, shrinking to whispers but gaining strength. She chanted with her mind more than her lips. The rhythm sent warmth spreading over her body, through her bones. She continued in a half trance. Warm tingles moved down her arms and into Galt in waves so strong that, at times, she felt as if she were joined to him. The fire ring dimmed and cooled as the spell began to draw upon its light and heat.

When embers landed on the edges of the bedding, she would pause to brush them off. They left burn marks, so she wouldl pause to wet the edges. Periodically, her fears emerged and disrupted the spell. She rebuilt the fire ring, recovered her state of mind, and continued.

She closed her eyes when she could, for it broke her concentration to look at Galt. Although she felt something happening, she wasn't certain it was doing much for him. He lay still, his first night of peace after nine consecutive nights of unrest. But there was no change in his appearance.

By the cock's crow, hours after she had expected to see some improvement in his burns, there was little. They appeared less raw but remained hideous, perhaps even more so, for they now appeared permanent. She feared she might have erred somewhere in the long task. Though she'd seen her parents use this spell before, and had even helped them, she'd never done it by herself, and never on such extensive injuries. Perhaps her fears were too great. Perhaps she shouldn't have interrupted the spell to wet the edges of the bedding. Perhaps the old asterium had lost its potency. She began to doubt.

The village stirred in the early morning, and, with rising nerves, she ceased the spell to avoid being caught. "I am sorry," she whispered. "It's the best I can do." She shoveled the logs back into the hearth, and swept up the ash from the floor. What she couldn't sweep, she scraped off and tossed into the hearth.

She sat on the floor by Galt and watched him wake, wishing she was a better sorceress and feeling sorry for him. The failed effort bound her to him somehow. When he opened his eyes, she had a tentative, hopeful smile for him. "Good morning, Galt. How do you feel?"

It took him a moment to come out of his confusion. He sat up and looked around, at her, at the cottage, at the floor, the hearth. As if realizing he had just awoken from a terrible nightmare, a bright smile popped onto his disfigured face. She didn't know what to say.

He felt no pain. He talked normally, asking what had happened and how long he had been sleeping, sounding happy and excited. When he removed the blanket and saw his scarred hands, the smile died on his burned lips. He bent to look at his reflection in the kettle of rain water, running his fingertips over his face. He fell silent and refused to talk any further.

11

Subjugation

On Dragon's Ridge, no man would see Isodore cast the healing spell. In that way, at least, she need not fear. Hatred and helplessness were what she felt. The savage beast was her captor, an enemy of the Church, and a tormentor of men. The asterium it gave her changed nothing.

The small egret it had brought her wasn't enough, but she wouldn't ask for more. As in the hungry years, she ate the cartilage and dragged the bone between her teeth to scrape off remaining bits of meat. She cracked the bones with a rock to eat the marrow. Nothing remained for the crows.

The dragon brought a new block of ice, its name for the miraculous white rock. These rocks melted a little each day and eventually disappeared. To collect enough water to soften the asterium, she melted ice in the dented Norman casque placed in the hot coals.

She used some of the water to wash the asterium. Holding the plant, she wondered how the beast had found something it would have taken her months to find, if she was lucky.

"You have been searching for this plant," she said, staring as she waited for an answer.

"Yes."

That explained why it had brought back no food for days. It was intent on finding the asterium.

"Where did you find it?"

"The forest."

Curiosity got the best of her. "Where in the forest? Which part?"

"In the foothills to the north."

"How do you know what to look for?"

"I will tell you . . . in time."

It seemed to know how valuable the knowledge was to her. Her parents had always looked for asterium in the trees near rivers and meadows. They often searched for months without success. She wondered if her captor was gloating, but she couldn't read its dragon face.

She proceeded with the spell's preparations under its watchful eye. She had no choice. If she didn't use the asterium, death would have her soul, and the dragon would have her flesh. She must deny death so she could deny the beast.

Hope was a strange thing. When she had none, she was ready for death. Now, she had hope and feared death.

She chewed the chalky, bitter plant and soaked it in the remaining water. The dragon set a big wood pile burning, then yielded the ground so she could arrange the fire into an oval. She brought the helmet with the pulverized asterium into the center and lay down in the fire ring. She unlaced the neck of her tunic, brought the paste to her swollen flesh, and began her chant.

The dragon tended to her as she had, not long ago, tended to Galt. She chanted through most of the night, while the stars turned across the deep blue sky. The beast fed the fire. When embers landed on her clothes, it pressed its wing-tip finger down to put out the glow. Occasional embers landed on her skin, and she felt the dragon's finger on her thigh, on her belly, on her arm. Gentle touches that she despised.

Death didn't try to wrestle her life away that night, and her pain vanished, as Galt's had. The dragon left, flying toward the distant predawn horizon, leaving only the sound of wing beats fading into the absolute silence of the mountain morning.

Feeling whole again, she stayed to greet the new day. She swept the coals together on each side of her and added more wood. Balanced by the fire's heat, the chilly morning soothed her.

She sat at the precipice, watching the twilight glow. The peaks above her caught the first orange light of sun reaching across the vast plains. Her first sunrise since being captured brought a new day, with promising skies and a fate dire beyond anything she had ever known. The pain and swelling in her chest and wrist were no more. Gone, too, were the fever, chills, and debilitating fatigue. The chest wound was a dry and ugly hole she knew would fade in the coming months. For her life, she had given away the secret her parents had taught her to keep at all costs: "You must never, ever, tell anyone," they said.

But now, the dragon knew what she was.

And it could speak.

12

To Kill a Dragon

Galt remained in the small cottage, his mood dark. Isodore found him rolled up in bed linen or hanging his head at the trestle table, studying his burned hands and feeling the scars on his face. He wanted nothing from her, accepting but one small meal a day. Perhaps he would have preferred to die. She wondered if she had expended her asterium and risked her life just to ruin his.

Two days later, the regiment returned. While the villagers gathered around the triumphant men, Isodore wandered over to the carts to look upon the creature that destroyed Galt. Its gruesome head lay inside. The skin was dry and showed no sign of spoiling. A medium-large black dragon, its head was the size of a horse's, with a gaping mouth. Its lips were drawn back, baring pointed teeth. Its red eyes still burned with hatred and pain. A woodcutter's heavy ax was lodged in its forehead.

Eventually, some villagers wandered over to the cart.

"It don't smell like no dead animal. It smell like ash," said an adolescent boy making a close examination.

"Exactly," explained Sir Wilfred, the talkative knight. "That is the smell of a dead dragon. They are creatures of fire. Nothing will eat them, not even worms. Their flesh dries quickly. Their bodies turn to ash in time, even the skull. Dragonslayers used to bring back more of the beasts, but it took too much effort if we were far from a road. It's not worth it, because everything just turns to ash in the end."

He reached into the cart and lifted the head by the ax. The crowd gasped. "It is not as heavy as it looks," Sir Wilfred explained. "They're light for their size and strength."

"Can I touch it?" a man asked.

"Don't! Ye'll bring more dragons," hissed another villager.

"I touched it," shrugged Sir Wilfred.

"But yer a dragonslayer, blessed by the archbishop," replied the villager.

The man changed his mind about touching the dead skull. He studied it with a mix of curiosity, disgust, and fear, then crossed himself.

Later, the villagers gathered in the church grounds to make claims for things the regiment took from them in the rush to hunt down the dragon. The regiment clerk, assisted by Edwin's reeve, interviewed the villagers to record appropriated items, extra food, ropes, carts, clothing, pails, and so on. Time spent caring for the injured, burying the dead, and rebuilding what was destroyed was also recorded. The Church would compensate these costs.

Isodore would not be compensated, because she was under the Church's employment. But Father Serafin told her, "I want you to come to the nave this afternoon. Sir Dalton requested you."

"Has he spoken to Galt?"

"No one had spoken to Galt. His regiment had been asking how he had recovered so suddenly, but he refused to see or talk to anyone."

Isodore breathed a sigh of relief. She had recognized that had Galt not slept through the long hours during which she had cast her spell—he might know what she did. She had overlooked this obvious detail when she thought she could hide her act.

After a dragon battle, it was common for a regiment to provide an account of the battle to the local priest. If the local lord was cooperative, he was invited as a courtesy. It was to encourage more cooperation. Lord Edwin had been more than cooperative. That afternoon, his family and a score of dragonslayers gathered in the church nave, where Lord Edwin's servants served a fine meal.

Isodore wore the lace-trimmed tunic and necklace that Sir Rowan had given her. Sir Dalton, the handsome and chivalrous commander, thanked her graciously for tending to Sir Baret's squire. She accepted with the courtly manners appropriate for the occasion. "It is my honor to be of service to the dragonslayers, to whom we owe our lives and our village." Her manners had earned her the derision of her fellow villagers, and now she was concerned about the lord's family, who knew her only as a peasant. Their disapproving frowns went apparently unnoticed by Sir Dalton.

"I hope you will stay," said Sir Dalton. "Normally, only fighting men would have any interest in hearing the account of the battle, but I think you ought to know something about the man you looked after."

The commander turned to Lord Edwin. "You don't mind, do you?" he asked. "Galt was Sir Baret's squire, and I think the good knight would feel a debt of gratitude toward Isodore."

Lord Edwin nodded but his frown stayed. "Of course, of course. That is, if she does not find talk of fighting too disturbing or confusing. I know that fighting a dragon is no simple matter."

"Good point, Lord Edwin. But we have just the man to help Isodore. Sir Wilfred, might I take you from your admirers for a moment? There's someone I would like you to meet."

Sir Wilfred excused himself from Lord Edwin's daughters and grandchildren. A gentle man in his mid-forties, with black hair and an ordinary face, he sensed that Isodore wanted to be invisible.

"Don't worry," he whispered to her.

He walked Isodore to the back of the room, where they took their seats. Throughout the meeting, he filled in the details for her in low whispers. He didn't draw as much attention to her as she had feared, and he seemed to delight in his task.

Sir Dalton started after the men took their seats and the other women were ushered out of the hall. An enduring lesson from the noblemen's battles with dragons was that the standard battle tactics, from organized arrow volleys to pitched melees, didn't work. Dragons were too strong, their reach too far, and they projected fire. They were hard to kill and could take flight, either to flee or to attack from beyond the range of lethal weapons, or simply to return when the dragonslayers had moved on. Dragonslayers sought to fight on their own terms. Sir Dalton's ambush was staged to keep the dragon from fleeing, surround the dragon, make it fight, and subdue it for execution. By the time a beast realized it had been tricked, it would be too late.

The dragonslayers left a heavy old cow in the soggy field to bait the dragon. It was expensive bait, but it ensured that the thief wouldn't simply fly off with the prize. Shortly after the villagers had entered their underground shelters, the beast attacked.

About two hundred paces across, the field was big enough for the ambush, but small enough to let the men escape to the woods, should the dragon give chase.

Sir Dalton rode in, armed with a bow and two full quivers of arrows. To avoid alerting the dragon to the kind of foe it faced, he was dressed as a common warrior wearing Lord Edwin's crest, not in a straw suit. But his clothes were thoroughly wet, as were the horse's.

Sir Dalton's arrows irritated the dragon, but couldn't penetrate its tough flesh deeply enough to cause serious injury. That wasn't their purpose. He taunted and angered the beast, tempting it into a fight. Like all regiment commanders, Sir Dalton had fought in all positions of attack and knew how to read dragons. When it flew at him, he turned and fled. Unburdened by heavy armor, he let the dragon get close before signaling for his fast, agile courser to turn or accelerate into the woods. The frustrated dragon spat a single fireball before pitching up to avoid the trees, then circled and returned to the cow. In the woods, Sir Dalton pulled out a towel soaking in his saddle pouch and doused the burning mucus that had struck his saddle. Trained close to fires, the horse could be counted on to stay calm—as long as the fire wasn't too great.

Sir Dalton repeated his tricks to test the dragon and wear it out. It kept returning to the cow, but kept its eyes on him, exactly what Dalton wanted.

The arrows forced the dragon to face and watch Sir Dalton,

while the men positioned themselves in the woods behind the creature. They couldn't read the dragon and had to rely on Sir Dalton's signals. Perhaps it began to suspect. It peered into the trees. Dalton sent an arrow into its chest to remind it to pay attention to him. It hissed through a snarling grimace.

Sir Gustav emerged from the forest on the dragon's right, also dressed like an ordinary warrior. The dragon turned to threaten him, allowing Sir Wilfred and his crossbow formation to sneak up on its left. Sir Dalton moved toward Sir Wilfred's side, loosing an arrow as he went, and the beast's eyes followed. Its momentary surprise at the sight of Sir Wilfred's formation allowed Sir Baret's group to rush in to replace Sir Gustav, who repositioned himself at the dragon's rear. The trap was sprung.

The beast was surrounded by sixteen dragonslayers. The left and right formations each had three men armed with large tethered crossbows. A shieldman accompanied each crossbowman, protecting him from dragon fire. Dragon shields are as large as doors but thin. Laden with wet straw, they are heavy and cumbersome, requiring both hands to wield. The formations were on foot, to give them the best angle for using the tethered crossbows. Each formation was protected by a lance-wielding knight. To reach over the heads of the formation, dragon lances were much longer than the standard ones, and the knights often used two hands when aiming. They were difficult to aim, but dragons made big targets. Behind the formations, other dragonslayers brought loaded crossbows to replace the ones used.

The men on foot were dressed in full straw suits, including straw-lined helmets. Only the crossbowmen's hands were bare, to let them work their weapons and tethers. Though the beast's size and strength were formidable, the men were largely protected from its fire.

The dragon snapped at the men, feigning charges, blowing flames, and spitting fireballs. It looked for a way past them, testing their lines for a weakness. The crossbowmen counted on the knights to hold off an attack while they awaited openings to loose their bolts, sharp iron rods with tethers attached near the midpoint.

Launched at a dragon's wing, they threaded the tether through the vulnerable membrane. By controlling the tether, the men could restrain the beast. The dragon faced crippling wing damage should it resist or flee.

"For an instant, I thought it might take flight," Sir Dalton said. "Had it done so, our tethered bolts would have brought it down once and for all. But many dragons have learned to keep their wings folded when around us. The first bolt failed to thread the tether through."

Sir Wilfred explained to Isodore. "It pinned a wing to the dragon's side but didn't thread the tether through the membrane. The bolts can't penetrate far into the tough muscle. It fell out in the fighting. We rotated in another man, with a cocked crossbow."

"The dragon was growing impatient, and irritated by the arrows in its chest," said Sir Dalton. "I ordered the crossbowmen not to wait. They weren't going to get the chance they wanted. The left formation soon threaded a tether through the membrane. Ideally, the bolt would have struck near the knuckle, so it would make the longest tear possible, but that was a smaller target. The bolt was well placed, given the circumstances, halfway back."

"How close were the crossbowmen?" Lord Edwin asked. "Couldn't they have used a war ax to pull the wing open?"

Sir Wilfred told Isodore, "Never works. You can't reach around the dragon shield. And even if you could hook the wing, the beast would pull you off your feet, and that's the end of you."

While Sir Dalton gave a more tactful answer and weaved around the lord's suggestions, Sir Wilfred continued whispering. "A man rode forth with a rope. Its other end was already secured to a tree. He met the crossbowman and joined his rope to the tether, so the tether was secure, no matter what happens. The dragon tried to take the tether in its teeth. I drove my lance into its shoulder to prevent it. The lance with the weight of a horse behind it is the only weapon that can hurt the great beasts. This creature then tried to burn the tether, but the cord was wet. I could see the steam. The creature's fire was exceptionally hot. But I thought—"

Sir Wilfred stopped himself and turned to the front of the room, where Sir Dalton continued, after the questions.

Isodore liked the knight sitting next to her, despite his youthful presumption that she had much interest in dragonslaying. She was more interested in his kindness than in the knowledge he imparted, but her fascination with the dragonslayers' clever scheme grew quickly.

The dragon bit Sir Wilfred's lance, trying to break it. Sir Baret drove his lance into the creature's other side. It feigned a leap at his horse, then threw a spray of flaming mucus across his formation. The shields protected the men on foot. Sir Baret withdrew his lance to douse the fire before the heat got to the horse. The dragon turned back to Sir Wilfred's side. With a deafening roar, it threw another spray at his formation. Already committed, Wilfred kept his lance in place with one hand while dousing fire with the other.

The rope slipped backward through the pierced wing until the bolt stopped it. The long, slender wing fingers weren't strong enough to fight the horse's tug. As the wing was forced open, the other crossbowmen in the left formation took aim.

"The way the creature roared, the way it looked at its wing being forced it open—it wasn't rage, but fear. Panic. It knew what was happening."

On the other side, Sir Baret had snuffed out the fire on his horse and on himself. The formation rushed in while the dragon was fighting the tether. Unfortunately, the beast decided to spring.

"It sacrificed its wing," Sir Dalton said.

The creature lunged away from Sir Wilfred. The tether held fast and ripped the membrane to the back of the wing. The crossbow-men loosed their bolts, but without time to aim, all missed the membrane. The beast was free of the tether and of Sir Wilfred's lance.

Filled with rage, it threw itself into the right formation. Sir Baret placed his lance tip into the dragon's chest, but the force of the beast pushed his horse back and knocked over the entire formation, including Galt. The middle shieldman and his partner fell, obstructing Sir Baret's path to the dragon. The dragon's knuckle came down on a shield, pinning Galt's shieldman. Galt fell on his crossbow and lost it as he rolled away from the snapping jaws. When he got to his feet, he ran.

A bold, young crossbowman, Galt had taken the formation's front position, closest to the beast's teeth and flames. In an instant that would forever define his character in the eyes of his commander, he made a critical decision. Though he had dropped the crossbow, he held on to the tether. This coil of rope hung on an upturned lever attached to his belt. The rope was loose, so it could uncoil rapidly when the bolt flew. When Galt fell, the coil dropped off the lever. But he had the presence of mind to hold the rope over his head as he rolled, keeping it from winding around himself. He dragged the crossbow by the rope as he fled. Out of the dragon's reach, he retrieved it.

The dragon had killed Galt's shieldman and pinned the back pair under their shield. The middle pair escaped while Sir Baret's lance held the creature at bay. The dragon's keel stopped his lance from penetrating across its chest, preventing a deeper wound. The horse leaned into the lance while its master tried to push the dragon back, but a single knight wasn't enough. Galt took aim as the dragon clawed the shield aside to expose the dragonslayers it had pinned down. The shieldman screamed. Galt squeezed the trigger.

Designed to hit dragons' enormous wings, the tethered crossbow is not an accurate weapon. With a soaked tether dragging the bolt down, the crossbowman has to compensate for the rapid loss of speed. The bolt isn't big enough to weaken an angry dragon, unless it hits a sensitive spot. To accomplish this, Galt had to be close. Before the dragon snapped its jaws around the downed man, his bolt struck it in the throat. The beast recoiled from the shieldman and unleashed a fierce jet of flame at Galt. The wet straw and hide clothing he wore protected his body, but his hands had been left bare to work the crossbow. And his straw-covered helmet had tumbled away when he was knocked down. He turned and ran but, blinded by the scorching flames, he stumbled on the uneven ground and fell. Dragon fire ravaged him while he rolled, that hot blue fire that can boil water off the tether. Green grass around him wilted and turned to smoke as the flame swallowed Galt.

Sir Baret was the newest knight in the regiment, but the eldest, a veteran of many campaigns and known for his fierceness in battle. He made the dragon pay for its attack on Galt. The lance's barbed tip hooked onto the dragon's tough flight muscle. He wrenched the weapon back, pulling on the dragon by its own flesh, letting Galt roll away. When Galt was out of its range, the dragon roared with pain and bit down on the lance, fighting for control of the weapon. The lance broke.

From the dragon's back and left sides, Sir Wilfred, his mucus fire now doused, and Sir Gustav drove their lances hard into the beast. The dragon spun toward the two knights. Sir Baret left the barbed lance head in the creature and turned toward the woods for another lance. In his haste he didn't notice the dragon's tail whipping around the legs of his horse. The animal stumbled and fell, throwing him to the ground.

The dragon twisted away from Sir Wilfred's and Sir Gustav's lances and leaped at them, spitting fire. The knights couldn't raise their long, heavy lances fast enough. The lances broke when the dragon landed on them. The knights rode off for replacements, trailing flames from the mucus that struck them. Sir Dalton called them back to lure the beast away, but this voice was lost over the dragon's roar and the men's screams. The commander was left trying to drive the dragon away from Sir Baret with nothing more than arrows and feigned charges. It almost worked.

When Sir Baret attempted to mount his horse, the stallion stepped aside, refusing to let him. Its ribs had broken when it fell on its stirrup, but the straw-lined blanket it wore hid the gross injury. By the time Sir Baret realized this, he had wasted precious time.

The dragon covered Sir Dalton and his horse with burning spit, forcing the knight again to fight the fires and keep the horse calm. The dragon then turned to Sir Baret, who by that time, had made his way to the horse's other side, to try to mount.

A spray of fire and spit struck him and the horse. The already injured animal finally panicked and bolted. Knowing the futility of trying to escape on foot, Sir Baret, his back aflame with burning dragon spit, drew his sword and faced the beast. Following an old habit developed when fighting other men, he carried a sword even when ambushing a dragon, defying dragonslayer wisdom that swords were of little use against the dragons' much greater strength and reach.

The dragon sent a flame at him. He brought up an arm to protect his face. Enclosed by the curtain of fire, he never saw the bite coming. But he must have felt the teeth on his leg. He swung for the dragon's neck and missed, as it yanked him off his feet and whipped him into the ground. He dropped the sword. The dragon pushed itself up by its forelimbs and with a flick of its neck, threw the knight's limp, flaming body at Sir Dalton.

The battle was a disaster.

Sir Dalton yelled for the survivors to reform. He took a lance, but without the straw suit, he could only attack the rear, away from the dragon fire. When the dragon turned to face him, he had to retreat and circle. Sir Wilfred and Sir Gustav returned with new lances, but without the crossbowmen, the dragon was free to open its wings. It swatted the lances away with ease and forced them into defensive retreats.

"Keep it surrounded!" ordered Sir Dalton. "Crossbows," he roared.

The remaining crossbowmen and shieldmen reconstituted into three pairs as they ran back into the fight with newly drawn crossbows. One shieldman was a slow and nervous squire, with little training behind the big shield. But it was enough. When the dragon saw the shields closing in, it leaped over Sir Gustav's lance and escaped across the field. It took to the air with rapid, awkward wing beats, one wing torn and the other weakened by a pectoral wound.

The crossbowmen chased the beast and pulled their triggers. Three bolts rose and fell, drawing their tethers in two smooth arcs over the meadow. The third bolt found an outstretched wing, but having lost so much speed, it failed to pass through the membrane.

"Coward!" Sir Dalton yelled after the fleeing creature, sending two arrows into its belly and wing before missing on the third.

The dragonslayers on the church roof watched the creature

escape as long as they could, noting the direction it headed and its distance. Certain it couldn't go far in its condition, Sir Dalton regrouped his men and left to hunt it down.

"The dragon has faced tethered crossbows before," Sir Wilfred told Isodore. "It wouldn't be fooled again. If we didn't catch it, we never would."

Sir Baret never stood again. Sir Wilfred dropped a sopping towel on his back to put out the burning mucus. The downed knight regained consciousness and tried to crawl to safety but didn't make it. They found him with his leg soaked in blood, his back broken, and his heart still.

After three days of searching, the men found the dragon nursing its wounds near a meadow. Weakened by injuries and hunger, it relied on its fire to keep the dragonslayers away. When its fire reserve was depleted, the regiment closed in. It fled before the men could encircle it. In its earlier escape, the left wing membrane had torn to the knuckle and flapped like a piece of cloth. Tethered bolts flew at the open wings. One struck and caused a small rip, but that, too, would worsen as it flew.

The dragon had trouble staying above the treetops. They found it the next day in another meadow and replayed the battle without the fiery breaths. It escaped again, flapping its torn wings furiously.

"Pathetic sight," said Sir Wilfred. "The creature couldn't right itself. It flew in circles until it wore itself out and fell into the forest."

The dense wood trapped the dragon on its side but also protected it from the charge of lance-wielding knights. The regiment used the rare tactic of engaging the dragon with swords, spears, and axes, hacking the trapped beast to its grizzly end as it struggled, unable to bring its teeth around the trees to its attackers.

"I wanted to put it out of its misery," Sir Wilfred whispered. "Not even a dragon should suffer such a death." That was why he buried the ax in its forehead.

Thanks to Sir Wilfred, Isodore felt she understood dragonslaying far more than she had ever expected to, perhaps more than Lord Edwin and his sons did. All they asked about was the fighting. The planning, cleverness, and bravery it took to face and defeat such a foe made her shiver with gratitude. She understood Galt better too. He wasn't just an unfortunate victim of a battle gone wrong. He was brave. She wished she had known and had told him when he was suffering. She would still, though she doubted that it mattered to him.

THE NEXT MORNING, the regiment gathered at the steps of the church to depart. The villagers saw their heroes off with flowers from their gardens. The knights paid their respects to their lord host, and a formal farewell was given by Father Serafin, with Isodore behind him. The priest was brief and nervous, but clearly honored to have the role. As he spoke, Isodore saw a few young dragonslayers straggling to the line, with backward glances at pretty lasses. Sir Dalton thanked all who helped his regiment accomplish their task. Sir Dalton thanked Lord Edwin's family and the villagers for their help. He thanked Isodore publicly for tending to Galt. He even kissed her hand. When he named Isodore, the crowd's cheering deflated enough for Isodore to hear faint snickers.

GALT DIDN'T ATTEND, and she would have been surprised if had. She had last seen him two days ago, walking away as she went to watch the dragonslayers' triumphant return, his head hidden in the dark hooded robe she had borrowed from a monk.

After the regiment departed, she returned to the orphanage by walking around Savelle's perimeter, to avoid seeing the villagers, particularly the women who had whispered to each other when Sir Dalton bowed his head and brought her hand to his lips. Even though he had also kissed the hands of Lord Edwin's wife and daughters, she knew the villagers regarded her differently.

13

Dragon Lord

Warm thoughts of safety in the dragonslayers' hands alleviated some of Isodore's misery on Dragon's Ridge. She imagined hearing her children singing dragonslayer songs on a Sunday afternoon. She gazed at the indiscernible distance where she thought Savelle lay, under the tattered blanket of clouds stretching across the sky.

She was healthy again, feeding on meat that the dragon gave her. It tasted bland without spice, but it was plentiful enough to feed her on days the dragon didn't hunt, if she stored it in the cave, wrapped tightly in the surcoat remains to keep it away from the crows and flies, and recooked it each night.

She learned the habits of the dragons in the vicinity, particularly those of her captor. On most days, she saw dragons circling upward on invisible columns in the distant sky. She knew they were dragons because their wingspans were five to ten times greater than the eagles and buzzards soaring with them. She noted a peculiar pattern. While eagles and buzzards spiraled upward with no effort, the dragons had to flap their wings. Perhaps the smaller, lighter creatures ascended more easily.

Most afternoons, when the wind picked up, she could see dragons gliding along the ridgelines. She had learned to find them, even against the textured backdrop of meadows, forests, and rocks. But it remained hard to tell which was her captor. They were all small dragons and looked dark at a distance. She knew her captor by its behavior. When a neighbor came too close to its mountain, it would intercept, and the trespasser would steer away to avoid the confrontation, a routine familiar enough that she no longer felt fear or awe at the sight of dragons. Eventually, the neighbors stayed away.

Between morning and afternoon, there would be a period with few dragons in the air. Perhaps the winds were unfavorable for flight, or the animals they hunted were in hiding. Her captor rarely went out or returned during this time. If it was away, she had the time to herself.

One day, with an eye out for it, she paced the length of the precipice, studying her options for escape. The southern route remained impossible. On its barren slab, she found one crack her fingertips could cling to, but nothing to help her traverse to safety. She spent an hour trying the small ledges past the north end of the nest. Though she discovered more ledges than she had when she had first arrived, they were all false hope, each one narrowing to nothing. Climbing down the cliff had the same outcome. Clawing her way back up, she lay on the ground, dispirited.

She considered the climb up the mountainside. Even when injured, she had been able to scale the edge of the slab that formed the cave, but that was only halfway to the ridge, with a sheer wall remaining. She climbed to the slab's apex to reexamine her possibilities. There were footholds that worked well enough. Four feet above the apex, there was only a crack, too small for her toes to find purchase. She climbed down, found a femur from the bone pile and pounded it to fragments, which she brought to the apex and selected one to pound into the crack to make a secure perch. She balanced herself on this makeshift foothold. The rest of the way was unworkable, with only the granite's rough surface to hang her fingernails on. Her attempts tired her. She sweated from exertion and the fear of losing her balance. She used her remaining strength to climb back to the relative safety of the apex.

Directly above, on the ledge she was trying to reach, was a small protrusion onto which a loop of rope might hook. She climbed back down and dug through the bone pile for the ropes she had seen when she first arrived. She found three segments, two of which disintegrated when she bent them. The remaining one partially disintegrated, leaving her with a three-foot section.

She removed her tunic and tied one sleeve to each end of the rope to make a loop. Wearing only her linen chemise, she climbed back to the apex, onto the precarious footholds and, clinging to the wall, swung the rope up toward the protrusion.

Excitement and hope gave way to sheer determination as she kept swinging the makeshift lifeline up to the protruding point. Her determination flagged after half an hour. The protrusion was more of a stub than a hook, and her loop barely reached it. Tired, her foot slipped from its little foothold, and she dropped back to the apex. She lost her balance. Catching the apex of the slab with her arms, she saved herself from the fifteen-foot drop. But the fright drained any remaining hope.

Back on the apex, she rested to regain her courage before another try. The windy hours had begun, and a few dragons were skimming the ridges. Out of caution, she abandoned her escape attempt, climbed down to the cave, untied the rope, stashed it, and put her tunic back on.

Isodore was trying to determine whether one of the dragons that she could see was her captor, when from the distance came a distinctly different dragon. The newcomer was larger than any she had seen on the ridge. It was traveling along the ridge southeast of her, taking short flights as though exploring, perhaps looking for a nesting site. She watched with absentminded interest as the wandering dragon made its way from point to point along the ridge. Catching sight of Isodore, it came straight for her.

Isodore ducked back into the cave. A massive shadow passed over the ledge. The wing beats were noticeably louder than those of the black dragon. Peering out, she saw it turning overhead, a green body with broad, dark stripes. It circled and made another pass.

Why had her captor not returned? It dawned on her. This was the reason the black dragon had kept her alive. This creature was its dragon lord.

And she was the offering.

The striped dragon flared its wings and touched down on the ledge, darkening the cave entrance. Isodore stooped under the low ceiling of the cave's far end, listening to heavy feet grinding the gravel as her heart began to race. A clawed knuckle settled at the entrance. The dragon head entered on the end of a hideously knobbed neck, extending toward her with widening eyes and mouth.

The dragon stopped, its shoulders blocked by the narrow entrance. It lowered itself to the rock pile, where the entrance was widest, but it couldn't extend its long forelimbs forward to move. The dragon stretched its neck, long tendons bulging from head to shoulders, bared its teeth, and growled, sending a warm breath toward her. It roared and she scrambled through the small opening, whimpering.

The dragon pulled out of the cave and crouched toward south end, narrowing its stance to fit on the ledge. It was twice the black dragon's size. She squeezed back through the little hole to get away. The creature returned to the entrance and flushed her out again. The game repeated. When the dragon crouched toward the south end again, flaming drool hung from its mouth.

Isodore crawled back in through the little hole. The dragon peered in after her and spat through the hole. She jumped back as mucus splattered before her and set up a wall of flame across the narrow cave. It sealed off her access to the hole. The dragon returned to the entrance to collect its meal.

Isodore grabbed the half-eaten deer leg she kept in the cave and frantically swept the burning spit aside, making enough of a gap to slip through, with the dragon snapping after her. Frustrated, it pushed its shoulders against the cave entrance and gave an angry roar. It spat again, scaring her back through the little hole for the third time.

Once outside, she looked past the striped body sticking out of the cave. Black wings glided down from the clear sky. Her captor had returned. She tried to crawl back into her hole, but the striped dragon had laid down a curtain of flames across her little passage.

There was nowhere to go.

She looked down the precipice, sweat dampening her neck. Yes, she decided, she would prefer die in a crushing instant than be torn apart by these two beasts.

The black dragon descended from the north. Its neck taut and its teeth bared, it passed the striped dragon, reached and bit its left forelimb. The black body continued past, swung around the bitten limb and slammed down on the ledge. Isodore leaped up to avoid the tail as it whipped into the wall behind her. She landed on it, her arms waving for balance, then fell off when the black dragon righted itself.

Jaws clamped on the captive forelimb, it pulled. Braced low, the black dragon stretched the bitten appendage straight, snarling as it strained. Its teeth slipped along the forelimb, raking away skin the knuckle. The big striped dragon fought blindly, its head stuck in the narrow cave. It pulled against the black dragon to back itself out. Its feet skidded; its free forelimb clawed at the rocks behind for something to hold onto. Its roars were ferocious.

Eventually, size and strength prevailed. When the striped dragon's head came out of the cave, it sprang forward and discharged a massive fire stream, engulfing the black dragon, leaving nothing but a yellow fireball with two black wings in a roiling bubble of scorched air.

Isodore turned her face from the heat, feeling as if she were standing too close to an oven. When the fireball flickered away, smoke was rising from the black dragon's back. A blaze smothered its face, neck, and shoulders. Black scales sizzled under the flames.

Yet the little dragon did not relent.

It wasn't the black dragon that was burning, but the spit sprayed with the fire stream. The struggle for the injured wing continued unaffected by the fiery breath. Globs of mucus boiled and flared on the black dragon's scales, until they burned themselves out. The only thing that remained burning was the wound on the striped dragon's forelimb.

Flames flickered and dripped from the green knuckle that was held tight in the black dragon's jaws. Fire spread back up its wing bone along the lacerations.

Isodore watched in horrified fascination. Dragon blood burned! Flesh, blood, and mucus. Each creature was a living vessel of fuel and fire.

Both dragons hunched low, bracing against each other on a ledge too narrow for the fight. Their limbs scraped on the granite. They took turns yanking on the taut, stretched wing. Isodore pressed herself against the rock to avoid being hit by the thrashing beasts.

The fingers of the striped dragon's bitten limb splayed. The black dragon flicked its neck to slap the splayed wing fingers into the ground to break them. Before it succeeded, the fingers folded back against the arm, rendering the tactic ineffective.

Despite its size, the striped dragon was in a painful, defensive fight, with its adversary in control of its strained wing. The intruder's eyes bulged. Its roar sounded like screams. But it had enough wits left to change tactics. Instead of struggling to take back its wing, it suddenly lunged forward, reaching its long neck, jaws agape. The black dragon relinquished the wing and withdrew just before the bigger jaws snapped closed on its neck. Her captor stumbled backward, slipped off the ledge, and fell away, its head whipping over the cliff like the loose end of a rope.

The intruder threw down its injured knuckle to stop itself short of the cliff. It lifted the knuckle again, eyeing the burning, mauled limb. It limped backward like a three-legged dog before steadying itself in the characteristic crouching stance. The wing was aflame where it bled, at the knuckle and along lines raked by the black dragon's teeth. Flaps of skin from its forelimb hung like burning rags.

The creature dragged its tongue along the arm wound, then took the burning knuckle in its mouth to snuff out the fire. It placed the wing back on the ground, shifting its weight cautiously. It was hurt, but not enough to forget Isodore. It crouched toward her, limping.

There was no time to climb back into the small hole. She glanced past the south end of the ledge. The only escape was to jump to her death. She watched the striped dragon's head extend toward her, teeth bared. She scooted to the edge, ready to spring away and end her life on her own terms.

A roar from above and behind stopped the intruder. The dragon looked up. Her captor dragon dove in, teeth bared and hungry for another bite. The larger dragon brought its own teeth to meet its attacker, forcing the black dragon to veer away. Her captor circled back and tried again while the larger beast fended it off and countered with its bigger teeth, neither one inflicting another wound. Meanwhile, the mucus fire in the cave had burned out, and Isodore climbed back in through her little hole, scorching her hands on the hot rocks, temporarily relieved, but feeling hopelessly doomed.

Soon the sounds of swooping wings and growling threats stopped. She peeked outside in the eerie aftermath of silence. The intruder was fleeing, or trying to, in a slow and awkward struggle to stay aloft. Its injured wing was partially extended, flapping quickly to stay airborne. Even stranger, its body was oddly curved into a C. She realized that it was trying to hold more of its weight on the side of the good wing. She had never beheld such a sight. Limping in flight.

Smaller, faster, and more agile, the black dragon dove at its adversary, the way crows harassed hawks. It came from the rear, forcing the striped dragon to turn and fend off the attack. It slowed and lost altitude, but continued toward the valley's outlet.

In the black dragon's next approach, instead of a high-speed dive from the rear, it crossed the striped dragon's path from left to right, taking aim at the good wing.

The big dragon merely flapped its wing deep, under the black dragon's passing mouth. Even more agile at the slower speed, the black dragon turned sharply into its adversary. It clapped its wings, arched its back, and reached with its neck. Held on the right side, the striped dragon's tail didn't withdraw in time. The black dragon snapped its jaws around it.

The striped tail straightened. The small dragon whipped behind the larger. The two swung around each other. Connected head to tail, neither could fly. The black dragon drew in its wings, rolled over, and dropped. It swung underneath and tipped the bigger dragon off its wings. The pair tumbled together. Panicked shrieks echoed up to Isodore as the beasts plummeted, fighting for control. Near the foot of the ridge, the black dragon released the tail. It spread its wings, rolled into level flight, and escaped. The large striped body tumbled with a flailing wing and righted itself. But too late. A sickening crash against the piled rocks showed just how soft the mighty beast actually was against the mountain. A circular cloud of dust puffed into the air. Two seconds later, a crescendo of boulders knocking into each other came ringing up from the valley.

The victor spiraled down, stirring up more dust as it landed. It examined the tremulous broken body, then stepped on the suffering head. It bit down on the neck, shaking as its teeth sank in. The striped dragon's wings flailed in their final throes. The black dragon's head suddenly came up, tearing a gash in the neck. The wound leaked blood, Isodore could tell, even at that distance, because flames danced for hours over it.

THAT EVENING, ISODORE watched the sky turn golden, terrified of how close she had come to death that day. Yet she could not fathom why her captor had kept her alive, if not to offer her to another beast. It had been three weeks since her capture. When the black dragon returned to the nest, it brought in its claws a wild duck. She stood, waiting for it to say something, but it only brushed together a pile of firewood to start her cookfire.

"What do you want with me, dragon?" she asked, before it flew to its perch.

It stopped. "To stay," it said. It studied her for a reaction.

She stood over the duck, arms folded. "How long before you kill me?"

No response but the stare from its silent red eyes.

"Am I your prisoner?"

"No."

"Your servant, then? Your slave?"

"No."

"I am your prisoner! Though I've done nothing to you. Driving away that dragon and bringing me the asterium change nothing. You're nothing but a cruel beast." She dropped to the ground and began to sob. The beast watched her.

"Why did you save me from that dragon? Why did you bring me here?" She drew her legs up and buried her head in her folded arms, her hands curled into trembling fists. She felt the dragon approach by the heat it radiated.

It lowered its horn-crowned head to her. "You . . ." it said in its slow dragon voice, "are beautiful."

She lifted her eyes, facing the crimson orbs smoldering in their black, skeletal pits. She felt the skin on her face pull back as if repelled by the sight, while the tingle of revulsion spread over her like a wave of squirming maggots.

14

In Different Forms

Isodore's revulsion turned to fear of what the dragon truly wanted of her, then festered overnight into anger. Taking her for food, she could understand, but taking her to call her beautiful was sheer torment. Not knowing what to say to it, she didn't speak to the dragon again. The beast didn't seem to notice.

She had become a castaway of the mountain, living in miserable conditions. Mud, dirt, and soot soiled her clothing. To keep her hair tidy, she held it in a bun with a slender bone, a futile effort as the dirt worked into her hair, caking onto the oily strands each time she lay down to sleep. The mountain's dry air cracked her skin and lips. A rough film covered her teeth. She could scrub some of it off with her sleeve, but her breath was pungent. To lessen some of her body odor, she scrubbed herself with chunks of ice. She ripped off a strip from the hem of her chemise to devise a loincloth to absorb her menstrual blood, but her clothing became stained anyway. Ironically, meat—a rare treat for peasants—was all she had to eat, making defecation painful. She relieved herself by the northern end of the ledge and swept the excrement off the ledge with a bone. When the wind blew from the north, and not too briskly, the stench would waft back to her.

A THUNDERSTORM DESCENDED one afternoon. She hid in the cave, shivering and lonely. When the sun shone again, she gazed over the giant mountainous maze, heartbroken, at distant Gascony. At dusk, while waiting for the dragon to break up firewood, she stood at the cliff's edge, peering down at the pile of bones below.

Her anger had turned again, this time into recklessness. Though the sheer drop toward the escarpment still made her dizzy, she no longer feared an accidental fall. The graveyard of the dragon's past victims beckoned to her, voices haunting the breeze that teased her hair and brushed her skin. It would be easy enough to end her misery—just lean and let her body topple like a log.

Lean out and topple ... Lean out and topple ... The world spun.

The thought of ending her life made her fear for her sanity, but it didn't make her step back from the precipice. The choice remained hers. Live on in misery or take a simple and irreversible step to escape everything.

God forbade throwing one's life away, she vaguely recalled Father Julian saying long ago, when she didn't care to question why God thought such a law necessary. Was death not a part of life, bringing it to completion so He might pass judgment? What else would God possibly need to know about her life?

She had given these matters little time or consideration when she sat through Father Julian's sermons, but on Dragon's Ridge, she had nothing but time with her thoughts. And it had come to this, the hell of God or the hell of this dragon.

Her captor paid her no heed.

"What if I jumped off this cliff, dragon? Would you care?"

Her captor stopped breaking firewood and looked at her, its head cocked. "You would die. Why would you want that?"

She spun around to face it, unable to believe it could be so blind.

"Because I might as well be dead!" she snapped, ignoring the danger of angering the beast. "This is no life! I do nothing each day but stew in my hatred of you. How can you stand to be next to someone who hates you so much?"

"Would you prefer to go back to the men?"

It took a few seconds before she understood that it didn't mean a specific group of men. It meant mankind. All men were the same to the dragon, but not to her. "I want to be with my people."

"People!" it spat. "Do they not hate you as you hate me?"

"No! They're kind to me."

"No," it countered. "They are not kind to you. They would kill you. Wouldn't they, sorceress?"

It stuck its face in hers, but she didn't back off at first. Then the dreadful realization washed over her as she stared into the crimson eyes and they stared back. The dragon knew more than her dangerous little secret. It knew the fears she had been hiding since long before their paths crossed.

"Why should you care what people do to me?"

"Because we are the same, sorceress. I know what they would do to you, and you know what they would do to me. They would kill every last one of us. You must know this. You are too old for such ignorance. We are creatures of magic, you and I, unlike them. And they have no love for us."

"What do you know of them? All you do is kill and burn. I had a life with them. I was happy and content. I just want to go back."

"A life based on lies, sorceress. You hide and live in fear of being discovered. Stay here, with me. You and I are the same."

"No. You are a monstrous beast and I am a human being."

The dragon straightened its back, squaring its eyes on her.

"I am a dragon, and you are a sorceress. We are creatures of magic, spirits forged into physical forms. You from blood, and I from fire. Look deep, sorceress. We are magical. We have always been and will always be."

"No. That's ridiculous. I wasn't forged. I wasn't conjured or beckoned with a spell. I was born of a mother. I had a father. And a brother. I saw him born!"

"As had I. Your parents—who created them? The people you wish to return to? No. Your parents were a sorcerer and a sorceress. Each of them born to a sorcerer and sorceress. Like you and your brother, they were forged in their mothers' wombs, from blood, by sorcery. We are of the same spirit, sorceress, in different forms."

She gave up arguing and wished only that she knew the truth.

In her life, so many things that sounded believable and reasonable had turned out to be false. Kind Father Julian had told her that if she lived a life of good deeds, devoted to God, she would join Him in heaven. Then he said that witches were evil, who would suffer eternally in hell. Sir Rowan said God was his Lord, then he sinned and ran from God. Archbishop after archbishop promised deliverance from dragons, but the dragons lived on, untouched in the mountains. Duke after duke swore land being resettled was free of dragons, but they kept granting estates deeper and deeper into heathen land, where the dragons roamed. Her parents said, as they gathered around the hearth fire, that if she could keep the secret, they would teach her all of their wonderful magical spells. But they never did.

After giving her time to reflect, the dragon continued, its deep voice gentler somehow. "If you do not know this, then your parents failed to tell you. They are dead, aren't they? Or lost. Tell me, sorceress. Were they killed by . . . people?"

For a moment, she was determined, out of sheer defiance, to tell the dragon nothing. But there was no keeping the memories from stirring in her mind once the question was asked. She bit her lip, fighting a wave of anger and sorrow that threatened to bring her to her knees. She trembled. Although thinking of her parents always made her sad, it had been years since the memory could make her cry. But cry she did.

15

Wings of Ash

In the village where Isodore had been born and raised, the villagers had a pen in a nearby field, like a small bailey with a short palisade. It kept forest predators from the sacrificial offerings to Ashwing, a vindictive little dragon named for its gray-black mottled wings. Provided that there was an animal waiting when it came, Ashwing left the village in peace. It even drove away other dragons scouting the area. It became the village's dragon lord.

Ashwing grew over many decades, as did its appetite. It expanded its domain to a dozen villages in the area, starving the peasants with increasing demands for food. The villagers begged the archbishop for dragonslayers, but the beast—seven feet tall at the shoulders, among the largest in the land—was so formidable that the task would require the combined strength of three regiments. With the diminished number of dragonslayers, it was a long wait. Wishing to rid themselves of the dragon sooner, the villagers schemed to poison it.

They coated the hide of an old black cow with all the poison they could think of. After devouring part of the animal, Ashwing flew away, and didn't return. The sheep they offered next remained untouched for months. Neighboring villages reported that Ashwing had not visited them either. More weeks passed. The villagers talked of festivities on the village green to celebrate their victory. Finally, Lord Maldon, a man initially skeptical of the plan to poison the dragon, declared the end of Ashwing.

During the celebration, the villagers danced and struck at a straw effigy of their tormentor. Troubadours sang. They even had a song to tell how they had cleverly defeated the beast. The lord came, speaking with great pride of how his village had risen to defeat the fearsome beast. There was even talk that the village would refuse to pay the archbishop's tax.

At the height of the festivities, Ashwing returned like a dark, vengeful spirit. It circled the village green, laying a wall of mucus fire around the stunned revelers. Once they were trapped, it widened the circle, throwing burning mucus into the surrounding orchards. Those not yet trapped didn't know which way to run. Ashwing snatched up thatch roofs and tossed them, burning, into the orchards. With an enormous fire reserve, the beast circled the village, sealing the gaps. By the time the villagers realized Ashwing's intention, it was too late.

The dragon attacked the castle, the church, then the smaller dwellings. It laid a ring of fire around the base of the keep, turning the wooden fort into a fiery tomb for those inside. It smashed mud walls, causing the sanctuary's roof to collapse. It knocked over the water wheel, tearing a gaping hole in the wheelhouse, then threw its fire inside. It spat fireballs at wood and swept its flames over thatch.

Then the carnage began. The dragon spewed streams of fire at panicked villagers, pinning flames on their backs. Succumbing to the pain, they collapsed, writhing on the ground and engulfed by fire, screaming for their God. They crashed into each other while dashing for safety. Wherever they ran, fire and spit followed. Separated family members called out for each other and died in their search.

The villagers had neglected their underground shelters during the century their sacrifices had kept them safe. Villagers now strained against stuck hatches until the flaming roof collapsed on them. Embers floated to yet untouched cottages. The conflagration was alive. Roof after roof caught fire or was torn away. When cottage occupants ran for their lives, the dragon clawed, bit, burned, or tossed them back into the inferno.

In their little cottage, eight-year-old Isodore stood, shaking, holding her little brother Tomas, as her parents argued over risking fire or the dragon. Try as they might, sorcerers had never found a way to protect themselves from fire, for fire was its own magic. Her parents started a concoction, then her mama ordered the children to cover themselves head to toe with soot from the hearth. She did the same, then slapped soot all over her husband while he worked. Isodore coughed and Tomas cried, but her mama yelled at them to continue. Isodore had never seen her mama so frightened. Her papa was hunched over the kettle, chanting incomprehensible verses from his spellbook. A foul smell rose from the concoction.

Her mama took the kitchen knife and sawed off Isodore's hair.

"No, Mama!" Isodore cried, lamenting the years it had taken to grow her long curls.

"Be quiet, girl!"

In a few minutes, all their heads were topped by nothing but short, uneven tufts.

An angry red hole opened in their roof. Burning thatch fell into the cottage. Tomas clung to Isodore, shrieking. She tried to comfort him, but she was terrified. Her mama dragged the trestle table to the back door, and her papa knelt under it to work as the roof fell in, bit by bit. Isodore joined them and gave Tomas to her mama to soothe. A chunk of thatch fell across the table above them. Her mama told her to sweep it away with the broom before it set fire to them. Smoke burned her eyes and filled her lungs. The straw beds caught fire. The cottage felt like an oven. Isodore watched the fire rain down and felt the heat rise. She began to panic.

Sweat etched a trail through the soot on her papa's face. He declared the mixture ready. It was a thick, buttery ointment, now clear as water and no longer smelling of anything. They rubbed it all over their bodies, their skin and clothing, even their faces. They scraped every last bit of it from the kettle.

Isodore's papa put the spellbook into the burning thatch beds and returned with a frightened look of finality. They all waited under the table as her papa peeked out the back door. A section of the roof fell and began to consume the cottage from within. Smoke filled the house and choked everyone. Tomas clung to his mama and buried his face in her chest. Isodore was so hot that she thought she was already on fire.

"Let's go, Papa! Please!" she pleaded, no longer able to pretend she wasn't afraid.

He made them wait. Outside, their neighbors attempted to flee. A family of five ran along the trees looking for a way through the orchard fire. Ashwing plucked their burning roof and dropped it on them. Three of them escaped the bombardment. Ashwing dropped down, crushing one, caught another in its jaws, and slapped down the third. It tossed the second man back into his burning home and gathered up the last man in its wing. The man fought against the membrane until Ashwing took him in its mouth. His bones crunched and he went limp. The dragon vaulted away for more.

When no one was in sight, her papa led them out. They were to run far enough that the house couldn't collapse on them, then fall onto the freshly turned dirt, away from anything that could catch fire, and lie still. If she was confused, she was to do what her parents did and be quiet. She saw her parents burning and looked at herself. She was burning, too. Within seconds, the entire family was engulfed in flames.

The fire wasn't hot—just ephemeral wisps of light and smoke released by the vaporizing ointment that billowed into the air. They dashed through most of the croft and lay down in the bare dirt. It was hard to lie still and pretend to be dead with the sounds of Ashwing and mayhem in their ears. In a few minutes, the concoction ran out. The magic fire and smoke stopped. The family was four blackened bodies lying still on the ground. Isodore's mama curled around Tomas to muffle the sound of his cries. Her father reminded her to be still. "It won't waste fire on the dead," he said. "Lie still. Make it think yer dead."

"It will eat us!" Isodore cried.

"Not if it thinks we're burned. No more talking."

She was afraid, but she knew what was expected of her, and she didn't argue.

After some time, the sound of dragon wings stopped, but she could still hear Ashwing roar and the sound of falling roofs and crumbling walls. The dragon was on the ground, tearing down what remained of the church and wheelhouse at the other end of the town. Screams came less frequently. Isodore wanted to run for the forest.

Some neighbors did just that, when Ashwing tore down their cottage. The dragon was upon them. It gathered them in its wings and released them as burning figures. It watched them run until they collapsed.

When all who hadn't escaped were dead, Ashwing skulked around the village, gorging itself on the unburned kills. It ate their neighbors but didn't finish—there was too much flesh, even for its appetite—but it took a piece of each body and left the rest to rot. Red blood dripped down its chin and neck. The sound of breaking sinew and snapping bones made Isodore want to scream. Her papa's hand tightened around hers, reminding her to stay still.

"If anyone moves," he whispered firmly, "it's certain we'll all die."

The dragon's footsteps came, louder and closer. A massive shadow slid over the entire family. The dragon's head passed slowly over them. It sniffed their soot-covered bodies then drew back with a grunt. The family remained still, lifeless. The footsteps continued past them and faded. When Isodore dared to open her eyes, she saw the hunched, mottled shape skulking through her neighbors' charred ruins. After another half hour, they heard the sound of leathery wings beating as the enormous beast lifted into the air. The family rose and ran past the torn bodies of their neighbors, into the dead, blackened orchard. Before setting out in search of food and shelter, they found a shallow stream and washed, but the stubborn soot remained.

THE FIRE SWEPT across the land, destroying three more villages and left the frontier burning for days. Most of the lord's family, his guards, and servants perished. Homes and crops burned; the surviving villagers gathered in makeshift hamlets outside those villages, competing for the generosity of those who could spare food. Upon arriving, Isodore's family received not relieved welcomes from their former neighbors but long, suspicious stares. Her parents' greetings were either ignored or met with hostile looks. Wide-eyed children stared. Her parents explained their soot-darkened skins. "'Twas from all the smoke. Much, much smoke. We were afraid te come out, ye see."

Two neighbors stepped away and pointed their accusing fingers. "Ye rose fro' the ashes! Ye devils! Ye rose fro' yer ashes! Jus' like the dragon. Stay away. Stay away, I tell ye."

The family was believed to have died.

Isodore's papa explained, "'Twasn't us. Whoever died, it couldn't have been us. We escaped. Praise the Lord!"

Their former village neighbors crossed themselves and spat on them.

Isodore knew it was bad to be called devils. Her family attended Mass and bowed to God to show that they were good Christians, but there were more stares and more whispers than they could sway, more fear than they could calm. They were said to have been spared by making a pact with Ashwing. Her parents made up a story of their escape, but no one believed it. Some of the belligerents pushed past her papa as he tried to shield her. "Is it true?" they asked her. "Tell the truth, or ye'll burn in hell!" She knew she had to lie. She nodded, but couldn't keep the fear off her face. "Liar!" they called. "Lock them up! Burn them!" Their former friends overtook Ashwing to become the thing she feared most.

The family was exiled to the woods. Her parents were refused work and the family grew desperate. No one would talk to them. With no means of acquiring food, her papa stole some fruits from an orchard. He was seen and attacked, suffering two pitchfork wounds in the belly.

The family fled to another village, but they were met with the same suspicion and hostility. The stories had spread of the family that Ashwing had spared.

It was in those weeks that Isodore learned two spells that would later help her survive on the road—how to restore putrefied food and how to bewitch woven cloth to fly into the face of a pursuer.

They foraged for food, but it was late autumn, with little to find. Isodore learned the poisonous plants to avoid. Hemlock, belladonna, foxglove, wolfsbane. Belladonna was the worst. Not only was it the deadliest, it tasted harmless and was easily mistaken for the edible black nightshade, which they sought. Life was miserable and sorcery couldn't fill their bellies. Food was far easier grown than conjured, her parents have always said, and she spent many days wishing it wasn't true.

Her papa's wounds festered on his weakened body, and they used the last of their precious asterium. They could no longer eat the dead animals they sometimes found floating downstream of the settlements. One day, her papa found a heap of cooked chard by the roadside outside the village. He rushed back to share it with the family.

Before they finished the meal, he stopped them. Something was wrong. Tomas was no longer eating and looked sleepy. He wouldn't speak. As they sat trying to get him to respond, the boy fell over. The chard was poisoned.

Everyone fell ill. All recovered except for little Tomas. Their parents desperately searched for asterium. The boy had a high fever, and his heart raced. Isodore worried. When their parents returned at dusk, Tomas's body was cold and stiff in her arms. Her mama threw herself to the ground, holding his body and kissing it as if she could wish it back to life. Her tears were endless.

Days later, the villagers came looking for them, accompanied by Lord Maldon's surviving son-in-law Melvin and Melvin's guards. They arrested Isodore's family. As they were marched back to the village, her papa's anger grew. "Aren't ye goin' te ask where's me son?"

They ignored him. Some of them smirked.

"No, o' course not. Ye already know, don't ye. Ye killed him! Ye poisoned us. Ye poisoned us, ye bastards."

He pushed one of them but quickly found himself facing the tip of Melvin's sword.

"Don't like the taste of belladonna?" said Melvin, who now called himself Lord Melvin. "Perhaps you should have let that dragon die."

They were jailed and charged with theft. In a testimony, their former neighbor said, "'Twas the dragon that gave back their lives. I saw 'em burn. But the dragon came te them. It did! I saw it all wit' me own eyes, as I hid in the woods. I saw the awful beast eat me family but spared them." The charges of witchcraft and colluding with Ashwing were added.

Lord Still, who ruled the domain, refused to try the family. He subscribed to the belief that it was unwise to make sacrifices to dragons. He cared neither for Lord Maldon's approach, nor for Melvin, nor for the mob's persecution of Isodore's family. He delayed the trial to consider the matter.

The village's priest convinced her parents that it would be best for Isodore to move to his orphanage. When little Isodore refused to leave her parents, he assured her that God would look after them. Soon afterward, her parents were accused of heresy.

She was too young then but when she grew up, she understood what had happened. Lord Still didn't care about her family or justice. He wanted a piece of Melvin's land, and he wouldn't allow the trial until he got it. For this piece of land, Melvin could blame the loss of his village on her family's treason, instead of the failed scheme to poison Ashwing.

A spate of witch burnings had come centuries before, when Archbishop Airardus tied the sins of men to the menace of dragons. Though the burning of witches was now forbidden in the Holy Roman Empire by the Church, it persisted on the southern frontier, where the threat of dragons was immediate and Rome was far away. To burn practitioners of witchcraft, one simply had to convict them of the burnable offense of heresy.

Her parents were tried and quickly convicted of all charges. The orphanage headmistress reassured Isodore, as the priest had, that God would look after her parents. They dismissed any speculation of burning. But a day after the conviction, a child ran back from the village square shouting with excitement, "They're goin' t'burn the witches!" The orphans streamed out, Isodore crying, "Mama! Papa!"

The headmistress shouted, "Get back 'ere, all of ye! Or ye'll all get a beatin'!" The orphans stopped, but Isodore ran on.

In the town center, she saw two stakes standing over two pyres. Her parents were being bound to the stakes. The priest had his Bible in his hand. Her parents were pleading with him, but he was impassive.

"Get that girl!" the headmistress shouted. The gathered townspeople grabbed Isodore as she tried to squeeze through.

She and her parents strained to look at each other for the last time, as two men helped the headmistress carry her, screaming and fighting, back to the orphanage.

Forbidden from leaving the orphanage, Isodore tried to run again but got caught at the door. She screamed, kicked and clawed at the headmistress, coming away with a clump of hair and leaving blood-oozing gouges on the woman's neck. With the help of two older boys, the headmistress bound her hands and tied her to the heavy trestle table. She cried for them to let her go, so the headmistress beat her to make her stop. When she didn't, a rag was stuffed into her mouth and tied in place. She collapsed, listening to her parents' screams, distant and muffled by the mud walls, the herald of her impending orphanhood.

The other orphans laughed, but in the end, the headmistress was true to her word: all of them received a beating for Isodore's escape. They blamed her for their suffering and sought vengeance by tormenting the witch child. The headmistress ordered them to leave her be, but they persisted and the headmistress grew tired of repeating her orders. The tormenting, teasing, and beatings went on while the headmistress ignored Isodore's tears and bruises. Isodore made no friends. After two years, she ran away and hid in the woods until the search parties gave up. Remembering only that her parents wanted to be as far as possible from their old village, she went north, away from the village, away from the frontier, away from Dragon's Ridge. She remained a child of the woods until the day she met Sir Rowan.

16

Name of the Fool

Isodore sat, her back against the cold granite, with her legs drawn up, fingers clutching at her tunic. Tears glistened on her face. She had buried the memories of her parents' deaths along with the sorrow and anger and hatred for the people who took everything from her. She had never mourned her family, never sought sympathy from anyone. But just now, she felt such a need to tell that story, despite her animus toward her sole companion. The dragon drew the story out of her. She didn't know if it felt sympathy or if she wanted it to.

"You owe the men no loyalty," said the black dragon.

"You're simplistic and one-sided," she said, too sad to be angry. "If not for that dragon, we would never have been exposed."

"That dragon wanted only revenge."

"Revenge . . ." She let the word roll off her tongue with the faintest whisper. The Jews, the Arabs, and the Moors believed in revenge, Father Julian had taught in his sermons, but not so the Christians. Christ said we should forgive even our enemies, she wanted to tell her captor, but she kept silent, for she, a sorceress, had no standing to preach Christ to a dragon.

"The ash-winged dragon would have killed you because you were part of the village that betrayed it. It would have killed you because of where you were. Your people killed your parents not

111

because of where they were, but who they were." The dragon lay down and looked out at the valley. "Tell me, how many people have dragons killed and how many people have died at the hands of their own kind?"

Her sorrow yielded to a familiar loyalty. "Some people are ignorant and cruel, but I know many who are good and kind. I have never known a dragon to be good and kind."

"How many have you known?"

She glared at her captor. "I know you, and I know you well. You are neither good nor kind. You were going to kill a helpless child. One of my children!"

The dragon nodded. "You are right, sorceress. I would have killed one of your children, and I nearly killed you. That was out of hunger, not hatred. Unlike your people, I do not hate you."

Isodore turned away from the dragon and looked over the distant peaks bathed in the red rays of evening. So, the dragon didn't hate her. Did it expect an outpouring of gratitude?

"And now, I know who you are, I can protect you. No man, animal or other dragon will trouble you again."

"Oh, how kind of you, dragon," she spat, glancing at it only long enough to convey her disgust.

The beast was unmoved. "I have a name. It is Pyramine."

She cared not at all what name it had. She had no intention of addressing the creature by name.

"By what name are you called?" it asked.

It had been too long since anyone called her by name. Her mind rang with the sound of Sir Rowan calling her name, even his nickname for her. Her youngest children had called out her name everyday, as they vied for her attention and sought her help for one thing or another. She missed the sweet sound of their voices. The dragon's voice was deep, hoarse, and hissing. She refused to soil the memory of those she loved by letting it speak her name.

"What do you want with me?" she seethed.

"Nothing more than you would want for yourself. What all creatures—even people—want. A mate."

"A mate!" Hysterical laughter burst out of her. She guffawed, distressed and aghast, bent over by a laugh and a cry.

A mate! She couldn't imagine a greater insult. She had been captured and imprisoned by a loathsome, monstrous fool. She staggered to her feet, red-faced and wheezing, stumbling like a drunk to the edge of the cliff, where she could take a good look at the fool. It didn't look so fearsome anymore, just a foolish little beast. It sat there, still and imperturbable.

"Are ye mad? Are ye bloody blind?" she yelled, sending spit from her trembling lips. "Can't ye see?" She stomped back to the dragon with two fistfuls of her tunic's skirt. She raised them to the dragon's eyes, shaking her fists as she roared back at the magnificently foolish beast. "Look at me! Do I look like a dragon to you?"

Patient and calm, the creature breathed deeply. "No. Not yet. Not without the work of sorcery."

17

Old Maid

Three months after Sir Dalton's regiment killed Savelle's dragon, the heroic deed had faded from the talk of the village, giving way to complaints of uncompensated appropriations. Father Serafin promised that the Church would be forthcoming with the funds, but each passing day weakened his credibility.

Since the beginning of the dragonslayer corps, the city of Auch had struggled for acceptance for its unconventional ecclesiastical tax. Unlike the lords, counts, dukes, and kings who taxed at will, the Church swore to minimize the burden on the populace. Dragonslayers were to live without extravagance and on occasion when they borrowed or appropriated from the peasants, they were to repay their debt. Their reputation depended on them keeping their word.

The villagers held back their services for Father Serafin and the orphanage. Podlum, Savelle's part-time carpenter, refused to replace the rotting legs in one of the orphanage's two benches without first receiving payment for a cart the regiment appropriated and never returned. The regiment took the carpenter's two carts when it rushed after the injured dragon. Its own carts were too big for the woods and not made for the uneven terrain of roadless forests. One of the borrowed carts broke during the pursuit and was abandoned.

Isodore crossed the road to Podlum's home to plead with him. He let her in and returned to work at the far end of his long cottage, forcing her to enter to hear him talk. Tools lined the wall and wood planks scattered about. The place smelled of stain and sawdust.

Isodore reminded him that he had agreed to fix the bench. He wanted the cost of the cart included in the price.

"The dragonslayers will compensate you for that," she said.

"What's takin' so long?" he demanded. "The Church taxes me every season, but when time comes for me t'be paid, there's delay after delay. What 'ave ye done with the taxes I paid all this time?"

"I've done nothing with it. I don't have it." She tried to remain calm. "You know well there were unanticipated costs because the dragon escaped. The regiment had to rush off or the beast would get away. But you will be compensated. The Church gave its word."

"Ye told me that last month! And the month before! Why should I believe ye? Yer scrapin' me clean. I 'ave t'pay taxes te the Church on top of m' lord's taxes. I'm taxed fer me crops. I'm taxed fer selling me goods. I'm taxed fer marryin' off me daughter. I'm taxed fer cuttin' wood. Fer the dragonslayers. Fer eatin' and sleepin'! Tax, tax, tax! Jus' because once a while, a dragon swoops in and takes a lamb. People should jus' take better care o' their lambs."

Isodore's knuckles went to her hips. "You're not taxed for eating and sleeping."

"I live on the frontier, don' I? We're taxed fer livin' 'ere."

"There's no tax for living on the frontier!"

"All frontier dwellers 'ave te pay the Church. Except those who are living off o' our pain, like ye an' yer priest."

"That tax is for the dragonslayers."

"As I say, it's a tax fer eatin' an' sleepin' on the frontier."

"You're counting that tax twice!"

"Tax twice, tax twice," he mimicked in a falsetto. "I am taxed twice! By the duke and by the Church. Why mus' I pay both? We never see the duke's men. What's 'e doin' with me taxes? That's what the Church oughta be askin'."

"The duke's men are in the north, to protect the Duchy against the Franks."

115

"Well then let the northern counties pay fer the duke's men. They don' pay fer the dragonslayers. Why should we pay fer the duke's men?"

Isodore gave up the argument with a sigh, regretting being drawn into it in the first place. Podlum smiled smugly. He had never persuaded her of anything but always took silencing her for a win.

"Podlum, all I ask is for a little more time for the Church to pay you. My children have been standing at the table to eat for months. We need that bench fixed. I know you've been looking for more work. You announce it every day. I will ask Father Serafin to ensure that when the funds come, you will be the first to be paid."

Podlum tilted his head and smiled, an expression that gave him the unsettling appearance of a happy troll. He had narrow eyes that looked at her not the way one looked at one's neighbor, but at one's possession. The dimness of the shop and planks of wood in the shadow reminded Isodore of a cave. "Well . . ." he said with mock contemplation. "That is a very nice gesture, and I know ye would do anything for those poor tired children. But ye can't bring the funds, me love. That isn't in yer power." He brought up his hand to give her shoulder a condescending pat. And a squeeze, rubbing her with his rough carpenter's thumb. "Ye must barter with me. We both know there is something within your power te offer me, isn't there? Hm?" He smiled wider, letting his hand run down her arm.

She pulled her arm away and took a step back. He was some twenty years her senior, though that didn't bother her so much. Sir Rowan was nearly as old. But Podlum had a wife. The carpenter had not made advances toward her in a year or so, when she reminded him that adultery was punishable by law. Since then, he had been making her life difficult in petty ways.

"Podlum, no. I will not be party to your sins." She folded her arms and turned a shoulder to him. "All I ask is . . . "

"Sin? What sin? Oh, heh, heh. Is that what you are suggesting? Well, 'ave no worry, love. I won't tell no one. Ye always known, I can keep a secret, and at the end of it, ye'll have a perfectly good bench for yer cottage. Hm?"

He advanced slowly toward her and she backed up to the door.

"Oh, very well. Ye know I was only jestin'," said Podlum in a soothing voice that didn't soothe Isodore at all. "'Ere. Te show me generosity, I will still repair yer bench for ye and those poor children, and you don't have to do anything Father Serafin would disapprove."

She waited for him to elaborate.

"As ye know, me son will soon be choosin' a bride," he began, as if Trand were some prince.

Isodore knew Trand was all too similar to his father.

"Although many women 'ave presented their daughters t'me, seeking to marry into wealth, I 'ave a kind of special sympathy for you, Isodore. Wit' no parent of yer own, yer at such a disadvantage. No family te back ye, no dowry te offer. And what people say about ye." He clucked his tongue. "I don' 'ave te remind ye, and ye don't need help rememberin'. Yer by far the oldest of all the unmarried women in Savelle. Much older than the girls flockin' te me son . . ."

She backed out of the cottage as he spoke and left him with his unwelcomed words.

THAT AFTERNOON, ISODORE checked with Father Serafin to see if he had received any word of when the payment would come.

"No," said the priest, "but the money should arrive any day now." He had an earnest and trusting nature that she found endearing most of the time. Today, she only wished he were a more forceful Church official. The payment was to have arrived "any day now" for months.

On her way back to the orphanage, she saw Trand moving a massive log to the carpenter's shop. The boy was fifteen years of age, but big and strong, like his father. Well fed, he had arm and leg muscles that bulged, glistening under a sheen of sweat as he heaved the log along. When he saw Isodore looking at him, he gave a confident smile and a wink. She ignored him.

Two years ago, Podlum suggested to Isodore that she marry his son. The lad was only thirteen, barely older than her oldest child. She had seen Trand down by the stream, sneaking through the bushes to spy on girls as they washed themselves. They sometimes caught him and chased him away. Isodore always made sure she knew where he was before she washed herself.

"Father said I should consider taking ye to wed," he had told her. "I might consider that. Yer better with the children than that 'ag before ye."

As the year passed, the idea of Trand pursuing Isodore caught on with the villagers as a source of humor. "Ye'd better bed 'im soon, before yer teats dry up an' leave 'im starved," joked a man who had an interest in her back when she rejected all romantic advances because she was saving herself for Sir Rowan.

Humorous or not, Podlum suggested that Isodore might treat his son with more deference if she didn't wish to be an old maid. "'E will move to Lovishar one day an' be a full-time carpenter. Ye'd be so lucky if 'e chose to wed ye."

Isodore ignored the jokes and Podlum's warnings for a long time, but the idea of becoming an old maid became more real the more people teased her. With each passing season, each birth, each death, each marriage in Savelle, she became more worried. She was twenty when she came to Savelle. Now twenty-seven, an age at which most women had borne many children, she looked back with some regret over her disinterest in Marcus, a decent and honest man, if not dashing or assertive like Sir Rowan. Marcus was now father to three young children and husband to a wife who forbade him to talk to any unmarried woman.

Down by the stream on rest days, Isodore watched the eligible men, all younger than herself, courting—in discreet and not-so-discreet ways—the young girls she could no longer compete with. In pairs, they stole away, while she remained invisible to them.

Much had changed in the years since Podlum suggested his immature son was her last hope. Savelle, like other villages, grew and brought more demand for carpentry. Trand worked more and played less. He grew. Podlum had more silver. He recently boasted that Lord Edwin had agreed to let Trand move to Lovishar to be a full-time carpenter after his apprenticeship under his father. "I'll be taxed fer it, o'course," he added, "but we'll be the wealthiest family in Savelle." Trand bought new clothing to wear on Sundays. Girls no longer laughed about him. The younger ones blushed when he turned his confident smile toward them.

Back in the orphanage's small cottage, cutting vegetables with the broken bench in view, Isodore couldn't wrest her mind from the dim future Podlum had painted for her. Trand had a good future, if Podlum's boasts were true. He would do well indeed, if he left the orchards for Lovishar. Marriage to him might be her best prospect, but she couldn't disregard the instinct to recoil from his family. Why would a father who believed she had little chance to find a husband be so willing to consider her for marriage to his son, who was supposedly much sought after? With Podlum, selfishness was the most likely explanation.

If she married Trand, she would never be free of Podlum. Even worse, she suspected that the carpenter had no plan to allow his son to marry her. Following Podlum's bait, she would lose what little time she had left to find a husband. When Trand finally married, she would be alone again with only the carpenter and his repugnant leer. Yet despite that, she found herself considering this fifteen-year-old boy and wondering if he would actually choose her over the village's other girls. Then warm tears welled in her eyes. She missed Sir Rowan.

TWO DAYS LATER, Isodore found Father Serafin in a jubilant mood. "The payments are on their way!" he said. "They will be here tomorrow." He waved a letter that a messenger brought that afternoon, four months after Sir Dalton's regiment had departed with the promise of compensation.

"Even better," the priest added, pointing to the words in the letter, "they're not just sending the silver. The whole regiment will come to rest a day and replenish its provisions."

Though the town of Lovishar, ten miles away with merchants and full-time tradesmen, would have served the regiment better, Sir Dalton had chosen to stay at Savelle, where his men had been both loved and mourned as heroes.

On the morning of a late winter day, a crowd gathered to welcome them, with villagers fighting to be close to the line of men riding down the village to the church. They momentarily forgot their displeasure over the overdue compensation. Those working in the orchards returned to join the welcoming crowd. Isodore, aware that her reputation as a pretender deepened when the villagers saw Sir Dalton's special regard for her, watched from across the road, behind the crowd, while villagers who had no concerns about blemished reputations elbowed each other to touch the clothes of the heroic knights.

She watched Sir Dalton until he dismounted on the church grounds. He looked more handsome than the haggard commander who had lost five men and a knight. Behind him followed Sir Wilfred, Sir Gustav, and the other dragonslayers, all on horseback. The regiment's younger squires brought up the rear, driving carts loaded with equipment. Isodore watched the last of them enter the courtyard but didn't see Galt.

Lord Edwin opened his home to the dragonslayers, and most took his offer. But many, including the knights, chose to camp in the church grounds. Since their early days, dragonslayers saved their precious funds by avoiding extravagant expenses such as inns. Over time, more noblemen invited dragonslayers into their homes, out of gratitude as well as a desire to be associated with the popular regiments.

Isodore went inside and worked as she did other days. She listened to the sounds of the men in the church grounds, their horses and carts, striking weapons, shouting, cheering and merry laughter. She fought off the envy she felt toward those who provided goods and services to the regiment, while she, one of the few villagers actually affiliated with the Church, could find no excuse to visit them. Seeking to distract herself, her thoughts wandered to another unhappy subject. What had become of Galt? Had he died in spite of her efforts? Had she saved his life only to let him live in misery, wasting away with terrible scars and a broken future, excluded from the world of the dragonslayers?

"Do not envy," she scolded herself. "You've no reason to lament.

You're not the one who was burned."

She finished cutting vegetables and set a kettle of pottage to cook over the hearth fire while she began her next task. She dribbled water into a bucket of hard clay that she had dug up from the far end of the croft. She worked in straw, then tied up her skirt and stomped the mix into dense daub. The mixture covered her in a muddy layer up her calves and splashed onto her clothes. She dug out handful of daub, slapping and pressing them into patches of exposed wattle frame in the orphanage's crumbling walls. Mud covered her hands and wrists.

Her mind wandered to Sir Rowan, as it often did when she needed comfort and belonging. She had never understood why he had committed the crime of sodomy, or why it angered God so much. Some time after hearing of his conviction, she found the Old Testament passage on which the conviction was based. But she couldn't understand why he would lie with another man. Could he possibly have thought no woman would have him? Perhaps she should have professed her love for him. He was dashing, and she was certain she wasn't the only girl who had dreamed of his touch.

The little boy Xabi ran into the orphanage with a message, breaking her contemplation. He shouted, "Isodore, ye must come te the church. The knight 'as sent fer ye."

She stood straight, her back aching, her hands untouchable, and her lower legs encrusted in mud. "The knight? Sir Dalton?"

"Yeh."

She dropped a ball of daub back into the bucket. "Oh woodness! Where is he?"

"At the church."

"When should I come?"

"I don' know."

"What does he want of me?"

"I don' know."

"Is it urgent?" She swept the skin of mud off her arms, leaving brown streaks in their place.

Xabi frowned heavily, full of serious consideration. "Umm . . ." He was old enough to be of some help, but young enough not to be very helpful in complicated matters such as delivering a summons.

Isodore sent Xabi to fetch Claudia from the orchard while she cleansed herself. She couldn't bathe in the stream because of the number of dragonslayers wandering about. She scrubbed mud off her arms and face, but attempts to sweep hair out of her face left brown streaks across her forehead. She rubbed sweat off herself with a damp rag, brushed her hair and put on the tunic that Sir Rowan gave her as a farewell present seven years earlier.

She instructed Xabi and Claudia to stay and look after the toddlers. "If they cry, tell them I will be back soon. Will you do that? Will you remember?"

Claudia nodded. Xabi said, "Of course! Why're ye wearin' yer Sunday clothes? 'Tis not time."

"Is there mud on my face?" Isodore asked. Claudia wiped off the smudges that Isodore had missed. They laid the broken bench on its side next to the fire to block it off from where three small children were napping.

"Claudia, I have stew cooking here. Don't touch it and don't let the children get past the bench. Keep the fire burning, but not too hot."

"Yes, Isodore." Claudia and Xabi answered together.

"She's talkin' te me, Xabi."

When Isodore came to the church grounds, she found Sir Gustav and some dragonslayers practicing combat with wooden swords and blunt spears in the courtyard. Some of the village girls were mingling with them. A dragonslayer on the outer circle greeted her with a smiling nod as she came to his side.

"Greetings, good man," she said. "I'm here by Sir Dalton's summons. Where might I find him?"

"I believe he's with Father Serafin. He went inside."

She thanked him and headed to Father Serafin's study. There, she disturbed a young, clean-cut regiment scribe seated at the priest's table, hunched over a piece of parchment, a feather quill in his hand. He looked up when she stepped into the doorway.

She curtsied. "Greetings, good man. I'm sorry to disturb you, but I'm looking for Sir Dalton. Where may I find him?"

"He has gone with Father Serafin to see Lord Edwin."

"Ah, thank you." She bade him good day and backed out. She worried that she had taken so long to clean herself for the meeting that Sir Dalton no longer required her.

"Wait," the scribe called. He looked her over for a moment, though she wasn't sure he was really looking at her, or anything in this world, at all.

"Yes?" she prompted.

His brows drew together. In a hesitant tone, he asked, "Are you the woman who stayed with our burned man?"

"Yes!" She rushed to the table, so excited at the prospect of learning Galt's fate that she couldn't contain herself. "His name was Galt. How has he fared, can you tell me?"

The young man's eyes fell away, searching the table with some discomfort. "Galt, um, wishes to convey his immense gratitude for your kindness during his convalescence." He turned his gaze back to her, his eyes tentative.

She clasped her hands together, almost in prayer. "Oh, so he's alive! If you would, please tell him that I shall be so happy to see him, should he find himself passing through Savelle again," she said, leaning over the table with such eagerness that she sent the young man into the seat's backrest.

He straightened himself, standing the quill back in the squat ink bottle. "Isodore. That's your name, is it not?"

"It is."

The scribe released a fistful of coins on the table and rose, pushing the chair away. He stood taller and more formidable than she expected. The sword on his belt came into view. He was no mere scribe, but a fighting man of the regiment, a dragonslayer.

He bowed. "Then please forgive me," he said, straightening. "It's hard for me to recall those days, but . . . I am Galt, the man who was burned."

18

Debtor's Day

Galt's smooth, youthful face was an arm's reach across the table. Gone were all traces of injury and the anguished voice hissing through burned lips. Isodore had spent a week at his side but only now saw what he looked like. She was so happy to see him restored that she clasped her hands together to keep from throwing them around him. The man she had seen on the threshold of death, the man she risked execution trying to save, was alive, well, and beyond recognition in every way.

Unable to fathom that she herself had cast such an effective healing spell, her decorum lapsed. "What . . . happened to you?" She gasped and her hand flew to cover her mouth.

Galt waved off the blunder. "What happened to me, indeed."

He almost laughed as they looked at each other. "Well. When I woke up by the hearth, I didn't feel any pain. I thought my burns had all been a nightmare. When I saw my face and hands, and I knew it was true. But, I couldn't understand it. I didn't know how I would carry on, but I felt . . . like nothing had happened." He paused, looking at Isodore as though seeking her assurance that she did not think him mad.

She could feel his excitement. "Go on," she said.

He smiled. "I had never felt anything so strange before. I needed no medicine. The physicians couldn't explain it. I was strong and in good health. Not knowing what to do, I continued my training and duties. But . . . but my scars. They were so ghastly, even worse than what you had seen. I've seen men burned, but I looked . . . I shouldn't have lived. My face was half skin and half raw flesh, truly horrifying. It was . . . distracting to the regiment. People gawked at me as though I were a leper. Some were afraid of me. Even . . . even those who had known me most of my life."

Galt's eyes dropped and his jaws tightened. Isodore felt the horror of his pain as if it were her own, and she didn't bother to hide it.

"I couldn't see my face, as others had to, but my hands always reminded me. And I could feel that my face and neck had changed. The skin was thin." He shook his head.

His tone had changed, detached from memories of pain, yet fascinated by the remaining facts.

"It felt strange to move my mouth or face, as though something had stuck to them. Something I couldn't remove. I took to wearing a mask on my head, and gloves, to hide the scars and spare the people around me of the sight. I lived that way. I thought it would be for the rest of my life.

"But then, under the mask, the scars began to fade. Day by day, my face and hands recovered their old form. I thought I was dreaming. Each time I woke, I checked. Sometimes, I wonder if I'm still dreaming."

"You're not!"

"I told no one, because I couldn't believe it. I didn't want to make a fool of myself. I didn't know how much the scars could heal. After some months, they were completely gone, impossible as it seemed. I went to the archbishop. He knew immediately how it came to be."

"He did?"

"Yes! It was a miracle."

Miracle, thought Isodore. Perhaps. Perhaps she had not erred so badly with the healing spell after all. In any case, the moment they were sharing felt very much like a miracle. She nodded.

She knew that the spell's effect depended partly on the time spent, but she didn't know it could clear scars. Perhaps in her fear that her spell wasn't working, she had carried on too long. Her parents had used it for deadly fevers, which left no scars.

"Are you . . . all right?" Galt asked her.

"What?" His question snapped her out of her thoughts.

"It was a miracle, don't you think? As the archbishop said."

"Oh, absolutely. There could be no other explanation. You are doing God's work, after all." She beamed at him and he smiled back. As they looked into each other's eyes and the silence stretched out, she could think of only two choices. Either throw her arms around him or leave before she broke all protocols required of a proper lass.

"I'd better go find Sir Dalton. I mustn't keep him waiting. It is . . . such a happy day to see you in good health and spirits. I shall always remember it. I am so glad that your regiment decided to stop in Savelle."

"We had to settle our debts. The regiment, that is. I volunteered to do the task for Father Serafin, but I need someone who knows the people of this village. Sir Dalton summoned you because I asked for you."

"I shall be happy to take you to these people." She was certain he had no idea just how happy she was.

He picked up two triangular sheets of parchment, scraps left over from the making of books. The sheets formed a ledger, showing payments due from the Church to individuals in Savelle.

"You can be a witness to the payments as well. It's good practice to have a witness familiar with the recipients," he said in a conspiratorial voice as they left the room. "People sometimes forget that they have been paid." They exchanged a knowing smile. Then she turned from the unexpected heat of his pleasantly lingering eyes.

The ledger listed the villagers who had given time and resources to help the regiment. The villagers held signed notes the regiment had given for goods and services that had gone unpaid. One was for the sacrificed cow. She first took Galt to the house where he had convalesced, which was closest to the church grounds. She stood behind him and let him do the talking. The elderly couple didn't recognize his name. Isodore realized that the villagers, like her, had no idea the burned man had survived, let alone was standing before them. Galt, oddly, didn't tell them who he was. He paid them in silver coins and thanked them for their help. Through their round of the village and the orchards, he never volunteered his identity. She suspected he wanted to avoid retelling his story and the commotion that it would cause. She felt honored that he had chosen to tell her.

At the carpenter's house, they met Podlum, his mousy wife, Thera, and Trand. The couple's younger children came to watch, but the carpenter sent them out the back door with a wave of his hand. Like the other villagers, the carpenter's family greeted Galt cordially and ignored Isodore.

"I am here to settle a debt our regiment owes to you for a cart that we took," Galt said, glancing down at the line on the parchment he marked with his thumb. "The regiment is grateful for the loan and we regret the loss of your possession. The Church has determined your cart was valued at six silver pieces." He placed a hand into the money bag, picking out the right count.

The sound of shifting the coins was vindication for Isodore's trust in the Church's assurance. She watched Podlum, but his eyes were on the money.

"Six?" Podlum frowned and glanced back at Thera.

"Oh, it's worth more 'an that," she said, frowning.

"Yes. I would charge fifteen fer a fine cart like that," said Podlum, to the expressed agreement of Thera and Trand. "But ... in gratitude fer your riddin' us o' that beast, I'll 'appily settle fer, oh, ten."

"That price is more 'n fair," Thera agreed.

Trand nodded. He threw Isodore a smiling glance that bragged of more riches. She ignored him.

"Hmm ... very well," said Galt.

The family suddenly brightened.

"Here is what you are authorized to receive today," Galt said, dropping the six silver pieces into Podlum's hand. "For the rest, you are to speak with Lord Edwin the next time he holds court. He or his designated steward will judge. Whichever price is placed on your cart shall be the final price. The Church will authorize an additional payment if Lord Edwin's court rules that your cart was of greater value. If he rules it to be of lesser value, the difference will be added to your tax."

"Oh," said Podlum, clearing his throat. "I will certainly do that. Certainly." His smile half faded as he glanced back at Thera's blank face.

Striding to the next household listed on the ledger, Isodore whispered to Galt, "I don't think that old cart was worth ten silver pieces."

"I don't think he'll trouble himself to bring it up with Lord Edwin," said Galt, unbothered. "We used to have people come to us for their payments. It didn't work well. Some would inevitably feel cheated because they hadn't gotten as much as a neighbor. They'd demand more, and once that starts, everyone joins in. It's a rowdy crowd."

He is intelligent and above petty squabbles, she thought, unaware that a smile had formed on her lips—until she saw it reflected on his face. She turned away, blushing.

"Next is Jonah," said Galt, rolling up the ledger. "A baker, I believe. We owe him for bread and three chickens."

Most of the villagers were happy to finally receive compensation and didn't argue with Galt. Neither of the women who traded jobs with Isodore to get out of caring for Galt recognized him. She secretly resented them on his behalf.

The villagers took note of Isodore accompanying Galt. Her neighbors watched with disapproval. She tried to walk a step behind him but felt as though she was following him like a puppy. She tried walking abreast but she feared appearing to exceed her station. And she felt rude walking ahead of him. She couldn't help resenting the villagers for denying her the simple pleasure of walking with the man she had risked so much to help. They didn't know he was the burned man. To them, she was only latching herself onto a man above her station.

It was past noon when she and Galt finished the household visits. He apologized that he had nothing for her. "You spent many days caring for me when I was difficult company. But my instructions were to give money to Father Serafin, because you were under his employment. Perhaps I can speak to him about giving you additional—"

"I wasn't expecting anything!" She interrupted as soon as she knew where his words were going. Compensation for her time had never occurred to her. "Your good health is far greater a reward than all the payment the Church could offer," she said, exactly as a proper lass would.

On their way back to the church, he asked to visit her orphanage. The exposed wattle, bucket of mud, and other unfinished work embarrassed her, but she didn't want to turn him away. She was enjoying his presence so much that she felt guilty for it. He said nothing of the mess, the smell of wet straw from the bucket of daub, or the stifling dampness from the bubbling pottage, instead turning his attention to Xabi, Claudia, and the waking toddlers.

With a man in the cottage, she couldn't change back to her daily clothes and she didn't want to return to the messy repair work in her special tunic, so she looked after the pottage and prepared the remainder of the orphanage's dinner, hoping the smell of thyme could cover the smell of wet straw. She offered him a bowl of pottage and was surprised he accepted. She was certain that between the church and Lord Edwin's hospitality, the regiment was well fed. Xabi leaned over the trestle table, staring at the dragonslayer in their midst. Isodore scolded the boy for his intrusion, but Galt said it was all right. All of the children watched the dragonslayer as though he were an exotic animal.

After a few spoonfuls, Galt hesitated before putting more into his mouth.

"Is something wrong?" Isodore asked.

"Ah, no. No. It's fine." He smiled and nodded.

"Is there something else you desire?"

"Well, it is just . . . it would be better with salt."

"Salt? Oh, yes. I'll get some right away!" She dashed out to the church.

Salt! Of course! It was a luxury not available to the lowly orphanage, but perhaps he was used to it. In the church kitchen, she asked the cook for some salt. "It's for a dragonslayer visiting the orphanage. He's asking for it."

The cook, a resident monk practicing silence, poured a small amount on a saucer, eyeing her suspiciously. As she took the saucer, he didn't let go.

"You are certainly welcome to come check for yourself," she said, one fist returning to her hip. He released the saucer but narrowed his eyes.

She strode back to the cottage, protecting the precious pile of tiny crystals from her jostling steps and the oncoming breeze. Galt was waiting at the doorway with Xabi by his side.

"I must apologize," he said. "I didn't mean to put you through the trouble."

"No, you mustn't! The cook gave me no trouble at all."

She stole glances at Galt while he ate, relieved that he didn't reject her cooking. He talked to Claudia, Xabi, and the three toddlers. They relished the attention from the rare guest. One by one, each overcame shyness and competed with others to talk to him. Isodore reminded them to wait for their turn to talk.

"You should heed your headmistress," he advised them. "She is teaching you well."

Galt asked them many questions. What lessons did she teach them that week? What did she do when they misbehaved? When they made mistakes? How did she resolve their disputes? How did they like her cooking? Did they go to bed and rise on time? Did they attend Mass? What became of the older orphans? Questions about their headmistress were suspiciously prevalent. Xabi and Claudia competed to give their own versions of the answers, both positive. Isodore suspected that the children wanted Galt to like their headmistress. She couldn't help wanting the same.

Cleaning the dishes in a pail away from the table, she strained to hear every word. Essentially a servant since the days she lived in Father Julian's orphanage, she was accustomed to being questioned and talked about. But Galt showed unusual curiosity about her, and that made her terribly curious about him.

He finished every bit of pottage in his bowl, though in the end, he hardly used any salt, leaving it for Isodore to save for a special occasion. The children would be so delighted. They had never had salt before.

She walked Galt out. He stopped outside the door and asked, "Can you ride a horse?"

"Yes," she said hesitantly. She hadn't been in a saddle in years, but she didn't want to part with him.

"It's a beautiful afternoon. Would you care to come riding with me?"

She regained her poise. "I would be delighted to," she said, as a proper lass would, but inside, her heart was bouncing up and down. She put Claudia in charge again and crossed the road with Galt. She was so excited that she didn't notice the villagers' eyes on her. Galt waved to one of the younger squires in the church yard. "My horse. And a rouncy for Mistress Isodore."

Isodore was relieved to see the squire place a saddle on a small mare standing among the coursers. Though she had learned to ride on Sir Rowan's war horses, she stood less chance of embarrassing herself on the rouncy. When the squire brought the saddled animals, Galt said to him, "There are unfinished repairs on the orphanage walls. Lord Edwin has put his servants at our disposal. Send two of them there to finish the task. Tell them it was I who took the headmistress away from her work."

"Yes, Sir Galt," said the squire.

"*Sir*?" Isodore gasped. "*Sir* Galt? Oh, woodness! I am so sorry. Please forgive me, I beg you. I didn't know. I thought..." She had not been thinking at all, and it was too late to save herself. She dropped into a curtsy and bowed to hide her mortification. A dubbed knight was considered a nobleman, and she had been talking with him as though they were equals. When she recomposed herself and straightened up she found Galt and the squire grinning awkwardly at one another.

After the boy left, Galt apologized for causing her embarrassment. "I should have told you when I introduced myself, but I'm not yet accustomed to it and, well, you're not to blame."

No one had mentioned he was a knight, not even Sir Dalton when the commander spoke of his bravery during the dragon battle.

He would make an uncommon knight, she thought. She wondered why he didn't have the suffering-dragon blazon that identified the other regiment knights.

Galt steadied her horse while she arranged her tunic over the saddle and seated herself. Then he mounted and led them out of Savelle. The horses walked side by side on the narrow road that wound through the trees. On the frontier, no road could be made wide for fear of being seen by dragons overhead. The trees left little view of the sky. The riders were soon alone, sealed off from the outside world in a cool, shady tunnel.

Galt was a natural rider, very comfortable in the saddle, probably trained from childhood to be on horseback. Her riding lessons came back the more she observed him. She recalled how to hold her body, erect but not rigid, moving with the horse. She wanted to ride well so Galt wouldn't be disappointed to have her along. Sir Rowan's voice was in her head, the skills he drilled into her, and the habits he forbade. And she listened like she never had before.

"You have a good seat," Galt said.

She glanced at him, nodded, and looked ahead again.

"Who taught you?"

"Sir Rowan. He was a Knight of the Cross and a friend of Father Julian, the priest in Dorune. I grew up in Father Julian's orphanage. Sir Rowan was very kind. As was Father Julian."

"Where are they now?"

"Father Julian is still in Dorune. We don't know where Sir Rowan is. I fear he may have died." She added the last comment hoping Galt wouldn't ask further about Rowan's fate.

"How did you come to be orphaned?"

"My parents were killed as a result of a rampaging dragon," she said.

He asked of her parents, her family, and how she came to be headmistress of the orphanage.

"My parents were cottagers on the southern frontier. We grew figs and peaches. They supplemented their livelihood as a part-time seamstress and a salvager." Afraid of inviting questions too difficult to answer, she skipped certain parts of the story, as she always had. "Sir Rowan found me after they died. He brought me to Father Julian's orphanage. I helped Headmistress Janine from the age of twelve, and learned from her how to run the orphanage."

Galt listened to her history with a focus of someone assembling a puzzle. And she was hiding several pieces. When she finished, he returned the conversation to her parents and her family. He was polite but intent. "They were farmers?" he asked.

"Yes."

"And you escaped?"

The question gave her a momentary fright, not knowing whether he meant escaping Ashwing's attack or leaving her village without her lord's permission, or escaping from her first orphanage.

"The dragon destroyed our village. Burned it to the ground. And killed the lord and half his family. I lived on the road, and in the forest, for some years before I met Sir Rowan. He feared for my safety and took me to Dorune, where Father Julian took me in."

"You lived on your own in the forest? How old were you?"

"Ten."

Before Galt could put in another question, she told him of the years she had spent at Dorune's orphanage and how she learned to conduct herself. And of her baptism—she hoped, as her parents had, that her religion would shield her from suspicion. She spoke highly of Sir Rowan and Father Julian and what they had taught her, but she omitted how the knight had fallen from grace. Fearing Galt would ask more about Sir Rowan, she changed the subject again.

"I have not been on a horse in years. It brings me such joy to be carried away and feel the wind in my hair. And the rhythm of the hooves."

"Shall we go a little faster?"

"Could we?" She was afraid she might mishandle the horse but more afraid of revealing too much of her past.

They gradually brought the horses to a gallop and raced down the winding road, turning onto the shortcut that connected the road to Auch and the road to Bayonne. The rouncy, it turned out, was very forgiving. When they turned to head toward Savelle, the sun, low on the winter's horizon, shone heavenly red light on the patchy clouds she could see through gaps in the trees. They slowed down to let the horses rest. Unaccustomed to riding, Isodore's legs and back were tired and sore but she ignored the discomfort, happy to be engaged in an activity she had not experienced since she last saw Sir Rowan.

"Your friend, Sir Rowan was it?"

"Yes."

"He taught you well," he said. "I'm sorry he is missing."

She nodded and asked, "Sir Galt, are you a Knight of the Crown or a Knight of the Cross?" She pretended not to know that all regiment knights were Knights of the Cross so she could steer conversation away from Sir Rowan.

"Uh . . . Of both, actually, I believe . . . Well, soon anyway."

She had embarrassed him again.

Stumbling through his words like a man uncertain of his position, Galt explained that when the story of his actions in battle and his return to the dragonslayer corps had reached the duke, Galt was summoned. The duke decided to dub him a Knight of the Crown, conferring upon him the title of Sir. Months later, when his scars faded, the archbishop of Auch declared it a miracle from God, to bless his actions against the evil dragons. Just before the regiment embarked on its current journey, the archbishop dubbed him a Knight of the Cross as well. "He said that I was to be known as the Knight of God's Miracle. It was his command," Galt explained in what sounded oddly like an apology.

It was a fine story, though he was very hesitant.

"It must be a great honor to hold such a title."

Galt lowered his voice. "The honor belongs to God. I did nothing."

"Sir Dalton said you saved the lives of the other men who were knocked down by the dragon."

He nodded, and she took his silence to mean he didn't wish to talk about it. He wasn't wearing the golden cross on his surcoat. Perhaps he wasn't ready for knighthood. Squires qualified for knighthood after the age of twenty-one, and he appeared younger. Perhaps he simply looked young for his age. Or perhaps the healing spell somehow cleared the marks of age as well as the scars. She had never seen that before, but neither had she seen the spell used on facial wounds. Galt was boyish in some ways, an inconsolable child only four months before, and now, a young man uncertain of his status. Her heart went out to him. He was keeping some kind of secret, perhaps. She knew how lonely that felt.

"Sir Galt, may I show you something?" she asked.

"Yes, please. But before you do, I have a request. While we are in private, I would like it very much if you would address me the way you did before we went riding."

"As you wish," she said. "This way." When she was certain he could no longer see her face, she allowed herself a curious frown, mouthing to herself in a way a proper lass should never do, "What?" A dubbed knight who didn't wish to be distinguished by title from common knights? How odd.

She led him off the main road, down a path worn through the forest toward a stream. She had never gone this way on horseback before and didn't consider how low the branches were. While the horses lowered their heads, there was no graceful way for riders to slip through.

"I'm sorry," she said, struggling to push away the chest-high branches. "Perhaps this was not such a good idea."

"Allow me," said Galt, drawing his sword and urging his horse past hers. He hacked through the branches to clear the way for both of them.

At the end of the path, they came to a wide stream parting the forest canopy. The stream flowed gracefully over a bed of rounded stones, shimmering under a red-hued sky. Isodore pulled up next to him. The sun had set, but the sky was radiant, the air pleasantly chilly.

"I like coming here to rest on Sundays."

"It's beautiful," he said, looking around in silence.

"Depending on the time of day, one side of the stream is shaded and the other is sunny. I can pick whichever side I like. If it's a hot day, I put my feet in the water to cool them. Then I sit still and wait to see how close the fish will come to me." She fought off an urge to giggle. Such trivial things. She intended only to put him at ease, because he appeared nervous. She thought of pointing out the rocks where she usually sat but decided she had said too much. She pictured herself on that rock and wondered what he might be picturing.

It was late winter, so there was no reason to set foot in the water.

"If we follow the stream, there is another path back to the road," she told him, and they rode down the middle of the stream.

Galt looked around constantly, perhaps watching for dragons by habit. When he looked in her direction, his smile deepened ever so slightly.

"Would you tell me about yourself, Sir Galt... um, Galt, as I have told you about myself? I would be so honored to hear more about your life."

Galt composed his thoughts before starting, and he took a cautious tone that Isodore found odd, given how much she had told him about herself. "My father was a bishop and my mother is from Toulouse. Three of my uncles entered the clergy. Only one, Uncle Corvin, was a warrior. He became a knight of Laronde. He later deposed the lord there and rules that domain. I am the youngest of three brothers. My oldest brother died from a fever. He was Father's favorite, and Father was never the same again. Father wished to be closer to God, so he entered a monastery and lived a life of asceticism. My second oldest brother soon followed his footsteps and entered the Order of Saint Benedict. Father was always good at fasting and devotion. Not me. I'm like my Uncle Corvin. I chose the sword over the Book. My mother was very pleased about that. She sent me to be raised by my uncle. Perhaps she feared I would follow the other men in my family."

Isodore stole a glance at Galt, relaxed and comfortable in the saddle as the horses picked their way over the rounded stones in the stream bed. He made a good warrior, not as broad or strong as Sir Rowan, but still a convincing portrait of a Knight of the Cross, if she looked past his young face.

"I grew up just a morning's ride from Auch. I saw dragonslayers come and go. Heard songs and attended thespian re-enactments of famous dragonslayer battles. I admired the dragonslayers, their bravery, their methodical approach, their cleverness, and their chivalry. I wanted nothing more than to join them. My wish came true when Uncle Corvin found me a squireship under Sir Baret. I owe a great debt of gratitude to both men. My uncle was like a father to me. He began my training, and Sir Baret continued it."

Galt seemed modest. This wasn't bad in her eyes, for she had seen far too much arrogance in men, particularly knights. Sir Rowan had not been excessive, but he always loved to tell stories about himself and his exploits. Galt finished in a few minutes what Sir Rowan would have drawn out for an evening.

Isodore's curiosity grew. She wondered about Galt and found herself wishing that, somehow, he might ask her to come work in his house. She thought he would make a kind master.

They came to the path back to the main road, and Galt took the lead to hack through the low branches. At the road, she could ride abreast with him again.

"I have two questions for you, Isodore. Well, perhaps only one," he said. "I apologize for their intrusiveness, but I must know before the regiment departs tomorrow. Will you forgive me?"

Isodore swallowed, instinctively fearing Galt suspected sorcery despite the archbishop's explanation for his recovery. It was the curse of carrying such a terrible secret. Exposure and death were always just a word away. She would lie if asked, she decided. She had lied before by her silence, when Father Julian spoke of the evils of witchcraft. She lied to Sir Rowan and Father Serafin by hiding from them her reservations about Christianity. It was a long-running lie that felt comfortable and safe, but she wished she wouldn't have to lie to Galt.

Galt took his eyes from her, sitting erect in his saddle. His gaze wandered into the patchy red and gray sky. "Do you have a suitor?"

"A suitor? Uh, no. I have no one." She was glad he had turned away, as she felt her cheeks flush hot.

His back stiffened further as he asked the next question. "Are you a maiden?"

Isodore's own back stiffened in her saddle, and her eyes widened at the road ahead in disbelief. She answered quietly, but with confidence. "Yes."

She wondered if these questions were somehow routine for him. She stole a brief look at him, then looked away, fearing he might see her looking. He was deep in thought and his face had a look of determination. Perhaps he was thinking of more than having her serve in his household. Her mind whirled with preposterous speculations.

They arrived back in Savelle, sitting straight and proper in their saddles, with discreet rosebud smiles on their lips, hard to see in the dimming daylight. The villagers gawked, but she was too distracted to care. She and Galt rode to the orphanage, where she dismounted and gave him the reins.

"Thank you, Isodore, for your help in resolving the regiment's debts. And for showing me around your lovely village."

She curtsied. "The pleasure is mine, Sir Galt."

Galt turned the horses, and she slipped into the orphanage. She couldn't sleep that night, and didn't care to.

Before the regiment departed the next morning, Galt asked her to wait for his return.

She did, with great anticipation.

19

Beautiful Spirit

Isodore now knew that the dragon who called himself Pyramine couldn't read her mind. If he could, he would have known how vile the thought of being his mate was to her. She would never want to be a dragon, and never, ever to be his mate. But to buy time for escape, she pretended to consider it. Days later, she felt confident enough in her ability to mask her true feelings.

"Why me?" she asked while Pyramine started her cookfire. "Why not another dragon?"

"I have told you. You are beautiful."

"Beautiful," she repeated, pretending to think about it. No man had ever given her such a compliment, not even Galt. Sir Rowan sometimes called her beautiful, but it was in the same way he called her ragamuffin, not the way a man called a woman beautiful.

"But if I became a dragon, wouldn't I look very different?"

"I spoke not of your appearance."

An unusual cynicism overcame her. "What, then, do you find so . . . compelling?"

"Your spirit," answered the hideous beast.

Despite the game she was playing, Isodore stopped to consider his answer. Galt had been so hideous that the women taking care of him couldn't bear it. And yet, she knew he was still a person inside, capable of joy and sorrow, of pain and triumph. He was so pleased when she had asked after him even before she knew his scars had healed. Was it her spirit that Galt saw? Her spirit that drew him to her?

Isodore cocked her head and studied, for the first time, the glistening crimson orbs peering out of Pyramine's black skull. There was more there than mere hideousness.

"You have courage," Pyramine said. "You are strong of mind, loyal, and just. Not greedy, or lazy."

Courage? It was an odd credit from a creature who had instilled so much fear and despair in her. And yet, despite her animosity toward him, it was his apparent regard for her that gave her the safety to challenge him.

"How do you know I'm not greedy?"

"You are not demanding, neither of food when you are hungry nor of asterium when you are dying."

"And that's enough to make you wish to be with a woman?"

"You are not a woman. You're a sorceress. We are of the same spirit, in different forms. Women, and men, are our enemies."

"Women and men are not my enemies. Not all of them. It is true, they persecute sorcerers and dragons. But they persecute their own kind too: Jews, Muslims, heretics, and pagans."

She thought he might be considering her argument. Whenever someone fell silent, she always presumed they were thinking, like she did. But it was hard to tell with a dragon.

"So you find me a worthwhile companion?" she asked. He nodded. "Why then do you never stay with me? You're away all day. You stay with me only at night, and I think it's because I would die from cold otherwise."

"I am away to hunt, to bring food to keep us alive. And to find firewood that you demand. Is that not enough?"

"Enough? Enough to make up for my imprisonment? No. I could find my own food and my own firewood, if you would set me free. And I would get food that I choose, not your leftovers. All this meat is making me sick. How can you claim to seek a worthwhile companion when you don't care for companionship at all?"

"I also brought asterium. You would have died without it."

"That's not companionship. Perhaps hunting requires much of your day, but when you're here, you always sit up there on the ridge by yourself. When I cook or eat, you're never with me."

"I dislike the smell of cooked meat, and the smoke."

Though her parents had said the same of Ashwing, she found it amusing. "Smoke? You're a creature of fire. How can you dislike smoke?"

"All dragons dislike smoke. Smoke and fire are different things But they come in pairs, fire and smoke." She laughed, her first true laugh since she laid eyes on this dragon a month ago. "Look!" She stretched out an arm toward the cookfire billowing smoke past a fawn's leg.

"Not all fires give smoke," he corrected her.

"Of course all fires do! Every fire you've started gave smoke."

Pyramine issued a slender, smooth stream of fire at the ground before them. The fire flared where it hit the rock surface, flashing blue and orange, clean and smokeless. Befuddled, she stopped talking to sulk over her embarrassing ignorance. The conversation had been more enjoyable before, when he was praising her spirit. All those times Pyramine started fires for her, she had never guessed just how much he disliked smoke. But she understood now, why he always left his head in flames. He was avoiding the smoke billowing above.

"It's still peculiar that dragons dislike smoke."

"Smoke is the impurities of a fire. It is dirty. You are forged from red flesh and blood. Do you not dislike impurities in those?"

She gave in. Though defeated, she was satisfied with the conversation. It was the most companionship she'd had since he abducted her.

"It's too bad that smoke and burned flesh bother dragons so."

"Why?"

She gave up putting on a show. "When Ashwing attacked, so many people burned to death. Yet their deaths served no purpose. He was simply killing out of anger. He killed more with his own teeth, to feed on, but left the burned bodies untouched. I'd always wondered why. My parents told me, but I didn't believe it could be true."

"If dragons could live on burned flesh, it would make a dragon's life very easy. Lazy dragons like those who take men's sacrifices would burn down the forest and scavenge on the creatures killed."

The notion of lazy dragons was amusing. She'd always considered them beasts, like bears and wolves, horses and cows, and thus largely free of human vices and virtues. The insight Pyramine gave her made her feel, for the moment, less like a captive and more of an emissary between men and dragons. She possessed knowledge that no man knew, not even the most learned of dragonslayers. Not only did dragons share the virtues and vices of men, but Pyramine could differentiate them.

A smile crept onto her lips as she remembered him saying that she was neither greedy nor lazy.

"Are some dragons greedy?"

"Some steal, like the dragoness who attacked you. But that was perhaps laziness and hunger. No, I do not believe dragons are greedy."

That surprised her. "What about the valuables dragons take from men?"

"It soothes my hunger. And yours."

"I don't mean food. Valuables. Treasures. Like gold, and silver. Jewelry. Silk and spices."

"Gold . . . bright yellow stones," he said, perhaps scouring old memories.

"Not stones. Men can change its shape. It's a valuable metal. The duke's crown is made of gold."

"Metal?"

"Metals are hard, and shine when polished. Like swords and certain kinds of armor. That helmet I use for melting ice is metal."

"Yes, metal. I do not know what the others are."

She explained human treasures to him. He understood jewelry. He even said that there was some in the pile of bones, from people he'd killed. He had more trouble grasping the value of silk and spices. Cloth couldn't be eaten. And food had the power to sate hunger, so what was the value of spices? She lost her enthusiasm for challenging him. The point of her question was spoiled as she realized that she already knew the answer. He would never ransom her.

"Why would dragons take treasures?" came Pyramine's reply after his careful consideration. "What good would they do us?"

"Never mind." She stared into the fire, just to have something familiar to look at. Despite the claims of the tax collectors, dragons neither stole nor hoarded treasures. If Pyramine valued men's treasures, the jewelry of his victims wouldn't be lying neglected in a pile of bones. The nests of other dragons held no more treasure than Pyramine's, she was certain. The stories of stolen treasures had all been fabricated by conspirators to blame their thefts on a convenient enemy. Dragons took livestock out of necessity. Men hoarded treasures out of greed.

She was glad he couldn't read her mind.

The next day, he brought her a sack of plums.

20

Invitation

In Isodore's most outlandish fantasies, born in the difficult days
on the road, alleviated by occasional encounters with chivalrous
knights, she dreamed that such a knight would one day take her as
his bride, swear to protect and provide for her and give her children.
For a time, the knight of her dreams was Sir Rowan, with shoulder-
length black curls, a mustache framing his mouth and chin, and a
happy laugh. Lately, it was his contrast, a fresh-faced, short-haired,
modest young knight, inclined to hide as much as he could from his
fame.

In Sir Rowan's case, it was too good to be true, and in Galt's, she
began to wonder the same. He'd said his regiment would return in
two months' time. She had counted two months, three weeks, and
five days. She had kept silent about her excitement. Now, without an
explanation for Galt's overdue return, she was grateful that it was
her nature to be silent. She felt foolish.

She suspected that some people knew. The villagers had
mocked her less since seeing her ride down the village road with
Galt. Podlum kept his distance from her, no longer talking as if his
son were her only hope of avoiding an old maid's fate. However, as
time passed with no word from Galt, her reprieve from the villager's
ridicule approached its end. Recently, Podlum began to talk again of
his son.

"Surely ye didn't put yer hopes in that dragonslayer. Ye've enough difficulty attracting a man o' yer own station," said the carpenter, still unaware that "that dragonslayer" was a knight. "Trand still 'as not made up his mind who te marry. Yer fortunate that 'e is takin' 'is time t' decide."

The idea of being Trand's bride still didn't settle well in her mind and not at all in her heart. It added humor to the village gossip, however. The quiet mocking from villagers resumed. Even she began to mock herself. What knight would ever accept her, a lowly orphanage headmistress with no family and a history she hid behind false stories? What aristocratic family would ever approve? Perhaps Galt had simply realized this.

To alleviate her disappointment, she sought comfort in thoughts of Sir Rowan. Where could he be? Was he still alive? She imagined him walking through the door of her orphanage, perhaps with another orphan he scooped up from the roads nearby. "How wonderful to see you again, Sir Rowan," she'd say, certain he could explain to her how he was innocent of the crime for which he was convicted. Perhaps the witness whose account convicted him of sodomy had had some reason to disgrace him.

"Take care of yourself, Sir Rowan," she'd whisper when she was alone, before bed or when sitting by the stream. "How I miss you." Despite their rough start, she always knew where she stood with him. With Galt, she didn't have such certainty.

More days passed. Perhaps the regiment was late, or tied up. Ambushing dragons was never a predictable endeavor. If the regiment was late, would Galt not have sent word to her? Perhaps he had changed his mind and didn't care to tell her. Perhaps he found another, more suitable maiden.

She finished her wondering with a whisper. "Please, don't be dead."

GALT NEVER AGAIN returned to Savelle, but one day, Father Serafin brought four courteous guards and two servants who came looking for the headmistress of Savelle's orphanage. The servants were well groomed for their station. Their clothes were plain but of fine cloth and free of dirt, wear and tear. Their hair and skin were clean. All were very courteous.

Father Serafin said, "This is Michel, the chief steward of Sir Galt, the Knight of God's Miracle."

"Greetings, Michel. I am so pleased to meet you." She curtsied, her heart pounding like a hammer in her chest.

"Greetings, Mistress," said the man with neatly combed hair. "This is Lorraine, a servant in the house of Lord Corvin, Sir Galt's uncle."

The woman with twinkling eyes acknowledged Isodore with a bow of the head.

"I am pleased to meet you," said Isodore. Beneath her outward calm, she wondered if she was dreaming.

"And these are four of Lord Corvin's palisade guards."

The guards remained motionless.

"Lord Corvin cordially invites you to his home near Auch," continued Michel. "We are here to escort you."

"Lord Corvin? He knows of me?"

"Of course. Sir Galt had spoken of your invaluable service while he was injured. There will be a ceremony in Auch for him, and Lord Corvin would like you to witness the event."

"Is Sir Galt there?" she asked, just to show a semblance of control, lest the visitors see her jumping out of her skin.

"Not yet. His regiment was delayed in their last mission. The dragon they faced was much bigger than they had expected, but they prevailed, and Sir Galt was not hurt. They were celebrated by the duke and will be on their way back. The archbishop wished the regiment to proceed quickly to Auch, so Sir Galt could not bring you himself."

"When must we leave?"

"It is important for you to arrive three days from now, when Sir Galt is due to return. I can tell you more about that on the way, but we should depart tomorrow."

"Oh." Isodore's hand went to her lips, and she glanced at Father Serafin.

"Headmistress Isodore has ten children to look after," said Father Serafin. "We will try to find a temporary replacement for her, certainly, but on short notice, I don't know . . ."

"If I may, Father," Michel interrupted. "Lorraine is more than capable of caring for the orphans. She has raised many of Sir Galt's cousins and Sir Galt himself, since he was seven years of age. She has been with Lord Corvin's family for many, many years. She is from a Christian family and completely trustworthy."

Lorraine addressed Isodore and the priest. "I have cared for as many as twelve children at a time. You will be pleased with my work." She flashed an expression that was part maternal and part consociate, which Isodore found reassuring.

With Father Serafin's easy consent, they planned to depart the next morning, giving Isodore the rest of the day to prepare herself and her children. She introduced Lorraine to the orphans and went over their daily chores, her duties, the children's work in the orchard, and two apprenticeships. Lorraine won the young children over with a new dish and the promise of even more to come. The older ones accepted her with the courtesy Isodore had taught them.

Michel instructed Isodore to prepare for a week away from Savelle. When she folded up her fine Sunday tunic, Michel stopped her. "You will not need spare clothing. Appropriate attire awaits you."

She held up the tunic to show him, certain that he didn't expect her to possess such a fine outfit.

"It's an outstanding garment," he said, with the smile of someone who knew more than he let on. "You will have better."

Lord Corvin planned to provide her with better clothing than this? She gave in to her curiosity. "Michel, what do Sir Galt and Lord Corvin plan for me?"

"There will be a ceremonial dubbing for him at the cathedral. He wants you to be there." It was the same answer he gave before. There was, however, something about the way he spoke, the slight bow, holding his eyes on her. It left Isodore suspecting that he hadn't told her everything.

THE RIDE TO Galt's uncle's estate near Auch would take two and a half days on horseback. Isodore rode the palfrey that had carried Lorraine. An hour out of Savelle on the narrow winding road through the woods, with two guards well ahead of them and two well behind, Michel rode alone with Isodore, answering her questions. Without her asking, he admitted, "There is one more reason I am bringing you to Auch, Mistress Isodore. Sir Galt would like you to meet his family—Lord Corvin, in particular."

That prospect both excited and unnerved Isodore. Michel studied her intensely, as if he were about to put his life into her hands. He must have been satisfied with what he saw, because a conspiratorial smile came to his lips and grew. "Sir Galt wishes to wed you, Isodore. I could not tell you earlier because he forbade me to do so until after we had left Savelle."

This is rather sudden, she thought. Though maybe not unusual for the nobility. Some noble children were betrothed without their knowledge. Perhaps Galt had known all along he wanted to wed her. He had asked such blunt questions about her the day they spent together. Perhaps he was assessing her suitability.

She understood why Galt didn't want Michel to tell her this news in Savelle. During the day they had spent together, she found him astute. Though he didn't let on, he might have noticed how the villagers looked at her. Perhaps he thought it was best that they didn't know of his plans. She certainly didn't want them to.

"Mistress Isodore," Michel called her out of her contemplation. "He wishes to wed you," he said again, as if he thought she hadn't understood the first time.

"Oh, that would be fine. He's a very gentle knight," she said, her proper-lass demeanor stretched to its limit to contain a jubilance she had never before felt.

"Then you will agree?"

"Certainly!"

"Very well." Michel's smile was genuine but brief. "There will be much opposition."

She came out of her reverie then, to the tough reality that she would face. "I know." She expected that the choice of a young knight to court a twenty-seven-year-old orphanage headmistress would understandably bring attention and a certain degree of suspicion, if not outright hostility. But she thought Galt was different.

"Sir Galt intends to marry you if you accept, but out of respect for his family, he would have you meet them first. And out of deference for them, he wishes to keep his plans secret. Only his family knows, not even the house servants or those accompanying us. For your visit, you will be a guest of Lord Corvin, not Sir Galt."

Lord Corvin, the lord and knight. Though Galt had said little of him, she, by instinct, began to fear him.

LONG HOURS OF daylight facilitated their travel. They rode, rested, and camped under forest canopy the first half of the journey. The forest reminded her of her childhood, and riding through it with four guards and a servant, she imagined how she would look through the eyes of a starving orphan hiding by the roadside. She saved her meal in case one came to her asking for food, but she encountered none. When they were closer to Auch, safe from hunting dragons, the road widened. They passed expansive pastoral land that Isodore had not seen since moving to Savelle.

They arrived in Laronde in late-morning, a large village, with scores of cottages and a church across the road from the village green. On the west side, they passed through the palisade gates, where Michel and the guards greeted each other cheerfully. They dismounted in the bailey. Michel spoke to the stable hand while Isodore looked in awe at the motte beyond the bailey's cottages. It was more than twice her height, topped with a formidable keep that loomed over the domain from behind another palisade. The compound was more fortified than Lord Edwin's meager bailey in Savelle. On the frontier, the nobles didn't fight so much over land and peasants; the greatest danger came from dragons, against which mottes and palisades offered slim protection. But away from the dragons, these lords were each other's greatest threats, and a well-defended castle was indispensable.

Michel led Isodore to the cluster of cottages at the center of the bailey, passing the guards' quarters on one side of the open ground and the stable on the other. A long house and the keep were the biggest, sturdiest structures in the bailey. They had plank siding while the others were the common wattle-and-daub types, like her orphanage. Inside the long house, Michel greeted and introduced Isodore to a gray-haired servant with a soft smile. Margot had been expecting Isodore. Michel left to prepare for Galt's arrival later that day.

The lord's family wasn't home, but the house servants whisked her away for a warm bath in one corner of the great hall. A cone-shaped curtain gave her some privacy while she bathed, but she could hear and see through the curtain's opening.

House servants scrubbed clean the trestle tables and chairs, swept the floor, and cleared cobwebs from the corners. Margot, a firm but soft-spoken woman attended to her bath, but Isodore felt out of place receiving the service rather than helping clean the house.

After the bath, Margot dressed Isodore in a soft, white cotton tunic, with lace-trimmed bell sleeves, hem, and neck. A laced-up bodice showed her feminine figure better than the belt on a tunic ever could. The outfit far surpassed the Sunday attire that Sir Rowan had given her.

A servant girl named Sorrel braided Isodore's hair in two neat ropes. She reminded Isodore of her twelve-year-old orphan, Claudia. Sorrel complimented Isodore's long hair and gave her a strip of lace to tie high on her head. It wasn't a crown, just a white strip of intricate needlework, but it made her feel self-conscious, try as she might to ignore it. Were it not for the excitement of Sorrel and the other servants, Isodore would have removed it.

They gave her bread and soup, though she was too nervous to eat much. She sat to wait for the arrival of Lord Corvin. Filled with nervous energy, she offered her assistance in cleaning the great hall, but Margot said, "Please, you are m' lord's guest. You mustn't be seen working."

Isodore had seen a few longhouses before, but this was her first time inside one. It was ten times the size of the cottage she shared with her ten orphans. Along the walls were small tables set with vases, lamps, candles, baskets of fruit, and bottles of spirits. Four full bags of grains lay neatly in a wooden chest sturdy enough to keep out rodents. At one end of the hall, a loft provided the exclusive sleeping quarters for the lord and his wife. A curtain separated this solar from the rest of the house. Under the solar were two more large beds with mattresses. For the lord's family members, she guessed.

The great hall had room for six trestle tables and their benches. The stack of sleeping pallets at one end of the hall told her that a score of servants and guards lived there, though only half of the servants were in the hall, cleaning. The rest must be outside. She heard faint sounds of voices and people working there. Only four tables would have to be moved to make room for the servants' beds, leaving two permanently at the ready. Her tiny orphanage had just one table for her and ten children, and it had to be stowed each evening to make room for the sleeping pallets. It didn't have the abundance of food in this house.

She observed the wealth and watched the servants work. When the immediate novelty faded, she recalled the reason she was there. To meet the master of this place.

The instinctual fear she felt when Michel had told her she would meet Lord Corvin returned, making her sweat. This wasn't walking with Sir Rowan through a garden. She was meeting a master and warrior. Galt had told her in passing that his uncle became Lord of Laronde after defeating the previous lord. Unspoken was the fact that the man had likely killed every member of his predecessor's family, to prevent any possibility of them reclaiming the lordship.

Isodore prayed that he wasn't like some of the knights she had seen. She braced herself for a man who was fearsome, unforgiving, and prone to find faults in her. She hoped that Galt wouldn't put her through such an ordeal.

"I will not be afraid," she whispered, trying to calm herself. "I will not be afraid."

The sound of horses reining up outside Lord Corvin's home made her shiver and paralyzed at the same time.

21

The Lord Knight

"I will not be afraid. I will not be afraid. I will be a proper lass."

Isodore stood to greet Lord Corvin. Two armed guards entered and held the door for him. Two followed him in. A solid man of about fifty years, Lord Corvin was tall like Galt, but broader, with shoulder-length graying auburn hair and beard. He wore a thick white tunic, a gray vest, a brown leather belt, and brown boots. Though guards accompanied him, he carried his own sword. Unlike Lord Edwin, an administrator who relied on his knights for protection, Lord Corvin was a warrior. And he carried himself like one.

Isodore curtsied. "Lord Sir Corvin, it is my great honor to meet you. I am Isodore. Thank you for the hospitality of your house."

He studied her, his eyes went from her head to her toes and back, his face unreadable. "There is no 'Sir' in my title. I am not that sort of knight."

"Yes, lord. Please forgive me."

"Leave us," he commanded the guards and servants, then to Isodore, "Sit."

The guards turned and left through the front door. The servants filed out the back without delay. The great hall that had been bustling with servants fell quiet, the brooms, dusters, buckets, and rags all left behind.

Corvin removed his sword from his belt, passed the sheathed weapon to his right hand and stood it against the bench with a heavy thud. Isodore waited for him to sit before taking a seat on the opposite side of the trestle table. The great hall seemed dark, though it was likely no darker than the orphanage in which she always felt comfortable. She suddenly felt all alone.

Michel had told her about this man—warned her. Lord Corvin was a harsh but honorable man. He valued courage and integrity. Above all, he cared a great deal about Galt. He had agreed to meet her at Galt's request. "Show him the respect he commands from you," Michel had advised. "But try not to be afraid of him." Sitting across from the lord knight, Isodore thought she could do the former but feared she would fail at the latter.

Though Corvin was a lord, there was nothing dressy about his attire. His tunic was of an expensive heavy cotton cloth but yellowed with age, mended here and there. Grass and mud stains covered the elbows and knees. His leather vest was scuffed and superficially lacerated. Watching him, she became horribly conscious of the fancy tunic and lace headband she was wearing and prayed he didn't think her childish.

Lord Corvin placed his elbows on the table and touched the fingertips of his rough, thick hands together, staring over them. "Tell me . . ." he said with a pause, as if deciding where to start, "about your family."

She told him what she had told Galt.

"Your grandparents?"

"I . . . have no memory of them."

"Aunts, uncles? Cousins?"

"None, lord."

"You were raised in Dorune's orphanage?"

"Yes, under Father Julian." Fearing he would delve into Sir Rowan, she said as little as she could about the knight. When she finished with one question, Corvin went right into the next, not bothering to evaluate her response. She suspected he already knew the answers. He was simply testing her.

"When did you first see Galt?"

"In the field outside Savelle, after the dragon battle. Father Julian called the villagers to come help the injured dragonslayers."

He asked for the full story of what happened between them, and she recounted the events for him, except the casting of the spell. He seemed more interested in this story than in her background. When she told him that she had volunteered to care for Galt after others wanted to stop, she felt relieved, certain that her actions spoke well of her to anyone who cared about Galt.

"Did anything unusual happen when he stopped suffering?"

"No. Only that it was the first night he had slept quietly. Before then, he didn't sleep well because of the pain."

She wanted to see if he suspected her of sorcery, but she dared not look at him too long.

"What does my nephew see in you?"

"I don't know." She looked down at the dark, empty, and heavy table between them, searching for something of substance to put forth. "I have nothing to offer him but myself. No title. No property. I can give him children." Feeling better at this, she looked up. "And I can teach them, as I have been taught. I have the highest regard for Sir Galt, and so shall the children."

"Plenty of lasses in Auch can do the same. Highborn lasses. Why would he choose you?"

She shook her head, her brief spell of confidence slipping away, leaving her grasping for something to justify herself. She could cook and mend, but Corvin would only say that was the role of servants. She could take care of children. But there was something more substantial. "I am entrusted with the care of ten children in an orphanage. I believe I will be proficient in the running of Sir Galt's household."

"Proficient, lass? A noble household is far more complex. How will you keep record? Only fools trust their scribes."

"I will keep the records myself, as I do at the orphanage. I can write, lord. And read."

Corvin hesitated.

She was sure he didn't expect her to be literate. Her parents secretly taught her to read so she could one day use their spellbook.

She had continued learning from Father Julian. Sir Rowan convinced the priest on the point that her education would help Headmistress Janine, whose illiteracy had caused the priest many headaches.

For a second, Isodore thought Corvin might test her claim. "Well," he said. "I suppose that makes you superior."

"No, please. I meant no disrespect. But you must know, I am capable."

"What I want to know is what that boy sees in you."

Stumped again, she replied, "I don't . . . I believe he and I are kind-hearted people."

"Kind hearts do not rule, lass. They don't provide for their family's needs. They don't protect you from raiders. They don't bring justice, or shelter you from injustice. Or win battles. Or conquer lands. Kind hearts died by the hundreds in Paris and Bordeaux, in England and al-Andalus."

Nothing she could do would please the man. I will not be afraid, she repeated in her mind to calm herself. I will not be afraid.

She looked at him with all the respect she could show and spoke. "A kind heart is a virtue taught by the Lord Jesus. It is why the Knights of the Cross conduct themselves with such honor. And why they have the support of the Church and the people."

"The Church again," grumbled Lord Corvin, with a disdain that Isodore could clearly hear and see but hardly believe. Galt had said he came from an ecclesiastic family, so why such disdain? She stopped speaking, certain that whatever she said would only earn Corvin's ridicule.

Corvin stared. "You have nothing to offer him. No family, no title, no dowry, no land. And you don't even know what he sees in you."

"I didn't think to ask him that, but I believe he must have his reasons. He was in high spirits when he took me riding. I believe he will be happy with me as his bride. I . . . He and I . . . enjoy each other's company."

"Enjoy each other's company?" Corvin asked, slowly.

"Yes." She smiled, thinking he believed her.

He glared at her across the table, eyes narrowing, not quite hostile, but far from friendly, far from trusting.

"You claim to be a maiden?"

She nodded. "Yes, lord. I am."

Corvin pierced her with a stare so hard that she nearly doubted herself. She couldn't help thinking that he knew something she didn't, a damning fact she had somehow overlooked.

"There will be pressure for Galt to explain why the famed Knight of the Cross weds a woman so old and without family. A scandal on top of that will be the end of it. This archbishop is not known for his flexibility."

"I know how my age can cause you to doubt, but I have lived by the laws of the Church since before I came of age. I can swear to that." She had never come close to lying down with any man, but because that fact made her appear undesirable as a woman, she didn't speak of it.

Corvin glared before taking his eyes off her. He gruffly remarked under his breath, "We shall see."

Isodore didn't understand what that meant. Caught by his unmitigated opposition, she wondered why Galt wanted her to talk to him in the first place.

"As for Galt being happy," continued Lord Corvin, "we'll see how happy he is when he loses everything he has worked for. He wanted all his life to be a dragonslayer. He's earned that and is now a Knight of the Cross. Do you know why the Church expects its knights to be of high virtue?"

"To set an example for all knights."

"And what kind of an example would it be for a knight to wed a cottager's daughter eight years his senior? An aristocrat's sole remaining son wedding a peasant? An orphan who can't even recall her grandparents? He'll forfeit his reputation and his inheritance! He's set to receive his entire family's estate. Do you think he'll have any of it after this foolishness?"

"I . . . I didn't know. And it's not my place to question him."

"So you question me instead? You question his entire family?" She didn't understand, so he clarified for her, pointing a finger. "If you wed my nephew, you do more than question us. You'll be opposing us. All of us. Is that your intent?"

"I believe I am doing what Sir Galt wishes me to do," she said, but her voice trailed off in a whisper as weak as her position.

"He is just a boy! Not even old enough to be a knight."

Bewildered, she asked, "But . . . is he not a knight, Lord Corvin?"

"A knight? Bah! He'll be a good knight one day, but now? A Knight of the Cross and a Knight of the Crown? Only six men in all of history have held those dual titles. He's not of that caliber. The duke, the archbishop . . ." Corvin stopped, trying to calm his rising anger. He pounded his fist on the table. "Using that boy like a pawn."

Isodore tried to stop her gasp, but it only froze on her face.

"They're using him," Corvin repeated, his anger under control, but his resentment unmistakable. "The story will spread. The Knight of God's Miracle. Hah! Brilliant title. I suppose it didn't sound good enough to say the Squire of God's Miracle. The story will spread. The two of them will have my nephew in their courts, so they can ride the fame they crafted for him. 'Look what God has done! He has shown his approval for our cause by this miracle.' That is why they dubbed a nineteen-year-old boy a knight. That's the only reason!"

"I'm sorry," she whispered.

Corvin's voice also softened. "God may favor him, but he's no knight yet. I know him. I raised the boy! And he needs more time. He ought to be in training, not paraded around."

Isodore recalled how reluctant Galt was to identify himself as a knight. Perhaps he knew all that time what his uncle was asserting. She looked again at Lord Corvin. The man was looking not at her but at the empty table, for a long, long moment.

"Do you wish to wed him?" he asked, gritting his teeth.

"Yes, if that is his wish."

"Why?" Corvin snapped.

"He is brave. He is an honorable and intelligent man."

"Is that all?"

The question took her by surprise. Of course it wasn't all, but why must she tell him? Since her days living in the forest, she had dreamed of a rare knight who was brave, valiant, courteous, and sworn to protect her. In a world so dangerous, it was a comforting dream. But crossing social lines brought a great deal of scorn and suspicion, for both the knight and the peasant. Being a pretender was a reputation she had come to live with all her years in Savelle, but now, she could no longer say the ridicule was undeserved. And for the knight crossing his social lines . . . It occurred to her why Lord Corvin had asked her what Galt saw in her. Aristocrats, with their wealth and power, didn't wed peasants. They used them, then left them with bastard children to raise. Was that why he had questioned her maidenhood?

"Is that all?" Corvin asked again.

Startled out of her private thoughts, she stumbled over her words, "Um . . . Yes. That is all."

"Good," he said, some of the anger dissipating from his stern face and demeanor. "Then that is what you shall have."

"I beg your pardon?" she said, shocked and confused.

"Do you want more? Galt's fame, perhaps? His family's wealth?"

"No! Of course not."

"Then you will have such a man. Brave, intelligent, and honorable. He's still a squire, but a promising one. Someone closer to your age. I've no doubt he'll become a knight with a few years more training. But it's not a given, and few people recognize his potential. Therefore, his family will be willing to accept a lowborn bride. He's courteous and will make you a good husband. I will offer a dowry along with you to make the arrangement more profitable to him."

Isodore drew a slow gasp as she listened. "You . . . You wish to marry me to someone else?"

"It's for the best. He's all that you want and he'll fulfill all your needs. You can cook and clean, run his household, and bear his children. He'll be happy with that. And his family will be far more welcoming of you than Galt's. That is to your benefit. You will be grateful for that. They're small holders, so you will have land along with a fine husband. That's more than Galt will have if he's foolish enough to proceed with this plan. This man doesn't have Galt's but that's all the better. Less attention. Less scrutiny."

"Is that what Sir Galt wishes for me?"

"That is what's best." Corvin rose and grabbed his sword as he stood. "Come. I'll take you to meet his family."

Isodore didn't move. Too shocked to protest, she shook her head until she could get her mouth to work. "Lord Corvin, I don't know much about Sir Galt or why he wished for me to talk with you, but I don't believe it is to accept your offer. It's a generous offer, which none in my position should decline. I know that."

Corvin stared down at her, a stare so cold that she shivered, but he said nothing. She tried not to look at the sword in his hand.

"If you wish to send me away and explain to Sir Galt what transpired here, then I have no choice but to leave. I know you can make my life very difficult. I'm torn between my loyalty and friendship to Sir Galt and the respect you, as lord and his uncle, command. I am a lowly servant with no family. I have no choice but to do as you order. But I cannot betray Sir Galt this way. I cannot accept your offer without talking with him. And I know you will withdraw your offer if I—"

"Enough!" Corvin's fist slammed down on the table like a mallet. He leaned over her from his side of the table, shouting into her face. "Damn you, lass! I am giving you the wealth and position of a respectable family that can provide for you far better than Galt can. Without scandal plaguing you! Without the endless opposition of a family that despises you! Without scrutiny of everything you do!"

Isodore clasped her hands under the table to control her shaking. "Lord Corvin, please don't think me ungrateful. I simply can't bring myself to turn my back on Sir Galt! If you won't allow us to marry, then I beg you to send me back. I can't be at peace if I agree to marry another man without a word to the man who brought me here. I must speak to Sir Galt!"

"Galt is a boy!" roared Corvin, shaking his mallet of a fist before her.

Isodore drew back, afraid to see his hand coming as much as the pain of being struck. But she braced herself despite her fright.

Nothing she could do would prevent him from striking her, but something in her refused to be cowed by his strength and power. She would look at him as he struck her, force him to face the dishonorable act.

Corvin couldn't look at her. He looked left and right, rendered speechless by his rage. He passed his sword to his left hand, as right-handed swordsmen would before drawing the blade. Isodore fought back the urge to run, refusing to look for an escape because it would mean taking her eyes off his. If he wanted to kill her, there was little she could do to prevent him. The only protection she had was the man's own sense of honor, which she now prayed Michel and Galt had not overestimated.

The sword slammed down on the table, still in its scabbard. Corvin turned again and barked at the back door.

"Margot!"

Isodore shrank as seconds ticked away.

"Margot!" he called, louder.

The sound of fast footsteps rose outside, then Margot, in her kitchen apron, burst into the great hall.

"Yes, m'lord."

"Take her away!"

"Yes, m'lord." Margot took Isodore by the arm, and Isodore stood. Respecting Corvin's mood, the old servant hurried both of them out of his reach. "What shall I do with her, m'lord?"

"I don't know. Just get her out of my sight."

"Yes, m'lord."

As they slipped through the back door, Corvin's last words boomed after them.

"Check her maidenhead!"

22

Maiden's Match

Isodore stumbled out of Lord Corvin's great hall on shaking legs. She squinted in the daylight. Margot led her through a wide path lined with flagstones, past beds of cabbages and onions, to the kitchen. Inside the mud-walled, thatch-roofed structure that was bigger than her orphanage, a dozen busy servants turned their curious eyes to Isodore. Two cookfires glowed under huge, simmering pots, shedding the scent of thyme, coriander, and cardamom in their steam.

"Ilsa, come," Margot called. "The rest of ye, please, I want this kitchen cleared. M' lord is finished in the house, so ye can go back t' yer cleaning there." The servants filed out, glancing at Isodore in turn. She felt weak and dizzy. Her stomach tightened.

Margot patted her hand. "This is Ilsa, dear. She's the midwife. Delivered every one o' m'lord's children, and 'is grandchildren, too. She's very gentle. It won't 'urt at all." To Ilsa, she said, "M' lord wants her maidenhead checked."

"Yes, of course," said Ilsa, a woman in her mid-forties with a hooked nose, a scarf around her head and gnarled hands white with flour.

Ilsa rinsed her hands with water Margot poured. With a rising fear, Isodore watched the two women calmly work. She wanted to flee, but as with Corvin, she felt paralyzed. How she wanted to trade places with the women. Being a servant with nothing to gain would be better than trying to prove herself to people who didn't want her. But prove herself was what she had to do now. If she refused the exam, Corvin would surely declare her a liar.

The two women cleared one end of the long kitchen table and helped Isodore onto it. She lay with her knees bent high, feeling even more vulnerable than she expected to. Ilsa set herself on a stool at Isodore's feet and brought down a candle that Margot lit from one of the cookfires. Isodore's tunic and chemise came over her knees and bunched up on her belly. A slight breeze cooled her legs and crotch. For distraction, she studied the neat rows of herbs and spices on the well-stocked shelves, the cuts of pork being smoked by the ceiling over the cookfires, but when she felt Ilsa opening her, it brought her right back to her vulnerable position.

She grimaced, sucked a breath through clenched teeth, took Margot's fingers and squeezed. The woman patted Isodore's hand. "There now, lass," whispered Margot. "She's just about finished."

But Ilsa's probing and prying continued endlessly. Spasms jerked Isodore's legs and body each time Ilsa's fingers pushed and stretched farther. She wanted to say something out loud, to let the midwife know that whatever she was doing, it did hurt, and could she please be more gentle? She was never schooled for this situation, but she suspected that a proper lass shouldn't make a fuss of it. She squeezed her eyes shut and held on to Margot's hand and fought the urge to slam her knees together, call an end to the exam and run back to Savelle. High-pitched grunts escaped her clenched teeth on shallow breaths. At last, she felt Ilsa's hands release her. They went to her knees and brought her legs together gently. Margot pulled the folds of Isodore's tunic back over her legs to her ankles.

"Yer a maiden all right, lass," declared the midwife. "There's no question, oh no. I don' know 'ow a lass kin be a maiden at yer age, but ye are. Maybe ye should carry yerself wit' more confidence, eh? Yer not that ugly."

Margot backhanded Ilsa on the shoulder. "Les clean ye up. 'Tis not our place te wonder 'bout our guest."

"I was jus' tryin' te help. She's runnin' out o' time te get a 'usband."

Isodore sat up, relieved but still nervous. She leaned heavily on the old woman as they left the kitchen. Ilsa strode ahead, disappearing into the great hall. Servants began trickling back to the kitchen.

"Wait," Isodore said. "I'm still a bit . . . Let me wait a moment, please."

"O'course," Margot looked at her with kind eyes and a patient smile. "Why're ye so fearful, lass?"

Isodore's shaking returned. "He was so angry."

"Well, 'e . . . gets that way, sometimes."

"I thought he'd strike me."

"Oh, I don' think m' lord would do that. No. Not without good cause. Ye did na show him disrespect, did ye?"

"No, but . . ." She didn't know if refusing his offer constituted disrespect.

Ilsa dragged her feet coming out of the long house.

"Did ye tell m' lord what ye found?" asked Margot.

"Yeh."

"What did he say?" Isodore asked, preparing for the worst.

"'E asked me if I was sure, and I says, 'Yes, m' lord, I checked and checked again an' I checked that the barrier isn't jus' partly broken, as it sometimes gets, ye know. She's definitely a maiden, m' lord,' I says. Ye know, I thought 'e'd be 'appy, but 'e jus' waved me awayWhen Isodore felt she could delay no longer, she nodded for Margot to lead her back to the great hall. It was busy again with the cleaning crew.

"Where's m' lord?" Margot asked a servant.

"'E left."

"Did 'e say what we should do wit our guest?"

"'E said she's a guest an' treat her like a guest."

ISODORE SIPPED WINE and nibbled on a thick slice of cheese to help calm her nerves. It was the most delicious wine and cheese she'd ever tasted but she couldn't enjoy the food. Anxiety gnawed at her.

She waited for Galt who, according to Michel, was on his way and would arrive that afternoon, if all went well on the journey home. She hoped he would arrive before his uncle returned.

Unable to eat anymore, too nervous to sit still, Isodore took to wringing her hands and watching the servants work. After some time, she realized they were up to something, laboring endlessly to clean and cook. She didn't think any house required that much work in one day. Likewise, the amount of food being prepared in the kitchen would feed multiple families. When Margot came along, she asked and learned that they were preparing for a feast later that day. Again, she offered her hand to help.

"Oh, no. O' course not. It won' do. And we don' need any help. We've done this before. Ye rest yerself. Would ye like another bath?"

Isodore sat back down, staring at the block of cheese that still could make her mouth water, even when no appetite remained. I would make a poor aristocrat, she thought. But she wouldn't have to be one, if Lord Corvin was right about Galt losing his inheritance for defying his family.

She would be the cause of much discontent if she and Galt wedded. Perhaps she should do him a favor and decline his offer of marriage.

She spun around at the sound of horses reining up hard outside. Her heart pounded and she wanted to run out to the croft to hide, in case Lord Corvin had come back. She backed up and bumped into one of the servants.

"I'm sorry."

"It's all right, lass."

The doors swung open and in strode a knight with shoulder-length dark brown hair and a thin beard, wearing a vest like Lord Corvin's, but new, ornate and emblazoned with the crest of the Duchy of Gascony: quadrisect fields with two standing lions and two sheaves of wheat—a Knight of the Crown. He stopped and scanned the room full of busy servants until he spotted her in the back.

"Isodore!" His face shifted into unrestrained jubilance.

"Sir Galt!"

She checked an impulse to run up and throw her arms around

him, waiting like a proper lass for him to come toward her first. Boy or man, she tried to determine as he crossed the long hall. At nineteen years of age, he was a man by most standards, even if his uncle asserted otherwise. He walked tall, his head held high, one arm steadying the sword on his belt and the other reaching out to her. His hair had grown out to a normal length, erasing the last vestiges of the horrific injury that had brought them together.

Halfway to her, the servants swarmed around him, bursting with cheerful greetings. They freely patted his shoulders, squeezing his arms and running their hands over the ornate vest. Isodore watched them welcome him back, humbled and elated to see how warmly he spoke to them. They addressed him as Master Galt, rather than using his knightly title.

He mussed the hair of Sorrel, the young girl who gave Isodore the lace to tie around her forehead. The girl looked at him, infatuation written on her face. Isodore wondered if she had ever looked at Sir Rowan like that, and whether anyone noticed.

"Has my uncle told you who Isodore is?" he asked the gathered group. No one knew.

"She's m' lord's guest," said Sorrel.

"But why?" Galt asked, engaging the girl. Sorrel shrugged, and Galt continued. "Isodore is the woman who looked after me when I was burned. It was she who helped relieve my pain. She kept me as comfortable as she could."

"Ahh," said some of the servants. A glow came to their faces, warming what had been, to that point, formal and cordial smiles. After a prolonged welcome home, Galt stole Isodore away to Laronde's church, where they strolled through the garden, through rows of flowers among broad plane trees and oaks, seeking shelter from the hot sun.

"I was relieved to hear that you were unhurt," she said. "How went the battle?"

"I was not harmed . . . but we lost more men."

Isodore's joy shrank. The dragon battle, she learned, was far more difficult than Michel had summarized for her. Galt's regiment joined with another because the dragon they had to kill was reported to be unusually big. It was even bigger than they expected, so they devised a new ambush plan and worked out extra contingencies.

Galt sighed. "We should have had three regiments. The dragon was not just fierce. It was nearly seven feet tall. It was . . . hard to trick." He shook his head. "Sir Wilfred believed it could understand us." Galt looked up, frowning, and Isodore frowned back in sympathetic bewilderment.

"It was as if the beast knew our plans. Whatever we tried, it was right there with us. We lost nine men in all, and we were tired. When Sir Wilfred rotated to the front, he gave us instructions in Latin. It just made things worse until we realized a few of us understood Latin, and we followed them. Perhaps the dragon was as confused as we were, but we managed to position our crossbowmen to capture one wing. The dragon seemed to panic after that. It went after the tethers and left itself blind to a lot of lance attacks. Sir Dalton drove his lance into the other wing and pulled it open for the crossbowmen. We finished it off with seven lances in its neck." Galt smiled wryly, apparently still astonished.

"We rushed to present the duke with the dragon's head. I'd expected a dubbing ceremony, but there was a lengthy banquet, as well. We couldn't refuse. After that delay, the archbishop wanted us to proceed directly back. That was why I sent for you. How did you find my Uncle Corvin?"

For a moment, no words came to Isodore that she dared to speak. Those in her head would open doors she was sure she didn't want to enter. "He was . . . enlightening."

Galt smiled as though he understood her. But she doubted that he did.

She swallowed a lump. "Have you . . . spoken with him?"

"Briefly. He was at the river, by the bridge."

"What was he doing?"

"Combat training. He has a couple of new knights."

She knew, from time with Sir Rowan, that this meant donning full armor and fighting hard with blunt swords. It was exhausting the way Sir Rowan did it and probably even more so with Corvin.

"Combat training? With a feast coming soon?"

Galt shrugged. "It helps him calm his mind in the face of difficulties."

"What . . . difficulties does he have?"

"I didn't ask, and neither should you. He has his way of dealing with these things."

"I see. Did he say anything . . . about me?"

Galt thought and frowned. "He said you were fine. You were loyal. Well mannered, for a lowborn. And respectful."

Isodore was shocked. "Was that all?"

Galt hesitated, a worried look spread across his face, but he cleared it with one that was merely amused. "Well, he said you were stubborn. What did you say to him?"

Isodore could think of no explanation to give. She dared not reveal his uncle's treachery.

Galt laughed. "He says that about many people. He has impossible standards."

Isodore sank a little but quickly realized Corvin's criticism was much better than what she expected from the man she thought was about to kill her. She no longer knew what to think of Lord Corvin, but she didn't feel right talking poorly of him in any way to Galt. "Why did you want me to meet him first?"

"He wanted it. I asked for his help to convince my family to accept you. They—"

"And he agreed?"

"Yes. He asked only to see for himself what kind of lass you were."

"And you thought that would be good?"

"Yes," he said, as if he was never in doubt.

Isodore blew out a breath and fell back, leaning against the ivy-covered wall behind her. If Corvin's conversation with her was his way of helping, what were his true feelings about her? Her fear and doubt weren't lost on Galt.

"You're concerned, Isodore, and I don't blame you. Michel did say we face much opposition, didn't he?"

Isodore nodded. Michel had warned her that Galt's family was against his courting a peasant, let alone marrying an orphan with no history, no longer a girl. She asked him if it was true.

"It's true. But I told them that your station doesn't matter to me." He rested a hand on his pommel and brought one foot up to rest on a stone protruding from the stonework wall.

Isodore looked at him, dumbfounded for a few seconds before it finally dawned on her why his view of the situation was so different from hers. Galt, she realized, was simply, blindly naive. Did he truly believe that his family would give in just because her station didn't matter to him? Had he any idea what his uncle tried to do?

Sensing her doubt, he reassured her. "In time, they will come to see that it is you that God wishes for me."

She waited for the rationale of his conviction, something to let her believe him, because she desperately wanted to. But his quiet faith was all that he offered. She wished she had his confidence in God. She had lived her life without seeing God on her side and was unsure God could look upon her any more favorably than his uncle did. In any case, God would have to wait. It wasn't His judgment that would soon bear down on her but Galt's family's.

"You will lose your inheritance. Your uncle said you will see none of your family's estate."

He studied her, not with Corvin's suspicion, but with trepidation and uncertainty. "Does that matter to you?"

"No."

Their eyes locked, as if bound by a knot pulling close with the passing seconds, a knot that could hold them together as one, or strangle them as one. She offered her own conviction. "Only you matter to me. I am accustomed to living with little means, so I don't need great wealth. None. You are far more than I had ever hoped for. A good man. A man of character. I am concerned only for . . . only for your future."

"Don't be! I'm not concerned. Not about that." His abruptness startled her. She thought he might be angry at her, possibly not believing her. He turned and paced away but continued to talk. "I'm not afraid of that. I have seen wealth and poverty. Strength of will and weakness of the heart. Courage and cowardice. My father and brother had given up their earthly wealth. I can face poverty as well as they can. But I will never again live with weakness or cowardice!"

He was so firm, so passionate, she almost thought he was angry. His face was flushed red when he paced back to her. Instinctively, she feared he was displeased with her, though she was certain she hadn't presented herself as weak or cowardly, to him or his uncle. He had looked down when he spoke, as though he was addressing himself or someone far away. Not her. She wanted to ask him what he meant. Whose weakness? Whose cowardice? But it wasn't her place. Perhaps it was someone important or powerful. She didn't want to know.

She wanted to reach out and touch his arm, to bring him into an embrace the way she would whenever one of her children was troubled, but she held back. He was, after all, little more than a very kind stranger to her. She had spent days by his side but only one day in conversation with him. She was still learning who he was. A boy, his uncle called him. Naive, she now believed. Perhaps he was, partly. No boy ever became a man overnight. He became a knight through courage, resourcefulness, and quick thinking in battle, not by triumph of wisdom over innocence.

He reaffirmed that marriage was what he wanted and told her his plans. "We can be married in four months, when the regiment returns from our next tour," he said with his earlier enthusiasm. "Michel will have the banns posted in Laronde and Savelle."

These banns, and other required public announcements, would give those with good reasons to oppose the union a chance to step forward. When Galt's regiment returned, if no one had come forward to block the union, the vows would be spoken and the marriage sealed.

"I expect that no one will have any reason to prevent our union," said Galt, blissfully oblivious to his uncle's attempt to dissuade Isodore that morning.

"What about your family? I am . . . only a lowly church servant."

"My family can't use your station to prevent the union."

"They must have their reasons for opposing. You must consider that."

"I have. They claim that you are only after our wealth, but—"

"But I'm not."

"Of course not. And they believe that one of your orphans is actually your own child and will come forth to lay claim to our land and wealth, going so far as to murder me to hasten the opportunity." He laughed. "As if I were Louis the Pious."

"But I've borne no children!"

"Of course not!" Smiling brightly, he reassured her, "I told them you're a maiden!"

Clearly, he thought his family would simply take her word for it, as he had. Had he any idea the degree of their opposition?

23

Dragon Inheritance

On a clear, warm afternoon, Isodore sat in the shadow of the ridge above the dragon's nest. Legs extended, her back against the cool granite slab, she gently flipped through the thin browning pages of a spellbook. She had received the thick leather-bound manuscript from Pyramine, who said it once belonged to a sorcerer who had transformed himself into a dragon.

The book was ancient, its pages made from papyrus, like the centuries-old Bible that Sir Wilfred once showed her in the Auch Cathedral. But the spellbook was in much better condition, like new, except for flattened bits of dirt and herbs between some pages.

Although she only planned to feign interest in transforming herself into a dragon to buy time for planning an escape, the pages enticed her. It was a trove of carefully preserved knowledge. It must have belonged to sorcerers far more advanced than her parents, for it contained a variety of spells her parents had never mentioned, all of which were described in detail, albeit in Latin.

Numerous notes, made by many hands, were squeezed into the margins and between the original lines. The additions were in modern Gascon, which she had learned to read, first from her parents, then from Father Julian. The spells' names were translated, but not all the spells. The translations given were terse.

The spells were sorted by complexity, from the easiest to the most difficult. Seeing some familiar spells reminded her how useless certain ones were. In happier times, her parents often poked fun at ancient sorcerers for devising elaborate spells to conjure food. "I have an easier one you can try," her father once told her. "First, you get a cherry, or just the part nobody wants to eat. You throw it on the ground and dump dirt on it. Keep the squirrels and rats away and it will give you cherries for the rest of your life!" Indeed, she found food-conjuring spells in the latter half of the book. Being pointless, they didn't merit translation. Farming was the superior magic.

Some of the familiar spells reminded her of her parents. Her mother, a part-time seamstress, often thrilled her by changing the color of thread, but she didn't use the spell often, lest it bring scrutiny from competing tailors. Her father could mend wood and leather, allowing him to reuse the refuse of others. After Ashwing's attack rendered them homeless, they survived by restoring putrefied food and dead animals they found near settlements. Restoration was a useful spell that later helped her survive in the woods, whenever she could find the asterium the spell required.

With the comfort of familiarity, she scanned the spell for bewitching woven fabric so that it flew into the face of a pursuer. The book noted that it was an easy spell to teach young children, a safe spell to use, because to unsuspecting people, it looked like the hand of luck rather than the work of sorcery. There was a spell to preserve food, which was easier than restoring food and required less asterium. Her parents never used this one, preferring ways that wouldn't attract attention and risk suspicion. Preservation would be useful now, however, because Pyramine hunted only every few days.

Oddly, she couldn't find any spell to make rock melt into water.

She flipped toward the complex spells. Halfway through the tome, she found the healing spell, the most complex she'd ever used. She read it with a sense of pride for having successfully cast it twice without the guidance of her parents. It wasn't until the very end of the book, however, that she found transformation spells. These spells were lengthy to cast, required multiple, simultaneous tasks and used more material, such as fire, asterium, rare creatures, rare minerals, precious metals, blood, and body parts.

She skimmed the section looking for the spell she needed. The one labeled "Sorcerer to Dragon" was the last and most complex of them all. It took twelve pages to describe and required a specific mix of wood for fire, wordy chants, six ounces of gold, twelve ounces of silver, and the head of the creature being transformed into. The book remarked that, because the sorcerer was also the subject, it was an exceptionally complex task. It referred the reader to an easier spell, transforming another person to a dragon. Easier it might be, but it was still an immensely daunting task.

The "Sorcerer to Dragon" spell would take five days to cast. Five days of work with little rest, risking a grave mistake by the sorcerer. She grew tired just reading it. It was too complex for one who had so little teaching. Though it had been translated to Gascon, she didn't know all the words.

Pyramine couldn't read and was not a sorcerer, but he was more familiar with sorcery than she. "I am a creature of magic, like you," he reminded her. Through context, they figured out as much as they could. He sat with her as she pored over the pages, and he answered her questions as well as he could, guessing when he needed to. She had never spent so many waking hours next to a dragon, never had to remember so much. When he left her alone to hunt, she forgot much of what they figured out and anxiously waited for his return. The process was slow and frustrating.

"I don't think I can cast this spell, and you can't help me," she complained one afternoon, dejected to the point of forgetting that her plan didn't require her to cast the spell at all.

Pyramine had been at a loss to decipher a number of terms that came up that day. He turned his head and looked out over the valley. A taste of defeat soured in her mouth. They both rested in silence. Isodore shifted position, drawing her knees in, hugging her legs, then stretching them out. Pyramine sat as still as a stone gargoyle. It was a long time before she could think beyond their limitations in the endeavor.

"Will the spell change who I am?" she asked.

"The sorcerer said only the physical body is transformed. The spirit is untouched."

She closed the book in her lap, running her hand over the old leather cover. "Why do you have this book, if dragons can't practice sorcery?"

"The sorcerer had no need for it, after he became a dragon. He told me where he hid it."

"Why didn't he give it to another sorcerer?"

"All his friends had died. Burned by men. He didn't want men to find it."

By now, she had accepted that Pyramine differentiated men from sorcerers and women from sorceresses, even though she didn't. Dragons, sorcerers, men—so different, yet so alike.

"Why did he want to be a dragon?"

"To be with another dragon," replied Pyramine.

"He knew this dragon while he was still a sorcerer?"

"Yes, for many years. Dragons and sorcerers are not natural enemies."

She was astonished that turning a person into a dragon for the purpose of mating had precedence. But astonishment was commonplace on Dragon's Ridge. Was she not sitting on a mountain talking to a dragon? For a while now, she had forgotten to be incredulous about his speech. Their companionship had become almost normal; even this lengthening moment of silence between them was now unremarkable.

"Do all dragons talk?"

"Many can, but most don't."

"Why not?"

"Dragons think that men talk too much. Their words are unpleasant to the ear."

"I'm sorry to cause you so much misery," she said, but neither irony nor sarcasm penetrated him. He appeared to accept her apology.

"Who taught dragons man's language?"

"No one. We inherit memories from our parents."

She gasped and sat bolt upright, turning to him. The book slid off her lap. She stared, peering deep into his eyes, as if searching for the astonishing truth, or the cracks of a lie, or the admission of a joke. "Inherit? You inherit memories?"

"Yes. It's easier than reading a book."

Dragons didn't joke any more than understand sarcasm. Questions called out from many corners of Isodore's mind. "What memories did you inherit?"

"Many. Countless hunts. Dangers to avoid. Shapes of mountains and rivers. Distant lands where I have never been."

"Oh, so you didn't need to learn to hunt? You just knew how?"

"Learn . . ." Pyramine thought before answering, as though he had no ready answer, at least none that had been put into the language of men. "Yes, I had to learn, and practice, but not be shown how to do it."

He was right. That would be easier than using a book. She wished she had inherited even her parents' limited knowledge of spells. "Do you recall the hunts as though you'd carried them out yourself? Is it like your own hunts?"

"It's different. I recall, but I know the memory isn't mine."

"How do you recall them?"

"The same way I recall my own memories. Some come when I need them, some while I sleep. Some for no reason. It was confusing at first, but once I knew what they were, I found them useful. I made sense of them. Then I began to search for them."

"Do you . . . remember things that your parents inherited from their parents? And their parents? And from all your ancestors?"

"Yes. Some are clear, those that are important or useful. Others fade with time. They become vague and fragmented. In that way, they are like my own memories."

"So you recall the words of men. Words you find so unpleasant. Why are they interesting to a dragon?" She was certain that conversing with a human captive was not of particular interest.

"It allows us—those of us who recognize their value—to learn the ways of men and defeat them."

"Do many dragons value the words of men?" She flipped the page in the book and examined the writing, to hide the interest she had in his answer.

"Few do, but they are the ones who survive. Those who reject the knowledge fall easily to men's traps. Men are very clever, but they think we are beasts."

Beasts, thought Isodore, her eyes on a page of incomprehensible Latin. The terrible secrets he naively entrusted to her found their way to the unspoken voice in her head. *If you only knew the dragonslayers' minds, Pyramine. If they only knew yours.*

Only she knew the minds of both sides. If she became a dragon and passed memories on to her offspring, it would be the dawn of a new breed, more learned and dangerous than the dragonslayers would ever expect. It would be the dragons who tricked and ambushed the dragonslayers.

24

The Feast

Isodore didn't recognize Lord Corvin when she saw him at the feast. He'd changed out of his rough clothing and shed his threatening manner. A different Corvin, a jolly and affable statesman, welcomed his guests wearing a clean, white tunic, brightly embroidered tabard, polished boots, and jeweled belt with nothing but a dagger by his side.

He embraced his sister, Galt's mother, when she came through the door. Galt's two sisters greeted their Uncle Corvin playfully. One sister was just out of childhood and the other was married, with two small children. The sisters swung into comfortable conversations with Lord Corvin's daughters. The children quickly found places in the back, where the servants offered them bread and honey. Corvin greeted the knights of Galt's regiment with open respect, particularly Sir Dalton, whose hand he shook heartily.

In attendance were many from Corvin's household, including the steward and chaplain. From elsewhere in his domain came the seneschal, bailiff, bishops, deacons, and the five vassals he retained outside his compound. In the back, where the children sat, there were a dozen laborers. They came through the back door, but the servants treated them as guests. Some wealthy lords occationally allowed a few workers into their feasts, but Isodore had never received such an invitation.

After the guests had arrived, Lord Corvin welcomed them one and all. He formally introduced Galt, though everyone already knew the famed young knight. Corvin mentioned Galt's title, dragonslayer and Knight of the Cross, but not Knight of God's Miracle or Knight of the Crown.

Isodore took in the regiment's newest knight, his bright but hesitant smile, his passionate eyes, his warrior spirit, and youthful optimism. Neither she nor Corvin were completely wrong about him. He was a boy, about to become a man, both intelligent and naive. He was perfect. If he were younger, he wouldn't have been drawn to her. If he were wiser, he might not have risked his family ties for her. She didn't know if it would be enough, but as long as he was willing to fight for her, she would stand with him. And if he gave in to his family's wishes, she would gracefully do the same.

Corvin's introductions continued in order of importance, so Isodore was last. Not expecting one at all, she was surprised. He said, "Isodore is the good lass who stubbornly stayed by Galt's side when he was at death's door after a fierce battle with a clever dragon. The regiment and I are grateful for her service, and I've invited her to come and witness Galt's knighthood ceremony." He smiled and nodded to her. She curtsied and hoped the crowd would mistake the shock marking her face for nervousness of a lowborn lass in the presence of noblemen.

Mercifully, Lord Corvin wasted no more time. "Let the feast begin!"

Joining the lord at the head of the table were his wife, his eldest son and his sister. Below them were the vassal lords, the bishop, and other family members. Galt sat with the other regiment knights just above the salt. He beckoned to Isodore and offered her the first seat below the salt. The knights warmly welcomed "Headmistress Isodore," and their gestures sheltered her from the multitude of strangers.

The servants brought wine and cheese, crackers and honey, soup and bread, ale and mead, roasted pork and meat, and sweet vegetables. Isodore had never seen such plenty. It was a pleasure just to breathe in the mouthwatering aromas.

When the meat was served, the knights reached for their daggers and the other guests produced their own knives; Isodore was left without a cutting utensil. Galt gave her his dagger and called Sorrel to bring him a knife from the kitchen. He sprinkled salt onto his soup and meat, then handed the salt dish to her. She gasped, smiled, then, in a world of their own, exchanging no words, reminisced with him about the meal she had given him at the orphanage.

The dinner conversation between the regiment knights turned to Sir Wilfred's Latin commands during the recent dragon battle, specifically his claim that the dragon somehow understood Gascon commands. Sir Dalton, the most senior and experienced of the group, wasn't so easily convinced that the dragon literally understood Gascon words.

"Horses and dogs can recognize our commands," Sir Wilfred argued. "Why should dragons be different? Beasts that hunt have to be intelligent."

Sir Dalton countered, "Horses and dogs must be trained. Should it even be possible, it would take many encounters for a dragon to even discern any words, let alone learn how we work. We don't kill every dragon we ambush, but no dragon gets away that many times. We get them before they can figure out much of anything."

"Then how do you explain dragons becoming more dangerous and harder to kill?"

"We have simply killed all the ones that were easy. The remaining ones are, of course, the hardest to kill."

"If that were the case, my commands in Latin would not have made a difference. These beasts have learned over the years to recognize our tactics and commands. They teach their young."

Sir Dalton laughed. "They aren't wolves or dogs, Sir Wilfred. They're dragons. Solitary creatures. Like snakes. Have you ever seen a dragon teaching its young how to fight? Of course not. How could they teach if they never venture out together?"

"There must be a way," Sir Wilfred insisted, but he couldn't a convincing explanation. Nevertheless, he went beyond advocating

Latin commands. He advocated a rotating system of command codes to confuse the beasts, an "unnecessary complication," according to Sir Dalton. "They know our tricks," warned Sir Wilfred. "At the very least, we should revive the old techniques that have not been used in years, for variation."

"And which do you propose, my friend? The Hidden Ballista perhaps?"

Sir Wilfred paused. Sir Gustav covered his pained expression with a hand and shook his head.

Galt saw Isodore's puzzled look. "The Hidden Ballista is a tactic we haven't used in a hundred years. Dragonslayers would hide ballistae—giant spear throwers—inside a row of cottages and send a runner to bait the dragon into a chase. The timing had to be perfect. When the bait called out, the ballistae would launch long, heavy spears—more like sharpened poles—through the cottage walls. If the dragon was in the right place, they could mortally wound it."

"And if the timing was off?" prompted Sir Dalton.

"After killing the bait, the dragon would tear open the cottages and burn the ballista crew."

"It's no knightly way to fight," said Sir Dalton.

"But it worked for many years," Galt told Isodore. "We stopped using it because dragons learned not to fly into villages. That has kept the villages safe."

"Exactly!" said Sir Wilfred. "To this day, dragons hesitate to enter villages. And if they end up there, they get out as fast as they can."

"It merely taught them to fly over the cottages instead of next to them," said Sir Dalton. "Besides, we lost too many men with that tactic."

"No, I'm not advocating the ballistae. But like Sir Galt said, we haven't used that tactic for a hundred years. The dragons of today have never seen it. Yet they still won't linger in villages. How do you explain that?"

"They've learned to fear people. Take bears. They may attack weak individuals, but not those who fight back. Not traveling parties. Not occupied camps and certainly not villages full of people."

"But they once did."

"They did, and it worked, so they kept at it until it got them killed. Today's dragons don't, because they've developed a fear of people—thanks to our work, mind you."

Neither Sir Dalton nor Sir Wilfred were was willing to give in, each arguing passionately. Isodore listened along with Galt and Sir Gustav, who seemed willing to defer to the opinions of the older knights. One thing all four knights agreed on was that what had once been "the most dangerous dragons" were now commonplace. They were harder to surround and they knew to keep their wings tightly folded during the fight. "We will lose many men to these beasts," predicted Sir Wilfred. "We have to put ourselves at greater risk to tempt them into fighting. They know something we're not giving them credit for."

In contrast to Sir Wilfred's dark warnings, musical instruments sounded softly during the meal. Between courses, balladeers sang a number of dragonslayer songs, from triumphs that turned the tables on the dragons to painful, tragic losses. Most tragic was a battle that had devastated the corps.

The ill-fated expedition was launched more than a century before. Sir Wilfred, voluble as ever, told the story that had passed down through generations of dragonslayers. "The corps had perfected a number of techniques to subdue and kill dragons. The dragons' numbers thinned. Regiments were waiting longer and longer for the beasts to come. People complained that the Church was overtaxing them. Because so few dragons were being killed, they said that their tax should be reduced.

"Perhaps they were right. But until the last dragon died, their numbers could return. The archbishop at that time believed we had to wipe them out. It wasn't enough to ambush them one by one in the frontier counties. We had to go to Dragon's Ridge. Some dragonslayers questioned the wisdom of that adventure, and the supreme head of the dragonslayers had strong reservations, but the archbishop replaced him with another who was more agreeable.

"They called it the Deleret Expedition, and it was undertaken during the reign of Duke Sancho. He and Archbishop Hidulfus launched the expedition with fanfare. It was the first time dragonslayers ever ventured into Dragon's Ridge, and it turned out to be the last. Only three returned. They'd gone so mad that they could hardly say what had happened. The songs were written by piecing together the events of the massacre."

The ballad described how the expedition had met with a tempest of dragons high on the mountain. The men fought bravely and sacrificed everything, the balladeer sang.

Galt was skeptical. "The poets made that up. They couldn't have known that from the three men who returned."

"Regardless of how the defeat happened," said Sir Dalton, "the expedition should never have been launched."

The other knights agreed.

"But how could the dragonslayers have been defeated?" asked Isodore. "This was long before the dragons learned the tactics of your crossbows, wasn't it?"

"It was," Galt said. "We don't know what happened. The survivors spoke of being surrounded by a horde of dragons. Dragons on the ground. Dragons in the air. Even in the woods. Closing in on the regiments. It's hard to believe. As Sir Wilfred said, the men had gone mad. We never see two dragons together, except when there is more kill than they can carry away. Even then, they don't work together, not the way we do. Each creature attacks on its own. So the claim of a coordinated attack is extremely farfetched."

Sir Wilfred said, "I believe that the dragonslayers simply could not find conditions favorable to them. Our victories come from battles fought on our terms, when the dragons come to Gascony. We fight in places we choose. We trick them into coming and ambush them when they do. Going to them, we lose all of that. We would never send a small band of fighters against a deep line, but that was what we did at Dragon's Ridge."

The other dragonslayers nodded grimly, even Sir Dalton, who had spent the better part of the conversation arguing with Sir Wilfred.

"The duke and the archbishop blamed each other for the failure," Galt said. "The dragonslayer corps lost half its strength. We've never recovered. At the height of our strength, there were seventeen regiments. We were down to twelve at the time of the expedition. And six, after. Now, there are only four regiments, each barely big enough. We move continuous to respond to calls for help from the frontier."

The doomed expedition instilled in the dragonslayer corps an enduring lesson, which Galt explained while the others nodded. "The only way to rid the world of dragons is to lure them down and kill them faster than they can produce offspring. Dragonslayers will never again venture into those mountains."

25

The Lost Battle

How wonderful it would be, thought Isodore, to possess the memories of one's parents, to see the world and to live through their eyes. The hours she spent trapped on Pyramine's nest made her long for these memories. The memories of her last days with her family had been the most vivid all these years, and the saddest. She longed to know more of her parents' happier times, like when they had met. How did two sorcerers find each other while hiding their secrets? Did their parents force them to marry or had they chosen each other, as she and Galt had?

She asked Pyramine while he broke wood for her cookfire, "Do you recall whether your parents chose each other?"

"My father chose my mother."

"She didn't choose him?"

"She did, after he defeated other dragons wishing to be her mate."

They were like roosters facing off in the yard, she thought with a laugh. And some men. But her curiosity toward dragonkind had outgrown her hatred and fear of Pyramine. "Then your mother gave herself to him?"

"No. She fought him too."

"Why?"

"To test his strength. A dragoness must find a strong mate who can protect her and her nest, not a weakling she has to defend."

Isodore gathered that Pyramine knew this not because his parents told stories but because of the memories he inherited. It was remarkable that he could recall both his mother's memories and his father's. Dragons might keep secrets from their mates but apparently not from their offspring. That must influence their conduct, perhaps forcing them to be more honorable. Men often spoke of honor but acted dishonorably when they thought no one would know. If men feared their offspring would know their deeds, they might be truer to their preaching. Perhaps the tax collectors and ministers wouldn't have stolen and blamed the theft on dragons.

Pyramine didn't fly away after starting the cookfire, as he normally did. He settled down and gazed out at the evening sky over Dragon's Ridge and Gascony.

"Where are your parents?" Isodore asked in absentminded curiosity.

"I do not know."

"Can you recall where they've been?"

"There is no new memory. I only inherit what they had when they conceived me. And a little more from my mother, while the egg that would bear me grew in her body."

That made sense, she thought, strange as it was. Perhaps the memories were carried in his father's seeds and his mother's blood. "How far back in the ancestral lives can you recall?"

"I do not know when the old events took place, other than very long ago. They are . . . difficult to discern."

"What are the oldest that you recall?"

"A time when dragons hunted to the south, in the place men called al-Andalus. Before that, I know little."

"Why don't dragons hunt in al-Andalus anymore?"

"It became too dangerous. The men there devised contraptions to bring us down, by tearing our wings as we flew over."

"Men have those in Gascony, too."

"It is dangerous on both sides of the mountains, but more so in the south. Few men in the north possessed the weapons, but many in the south do. The nests of the south are better defended, and they are harder to break through."

She nodded, recalling that al-Andalus was wealthier than Gascony. Its wealth meant more arms and stone dwellings. "Have you gone there to see if it is still dangerous?" She thought that if she could trick him into hunting in al-Andalus, perhaps one of the Muslim crossbows would bring him down. It was the seed of a plan that formed suddenly in her mind with unexpected cleverness—and shame. Alas, he was already wise to the danger.

"I never have," he replied, "but I recall the attempt of my mother's parents. When the men of the north learned to bring down dragons, many of us turned to the south again. My mother's mother wandered over their skies. She stayed high, but her mate was bold and impatient. He dropped fire on their nests to send them into hiding, then he went down to take an animal that the men abandoned in the middle of butchering. But the weapons were hidden inside their nest. The men snagged and tore his wings as he descended. He went down, like many others who tried the same. The fear of al-Andalus remains in dragonkind."

Fear wasn't a word she thought dragons knew. "What else can you recall of ancient times?" she asked, wondering what she could draw from his ancestral memories that she could pass on to the dragonslayers, if she ever escaped.

"I recall living in a nest of men, so perhaps one of my ancestors was in the form of a man. But I don't recall whom or which nest. I recall a great battle against men who came to these mountains to kill us. My father's father took part."

"What happened?" An eerie feeling filled her, as though ghosts of the Deleret Expedition's massacred were gathering.

"It was a time of great distress for dragons," Pyramine said, his head lifting to look out at the horizon as if there lay the past. "Men on both sides of these mountains attacked us wherever we went. Many dragons fell, and we thought the end was near for dragonkind. We were safe on the mountains, but we lost land. We hated the men, but instead of fighting them, we fought among ourselves for hunting ground.

"Not satisfied with killing us in the lowland, they came here. A mob of them amassed at the forest's end. Several of us saw them, and they saw us. We knew what they could do, and we were cautious, but so were they. My grandfather and the other dragons feigned an attack of fire but didn't carry through, lest it burn the forest and poison our home with smoke.

"The men grew bold. Their archers came out to sting us with arrows. Some dragons tried to catch the intruders. Two fell when the men sent ropes through their wings. Men's wing rippers were effective. Men on horses rushed in to kill the downed dragons with their long spears.

"It excited the men to kill us in our mountain home. They left the trees and marched up the mountain to tempt us down. More dragons came, so despite the fallen, our numbers grew. One dragon dropped the burning remains of a human carcass on the men. They were disturbed at last. We brought more old carcasses to set on fire and drop on them. We dropped rocks, too. The men feared rocks, but we could not hit them without flying close to the wing rippers. They spread out to make it harder for us. We struck some but lost more dragons.

"We thought there was nothing we could do to stop them. We used our fire on those who were far from the woods, but their clothing didn't burn. They cut apart the dead dragons to anger us so we would attack. Some of us did and quickly fell.

"By nightfall, all of us were arrow-struck and seven dragons had died. Never had so many perished in one day, and in our own home. It was not worth their lives for the few men we killed. The intruders retreated to the dense forest, where we could neither attack nor see them from the air. But we looked for them. We listened for the sound of their celebratory warbling, their work, and their preparation. We smelled the smoke of their fires. We knew where they were in the thick forest. Two dragons fell to wing rippers hiding in the trees.

"We talked about the men. There was a time when men settled near these mountains. Some among us recalled the men, their battles and their camps. These dragons could tell by how much forest the intruders occupied and the smoke from their fires that there were hundreds of men. A large mob, but no more. We had seen more than half of them in the battle. The rest had to be close, to bring the fighting men their weapons.

"Overnight, many more dragons gathered in the mountain above the battle site. It was curiosity that brought them, but when we showed the mutilated bodies of the dead dragons, they agreed to fight. The elder dragons wanted us to fight together under their command. Many insisted on attacking on their own, but by morning, we had agreed to the elder dragons' plan.

"When the men returned the next day, their arrows flew, the taunting began, and the battle followed. We stayed out of sight so the men wouldn't know our numbers. We took our turns hitting them with branches and rocks. It was ineffective as before, but our numbers let us rest longer between attacks. The rests gave us the strength to fly fast over the men, making it harder to hit us with the wing rippers. We came from all directions at once to divide the work of the wing rippers. The elders' plans worked, but many dragons still fell.

"We fought until daylight waned and the men retreated. By then, another eight dragons fell, and nearly twice as many men. But we had a gathering of some fifty, unknown to the men. In the dimming light, those of us who weren't fighting slipped into the forest far below their camp, through a hole in the forest canopy, and crawled to their camp. We killed the camp guards so they could not warn the others."

"Did the woods not hinder you?" asked Isodore, wondering if she should question the tactic of hiding in the trees. Men widely believed that the woods effectively hindered dragons. "Aren't dragons too big to move in the dense woods?"

"The overgrown dragons that you know could not have flown down the narrow gap in the trees, and they have difficulty in the woods, but none were among us. We were normal dragons. The forest slowed us, but there was no need for speed. We approached in silence and surrounded the camp. After killing the guards and horses, we crawled up to the thin woods. There, we could move more freely. We formed a line between the men and their camp, and lay in wait.

"While we saved our strength, the men had tired from the long day in their heavy covering. Many of them had returned their weapons to their carts and begun to shed their clothing.

"They celebrated the day's battle. It was the battle the fools wished to fight. The battle we wished to fight was just beginning. When they entered our trap, we attacked. We killed many before they found their weapons. We destroyed the wing rippers in their carts. The men fled back to the high grounds, where they faced the rest of us. They were surrounded, and we closed in. The more men died, the more confused they became. They couldn't regroup. Many were killed in the woods. Some were burned on the ground. Some escaped up the barren mountain. We found them the next day, weakened or dead from the cold."

Cold was coming back to the ledge, too—a shiver up Isodore's spine. She wrapped the remains of the surcoat around herself for comfort.

"We feasted well for days," Pyramine reminisced.

It wasn't he who had feasted well. It was his grandfather, but he told the story as if he had lived it. He hated men as much as his grandfather did. There was no remorse in his tone.

Pyramine's recollection left Isodore's mind restless. Once again, she possessed knowledge known to no other man. It was a long-lost secret finally revealed. A trove of information with no value, unless she could present it to the dragonslayers.

26

Dark Hospitality

After the elaborate meal, everyone stood to let Lord Corvin's servants rearrange the great hall. Many people, from Corvin's knights to his administrators, sought out Galt to offer their congratulations, wish him well, and admire up close the work of God in his hands and face. Feeling like she was in the way, Isodore stepped back to give them room.

Once away, however, Isodore felt utterly out of place, an inconsequential among nobles and people of high status. They passed in front of her and behind, but none saw her. She made her way, invisible like the servants, toward Galt's mother. Mereine, as Corvin had introduced her, was talking to one of the merchants. A beautiful, green-eyed woman, Galt's mother had an elegant jawline like Galt's and long auburn hair down to her waist. She wore a deep green satin tunic and brown vest. Waiting for her, Isodore felt even more out of place and in the way. Mereine didn't notice her and, it became clearer with each passing moment, didn't wish to. Isodore wanted to cry.

"Would ye like anything 'ere, lass?"

A serving woman behind her held out a tray of honey bread, dried cherries and wine.

"No, thank you," she replied. The servant offered the tray to Mereine and the merchant. They stopped to take pieces of bread, but didn't acknowledge Isodore. As the serving woman moved on, Isodore wanted to change places with her, or to disappear, or to run to the church and find Sir Rowan praying, and sit with him.

Perhaps Sir Wilfred would talk with her. He was always willing to talk. She stood on her toes, scanned the room and found him surrounded by several people. Then she felt the massive presence of Lord Corvin next to her, his hand coming up behind her and wrapping around her slender shoulder.

"Isodore, good lass, how did you find the feast?"

She couldn't believe her ears or her eyes. His voice was jolly, his smile wide and passably genuine. "Oh, it was wonderful, Lord Corvin. The food was delicious. And thank you so much." Her smile trembled. Who was this man?

"Tell me about the days you were caring for Galt. You know, the minstrels will no doubt want to write songs about it. Galt said he could not recall much of it, so tell me exactly what happened so I can educate them when they compose their poems. Eh?" He laughed.

Her sudden inclusion caught her off guard, but however unexpected, courtesy was far easier to adjust to than hostility. "I would be happy to," she replied, recalling that she had already told the story that day, albeit to a very different Corvin. He wanted her to tell it again.

"Let me recall. When we came to the field, there were perhaps a dozen men down. One of the dragon shields was burning with a glob of dragon spit. I was sent to help a man with a broken leg and a bite wound, so I didn't immediately see Sir Galt. He was surrounded by Father Julian and others. He was in great pain. I could hear him moan. When they carried him away, I could see the grass where he fell. It was wilted, scorched black in the verdant meadow. I was horrified. He convalesced in a small home near the orphanage I keep. There was much confusion as we organized the care of the injured dragonslayers. Sir Dalton took a small party to track the dragon, but other dragonslayers were re-provisioning to follow . . ."

Nearby, the merchant had stopped listening to Mereine,

instead paying attention to Isodore's story. Soon, Mereine turned to listen to Isodore's account of her son's struggle to stay alive. Some of the woman's beauty faded beneath her tight lips and clenched jaw.

When Isodore told of changing places with the two women who wished to stop caring for Galt, Corvin turned red with indignation. "What the devil? What sort of people are these? Where is their sense of obligation? He is a dragonslayer! The frontier would be ravaged without men like him!" Corvin shook his head. "Well, it is just as well they were removed from his care. People like that are of no use without a sword over them."

Corvin softened on hearing how Isodore attended to Galt, bringing him water to soak his burns and feeding him porridge. "Ah, God bless you, lass," he said. "Many people of all dispositions found it hard to look at his scars. Even I. He took to wearing that mask to keep us at ease, the good lad. Were you not put off by his appearance?"

Of course she was, but should she admit it? It might be a trap. Having lived a life carefully cloaking what she was, Isodore thought before answering. Recalling how she saw Galt lying curled up in that small cottage, she answered, "He was the one suffering, not I. I did not want him to suffer alone."

If entrapping her was Corvin's intent, he took her evasion well. He turned a satisfied smile toward Galt's mother. "Well, Mereine, I can see why our boy feels such a debt to this lass. In the depths of despair, that is when you see the true character of those around you. Eh?"

The merchant nodded. Jaw still clenched, Mereine glared at her brother. "Did her work do my son any good? I believe Galt progressed to the verge of death."

"Indeed. I had nothing to do with Sir Galt's recovery." Isodore shook off the irony of the lie.

Mereine turned her glare to Isodore, who curtsied in response.

Lord Corvin said, "But Mereine, you mustn't disregard the role of will in a fighter. Whether he is fighting men, beasts, or death itself, the last thing taken from a fighter is his will to survive. And an injured man who is forsaken will lose that will long before one who is attended to. Galt was hanging on by a thread."

Mereine's response was cold and articulate. "Given that dragonslayers with lighter injuries remained in the village, certainly one of them could have been assigned to tend to him if the ungrateful lowborns refused to meet their obligations."

"Come, Mereine, you cannot expect a man of arms to care for Galt the way Isodore had. She fed him, kept him warm, soaked his burns, attended to every need, prayed with him, changed his clothes, even emptied his—"

"Corvin! Dear brother, I am sure she made an exceptional servant. Margot is an exceptional servant. But I wonder if you would be so facile if Margot had been the one to bind your son's wounds. Or perhaps your grandson's?"

Mereine gave Isodore a swift glance, full of loathing, as she turned and strode away. The merchant jumped out of her way, then, with a frightened glance toward Corvin, faded into the crowd.

Corvin whispered to Isodore as they watched. "Her whole family is like that. I truly wonder at times if Galt is really her son. If his father were here, he would be no help to you either. Do you want to reconsider now?"

"No, Lord Corvin," she said, glancing toward him and once again wondering what happened to the tyrant she had met earlier that day. "Thank you for your help."

"It's not you I'm trying to help, but my nephew."

Isodore felt suddenly weak and mortified for presuming that someone like Corvin would ever care about the likes of her, reminded again that she had no place in Galt's family. She wanted to cry, but she bit her lip. She wanted to turn and go away but feared that even that wouldn't be permissible. She wished Corvin would just leave. Instead, he stood there, looking down at her as tears pooled in her eyes. He took a deep breath.

"But I promised Galt I would do what I could to change Mereine's mind, and that I will do." Corvin smiled wryly, looking directly into her eyes as if reassuring her of that one thing.

She lowered her eyes to the intricate embroidery on the chest of his tabard. The sight of his face was too much to bear. "Why did you offer me marriage to another then?" she asked quietly.

"I told you. It was best—for Galt, for his family, for the Church, and," he emphasized, "for you. But alas, you're as stubborn as he is. Perhaps you two deserve each other."

He thinks we deserve each other, said a tiny voice in a dark corner of her mind, but it brought no relief. Having just been humiliated for thinking Corvin could be kind toward her, she would not be fooled again so soon. "Would you not have betrayed your promise to Sir Galt," she asked in a voice only he could hear, "had I accepted your alternative?"

Slowly, and in a volume matching hers, he answered, "If you had, then I would have saved my nephew from a grievous mistake."

With that, he left her, clapped his hands and announced to the hall that the afternoon's entertainment should begin. The servants stashed four trestle tables and their benches to make room for a stage area. There were only seats enough for Lord Corvin and his highest-ranking guests. The rest stood. As they shuffled around, Isodore migrated to one corner, as far from Corvin and Mereine as she could get.

Entertainment consisted of troubadours and a thespian troupe. The troubadours and musicians played ouds, vielles, recorders, crumhorns, drums and other instruments, performing sweet and uplifting songs, promising deliverance from the dragons, calling the audience to dance and make merry.

Mereine spoke with Galt while she danced with him, words Isodore couldn't hear. Whether it was a mother's love or advice or demand, Galt only nodded and kept in step. In contrast, no words were exchanged when she danced with Corvin, only big smiles and merry laughter filled the space between them. Isodore wondered whom he would choose, if Corvin had to choose between Galt and Mereine. Perhaps he was playing both of them, agreeing to help Galt, while trying to wed Isodore to another man for Mereine. Isodore created a special title for him, to remind herself never again to trust him: Corvin the Schemer.

After the troubadours and musicians, thespians reenacted two famous dragon battles, closing with a new piece called "The Knight of God's Miracle," illustrating how Galt had fallen after his heroic battle. During his convalescence they depicted him spending much of his time alone and in prayer. Food was brought to him occasionally by a nameless boy. With clear, poetic words, unaffected by pain, he asked God to save him so he could return to be His servant. He never screamed out, "Why, God, why?" as he had in the cottage in Savelle. According to the reenactment, an angel came down one night, sang his praises and called on God to heal him, for he had so many more dragons to kill. Galt suddenly felt no more pain. His strength abruptly returned, and in the coming months, the burn scars from his face and hands were mysteriously erased.

Galt was restless during the show, shifting in his seat often as the last act played out on the stage. Afterward, Isodore eavesdropped on his conversation with the actors. "It didn't quite happen that way," he said. "Mistress Isodore was there day and night, so if an angel did appear, she would have seen him."

"Who is Isodore?" asked the actors.

Isodore turned and disappeared into the crowd.

At the other end of the great hall, Mereine, her two daughters, and a group of clerics were discussing the reenactment. They praised it.

Isodore shuffled away and settled along the long back wall of the merry hall. She waited with her hands clasped, hiding behind a pleasant smile. Watching others enjoying the evening gave her a welcome distraction from Mereine's poison and Corvin's questionable antidote.

THAT EVENING, AFTER most of the guests had left, Galt's mother and sisters remained in the house of Corvin the Schemer. Mereine had insisted that Galt not stay, by raising the spectre of unsavory rumors about her famous son sleping in the same hall as an unmarried woman. He would join the other regiment knights being hosted at the home of Sir Gustav's parents in a nearby town.

In his private goodbye, Galt assured her, "I know that my

family's opposition is difficult for you, and they have not welcomed you, but you mustn't lose heart. You're a guest here. Uncle Corvin won't allow any ill-treatment of you."

Isodore wished she could believe him. But it was enough to believe that since Corvin hadn't killed her earlier when they were alone, he wouldn't likely try with his family present.

The servants made a bed for Mereine next to Corvin and his wife's bed in the solar. They stacked six pallets to make a platform and topped it with two straw mattresses wrapped in a cotton sheet. Galt's sisters, brother-in-law, and the children slept below the solar, with Corvin's children, grandchildren, and Isodore.

In the darkness, she listened to the voices around her fade, giving way to deep slow breaths, sniffles, then snores. She lay still, afraid to make any noise that might keep someone from sleeping or give them more cause to criticize her further. She missed her children. She missed being someone who mattered, even if as just a servant.

27

Over the Edge

Isodore learned the habits of dragons as she had once learned those of bandits in the forest. Dragons living in the vicinity no longer encroached on Pyramine's territory. They had either lost interest in her or, if she believed him, were above stealing from their neighbors. No new strangers came to the area.

Isodore could guess whether her captor had been out hunting or patrolling, based on how recently he brought her food. He could return from a hunt any time, but when patrolling, he had a predictable return time. On this day, he was patrolling.

Pyramine had kept Isodore fed over the past five weeks with meat, a sack of peaches, and, recently, a sack of plums. She valued the fruits the most. They helped relieve the pain she experienced when defecating. More vitally, they provided her with material she needed for her escape.

She assembled her new lifeline. She removed her tunic and made a big loop by tying together the sleeves, sacks, and the salvaged rope.

She climbed to the apex of the triangular slab. She rebuilt the crucial foothold she had used before, by pounding the bone fragment into the small crack at chest level. The sheer rock face continued above that and ended at a weather-worn horizontal edge with a bulging protrusion. Her plan was to get the loop around the small protrusion high above the cave and pull herself up to the ridge. Her lifeline could reach it if she stood on the makeshift foothold. Balancing precariously on the bone fragment, she threw up the loop, trying to get it to catch.

She threw and threw and threw. Having started cold, she eventually became so sweaty that she feared slipping off her perch. After an hour, the loop had yet to catch. The protrusion was simply too blunt. While resting, she had another idea.

She climbed back down, disassembled a bag and filled it with rocks. She tied it to one end of the rope and her tunic to the other end. If she could get the weighted end over the edge above, perhaps it would catch on something.

Without being tied in a loop, the lifeline was longer. It could easily reach from her position at the slab's apex to the edge. She stood on the apex, a small but more secure platform from which to throw the weight.

She heaved the bag of rocks up toward the ledge. It rose short of the edge and bounced off the sheer wall. On the way down, it fell within an inch of her head, glanced off her shoulder, and tumbled down the slab. It split open on the ground and spilled half its contents. She had one bag left. She used less weight this time, to ensure she could throw it high enough.

Climbing up to resume her trials, she reminded herself to step aside when the bag came back down. On her first throw, the sack of rocks sailed over the edge and landed out of sight with a satisfying crunch. When she pulled on it, the rope slid a little then stopped. It had caught on something. She imagined the bag of rocks securely wedged between two solid boulders, but figured that it was more likely to be a minor bump barely enough to hold it in place. She didn't pull too hard lest it come loose. If she used the lifeline only for balance and didn't put her full weight on it, it might hold long enough for her to get a hand on something that could support her weight.

She climbed up to the bone fragment. From there, she had to claw her way up the virtually sheer, slightly canted surface. She proceeded slowly, pressing herself against the rock. Her fingers and toes trembled in the shallow cracks in the granite. She pulled on the rope just enough to avoid slipping back down.

Up she went. Her feet made it well above the improvised foothold, but her hands were still two feet from the high edge. She reached with one foot and pressed her toes down on a dark, peach-sized bump in the rock. She pushed herself upward and saw her hand inches from the protrusion that she had tried to get her loop around.

Her time was running out. She was out of breath and shaking. Her sweaty fingers lost traction. Sweat rolled down her temples. She could taste it on her lips. The toes gripping on the bump ached from fatigue.

As she clung to the wall, growing more tired with each second, she placed more of her weight on the lifeline. It slid down. She regripped it as high as she could.

Neither the lifeline nor her aching toes could support her full weight. She would have to use both in an attempt to jump for the ledge. And she would have only one try. There would be no landing back on the bump or swinging on the lifeline.

She pushed off, simultaneously pulling hard on the lifeline. For a split second, she was airborne. Her left hand slapped down over the protrusion. Her fingers curled up.

But there was nothing to hold on to. No handle, no crack, no firm edge. Down she went, fingernails scraping on granite. Clinging to the lifeline in her other hand, she pulled the bag of rocks off the ledge. She threw her hands up to protect her head and in a critical mistake, forgot that the real danger lay below.

She slid down the steep granite, scraping her bare legs. The bag, yanked off the high edge, flew away from the wall. Her feet hit the apex of the slab where she had stood securely to toss the rocks up. Distracted by the bag of rocks and unprepared for the landing, her knees buckled. Her feet slipped. Her buttocks slammed down in their place. She bounced down the slab's ragged edge, and her legs went over the side. She arched her back, reaching her hands behind for something to hold on to. Nothing. Her buttocks went over next, dragging her over the edge. Her back followed, scraping against the granite.

The back of her head struck the slab. Sky, mountain and horizon turned into a disorienting blur. She expected the ledge to hit her hard. She just didn't know from which direction.

28

The Road to Nobility

The cock crowed, and Isodore woke. The servants stirred on the other end of Lord Corvin's long dark hall. She lay still, clutching the blanket, waiting, dreading the day to come.

She glanced at someone rising on her end of the hall. Corvin's youngest daughter. Isodore rose and began to straighten her bedclothes, but stopped when she saw that the other girl didn't. Uncertain whether she should leave the bedclothes as expected of a guest, or whether she should put them away as expected for someone of her station, she glanced around to see if any other guests were doing, hoping to determine what to do before Galt's mother woke.

To her rescue came Sorrel, the young servant girl who, the day before, had tied the lace band around Isodore's head. "I will do it," whispered Sorrel, stepping between Isodore and the bed.

After a visit to the pit latrine, Isodore lingered in the herb garden between the great hall and the kitchen, to avoid Mereine. While Corvin's extended family members mingled, the servants put away the sleeping pallets and prepared breakfast. Isodore tried to gather strength for the call to breakfast when she heard horses reining up to the hall's front doors. She breathed a sigh of relief. Galt had arrived.

Galt didn't give Isodore the warm greeting he had given her the previous day, and she didn't want him to. It would undoubtedly upset his mother, and she intended to avoid that at all costs.

"How was your stay?" he asked her when they passed by each other in the shuffle to be seated.

"Oh, it was fine."

His eyes lingered on her, assessing her before giving her a wry smile. She waited until all were seated from Corvin on down, before she sat. Consequently, the grandchildren separated her from the adults. Everyone ignored her through breakfast, except for Galt, who cast occasional glances at her.

After the meal, the older members of the extended family proceeded outside, where Corvin's stable hands were bringing horses for the family to ride to Auch for Mass.

Twenty of Corvin's guards joined, armed and mounted under the banner of an ominous black bird gliding on a cloudy gray background. Two of the guards were Corvin's sons, undubbed knights around Isodore's age. Galt joined them at the head of the group, armed and armored, looking formidable in the circle of men who would protect Lord Corvin, if needed.

While others found their horses, Isodore stayed forgotten in the rear, waiting. Finally, a stable hand brought her a dapple gray. The horse either didn't like her or sensed her hesitation. It stepped away when she tried to mount. After a few tries, the stable hand took pity on her and held the animal still for her.

She mounted as the wooden gates creaked open. With a chorus of hoof steps, Lord Corvin rode through the gates behind his banner carrier and vanguard. The family followed, then the stable hands, a servant and the rear guards. Isodore struggled to control the horse beneath her.

The gray stallion was tense and jumpy, catching her off guard by charging forward when she cued it to walk. She panicked and yanked back on the reins to avoid crashing into the riders in front of her. It was the mistake of an inexperienced rider, which would be embarrassing if she had the luxury of time. The animal reared and shook, turning sideways, and she had to brace hard on one stirrup to keep from slipping off. She lost control and was left trying to calm the horse while the last of the party slipped through the gates. She heard snickering laughter from the departing group. Though she didn't have time to look or think, it was the high-pitched laughter of girls—Galt's two younger sisters.

"Woodness. Please, God. Not now. Let me survive this day," she murmured as she leaned forward to pat the horse's neck, speaking to it softly, the way Sir Rowan did when she had accidentally displeased his horse. The palisade guards eyed her, but she was too mortified to ask for help. She calmed the horse, but when she tried to turn it around, it bucked again. This steed wasn't the calm palfrey she had when she rode with Galt or the passive one that carried her to Laronde. It was much more like Sir Rowan's destriers, high-strung and disagreeable.

The sound of hooves returned, and with it, Galt's voice. "Isodore!"

She couldn't hide her frustration and embarrassment. She dropped the reins and slumped in the saddle on the verge of tears. Galt brought his horse up to the gray stallion and patted his neck with one hand while taking its reins with his other.

"Woodness! No wonder," he said, recognizing the horse. "Winter is not an easy horse to ride," he said. "I'll get you a palfrey."

"No! I think I can manage. I just have to get used to him."

"Perhaps you can, but it'll be better with a riding horse."

"No, it wouldn't." She recalled overhearing something earlier, when she was waiting for a horse. "Winter. Get Winter," someone had said in the same high-pitched voice that had laughed when the group left her behind. She hadn't known then that Winter was the name of the muscular gray stallion the stable hand eventually brought to her.

"Please, I have to try again. Just tell me what I should do. That is the kind of help I want."

Galt glanced toward the gate's waiting guards. He turned back to find Isodore staring down, her fists wrapped around the reins and her face tight with stubbornness. "Very well," he said. "You said you learned from Sir Rowan, right? Did you ever ride his warhorse?"

"Yes. That was all he had."

"Oh?" Galt seemed surprised. "Well, that's good. If you can do that, perhaps you can ride Winter."

The stallion was overly sensitive and unforgiving. He seemed irritated with her, but willing to restrain himself in Galt's presence.

Galt stayed by her side, calming the horse and adjusting her technique. Sir Rowan's lessons from long ago returned. Winter wasn't exactly like Sir Rowan's destrier, but Galt advised her of the stallion's nuances and preferences. She learned to bring the horse from walk to trot and back. That would be sufficient for the ride. They were out of time.

She practiced while they caught up with their party at Sir Gustav's family home. They were joined by the other regiment knights for the morning ride to Auch, on open roads, by pastoral lands under blue skies. Corvin's vanguard rode ahead, rear guards behind, with the stable hands. In the middle rode the family and regiment knights in a loose group. Riders chatted and enjoyed the pleasant day amid the clip-clopping of hooves on hard-packed dirt. Reacquainted with the task of riding, Isodore began to enjoy herself to some degree.

She watched her position in the group, neither too close nor too far from Mereine. She wanted to ride with Galt, but she feared his mother would feel taunted by the sight. Perhaps Galt felt the same way, for he avoided lingering by her side as well. The family left her out of conversations, but Sir Dalton and Sir Wilfred approached and asked after Lord Edwin, Father Serafin, and Savelle. It was nice of them, but she would have preferred to be ignored. She felt secretly watched by Mereine and had to choose her words carefully.

Lord Corvin eased into position next to Isodore and she felt his eyes on her. She greeted him with a nod, and seeing the statesman instead of the tyrant, she smiled back.

"You ride well, lass," he commented, apparently unaware of her earlier troubles with Winter. "How did you learn?"

"Thank you, Lord Corvin. Sir Rowan taught me when I was a child."

"Ah! He trained you on his horse, didn't he?"

"Yes. How did you know?"

"A destrier is a knight's steed. And Winter is one, through and through. He was sired by my best war horse and he takes after his father. Fast and strong, but not easy. I haven't yet seen a lass who could ride him well. You do a fine job."

"Thank you, Lord. Sir Galt helped me. I . . . had some trouble at first."

"Well, she's doing just fine right now, isn't she, Winter?" Corvin laughed, reaching out to pet Winter's neck. "He is a pleasure to ride, smooth, and powerful in a gallop. Let him show you."

Isodore wanted to say no, but she didn't dare. She had barely found Winter's timing when Corvin cantered his horse and pulled ahead. Winter followed as though he'd read her mind, though perhaps the cue had come from Corvin. Corvin let her catch up, then pulled ahead again.

"Come! Let's see how fast you can take him."

Isodore tensed up, fearing she'd misjudge the horse's rhythm as they accelerated. Her hair flew in the wind and the ride smoothed out as Winter reached a full gallop. It should have been a heavenly experience, but she was terrified.

The regiment knights, lightly armored on their fast coursers, took up the challenge. They surrounded Isodore and Corvin as the group hurled ahead. Corvin's vanguard heard the pack coming and matched their speed. It was an all-out race. Challenges were proposed and accepted with a mere glance. Laughter and howls mingled with thundering hooves.

Isodore felt Winter's massive muscles drive. He seemed more determined to keep up with Corvin than she was, and she couldn't slow him down. She was running a high risk of making a fool of herself. Galt had shouted some advice when he rode by but she couldn't recall what it was. She held on, praying for it to end.

After a couple of harrowing minutes, the group's speed flagged. Corvin's guards were dropping out. Carrying heavily armored riders, their horses were the first to tire. Corvin called an end when the last of his guard, his son, joined the thin line of riders strung out behind.

Isodore rested, slumping in the saddle until she caught herself and sat straight and tall again. She was the only woman. Corvin's family was nowhere in sight. He wanted to walk back to rejoin them, but Sir Dalton had to press on. The regiment was to meet the archbishop before Mass to receive instructions on the ceremony. Galt complimented Isodore on her riding, but had to go on ahead.

She had some time to worry before Mereine and her daughters caught up. Until that morning, Galt's sisters—fifteen-year-old Sevina and seventeen-year-old Christiana—had not been outwardly unkind to her. But that was before she had bested them in their game of horsemanship.

They met Corvin's wife, Glennis, who was accompanied by three guards.

"Where is Mereine?" Corvin asked.

"Your sister is making up for your speed and impulse," she told him. Corvin rolled his eyes.

Mereine, her two daughters, and her son-in-law came ambling along, in no hurry. But after reestablishing the marching order, with guards some distance in front and behind, Mereine wasted little time complaining about Isodore.

"Your contest is all well and good for men, but I don't see how racing in a group of men is proper behavior for a lass," Mereine told Lord Corvin, caring little that Isodore was within earshot.

"Well, you can blame it on me. She did what I challenged her to do. You thought she'd never learn to fit into Galt's station in life. Riding well is one thing that should no longer concern you."

Mereine replied with a huff.

"Mother is right, Uncle Corvin," agreed Galt's youngest sister Sevina. "Racing men-at-arms is not proper behavior. It is disgraceful. What will she do next, swing a sword?"

"What would you have her do? Cook? Clean? Tend the garden? If that's what a proper lass does, why don't you do it?"

"What? Why must I do that? That's the work of servants."

"Then what, pray tell, do you do as a proper lass, Sevina?"

Isodore looked straight ahead and kept her mouth shut. She regarded Corvin's argument with gratitude and increasing curiosity.

"Mother is teaching me to run the home," said Sevina. "My husband shall run the domain. That is proper."

"Isodore runs an orphanage with ten children. What makes you think she can't manage a household?"

Mereine turned toward Corvin. "You would compare your household to an orphanage? They're utterly different! There are servants to instruct, feasts to host. A noble house of any respectable size requires far more land and food than her tiny orphanage. She must be able to converse with noblemen, not hide like a mouse like she did yesterday. She must conduct herself with grace in respectable circles to find squireships for Galt's sons."

Recognizing an opportunity, Isodore spoke up. "I have found apprenticeships for my children, Dame Mereine."

Mereine sneered. "Sewing and sawing is not what I have in mind for my grandchildren, lass. Noblemen who seek squires do not ask servants."

Isodore shrank.

"Corvin, think what might have happened to Galt if you hadn't been there to take him under your wing?"

Corvin shook his head. "Galt's sons can always squire for him, or for my sons, as he did for me. And you can teach Isodore to run her home. If she can ride, if Sevina thinks she can wield a sword, why do you think she can't learn to run Galt's house?"

Sevina replied in an excited, squeaky voice. "Well, how can she if she spends her time frolicking about with men-at-arms?"

Corvin sighed and turned toward Isodore. "Will you let Sevina teach you to run Galt's home?"

Isodore maintained a shaky poise behind a courteous smile. "Yes, Lord. I would—"

"I refuse to do any such thing! She is a lowborn servant! It's futile to attempt to make her into something else."

Corvin rolled his eyes. "I don't believe her incapable of running Galt's household. Glennis can teach her then, if none of you will."

Corvin's wife, Glennis, glanced at him. She was a woman of moderate beauty, in her forties. She wore a rich blue dress, red vest, and brown shoes. She sat perfectly erect on her saddle and never shifted from that imperial posture. Her face held an indecipherable expression.

Mereine answered her brother with a loud declaration. "Impossible! She's fooled you with her pretentious title, hasn't she? An orphanage headmistress is but a servant. Have you ever seen any different? Servile stock will never rise. It's in their blood."

Without taking her eyes off the distant sky, Glennis casually observed, "The previous lord of Laronde claimed the same before my Corvin relieved him of his head." A woman of few words, she had been coldly cordial to everyone outside her family, though she wasn't entirely warm toward her own family, either. Isodore reminded herself to tread carefully.

"You're quite mistaken, Glennis," hissed Mereine. "We did not have to rise. We were born to power. Two bishops in our family, four archdeacons, a vicar, and three—"

"But none with noble blood," said Glennis with a calm that sharpened the mockery.

"We are related to the duke!"

"We're related to him by marriage, Mereine," Corvin corrected, "not by blood."

"You will be wise not to underestimate our alliance with the duke, Corvin."

"Alliance with the duke? Hah!" Corvin burst with sudden anger.

Glennis pursed her lips in a satisfied smile.

"Where was this alliance during my rebellion? Eh? A lot of good it did for his men to reach us after we had breached the palisade. Your infatuation with him had robbed you of your senses, Mereine, but I'll suffer no delusion. Remember this: they did not arrive until victory was assured. I lost many men by his delay. There's your ally. He believed in my victory no more than you believe this lass can host a feast."

"And yet, do you hesitate to pay him tribute? No. You still place great importance on your alliances with noble families. You ceded part of your domain to Glennis's father to marry her. All for the alliance with her father, I believe? To give your children her noble bloodline?"

"Exactly!" said Corvin, notably defiant.

"You, yourself, arranged the marriages of your children to other noble families. You understand the necessity. Galt's been like a son to you. Don't you see it is just as imperative for him?"

"Of course I do. I've made that clear to him. We all have."

"And you will stand by as he foolishly marries this woman? Who knows what foul blood runs in her veins!"

"I've done my best, Mereine."

"Given up is what you've done. She broke you."

"You're the one breaking me, woman. And I'm well tired of it!"

"You betray me, brother."

"You put me in this position!" Corvin barked. "I can side with you or I can side with Galt. What do you expect me to do? Command him to obey us? Yes, of course! Brilliant. We know well how that tale ends, don't we? Oh, yes. Just perfect! Perhaps you care to command him yourself? Do you think he's any less stubborn than his mother?"

The anger gripping Mereine's face tightened under Corvin's assault. But while he vented, her anger had nowhere to go. Slowly, like a tired muscle, her face changed. It softened to an expression Isodore recognized even as Mereine turned away. Isodore slowed Winter and fell back to give the woman some privacy. Corvin's children, she noticed, seemed uncomfortably bored, pointedly observing the countryside. They'd likely heard this argument before.

Corvin looked around the pastoral land, having calmed after his outburst. He brought his horse closer to his sister's and put a hand on her shoulder, squeezing. Angry as she was, Mereine didn't shake it off. Isodore could see the woman's vulnerability in the way Mereine slumped in the saddle. "That is not how a proper lass sits a horse," Sir Rowan would have said. Beneath Mereine's antagonism, there was fear and weakness enough for a peasant to pity.

29

Mysterious Beauty

With each village that Lord Corvin's party passed on the way to Auch, more travelers appeared on the road, largely peasants on foot, with occasional riders. When another armed party appeared, Corvin's guards, who had split up to ride well ahead or well behind, rejoined and surrounded the lord's family. Private conversation and contentious arguments stopped. Corvin eyed the banners of the other parties and they eyed his black-bird banner.

Towns had been appearing in Gascony's rural countryside in recent decades, as merchants gathered to trade. Auch was a hub in southern Gascony. Its roads, inns, and taverns hosted a steady stream of merchants, pilgrims, and men-at-arms. It was also the home of the dragonslayers. A disproportionate number of fighting men sported surcoats with the insignia of a gold cross over a suffering dragon. Auch was cleaner than most towns and suffered less from the scourge of murder, theft, and prostitution. Its wealth was displayed in construction. No wattle-and-daub cottages remained in the town center. All inns and domiciles were made of wood and stone. The cathedral, the biggest that Isodore had ever seen, was surrounded by beautiful gardens. Its transepts had been torn down and were being reconstructed, stone by stone, larger to accommodate the growing population.

The group left its horses with Corvin's stable hands and proceeded into the cathedral's courtyard. A few important-looking people greeted Mereine. More greeted Lord Corvin and Glennis. Other knights and lords were in attendance, each with their own entourage of family, stable hands, and guards. Isodore kept her head down. Though dressed like an aristocrat, she felt distinctly out of place in the gathering.

In the niches along the walls, where other cathedrals might house statues, Auch's cathedral housed the skulls of beasts that fell to the famed dragonslayers. Isodore gasped at the sight, but few of the attendants showed much awe.

Important, well-dressed families filed into the benches in the nave. Lord Corvin, Mereine, and their families took up two benches, Isodore in the back, on the outside. A score of Knights of the Cross had special places at the front, and Galt and his regiment sat just behind the crossing. The benches filled up, leaving peasants to crowd into the aisles.

After her group settled in, Isodore took note of a beautiful young lass on the other side of the aisle. She had long, silky brown hair covered in a white, lace-trimmed headdress, and she wore a ruffled white tunic with a burgundy laced-up vest and tanned leather shoes. She had a lovely figure. Accompanying her was a tall and handsome Knight of the Cross. The beauty and her companion came in behind Isodore and might have been among those who greeted Corvin and Mereine. At the time, Isodore had not thought them any more than acquaintances of the family.

Since taking their places, however, the brown-haired lass kept glancing across the aisle. Though very beautiful, she stood out for her cheerlessness on this bright occasion. She tried to be discreet as she glanced across the aisle, but she eventually got lost in herself and gazed blankly. Isodore wondered if the lass was looking at her. Christiana, in the row in front of Isodore's, looked across the aisle and shrugged, acknowledging something to the lass. Sevina did the same. Wishing not to be seen intruding on their private conversation, Isodore stopped peeking at the sad lass. But it was hard to stop thinking of the mysterious, forlorn beauty.

The archbishop's sermon that morning centered on the deeds of Saint George, the dragonslayer. He highlighted the bravery of the

Knights of the Cross and the ethics they upheld. The success of the dragonslayers, he said, showed how God had rewarded a society that adhered to His laws. He implored people to renounce sin. He promised that the end of days for dragons was near. Lord Corvin was restless in his seat, stretching his neck right and left during the long sermon.

The Archbishop called Galt forward, referring to him as the Knight of God's Miracle. He retold a version of Galt's story that was close to the thespians' version of events, referring to Isodore only as a servant of the Church.

"The dubbing of a Knight of the Cross is a rare event," declared the archbishop. "These knights are far rarer than all other knights in the kingdom. There are only eighteen, but they are examples for all knights to follow. We are gathered today to celebrate the latest addition, a knight marked by God Himself with the miracle of his healing."

Galt sat still, listening with either profound solemnity or a lack of excitement, Isodore noted. Perhaps he didn't like the attention. Perhaps he thought, as his uncle did, that he didn't deserve the honor, or that he was a mere pawn in the political game between the archbishop and the duke.

"The training of a dragonslayer is a long and dangerous endeavor, requiring dedication, bravery, and skills honed in the heat of battle with beasts once believed invincible. Beasts in whose throats burned the fire of Hell. How can we possibly train a man to fight such a beast? An ordinary knight is subject to increasingly difficult fights and has the benefit of mock battles fought with blunted swords and spears, against opponents who do not truly wish him harm. One cannot ask a dragon to partake in such a practice, with blunted teeth and claws and autumn leaves for fire. There is no rehearsal for the dragonslayer. Each time a dragonslayer faces a beast, it intends to kill him.

"The battle that left Galt severely burned injured four men and killed five, including Sir Baret, a knight with a long history of victories over men and beasts. While this does not seem like many lives compared to those who fall on the battlefields of men, we must not forget a time when dragons infested the skies. Men died by the hundreds trying to bring down a single beast. The men Galt saved are among the few capable of successfully facing a dragon. The five who gave their lives and those who can no longer fight have engaged in dozens of dragon battles, saving thousands. They will be difficult to replace. The Church requires more resources to continue the fight and rid the world of dragons, once and for all."

Corvin sighed as the archbishop began a defense of the ecclesiastical tax. Following that was a ceremonial presentation of Galt's new surcoat bearing the golden cross standing over a suffering dragon. The archbishop put it on Galt, buckled the belt over it, and blessed him with a cross drawn on his forehead with holy water.

After the service, Isodore waited for Galt, who was kept from rejoining his party by a crush of admirers. Lord Corvin, Mereine, and their families mingled, giving Isodore a break from their judgment. She walked and admired the flowers and sculptures in the gardens, protected by her anonymity as she meandered from one row of rosebushes to another.

In the corner of her eye, she recognized a figure watching her, and she turned. She didn't know how long the beautiful brown-haired lass had been standing there. She glanced behind, convinced the lass must be looking at someone else, but she saw no one looking back in the direction of the lass. Isodore smiled and thought she might receive a greeting, but the lass turned and rushed away.

Isodore wandered further before returning to her group. She found Corvin and Mereine under the banner showing three hunting dogs. They were talking with a Knight of the Cross, the same one who had accompanied the brown-haired lass. Isodore waited and watched at a distance. Whoever the knight was, Corvin and his sister spent a long time in conversation with him. Corvin the Schemer.

A friendly greeting came suddenly from behind her. "Mistress Isodore, I see your famed knight is still trapped by his admirers, eh?" A knight with a trim beard and a bright smile strode toward her.

"Sir Wilfred!"

A sudden exuberance freed her from nervous isolation as she recognized the chatty knight who'd shielded her from Lord Edwin's objection to her presence during Sir Dalton's account of the battle with the dragon. The one with strange ideas about dragons.

"Such a glorious crowd today, isn't it? Already seems the new transepts won't be large enough. We would have to sit on each other's laps in the nave!" He laughed.

"It is not normally this full?"

"Heavens, no. They've come to see Galt! He is a legend. Those of us who saw him when he was scarred still can't believe our eyes."

"Is he all right? He doesn't seem particularly fond of the attention."

"Ah, well, no, he doesn't care for it. But I'm sure he tolerates it better than those scars. And he'd better get used to it."

"Why is there a ceremony for him today? Did he not become a Knight of the Cross months ago?"

"Well, he was actually a Knight of the Crown even before he became a Knight of the Cross. That was the duke's decision after we returned from the battle in which he was burned. When he revealed that his scars had healed, the archbishop declared that it was a sign from God, as you heard today, and made him a Knight of the Cross. We were about to embark on another mission, so there was no time, for ceremony. I think the archbishop wanted a big ceremony this time because of the miracle. I've never seen such extravagance. With the duke holding us in Toulouse for days, and now this, it's as though they . . ."

"They what, Sir Wilfred?"

"Oh, I shouldn't say. It's not my place." He waved away the question.

It was as though they were riding Galt's fame, as Lord Corvin had asserted, thought Isodore. She wondered how many others believed that, but kept quiet in public.

"Do you think Sir Galt is too young for knighthood?" Isodore asked.

"Urr . . . Well, he is only nineteen years of age. There have been young knights before him. It is not common, but it does happen. But ... I think he will be a good knight." Sir Wilfred strained his neck to see the crowd gathered around Galt. He was trying to change the subject. Isodore recognized the tactic because she often used it when a conversation steered toward her parents or childhood. "Isodore, it will be a while longer before he is free. Have you seen the storehouse yet?"

"No."

"Then it would be my privilege to take you there and show you the dragon skulls. The regiments have a friendly competition to see how many skulls each has displayed in the archbishop's halls. We are in second place, but it is very close. There's one so old that what is left of it sits in a pile of its own ash. And by the pulpit, there is an ancient Bible made from papyrus. Have you ever seen papyrus? Will you accompany me?"

"No. I mean yes, of course. Uh . . ." She hesitated, wishing to observe longer the conversation between Lord Corvin and the unknown knight. The brown-haired lass had taken her place next to the knight, where she and Dame Mereine exchanged an embrace, a loving gesture Isodore thought Galt's mother incapable of.

"What is it?" asked Sir Wilfred.

"Sir Wilfred, I was just wondering who that knight is talking with Lord Corvin."

"That's Sir Reginald. He's a friend of Lord Corvin's family."

"How so? If I may ask."

"His father and Lord Corvin are old friends. Sir Reginald's father, Lord Harold—he is not here today—was the first to back Galt's uncle during his rebellion. That was crucial, because Lord Corvin was a strong knight, very well respected and popular. And popular knights have a way of, well, disappearing. The man he overthrew was a jealous lord who was getting more paranoid every day. If Lord Corvin hadn't taken up arms against the former lord of Laronde, his time would have eventually run out. But Corvin could do little without a strong ally. That was Sir Reginald's father."

"Is that Sir Reginald's wife standing next to him?"

"Oh, no. That is Aida, his sister."

"She seems so . . . sad."

"Yes, she does, doesn't she. Yes . . ." Sir Wilfred's voice trailed off, and the most loquacious man of the regiment seemed unable to find any further words to make use of his lips.

"What were you going to say, Sir Wilfred?"

"Ah, nothing. I would say nothing."

"Please, I beg you."

"No, Isodore." Sir Wilfred stepped away, then after considering for a few seconds, stepped back to her and lowered his voice. "If you would permit me, however, I have some words of advice. Will you heed?"

"Yes, of course. Please."

"Lord Corvin and Lord Harold have known each other since they were both young warriors. Their alliance is important to both of them. And the rebellion only strengthened that. I was therefore rather surprised that none from Lord Harold's family were at the feast yesterday. I think it was wise of Sir Galt to leave you with Lord Corvin's family and arrive here with the regiment today. It avoided some potentially awkward meetings. Isodore, you must examine carefully your curiosity regarding the people you see, because that is how curious others are about you." He paused to let her absorb his cryptic remarks then stepped even closer, whispering in her ears. "My advice to you is this: Inquire no further about Aida. It can do you no good and quite possibly make you more enemies than you already have."

30

Retribution

I sodore lifted her head from a perfectly shaped indentation in the dry mud. She was lying in the shadow of the mountain. Her shoulder, hip, hands and knee each was in its own indentation. Her tunic was draped over her like a blanket, keeping her warm in the shade. She sat up, gathering fragments of her memory as to how she had gotten here.

Rubbing a painful lump on the back of her head, her fingertips came away with dried blood. She looked up the slab and began to remember. She had been trying to escape by going over the ridge above. She had made a lifeline out of her tunic, a piece of rope, and two empty sacks.

It was morning when she attempted her escape, followed by the fall, and it was now afternoon. Checking herself, she found her back and hip scraped and bruised. Her ankles felt strained; the nails on her left hand were shredded. Her forehead, which had struck the ground, was oddly unscathed. The fall that could have killed her only knocked her out and left her with aches and pains. The layer of dried mud had given way to cushion the impact. She held her tunic against her bare chest as though someone might be watching. Her eyes found the sleeves and followed them down to the wrists. They were still tied to the rope, but the rope was a mere stub tipped with a burn scar. The sacks were gone.

"Pyramine," she whispered.

She didn't see him, but she knew he had been here and gone.

When he returned later, there was only silence between them as he started her cookfire. He wasn't angry, but watching him, she almost wished he were. She knew what to do with a cruel, angry beast, but not with this quiet companion. A part of her hated him for not being angry, a part hated him for what he had done to her, and a part of her wondered about him. Didn't he hate her, too? Did he think himself above hatred?

Lying in the dark quiet of the cave that night, after a long evening with too many thoughts and no words exchanged, Isodore felt control over her fate slipping through her fingers. If her attempted escape were to pass unmentioned into the past, if blatant defiance of her captor had no consequence, then his power over her was complete. Her actions, whether wise or foolish, had to have a consequence, or nothing she could do from this point on would. If she had fallen to her death in her escape, she would have had one victory, depriving him of the one thing he wanted. As it were, she had failed to gain so much as a small insight into the creature who had so tormented her with silent imprisonment. She couldn't bear it. With her rope burned, it was a total loss. She had nothing else to lose.

"I tried to escape today," she said.

"That is the reason I burned your rope," came the dragon's voice in the dark.

"Will you not make me suffer for it?"

"No."

"Why not?" she demanded, as though she were his master and he had erred.

"I would do the same if you held me captive. Would you make me suffer?"

She devoted the rest of her waking thoughts and the next several days to his question. However, an answer that satisfied her morality and sensibility eluded her.

She had nearly died in a fruitless attempt to escape, but, without any effort, she escaped retribution. Archbishop after archbishop had said that dragons were God's retribution for the sins of men. Yet in a world of men eager to burn sorcerers alive, this fiery creature had seemingly forfeited that right. Perhaps her sins were not the reasons for God's retribution.

31

Rebel's Folly

The head of Savelle's dead dragon looked down from one of the arches into the hall of Auch's cathedral. The ax that Sir Wilfred buried in the forehead remained, to remind viewers of the dragonslayer's indomitability.

"It's the most menacing one here, isn't it?" asked the beast's executioner.

"Yes."

"That's because it's one of our newest." He waved his hand at the other mounted heads. "All those others, their skins have nearly fallen off, and the bones break with the strike of a fist. Incredible that the remains of such mighty creatures should weaken so fast, wouldn't you say?"

Sir Wilfred was treating Isodore to a tour of the cathedral. In the fancy borrowed dress and shoes, strolling with her hand in the crook of his elbow, she felt very proper and privileged. She knew many eyes were on her, but for the first time in her life, it didn't bother her. In Auch, a regiment knight commanded the highest respect, and Sir Wilfred was in full regalia, the dragonslayer's crest emblazoned on his surcoat.

He walked her to the six skulls in the hall, telling her the story behind each. They stopped in the pulpit, before something even more rare. On the table was an opulent, antique leather-bound book, with a beautifully stenciled cover.

"This is the archbishop's Bible. It's written on papyrus, which is made from plants. It's the only papyrus Bible in Gascony. The Romans wrote everything on papyrus, but Gascony has not seen any since the Romans left. Most people don't know what it is."

Isodore certainly didn't. The Bible's pages were much thinner than parchment, so the volume lacked the unwieldy bulk of other Bibles.

"I have seen the pages, but I can't show you, unfortunately. Only the archbishop is allowed to touch it. Old papyri are brittle and fragile, not supple like parchment. You can tell it's old by the browned edges."

She admired it while the garrulous knight talked wistfully about lost Roman craft. Next, he led her from the hall, down a corridor that was empty despite the day's crowd, through a door that seemed not meant to open. A shaft of sunlight from the lancet window lit the large room. Waiting in the shadows were stacks and racks of old bones and lines of skulls, all of extreme sizes: a graveyard where dragon bones sat, collecting thick layers of black dust, or so she thought.

Sir Wilfred picked up a slender ten-foot pole as if it weighed no more than a broomsitck, shaking off the dust.

"That's not dust. It's ash. This is the wing bone of the biggest dragon ever slain. It's very light—all dragon bones are. Light as a bird's and strong as a bear's, at least until they die. Then they turn to ash. The skin is gone within months. The bones are harder, so they last longer. This one was killed about thirty years ago. There's its skull." He pointed to a long, black, tapered shell that hardly looked like a skull at all.

"Sir Wilfred, why are the bones that dull black color?"

"I don't know. They are just that way. Some people say it's because they are creatures of Hell. I certainly hope not all things black are from hell. You and I should have to tonsure our heads! There's much we don't know about the beasts, though. Like how they learned our tactics."

She didn't think he meant to talk at length about how so many dragons had adapted to the dragonslayers' tactics, but that was what he did. Incredible by his own admission, he was positive that they understood the words of men. She didn't know what to think, but she soaked up the conversation, amused and delighted at the attention from such a chivalrous knight, like the old days with Sir Rowan.

The tolling of a bell interrupted him. He counted the sounds. "Oh, dear. I'm afraid I must leave at once. I'm expected at Beardsley's Den. I am to show Sir Dalton that I can teach the men enough Latin for use in battle."

His company had turned a long, lonely wait into a time of education, fascination, and companionship, so much so that Isodore nearly forgot to disguise her childlike disappointment.

"Of course. I have taken much of your time, and I do not wish to take you away from your duties. You have been very generous with your delightful company."

He waved off her comments and blushed slightly. "The generosity is yours, good lass. And I must beg your forgiveness for my tendency to blabber on."

"It's very kind of you to keep me company, Sir Wilfred. And you do not blabber."

She walked out with him and watched him ride off, then, with dread, returned to the black-bird banner. Corvin's family wasn't there. She found them by the hunting-dogs banner once again. She studied the faces in the gathering. Somewhere there were the potential enemies Sir Wilfred had warned her about.

After Sir Reginald's group departed under the hunting-dogs banner, Corvin's family returned. Isodore mounted Winter, pretending she had not been watching them.

The lord knight came to her side and looked back at the group, where Galt sat his horse, saying goodbye to his mother and sisters. Mereine was begging Galt to delay the wedding announcement and reconsider his decision. She tried to be discreet, but to the few who knew her feelings, it was not hard to interpret her body language. Her hands were too tense, too firm. Her face was one part frustration and one part fear. On a day when all of Auch gathered to celebrate her son, she showed no joy.

Mereine's careless words drifted to Isodore and Lord Corvin as the two waited on their horses. Isodore couldn't bear to spend another minute in the woman's presence.

"With your permission, Lord Corvin, I beg to decline the hospitality of your home tonight. You have given me the best meals and warmest bed I had ever known. But . . ." She didn't want to say the wrong thing. To her, his home was a cold and hostile place. "Sir Galt said he would show me the dragonslayer compound. Perhaps I should return home directly from there."

Corvin nodded, but said nothing. She thought perhaps he had sympathy for her, because he, himself, had no noble blood, yet he proved himself a better fighter and more popular ruler than the nobleman he had overthrown. Corvin must believe it was possible to rise above one's station. On the other hand, he had, with calculated purpose, married into a noble family. He knew what the rules required. It was difficult to guess what went through the mind of Corvin the Schemer.

"Farewell, Lord Corvin," she said, to get on with it.

She nudged Winter forward and left him. There was a brief whistle behind her, and the horse circled back, bringing Isodore face to face with the lord knight. Corvin patted the neck of his loyal horse.

"You would be wrong to think that my sister's opposition to you is purely from prejudice," he said. "On the contrary. She understands you . . . and Galt . . . all too well." He didn't look at Isodore, and his words didn't come to him easily. He paused often as he spoke, this man who, until now, had always commanded with quick and unchallenged authority. "She was a willful, independent child, my sister. Headstrong and brash. She defied our parents as much as she loved them . . . exactly what Galt is now doing to her."

Isodore dared to look into his eyes, but his gaze was elsewhere.

"She rejected the accomplished noblemen favored by our parents and wedded a man of her own choosing. Galt's father was a pious and devoted man who loved his family very much, and his God even more. When their eldest son was taken by a fever, she couldn't comfort or make sense of it for her husband. Only God could. He entered the monastery and devoted himself to the Lord. Their second son followed him. Mereine forbade him to go, but like her, he was not one to bow to the wishes of parents. Galt is the only son left. She has no other worthy heir. Christiana married a simple bailiff. There's Sevina. She still has time to grow up, but . . . but hah that girl . . .

"Mereine's is a gloomy life, and Galt is the only light she has. She forbade him to enter the monastery, did he tell you? When he showed the slightest interest in swordsmanship, she sent him to me, to be raised a warrior. When he committed himself to the dragonslayers, she thought she had succeeded in steering him clear of her follies. She saw him becoming a knight, and marrying into a noble family as she should have done. That was Galt's life for a time, the life she wanted for him. Then you came along and unraveled it all. You, an orphaned daughter of cottagers, laid waste to that meticulous plan, and she's helpless against you. Galt is willing to live in poverty for you, to forsake all she's given him. That is a frightening prospect for a mother and a woman of her status. That's the reason for her hostility toward you. She wants her only remaining son to avoid making the same mistake she made." He sighed.

"Do you think Galt is making a mistake?"

"What I think, I've already told you." He looked her in the eyes at last. "Galt has sworn to your impeccable character. The boy has little patience for human failings, Isodore, even in his own parents. He can't see that his impatience—his intolerance of human weaknesses—is in itself a weakness. He sees it as strength. That is his true mistake. We're imperfect, all of us. You included. You should pray that when he learns, he is not mired in the regret that has entrapped his mother."

Isodore didn't know he had finished until the ensuing silence grew and ended the conversation on its own. Their eyes met once more.

Corvin nodded. "Farewell."

"Farewell, Lord Corvin." She stopped herself from adding,

"Thank you for your words of caution." She had nearly mischaracterized his motives again. What Corvin the Schemer had done, he did for his family, not for her. She would not be humiliated again. While she hesitated, his horse bore him away, leaving her alone with Winter.

32

To Be a Dragon

A full moon breached the horizon, floating into a pink pre-sunset sky over Gascony, out beyond the peaks of Dragon's Ridge. As the moon rose, its spectacular presence gave way to a steady transformation, shrinking, turning from pink to yellow to white. A distant lantern in the evening sky, perfectly round, beautifully ordinary. Isodore had come to Dragon's Ridge with a new moon, and this full moon marked six weeks of captivity.

It was the herald of her fate, the moon she might one day see through the eyes of a dragon. A part of her had given in. Perhaps being a dragon wouldn't be so terrible, she thought. It was certainly less frightening than death.

Yet another part of her couldn't help but think of ways for Galt's regiment to come to her rescue. The impossibility of it remained staggering. Galt would have to believe against all common sense that she was alive, and against hard-earned wisdom from the Deleret Expedition, convince the Church to sponsor another expedition to Dragon's Ridge, in the face of resistance to its tax. Even if the regiment pared down its arsenal, it would take many days to cross the forests, where old roads had given way to trees and brush. Galt would have to know where she was in the immense, convoluted landscape, when she herself had no idea. How would he ascend these towering ramparts with his crossbow and dragon shield?

How would he fight Pyramine on a steep mountainside, where the dragon had all the advantages and the man had none?

It would be an enormous undertaking, just to end in slaughter on a desolate mountain, for a peasant the world believed dead and long devoured.

Accepting Pyramine's offer would mean forsaking any chance of rescue, though she could hardly forsake what she never had. The only thing she still had and could relinquish was her tenacious commitment to her brave, stubborn, naive young knight. Being a dragon meant giving up on him. It meant releasing the last link she had to Galt, one that he had surely released weeks ago, when he would have received the news of her death.

"Farewell, Galt," she whispered to the lantern in the sky. It was never easy to say, but it became easier each time she tried.

To be a dragon was to fly free and see God's earthly kingdom the way He saw it. It meant being fearless, something she had never experienced. She would never be cold or hot. She would be free to go as far as she wished any time she pleased, to jump off the cliff and float away on outstretched wings. She could skim treetops and follow rivers. She would fly with the eagles and chase the bears and wolves for fun.

Yes, she would hunt the animals of the land, but she wouldn't be a greedy dragon, and she would leave men and their villages alone. If she met Galt, she would talk to him and explain that she would never harm any person. She would have to hold back her tears. She would let him onto her shoulders and show him the world of a dragon. If he were married or loved another, she wouldn't be envious but wish the best for him. They would be friends, as they were that day she had helped him distribute the compensation. She could bring peace between men and dragons.

For moments that lasted longer each time, she began to think she could do it—to be a dragon. But to give up her life as a woman was the least of her difficulties. There were still obstacles and uncertainties, as the reading of the spell's instructions reminded her.

"Do you have all the materials?" she asked Pyramine when he returned to the ledge one afternoon.

"No, I am still searching."

"What if I cast the spell incorrectly?"

"I don't know."

Even when he knew an answer, it often raised more questions. "What does this word mean?" She sounded out strange words and he explained them to her. "How did you come to know so much about sorcery?" He'd lived a long time. "How long?" He didn't know, but he was alive before her "nest" had appeared on the frontier.

Savelle was built under the rule of Lord Edwin's grandfather, so it was perhaps fifty to one hundred years old. "Is that old for a dragon?"

"Old," he mused. "Not old, but not young." He turned to look out over the valley.

"You've not grown as big as the dragons I have seen."

"Such as the striped one who attacked you?" He glanced at her, then turned back to the empty distance. "I am older than she."

"How do you know how old she was?"

"By her appearance. Her face, in particular."

Exactly how men knew, thought Isodore. Only she couldn't tell with dragons. "Why was she so much bigger?"

"Her size was unnatural. Your people fed her."

Shocked, then bewildered, Isodore could only ask, "What?"

"Your people. Their offerings let dragons gorge greedily. Dragons grow on these excesses. Their feeding is not limited by the difficulty of the hunt, but only by their weight, when they become so big that flying is difficult. It's dangerous for them. A grounded dragon cannot defend himself."

She recalled the enormous Ashwing, a dragon that stood two feet taller than Pyramine, coming often to the frontier, and stories of large dragons lifting heavily armored knights to drop them into the infantry ranks. Pyramine, she thought, must be mistaken. "I have seen big dragons fly. I've heard of them carrying off things heavier than me, more easily than you carried me."

"Those dragons possess great strength, true, and a man is small in comparison. I speak not of their prey's weight. It's their own weight they cannot carry."

"Their wings are bigger. And stronger. Aren't they?"

"They have to be strong, yes, just to lift themselves into the air. But to keep so much weight aloft is tiring. A great dragon has no stamina for long flights, or for ascending the mountain to these heights. You have surely noticed that the dragons nesting in these peaks are not the overgrown giants in the lowlands."

"But the dragon you killed was big."

"It is not impossible. It just takes longer. Resting far more than flying. She would have crawled much of the way. Great dragons are poor fliers, unable even to find their own food."

"Why is that?"

"It takes too long. Too many tries. Those dragons tire quickly. People who clear forests are easier to hunt, but they live too far from here."

She wasn't convinced. It was difficult to change beliefs she had held for so long. The large dragoness that Pyramine killed had flown poorly, but she'd thought the reason was the injured wing.

"See those birds?" Pyramine motioned his head toward a dozen eagles and vultures circling lazily in the sky. "The great dragons cannot fly as far as I can, for the same reason I cannot fly as far as those birds do."

Two dragons circled in the same column, ascending sluggishly despite pumping their wings. In a short time, the birds below rose past them, and those above were higher still. Size, the villagers of Savelle often whispered, was the reason Lord Edwin no longer ascended his own motte without help of a horse. He was once known for his strength, but she was certain she could run up the motte faster than he. She was the eagle, and Edwin, the dragon.

"If there are dragons nesting in the lowlands, then why didn't I see any when you carried me over the forests?"

"They hide in the trees and only come to open ground to spread their wings. I avoided the nesting sites I knew of. Carrying you, I lacked the speed and agility to fight back, should they try to take you."

"But you could flee, couldn't you? You said they were poor fliers."

"Avoiding is better than fleeing."

She conceded, wondering what else she knew about dragons that had been wrong all along. For the first time, she felt a shred of pity for the great Ashwing, whom she had blamed for her parents' death. She knew how he must have felt, having to rely on others to stay alive.

"Why don't you take sacrifices?"

"I enjoy the hunt."

He seemed happy at that instant, as he looked out at the evening. She wondered if dragons dreamed, and what they dreamed of. From there, her curiosity about them grew with each question.

"Where are your brothers and sisters?" He didn't know; dragons were solitary creatures and he had left his nest as soon as he could hunt on his own. "Do dragons and their mates share the same nest?" Only when it was time to mate or to protect their dragonets; otherwise, dragon pairs typically nest nearby. "What if I wish to share your nest?" He would grant her that peculiar human custom. "Would you not eventually find me shrill and irritating?" He could bear her; he had already talked with her more than he had with any creature. "How do I know you will not kill me when I no longer suit you?"

"Dragons are loyal. Only one thing can break my loyalty."

"What is that?"

"Betrayal."

A chill passed through her. She wondered whether he could sense the sudden change in her breathing. She tried to hide it, then changed the subject.

"Why don't you choose a dragoness to be your mate?"

"I did, once."

"What happened to her?"

"She was killed hunting too far north. There are very few dragons left. Men killed them, like they kill sorcerers. The end is near for us."

The end was near for dragons. Another chill went up her back.

"How do you know?"

"Much has changed. At one time, dragons were abundant here.

Now, we are nearly gone, while men have spread like rats."

Isodore recalled songs telling of a time when dragons filled the sky, songs she had thought were largely exaggerations by the poets. It was eerie to hear the same thing from a creature who held the memories of firsthand witnesses. It must be sad, seeing the decline of one's own kind.

"Where did dragons come from?"

"I do not know. Where did man come from?"

"God created man," she said, feeling strangely superior for knowing something he didn't.

"Why?"

"To give him dominion over the world."

Pyramine considered this, gazing out at the world below his mountain. "Does the world belong to God?"

"In a way. God created the world, and the air, and the clouds. The sun, the moon and the stars. And light. Everything."

"Everything belongs to God? These mountains, too?"

"Yes. Everything."

"Then, perhaps God created dragons," he speculated.

Of that, she wasn't sure, and the uncertainty reminded her that she was never truly sure of God, despite the confidence of her answers. Her sense of superiority wilted. She felt like a pretender.

Many said that dragons were God's punishment for the sins of men, so perhaps God did create dragons for that very purpose. But if dragons were serving God's purpose, why did the archbishops support the dragonslayers? She pondered the question but could find no answer. "Perhaps," was her only response to Pyramine's speculation.

Then she wondered who had created sorcerers. And why God felt it necessary to kill them. Perhaps, unlike dragons, sorcerers served no purpose.

33

Beardsley's Den

The Duke of Gascony owned one of the castles near Auch, an imposing wooden fortress atop a hill. On the castle's south wing, masons were constructing a new keep, a formidable structure unlike any Isodore had ever seen, made completely of stone.

"The duke is building stone keeps in all of his castles," Galt said. "King Louis is doing the same. Half his keeps and palisades have been rebuilt with stonework. Even his great hall." Isodore couldn't imagine such wealth.

Galt escorted her around the castle grounds, where there were many knights. Some were gruff, some jolly, some quiet, many boastful. Some knights were dubbed, their surcoats sporting either the duchy's crest or Auch's golden cross. The Knights of the Cross tended to be more courteous. It made her happy to count the regiment knights among her friends.

Some of the wealthy knights showed off tough new mail coats from al-Andalus, polished helmets from Milan, and exotic striated blades from Damascus. The very wealthy had simply beautiful armor, polished to a bright shine or ornately decorated. These, too, came from elsewhere. The world had everything before Gascony did.

The dragonslayer compound was located on the flatter ground below the castle. It was encircled by a palisade and had living quarters, a dining hall, and a kitchen for the dragonslayers. All of this was constructed by past dukes in gestures of solidarity with Auchan archbishops.

As Galt showed Isodore a small reading room, they heard shouts out the window, in a language Isodore couldn't understand.

She recognized the voice. "Is that Sir Wilfred? I thought he was going to Beardsley's Den."

"This is Beardsley's Den," said Galt. "That's what dragonslayers call our compound."

"Who is Beardsley?"

Galt had a sly smile. "Before I tell you, you must try to guess."

The invitation was happily accepted, and the game was on. Galt led her outside.

At the center of the compound was a small field of trampled grass where a group of dragonslayers battled a mock dragon with wood-paneled wings. Its body, neck, and head consisted of bags, stuffed tight with hay, strapped together. She could tell it was hay inside, because hay leaked through a number of open wounds. Sir Wilfred was on horseback with bow and arrows, taking pot shots at the dragon head while commanding the dozen men. The men were shifting and moving in formation on his orders, and loosing their bolts on the run. The mock dragon suffered from a cluster of arrow shafts at its throat.

The practicing dragonslayers arrayed themselves into left and right formations, flanking the patient beast.

The dragon was bolted to a platform that rotated on wheels. Sir Dalton and three other men pushed and pulled on shafts extending from the platform to turn the dragon. They were fast enough that the formations had trouble reacting.

Sir Wilfred charged the mock dragon, sending another arrow into the cluster by its throat as he shouted a command. He feinted toward one side before shifting to the other. It turned toward him. The left formation turned and retreated. Fooled by his feint, the men were slow, crashing into each other. Sir Dalton shook his head.

"What happened?" Isodore asked.

"Sir Wilfred lured the dragon to their side. They were supposed to move back before that, but two crossbowmen failed to move. It's the Latin. Only Sir Wilfred and Sir Gustav speak it. See? Sir Gustav's group was in the right place."

"Ah."

"Sir Wilfred will not be popular this evening," Galt predicted.

The dragonslayers paused and conferred. They nodded as Gustav reminded them of key Latin words.

They tried again. Sir Wilfred galloped the same path, sending another arrow into the effigy. The dragon turned. Sir Gustav, who had taken a head start upon hearing Sir Wilfred's signal, rounded to the front of the beast and drove his lance into its shoulder. The lancer from the rear came forward to protect the formation. The formation on the left backed away without bumping into each other.

They continued to watch the practice. Many of the men had beards, but Isodore suspected a trick. She pointed above their heads at the effigy, whose throat bristled with arrows.

"Beardsley is the dragon," she said.

Galt smiled but shook his head. "Beardsley is long gone, slain after many years of good service. That beast is his great-great-great-grandson, Beardsley VI."

From the look of him, the reigning Beardsley might not be long for this world. Hay spilled from dozens of holes in his sides. His wings were bolt-pocked. The bolts had chipped a hole through the wood panel where the crossbowmen aimed. The men cheered each time a bolt threaded through the hole. As they watched, four more arrows struck Beardsley's chin, seconds apart, from different directions, as Sir Wilfred galloped across the field.

"Sir Wilfred is an impressive archer!" Isodore commented.

"Well . . ." Galt smiled with unusual coyness. "Not all of those shafts are his."

GALT AND ISODORE strolled to the workshops along a section of the field's perimeter. In one, two women wove small bundles of straw together and attached them to shields and clothing of goat and swine leather. In others, women twisted hemp fibers into tethers.

Cowhide helmets with straw all around were stacked against the wall. A straw curtain ringed the bottom of each helmet to shield the wearer's neck from fire. Dragonslayers' shoes were lined to the toes with straw. Another shop made similar covers, but for horses.

In the forge, Isodore watched a blacksmith pour molten steel into a long slender mold to make the bolts. Once cooled, the rods were filed clean. Behind its midpoint, each rod had a stubby fin with a hole, where the tether was attached. The bolts weren't fletched and didn't spin when they flew, to avoid winding the tether around the shaft. It relied on the tether's tug to keep the bolt pointed forward, another reason for the weapon's poor accuracy.

In the field, Sir Wilfred and Sir Gustav had changed places. Gustav shouted a Latin word. Bolts flew toward the thin wings of the wooden dragon. A brief thrum sounded when they struck their targets. Several bolts punched through. Six tethers were left dangling.

The armory was lined with rows of long spears, dragon lances, crossbows, bolts, and coils of tether, but no armor.

"Heavy armor like what you saw on the other knights is of no use to us," Galt said. "Armor slows us down but won't keep the dragon from killing us." He showed her a mail coat with a frayed and blood-stained hole where a man would have put his arm through. That arm had been ripped off—bone, flesh, and steel links.

Isodore took pleasure in Galt's youthful enthusiasm. She was not the only one. Sir Dalton left the exercise to Sir Wilfred and joined them.

"Please, do not let me disturb you," he said with a wide, mustached smile.

Galt continued, sheepishly at first, but soon regained his natural enthusiasm.

"The tethered crossbow was invented during the reign of King Charles the Simple. It could bring down low-flying dragons. A single hit near a wing's knuckle would immediately tear a long rip through its wing and send the beast crashing down," he said and smiled. "And dragons crash hard. Fast-moving knights would inflict fatal wounds before it regained enough sense to fight back.

"The crossbow was more accurate and had greater range in its original form as a defensive weapon. The tethers were lighter and more supple. They needn't be wet or very strong because dragons had no time to burn or break the rope before it did its damage. Many dragons fell in the years immediately after the tethered crossbow was added to the arsenal. Now, most dragons avoid targets defended with tethered crossbows, especially if they're not prone to fire. That was how al-Andalus rid itself of dragons long ago."

"There were dragons in al-Andalus?"

"Yes. It was al-Andalus that gave us the tethered crossbow."

Having always believed Gascony's dragonslayers deserved credit for all dragonslayer victories, Isodore was disappointed. Like the knight's equipment, the world had everything before Gascony did.

"At one time, we acquired tethered crossbows from al-Andalus. We used them effectively, but the dragons remained. As effective as they were, defensive weapons just aren't enough. We made our own modified crossbows, attack weapons. The tethers were made stronger to hold the wings and wetted down to avoid burning. That worsened the crossbow's range and accuracy even more, so we had to get very close and be on the ground for the best angle.

"We created the dragon shield to protect the crossbowman, then added the dragon lance to protect the formation. We trained the horses to ignore fire. We honed the tricks needed to make the dragon fight rather than flee. It was a difficult task and took many trials, and many failures. But it proved to be our most successful tactic."

"He has a true passion for this," Sir Dalton commented.

Isodore agreed. Galt might not be the frightening warrior that his uncle was, but he was well educated and passionate. His enthusiasm was natural and copious.

"It's the marvelous innovations that interest me so much," he said. "The tethered crossbow, the battle tactics. The fight was so daunting, so hopeless. Yet, we persevered."

"Speaking of innovation, Sir Galt, you must show her your invention."

"Uh . . . of course." Galt proceeded with some caution and a shade of embarrassment. He pulled the covers off a box containing small, cylindrical pieces of carved wood and picked up one. "This is a . . ." He laughed impishly. "A whistle that dragonslayers could use to signal each other as we wait to ambush in the cover of trees. It makes a sound like an eagle's call, but dragons can't hear it."

Isodore gasped, her eyes fixed on the small, miraculous piece of wood. A secret signaling device!

"The name, Sir Galt. The name."

Galt sighed. "If you must, Sir Dalton, you tell her."

Sir Dalton laughed. "I call it the ghost whistle. When you blow into it, ghosts come!"

Isodore was amazed. She herself was unsure of ghosts, but she was surprised Sir Dalton believed they existed.

He laughed hard. "You can't see the ghosts, of course, but neither can you hear the whistle!"

Galt laughed as well. His sense of humor filled her with warmth and a sense of security she had not felt since Sir Rowan. She understood Sir Dalton's joke when Galt demonstrated by blowing so hard into the whistle that his face turned red.

"I can hear that," Isodore said of the modest sound.

"So can I!" exclaimed Sir Dalton. "But not when I need to. Not through the trees. Not in the rush of battle, alas."

"Well . . . you do have to listen carefully." Galt sighed. "And that's hard to do in battle." But he hadn't given up. From the drawer, he retrieved illustrations he had made for a large, hollow wooden tube with scores of holes where the small whistles would be inserted. It allowed one man to sound all those whistles at once.

Isodore read the drawing's heading and commented, "I think 'ghost whistle' is a better name than 'secret signaling device for dragonslayers.'"

The knights turned to her, stunned.

Galt asked, "You can read?"

"Yes," she said with pleasure.

Lord Corvin had poorly veiled his surprise when she told him she was literate. Her ability made a clear impression on Galt. It was the second time her literacy had made a vital difference in her life. The first was when the news of Sir Rowan's fall from grace came. No one had to read the letter to her.

She spent part of that afternoon resting in the shade, watching the regiment train. Squires practiced lancing targets. The knights rode new coursers through a bonfire-marked obstacle course. Shieldmen raced the same course, carrying their cumbersome panels. Crossbowmen running at full stride loosed their bolts at targets.

Sir Wilfred kept her company while she watched her betrothed command a mock battle. Galt added more arrows to the dragon effigy's beard. He was an excellent tracker as well, Sir Wilfred told her. "Good for finding dragons that escape our ambushes." Later, Galt taught her to use the bow and the tethered crossbow, while Sir Wilfred gleefully overpraised her mediocre performance. Despite the forceful objections from Galt's family, Isodore's future looked bright.

TWO DAYS LATER, Michel and a group of guards escorted her into Savelle. As the tiny entourage rode in, the villagers gawked with an expression she had never seen on them before—fear. They didn't mock her, even after her escorts left. They hardly let their eyes meet hers. Her children said that Lorraine had not only taken very good care of them but also told the villagers of Isodore's host, Lord Corvin. Lorraine gave the impression that Corvin was a powerful lord who didn't take kindly to anyone mistreating a friend of the Knight of God's Miracle. The fear and respect they had for him protected Isodore as if the man himself had been there with his arm over her shoulder.

One afternoon, a week later, while she was cutting vegetables for supper, shouts of alarm rose in the village. A dragon, the peasants' worst fear. Within seconds, the alarm repeated, clearer and more urgent.

She ran to the door to look. People were dashing to safety. Her children were racing back to the orphanage from the end of the road. Broad black wings sailed high over the west end of the village.

Xabi was a lump on the ground in the field, hurt and dazed. For a second, she frantically waved the children home, as if it could make them run faster. Then something took hold of her. She had been with the dragonslayers. Her heart swelled with the courage that she had seen in them. She decided, without thinking. That beast would not have her little boy. She could get to him and bring him back before it came around again.

The dragon was far faster than she had expected. She kept one move ahead of it, driven by strength and speed that she had never before known. But it wasn't enough. A moment later, she was lifted off her feet, a life on the cusp of deliverance thwarted by a single perilous act.

34

Terminal Prayer

A cold wind rolled across Gascony and over Dragon's Ridge in the last days of summer, ending a long streak of clear skies and hot weather. Clouds bloomed in tall columns over the distant plains. Their shadows covered more and more of the lowland until Isodore could hardly see land at all.

She sat at the edge of the precipice, looking toward Gascony, trying to find the words to say farewell. Then Gascony, drenched in the downpour of thunderstorms, disappeared under the clouds.

In the afternoon, massive storm cells churned over a slowly boiling sea of clouds. While birds had gone into hiding, dragons reigned over the sky with grace, no longer cumbersome, heavy fliers. They disappeared into the cumulus bodies and emerged from the thunderheads to swoop through loop after loop downward, before reentering the clouds to do it all over again. It was as if they celebrated the end of summer, by roaming where none other could. With evening's approach, they glided across the sky, meandering aimlessly back to earth through the last rays of sunset. Creatures of brutal mountains and stratospheric clouds, of wind and fire, masters of the storms, they moved through the heavens as though they belonged so close to God.

After sunset, the storm cells remained visible. Like day turned inside out, they glowed by flashes from within, while jagged bolts of lightning arced down their sides. Thunder rolled into Dragon's Ridge like muted sounds of distant crowds toward a lonely sentry.

Isodore received the hindquarters of a small piglet from Pyramine on his return. Her anticipation of this provision made her realize that she had not feared her captor for some time. She had even blocked off her small escape hole with rocks and clothing remains to keep cold wind from passing through the cave. She slept closer to Pyramine for the warmth. She thought about being a dragon more, and longed for rescue less.

"Should I become your mate," she said as her supper cooked over the fire, "you must promise that we would never hurt people, or steal from them."

"This pig did not belong to people," said Pyramine. "It belonged to its mother."

"Men raised these animals. They fed the animals, so the animals belong to them." She tore off one of the piglet's legs and touched the meat to gauge its temperature.

"If that were so, sorceress, then you belong to me."

Isodore stopped just short of taking a bite. "I am forced to eat what you bring me because you're holding me captive. I have no choice."

"I took you for food. It is no different from what men do to the animals. If men's creatures belong to them, then you belong to me."

"It's not the same. God gave men dominion over the earth and its creatures."

"God is very partial to men. And unfair to dragons." Pyramine lowered his chest to the ledge and lay down, curving his neck toward the cliff to hang his chin over it, looking out over the valley. He exhaled with a measure of disgust—at God, she presumed.

"Where is God?" he asked as though he aimed to go challenge the Almighty Himself.

"Up there, in heaven." She looked up.

Following her, he scanned the indigo sky. "I have been there. There is no one."

"You can't see Him."

"Is he hiding?"

"No, He . . . He just does not want to be seen, so you can't see Him. He's very powerful."

Pyramine narrowed his eyes and swept his head from one end of the sky to the other, straining to look for God. His arched neck reminded her of the suffering creature on the dragonslayers' surcoats. She felt sad for him, born a dragon, on the wrong side of God's grace. Like sorcerers. Kindred spirits in persecution. God's unwanted children.

The dragon had such trust in her words. More, it seemed, than she ever had in Father Julian's. She, too, scanned the sky but saw no sign of God or heaven. Was God hiding? She'd always wanted to ask Him why He hated sorcerers so much. Her parents had that very reservation even as they converted to Christianity. They had converted partly because the success of the dragonslayers proved the power of God, and partly because Christians attracted less suspicion than pagans did.

"Why should we worship a god who hates us so?" her mother had asked in the days leading to their conversion.

"It's not that I want to worship a god like that," her father said. "I just don't believe everything the Christians say about Him." Her father had an affinity toward God and the Christ Jesus. Christians were a different thing, however.

"Where shall we find food then, if all the animals are for men?" Pyramine asked.

Isodore took a moment to recall their conversation. While she had been contemplating God, Pyramine was still working out plans for their survival. She hid her uncertainties about God under a confident reply. "We shall hunt animals in the meadows below these mountains."

"Is that not also the dominion of men?"

"It should be all right as long as we don't take what men would." She felt guilty for passing a guess off as the real answer, and simultaneously justified, for she must know more about God than he did.

"Men once claimed that land. They left only because dragons came. Now that so few dragons remain, they want it again. They will take it all, if we let them."

They both spoke as if she had already decided to become a dragon, as if all that remained was the chanting of the mystic words.

"Then we shall go elsewhere. We can find a new home easily from the air."

"Why must we? They have taken enough already. They are insatiable, sorceress, like the dragons they feed."

She thought it was the kind thing to do, not kill or steal from men, as the priests and their Bibles taught. Christians, pagans, Jews, and Muslims all agreed on this point. It must be what God wanted.

Pyramine continued, oblivious to Isodore's internal debate. "Men steal and kill. Your people took the forests from the woodlanders and other creatures that lived there. They kill, not just out of hunger but out of greed, not only their enemies but any men who stands in their way, their own kind, their own tribe, their own family. Besides, the world already has too many men."

Pyramine's disgust hung in the air while Isodore contemplated whether men were any better than the dragons they hated.

"The sorcerer who left you the spellbook, did he kill and eat men when he became a dragon?"

"Yes. Creatures of the forest are difficult to catch. Men are easier." After a moment, he added, "He sought out and killed those who were his enemies. Your spirit is loyal, sorceress. In time, you will be loyal to dragons."

Isodore was certain he meant to calm her fears, but instead his words plunged her back into doubt.

She glanced toward the pile of bones, joined by the severed head of the striped-green dragon. Pyramine had retrieved this key ingredient for use in her transformation. By shortening three chanting periods in the fifteen-part spell, she would avoid acquiring the striped dragon's excessive size. But the book was clear. She would otherwise become the repugnant, thieving creature that had tried to kill her. Would she become loyal to dragonkind? The striped dragon's head sneered at her, as though enjoying a last laugh.

She would prefer to become Pyramine's neighbor on one of the eastern peaks, like the dark red dragon. It used to wander near to investigate her when she first arrived. It hadn't for some time. She once asked Pyramine why. He said that the red dragon, like others not corrupted by men, was above stealing from him. That made two dragons who didn't want to harm her. Perhaps her loyalty to dragons would be well earned.

What she once thought was a necessary choice to save herself had turned foggy, like the heavy mist that descended on Dragon's Ridge the next day. Pyramine appeared out of that mist, preceded by the sound of his body sailing through the air, the rhythmic "whoosh, whoosh" of his beating wings. He swept up the cliff, dropping a sack on the ground before placing his feet gently on the edge of the precipice.

The sack contained figs, supplementing the leftovers from the piglet they'd had yesterday, a piglet so small that there should have been no leftovers to save. Except that there were, because he had given her the animal's entire hind quarters. After discarding the entrails, there was hardly any food for him at all.

The mist turned to rain, and to avoid it, she tried to recook the pig's leg in the cave. Smoke filled the chamber from the top down, leaving only a shallow layer of clear air over the floor. She lay down, so she could breathe, and held the meat up over the flames. Her arms soon tired, and the smoke choked her. She abandoned the cookfire, coughing and blinking her eyes as she felt her way out. She sympathized with the dragons' dislike of smoke. How could she have questioned it?

She retrieved enough wood to cook, leaving the rest to stay dry in the cave. Pyramine started another fire for her. He set himself down, extending his left wing to protect the fire—and her—from the rain. The sound of rainfall on his wing reminded her of something she had not heard in a long time, rainfall on thatched roofs, and for a moment in that damp darkness, she could imagine she was cooking in the orphanage.

Soot from the fire dulled the underside of Pyramine's wing, but he was unbothered. They watched the rain around them while the fire kept her warm. Pyramine's wet scales glistened black and orange in the firelight, his body still, except for breathing. He stared out into the dark, blank haze at the emptiness, while rivulets ran down his enigmatic dragon head. Sharp teeth showed between his open lips. Traces of blood covered his chin, mixed with rainwater, and dripped down onto the ground.

This will be my mate, she thought. It will be me. This was the life of a dragon, to sit alone as rain fell and darkness deepened on a desolate mountaintop. No warmth needed, none received.

She would never again have the pleasure of brushing her hair, or wearing new clothes, or holding a child. She would never hold a man or be held by one. For the rest of her long life as a dragon, she would nest among rocks and sleep curled up, by herself. Knowing this, the joy and freedom of being a dragon was little consolation. These things had occurred to her before, but tonight, perhaps because of the rain and fog that confined her views, she felt more isolated than ever.

She willed herself to see the good in being a dragon, but she could only see Pyramine's face: black, rain-soaked, glimmering in the firelight, blood on his lips dissolving in the rain and washing away.

Why was there blood on his lips? He didn't bring back an animal, only the sack of figs. She looked at the sack's hemp weave, ripped in places, wrinkled, and on one side, dark blood stains.

"You stopped to feed before you came back, didn't you?" she wanted to say. It was more an accusation than a question, the way he once asked her about her apron: "It was you who cast the cloth at me. Wasn't it, sorceress?"

The words never left her throat. What would be the point? He was a dragon. Dragons had to eat, especially after giving her most of the small piglet yesterday. And why not raid a human village? Wasn't it she who wanted fruit? At least he had the courtesy to not bring the body of a human being back to the nest.

She could no longer pretend that becoming a dragon was merely a change in form. What did it mean to be loyal to dragons? Would she become an enemy of men? To keep herself alive, would she, for the rest of her time, put men to death? Would she remember all she had learned from the dragonslayers and render their tactics ineffective against her? Would she become the beast that dragonslayers feared? Would her children, as well? All doubts, everything she ever feared about being a dragon, came back to settle again in her terribly unsettled mind.

She conjured up the sight of Galt and her orphans lying crushed and dismembered at her dragon feet. She swore to herself that she would rather die than let that happen. It brought her an unexpected calm, seeing her fate that way. She listened to the rain, in peace, for a long time. Her choice became clear. She would face death if that were God's will, but she would not become a dragon. Never.

It only remained to tell her captor.

"Will you kill me if I refuse?" she asked.

He didn't answer.

"I know I have no choice, but I can't look upon your face. I only see the dragon that took me away from everything I had and would kill me if I refused. I don't see a creature I could bear."

"Perhaps," Pyramine said facing the emptiness, "there is a spell to transform me into something you find more beautiful."

"I don't know if that would change anything. You are ... perhaps not so terrible as other dragons are. But I don't know how I could live on as a dragon. I want to fly. And the world is so beautiful from up here. But it's not my home. I don't want to live my life on a mountain with no one around. I want to hear songs and the laughter of children. I want to be with kind people. I'm lonely here. I don't want to be lonely for the rest of my life. I don't want to live that long, if life is like this. Every day, I think about throwing myself off this cliff so I won't have to go on. I'm so unhappy."

The courage she thought she had gathered was gone. She trembled and cried. She was pleading, not defiantly declaring her willingness to die. She couldn't bring herself to speak of the other reason for not wanting to be a dragon, her loyalty to some men and her refusal to become their enemy.

Pyramine's response was a deafening silence.

She swallowed the heavy lump in her throat. She could ignore fate no more than believe that his silence was the end of the matter. He had brought her here for a reason, and though she had managed to delay him, that reason remained. Her moment of truth was near, and something in this drizzly night, she felt, would bring it about, whether or not she faced it with courage.

When she entered the cave, she saw that the abandoned cookfire had left a swath of soot stain on the wall. It had heated the granite and burned down to small coals. She swept the coals away and lay down.

When Pyramine entered, he stopped to scrape the soot from his wing's underside on the tall slab. Then he burned the remaining soot off with an intense breath of blue fire. The rain on his wing turned to steam. He settled down in the cave.

Isodore lay still, imagining her body lifeless, searching for the courage she needed for what she was certain would be the last night of her life. It took a long time, an unaccountable moment of dark, dead stillness, but not enough for her to gather back her courage.

"Is it your decision not to become a dragon?" Pyramine asked at last.

"Yes, but . . ." It was all she could do to keep from falling apart, from crying out loud, begging to be set free.

She waited for the answer, feeling death returning to the dark cave, its cold finger stroking up her back. Tears wet her eyes. She closed them and imagined herself kneeling at the altar of Father Julian's sanctuary. "Oh Mighty God," she prayed in a whisper only her maker could hear. "I lay myself down in your service. I am refusing the dragon so that I will not become a killer of men. I will not kill your dragonslayers, nor will my offspring. Please have mercy on me when I come before you."

The prayer gave her courage. She turned to the dragon to speak while she still could.

"Pyramine. If you will not release me, then I have one request. Please, kill me in my sleep, and kill me quickly, before I wake. I don't want to be in pain for too long. And I don't want to see death in your eyes."

Her task complete, at peace again, she felt a calm wash over her. She didn't know if it was courage, but she was ready to leave this earth with her fears contained and her poise intact.

It was a sign of how well she knew Pyramine that she could tell in the dark he was nodding. He exhaled a long breath that swirled in the confines with a comforting warmth.

"If you do not wish to be a dragon, sorceress, then you must turn me into a man."

35

Divine Signals

The air was stale in the small armory of Beardsley's Den. Racks of crossbows, dragon shields and dragon lances against the wall left a small space at the center for a table. The room's sole occupant sat hunched at the table, bore in hand, enlarging a hole in a wooden cylinder. Wood chips, sawdust, bores, and files littered the tabletop, lit by two oil lamps. The mess covered most of the drawing titled *Secret Signaling Device for Dragonslayers*. That title had been crossed out and replaced with *Ghost Whistle*.

The sun shone brightly outside the small, high window, through which filtered Sir Wilfred's commanding voice, shouting out three words in Latin. There was a rush of footsteps, then a thrum of four bolts striking wooden boards.

Sir Dalton's voice offered, "They must move faster, but at least they remembered where to go."

Undisturbed by the outside world, Sir Galt put down the file, picked up a small bore and began a new hole. He was thin, with bags under his eyes, his hair uncombed, scraggly beard untrimmed.

The cylinder in his hand was a hollowed-out pine branch, similar to the one in the drawing, but bigger and twice as long. Though the drawing specified twenty holes, sixty holes had been marked in four rows along the tube's length. A prototype, made according to the drawing specifications, lay discarded. Twenty-six holes had been drilled into the larger prototype and filed smooth. As Galt drilled the twenty-seventh, a knight appeared at his door with several scrolls in his arms and a stack of letters in his hand.

"Messages," said Sir Gustav. He was twenty-five, with wavy blond hair down to his shoulders, an image of vigor if it weren't for the dim light of the room. The second-youngest knight in the regiment, he carried his solid body with calm sways.

Galt glanced down at the table, the mess, and the tube with thirty-three holes yet to be drilled. There was no room for the parchment. His voice was tired. "Isn't it your turn to read our messages?"

"It is. These are dragon sightings you wanted from the field. The courier came."

"Yes, right. My apologies, Sir Gustav."

Gustav nodded, approached, scanned the table and laid four small scrolls and a dozen wax-sealed letters on the least littered corner. "You've been at this for a few days."

"Yes," said Galt, putting the tube down and picking up one of the scrolls to read.

"You need some rest."

"I've been resting. You didn't miss me at combat exercises?"

"Well, yes. Perhaps you should get some exercise. The feel of a sword in my hand always helps me clear my mind for fresh ideas."

"Thank you, but I want to finish boring these holes."

Sir Gustav looked back and forth between the drawing and the wooden tube. "Will it be loud enough this time?"

"I'll know when it is finished." Galt scanned the scroll as Sir Gustav looked on with interest.

"Anything?" asked Gustav.

"No. Red, green, red, gray, black but a big one, gray, mottled. They're all big these days. Here's a medium black . . . I suppose this could be the one. Dragons often look much bigger to people in the grip of terror."

"Shall I look through these?" Gustav waved a hand at the other scrolls.

"Yes, please."

They went through the scrolls, mumbling colors, markings and sizes as they went. After the scrolls, they started on the folded letters.

"Here's one," said Gustav. "Small black dragon. It took a girl and a . . ." Gustav frowned at the parchment.

"A what?"

"A bag . . . ?" He showed Galt the letter. "Does that say a bag of figs?"

Galt cocked his head. "It does."

"That can't be right."

"No. If only dragons preferred fruit, we could end this conflict by teaching them to farm."

"That makes me wonder," said Gustav, frowning. "Even if someone claimed to have seen the dragon that killed Isodore, how can we trust these reports? If you go to the archbishop and request a mission to hunt down a fruit-eating dragon, he'll think you've gone mad."

Galt gave a weak laugh. "That was exactly what Sir Wilfred said."

Gustav laughed, too. "He said that, did he?"

"Yes. A man claimed a dragon took a sack plums off his cart—" Galt froze, his eyes unfocused. "Wait . . . No, this is not the first report like this. We've seen this before. When was that . . . a short time ago. And we were in disbelief, Sir Wilfred and I. We dismissed it."

"You lost me. Are you saying you believe there is a fruit-eating dragon?"

"No. But there is something odd."

"You believe these reports?" laughed Gustav.

"Sir Gustav, both of these incidents involved a small black dragon—"

"And a witness most likely panicking senseless."

"A good point. But how often do we see young dragons? Each of these incidents involved a small black dragon. It's peculiar indeed to have two dragons acting like this. But not so unlikely if it turns out to be the same odd creature."

Sir Gustav held up his letter. "My friend, both of these reports are outlandish. Their similarities don't make either of them less so." He took a quick glance at the door and lowered his voice. "People accuse dragons of all kinds of theft. You've never believed dragons looted tax collectors. Why would you think they'd steal fruit? Dragons have no use for gold or fruit. They want flesh. This was just a starving laborer stealing food and blaming it on a convenient villain."

Galt sighed, tapping his fingers on the report, frowning deeply. "If you stole something and wanted to blame it on a dragon, Sir Gustav, why would you claim it was a small dragon? We rarely see those. Why not something more believable? A full-grown one. And if two thieves blamed their crimes on a dragon, why should their imaginary thieves both be small and black? Of all colors and markings. Of all sizes."

"Perhaps they coordinated their stories?" offered Gustav, only to retreat when Galt faced him. "No, not likely."

Galt picked up the next envelope and read it. Gustav followed, in silence.

Through the window came Sir Wilfred's unhappy voice. "Good God. I've never seen that move before. If this had been real, you three would be dead. And you'd be next."

Gustav glanced out the window, but Galt kept on reading until he finished the letters. He slapped the pile back on the table, dispersing a wave of sawdust.

"Nothing?" Gustav asked.

"Nothing. Were there any more reports of a small dragon?"

"No."

"At least we don't have to decide among dozens of dragons which is the one," reasoned Galt. "There are very few young dragons strong enough to fly all the way to the frontier and very few of them would be bold enough to commit multiple raids. I would estimate there is only one that is also black, and it will be back."

He looked at the report of the stolen figs again. "This is very recent. Just three days ago, in Feranwick. Perhaps the dragon comes once a month. Perhaps more frequently, but it took the fruit without notice. I don't know if we can predict this beast. The plum thief struck far from Feranwick. It is not following a routine. Intelligent for such a young dragon. Or very fortunate."

"Well," said Gustav, "at least we know how to bait it. Fruit is far less costly than cows."

"Bait it? With fruit?"

"I was joking about the fruit. You've forgotten how to laugh, my friend. But yes, bait it. If this is the dragon, you'd want to avenge Isodore, wouldn't you? Isn't that the reason you wanted these sightings?"

Galt frowned, the bags under his eyes growing deeper.

"That was the plan, but I don't think that revenge will be needed just yet, Sir Gustav. And I do not think this is a fruit-eating dragon. I believe all this fruit is . . . for a captive."

Gustav's eyes narrowed. "You think the dragon is keeping her alive?"

Galt thought deeply, intensely. "I think God is keeping her alive."

"Why?"

"A test, to see if I'd come to her rescue."

Gustav's eyes popped. "Woodness, Sir Galt!"

36

Book's Apprentice

Isodore leafed through the thick spellbook with one hand and licked the fingertips of her other to remove the fig residue. She wiped her fingers on her tunic. It was unfit for a proper lass, but so was possessing a forbidden book. She picked up another fig, judged it too moldy and tossed it at the bone pile, where it joined scores of dried peach and plum pits. She took another. She'd gone through more than half the bag in one week and wanted to finish it all before it went bad, but she was very full.

Far back in the ancient volume, there was a spell with a translated heading, "Dragon to Man." Though not as daunting as transforming oneself into a dragon, this procedure was extremely complex, requiring four pages of arcane description, and a list of materials as varied as that for the "Sorcerer to Dragon."

Pyramine searched far and wide for materials, leaving her to study the spell. She tried to memorize parts that must be executed one right after the other, without time in between for her to consult the book. Without an assistant, she would have to prepare multiple ingredients simultaneously, to be ready at the right time, in the right places. It was like cooking a complex meal while repairing the cottage, tending the garden, begging for apprenticeships, arguing with Podlum, and caring for ten children of all ages, something she felt very capable of doing. The spell would take a day and a half, with no time for sleep. That would be exhausting, though she'd have to do it but once.

A small price for life and freedom. She took a break to look out to the horizon. A bitter taste crept into her mouth.

Two nights ago, she had lain down in her own grave only to rise again for no more than a promise to transform her captor into a man and become his mate. For a full day, she had been grateful for that easy choice, for her survival. She had almost liked the dragon.

Today, she wasn't so sure. Her life had been stolen, then returned as if it were a gift. That was an illusion. From the start, she had been on her own. She had made this opportunity herself, through the dreadful task of lying in that grave. She owed him nothing.

She must make the best of it. She would be clever in her deception while navigating to freedom. She would rid herself of the dragon, then the man. The dragon first. A man was far easier to kill.

She avoided thinking about the gruesome task by returning to the spellbook. Even if she couldn't escape Pyramine the man, she would still be rid of Pyramine the dragon for good. As she re-immersed herself in the spellbook, yet a third choice appeared to her, a blessing she had not seen before.

Her life could be safer with Pyramine than with mankind. If the mighty dragons were facing annihilation at the hands of men, what chance did a lone sorceress have? The bargain saved her life and gave her a husband. He could protect her. She didn't need to hide her secret from him, as she must from Galt.

She only wished she had been courted and asked, and given a real choice. Not everyone had this choice, she knew. She herself had faced the prospect of being an old maid, considered accepting an adolescent son of a dirty old carpenter, and was nearly forced to wed a squire she'd never met. Noble families, like Lord Corvin's, rarely allowed such choices. Children with their own ideas of who to wed were not to forget the story of Queen Radegund. She had been forced to marry Clothar, the Frankish ruler who killed everyone in her tribe, including her family. But because Isodore had come so close to marrying a man she had chosen, having to decide between death and marriage felt like coercion.

She watched Pyramine return, a dark speck in the distance with a cluster of dead branches bristling in his clutch. His wings flapped hard, fast, and inelegantly. His struggle against the weight reminded her not of a majestic eagle carrying prey but of a child lugging a pail of water back from the village well.

Having reached the ledge, Pyramine turned to face the valley and collapsed on his belly. He hung his chin over the precipice to rest, breathing heavily. Carrying wood was exhausting work. This spell called for a fire ring big enough to encircle a dragon and be maintained for a day and a half. He'd had to sweep the bone pile off the ledge to make room. It took many trips. After each haul, he lay down for a break before flying again.

Ironically, the rarest materials the spell required, gold and silver, she'd found discarded in the pile of bones. The jewelry, forgotten for who knew how long, was more proof that dragons cared not at all for the riches of men. There was more jewelry than what the spell required. The remainder would help her and Pyramine in their life together.

The most critical ingredient for the spell, a human skull, he acquired with no effort at all. He had chosen it from among many bones below the cliff. "You will be pleased," he said, dropping it at her feet. "He was a strong warrior and beautiful." Just as the "Sorcerer to Dragon" spell would have turned her into the striped beast whose skull Pyramine retrieved, the "Dragon to Man" spell would transform Pyramine into the man who once owned this skull.

The skull was dry and bleached white, missing the jaw bone. She handled it as if it still housed a human spirit. She wondered what he'd looked like. "He died long ago. You can still recall him?"

"I remember him well. He tried to kill me after I caught his companion. He was foolish."

"Or anguished. Perhaps you killed his wife or his child."

"Foolish," said the dragon.

Isodore consulted the spell's translated notes. "It says the missing jaw bone is not essential. And the skull need not be fresh, but it still should be wet with blood. This one isn't."

"I will bring you another."

"No! You will do no such thing. You will not raid another village or kill another person so close to becoming one yourself. This skull will be wet. I will use my own blood for it." She stared him down, and he backed off.

She might have been coerced, but it was her undertaking now, her responsibility. Trading her initial motive—to feign interest—for her new motive—to cast an advanced spell—she now worried whether she could actually succeed. She had never before executed a spell from a book. She flipped to the front of the volume to look for an easy one. The spell to preserve food was so much simpler than the one to restore putrefied food, and so practical in her circumstance. Her parents had never shown her this spell, however. Preservation could be accomplished by drying fruit and salting meat, methods that were slow but didn't expose their secret. Her parents had no salt, but it mattered not because they never had enough meat to save. Food preservation would have been useful when they'd lived in the forest, but there were no leftovers to preserve.

Isodore tried the preservation spell on a fig. Like the healing spell, preservation required a fire ring and a bit of asterium, which she took from the supply for transforming Pyramine. The chants differed, and that made sense, because rather than reversing degradation, this spell simply kept the subject from changing. She rubbed a thin layer of asterium paste over the food and placed it in a small fire ring built from the cookfire. She chanted the words exactly as written, just to be safe, though her parents had taught her that the words were only there to keep her focused and guide her mind. Spells were cast by the mind, not the lips. Anyone could chant, but only sorcerers could invoke the spell. She reached toward the fig. A warm tingle pulsed from her elbow down to her fingertips. For a time, she and the subject of her spell came closer together such that she could feel it in her hands, even as it lay still in the fire ring. The subject was small, so the spell ended before long.

The fig was unchanged and tasted no different. "Preserved food will not change except when touched by a being of much greater size," read the margin notes. Her food was essentially frozen in time, becoming edible to her but not to flies or maggots. Perfect. She just had to protect it from the birds.

She'd memorized the spell by the time she finished preserving the figs. Next, she preserved a small bite of the pig, to test whether it could be cooked after preservation. It could, because fire was its own magic. She proceeded to preserve the entire remains of the pig. She left the food in the cave, protected under a pile of rocks. It took some restraint not to constantly check on her work.

Over the next few days, she busied herself studying the transformation spell. The meat remained fresh. No slime, liquefaction, or disintegration. It remained moist, though the air had been dry. The flies laid their eggs but these shriveled and died. The figs stopped ripening and resisted mold, remaining soft and sweet. With each meal of her preserved meat and fruit came a feeling of anticipation she had not experienced since before her capture. She savored the preserved food as she did her accomplishment. She saved a small morsel of meat and a few fruits for continued observation.

Boosted by newfound confidence and her task, she soon forgot about her ambivalence and resentment over Pyramine's bargain. She looked forward to seeing what kind of a man he would become.

She ran her finger down the cover of the spellbook, a leather-bound papyrus tome. Of course! She understood now why this ancient volume appeared much newer than the archbishop's crumbling papyrus Bible. It had been preserved through sorcery. She could spot the use of magic!

She gained even more confidence when she spotted patterns among the spells, similar timing, chants, and material. Asterium, for example, was used in all spells that preserved or restored living or nearly living things. In the transformation spells, it was to be eaten by the subject midway through the spell and again at the end of the twelfth chant, while the new body took shape. The last third of the transformation spell was identical to the healing spell, save some modifications to block the tendency to reform the subject back to dragon flesh.

"Oh," she whispered, the thrill of discovery tugging at her

cheeks. "The healing spell is used to put the man's body together from dissolved dragon tissues." She flipped to the pages of the "Sorcerer to Dragon" spell that was still exceedingly daunting, but she could see the same general scheme. In the final day of the spell, there it was again, asterium, fire ring, and healing chants. It, too, ended with a healing spell. She sat back against the slab of rock, furrowing her brow. Until now, sorcery to her had always been step-by-step recipes, without rhyme or reason. The excitement of learning shook her from head to toe.

She understood. "There's logic to this!" Her face beamed at the blue sky as she let out a laugh of wonder.

If only her parents could see her now. The lost orphan had at last come into her own as a sorceress. The world of sorcery was hers.

37

The Last Dragon Rider

The day looked auspicious for the "Dragon to Man" transformation. No wind blew to strip flames from wood, no rain to douse the fire.

Isodore proceeded as if following a complex recipe, preparing the asterium paste in the helmet ahead of time. She arranged everything she needed on bare granite, where she could verify their presence and quickly find them when the time came. The book lay open, its pages held down by two stones.

While Pyramine broke the firewood into smaller pieces, Isodore looked over the precipice to the escarpment below, across the valley's meadow and out of Dragon's Ridge. Freedom. She thought she might miss the mountainous heights, but somewhere down there was her new life, a future with her new mate.

She then recalled a problem she had yet to solve. "Pyramine, once you become a man, how will we get off this mountain?"

"I will climb down, and I will carry you."

"Can you climb off?"

"Yes."

"As a man?"

Pyramine's wingspan surpassed thirty feet, wing tip to wing tip. Each arm, from shoulder to the clawed wing finger was close to ten feet. One could perhaps climb down with arms like those. But she had spent much time trying to get off the ledge safely, and she found the idea of a man accomplishing the task wishful. "Just how big of a man you will become?"

He looked over the cliff with her. Then he looked around, studying all the dead-end routes she had tried, and admitted to the same defeat. The task was impossible. A man, no matter what size or strength, couldn't bridge the distance between the handholds and footholds of the mountainside to escape the ledge. Once she changed Pyramine, they would both be prisoners.

They put off the transformation until Pyramine could find a safe place farther down the mountain. It took him three days, time which she spent reviewing the spell and testing her memorization of the most intense parts. The extra days of studying gave her an additional measure of confidence.

Pyramine found a suitable cave in the foothills. He flew the firewood down first. Though not as tiring as flying it up the mountain, it took three full days, with more trips than she cared to count. The following morning, it was Isodore's turn. She clutched the sack holding the spellbook, the skull, the helmet, dried asterium paste, the jewelry, and other materials for the spell. She nodded. He lifted himself and whipped up enormous swirls of wind as he hovered. He reached for her with open clawed feet.

"No!" she cried, pushing back on his ventral scales. "I want to ride on your shoulders. I am tired of being a captive. I am your mate, and I will not be carried like a fish!"

Pyramine landed and, after some hesitation, agreed. He backed up to the cliff's edge and spread his spidery arms to lower his shoulders. She hitched up her tunic and brought her leg over the base of his neck, sitting to one side to avoid resting her tailbone on the bumps of his spinal ridge. Her legs came down over his shoulders, in front of the wings. Her knees clamped tightly on his neck. His scales felt pleasingly warm on her bare legs.

When he straightened, their combined heights gave her a commanding view eight feet above the ledge, with the dragon neck extended before her. She felt powerful yet oddly vulnerable. The view over the precipice, to which she'd become accustomed, became vertiginous again. Her feet felt around for nonexistent stirrups. There was nothing to brace herself on. Pyramine rocked up and down.

"What are you doing?"

"Checking my balance."

She hooked her feet together under his neck. He lowered, sinking into the spidery arms. His elbows came together above his shoulders, squeezing her in.

He leaped with his arms more than his legs, springing upward on the strength of his pectorals and threw her off. Only her legs around his neck kept her in place.

The wings beat hard, scraping at the air and stirring violent whirlwinds. His shoulders rose and fell as his spine and neck flexed with each wing beat. His back muscles flexed and shifted. She tightened her legs. He backed up just past the cliff's edge. Seeing the long drop immediately below her feet, Isodore squeezed his neck tighter.

"What are you doing?" she yelled over the swirling air. Suddenly, he dove back to the ledge and landed hard on all fours, throwing her forward.

She wrapped her arms around his neck and tried to hang on. His neck ridges dug painfully into her arm and leg. She released her grip and let herself fall to the ground with a yelp.

He backed up, looking for her beneath him. "You are too heavy."

She brushed the dirt off her tunic and hands, willing herself past the indignation. "But you carried me up here!"

"You were in my claws then. On my shoulders, you cause me to plunge when I fly forward. You have to be in my claws."

That explained his earlier hesitancy. She reconsidered his long black toes and scythe-like claws, such an unappealing carriage to freedom and a new life. Wise or not, she wasn't willing to leave this mountain the way she came.

"A horse can carry me without tipping. Why should you find it so difficult?"

"A horse does not fly. And it does not carry you on its shoulders."

"Then I will ride on your back."

With the same reluctance, Pyramine lowered himself again. She mounted and scooted down over his back. Not the smooth cradle of a horse's back, it was hunched and lined with bony dorsal bumps. His shoulders were too big to for her hands to hold, but she spread her arms wider to take hold of the wing membrane that stretched out in front of his arm bones. His waist was much narrower than a horse's, allowing her legs to wrap almost all the way around him for security.

"I'm . . . ready, I think," she muttered.

He either didn't hear the hesitation in her voice or didn't understand what it meant. He leaped once more off his long forelimbs. The push from his back was not as jolting as it was from his shoulders, but other than that, she regretted everything.

When he spread his wings, the membranes she had absent-mindedly pinned under her feet pulled taut and threw off her legs. Her hands gripped the front membranes so hard that her fingers turned white. Each time his wings came down, they pulled her into his dorsal bumps. Then they came up as she came down, pushing against her hands. Her grip slipped a little each time. Air ripped and whirled. He backed away from the ledge to give himself room for the full strokes of his wings. She pulled into a fetal position.

Unable to keep her body against his flexing, pulsing back, Isodore floated off and crashed into him with each wing beat. On the upstrokes, his wings closed on both sides of her. She bounced to the left as they came up. Struck by the left wing, she was sent well to the right. When the wings came up again, she blocked the right one. They both rolled right and dropped. Isodore screamed. Pyramine lurched for the ledge. Only part of him reached it. His legs and tail slammed into the sheer cliff.

He slipped backward and down. Both wing claws dragged sharp lines on the ledge, raking dirt and scraping rock. Somehow, they managed to catch. He hung on to the cliff and Isodore dangled from his shoulders. She glanced down the precipice, completing her regret.

"Don't fall! Don't fall!" was all she could say.

From the beyond the lip of the ledge, came his infuriating, slow dragon voice. "You must get off. I cannot fly with you there."

"How am I supposed to do that?"

"Climb up."

She looked up at the long dragon neck that disappeared above the edge of the cliff. It was trembling, and the tendons bulged. He was supporting some of his weight with his chin. She failed to even pull her head up to her hands. Her tenuous grip on the front membranes began to slip.

"I can't!"

He released his chin, and she screamed as he sank under their combined weight. He bent his neck down to her and took the back of her tunic in his teeth. As soon as she felt him lift her, she released his membranes and threw her arms around his neck. He shook under the strain. A heavy grunt rumbled from his throat. He lifted her up until she could place one foot on his shoulder. She stood herself up, crawled onto the ledge and turned around, relieved but fearful for him. He was hanging on by his two wing claws.

"Can you climb up?"

"No."

He walked his feet up the precipice wall and sprung away. He fell backward, down to the ramparts and toward a fate similar to the striped-green dragoness lying headless on the boulders. His shadow raced down to join him. He curled and twisted onto his belly as he plunged. His wings sprung out and merged with their shadows. They slid over the boulder field. Dust swirled beneath in their wake. Pyramine peeled up and into the air, then returned to her side.

"You didn't stay on my back," he said, as though she had wandered off irresponsibly.

"You were bouncing so much I couldn't stay on!"

While Isodore took control of her shaking body, Pyramine stretched and crouched, raising and lowering his body as if still gauging his balance. He was lithe for his size, big as a yearling horse, slender as a log, nimble as a cat. He leaped into the air, hovered, looking at his feet. When he landed, he bent his neck to look at his back.

"On my back, you didn't push me off balance. I can fly with you there, but not if you move to one side."

"But I can't stay in one place while you bounce like that."

"I can drop off the edge to gain speed. With great speed, I need not beat my wings so hard. Though with your weight . . ." He peered down the cliff. "Yes, there is enough height to gain the speed I need to carry you."

Isodore crawled to the precipice for a look. She'd seen Pyramine launch off the edge and sail away after the harrowing drop, but he had been unladen with her weight. The bundles of wood that he carried to and fro were lighter. She might trust his judgment but not her ability to hold on. Between each wing beat, he was essentially falling, and she with him. She came off his back because they were in free fall, and a free fall off the cliff was what he had in mind.

It was too much.

She reluctantly agreed to be carried in his claws, after he reassured her that he wouldn't poke his claws into her if she didn't struggle. He faced the mountain again and launched himself into the air, hovering and presenting his legs to her. She turned her back to him and held the bag across her chest. His toes came around her chest and thighs. As he held onto her, she held on to him. He lifted confidently, straight up, his legs holding her steady as he stirred up a storm. She felt sick seeing the mountain retreat. It left her high over the bony graveyard. Pyramine banked and dropped off the precipice.

Isodore gasped as they plunged. The cliff came up and past her, then the bones at the escarpment. She was headed for the graveyard! He'd misjudged her weight. She jerked herself into a fetal position but was restrained by his grip. "Pull away, pull away!" she screamed. The wind blew her hair upward. His wings stretched wide. Her head felt heavy and she sank into his grip as they peeled away from the cliff. They skimmed the escarpment and lower slopes within reach of his shadow, exactly as he had done earlier. If he had barely cleared the ground by himself, how could he possibly avoid it carrying her? They sped up as they descended. Finally, with the ground a blur and a strong wind over his wings, Pyramine peeled upward to give himself room to flap those enormous wings. They were on their way.

Apparently unaware of the fright he'd given her, he didn't check on her. She had a good mind to demand to know why he must always skim so dangerously close to the ground.

He headed toward the notch in the ridge north of the nest. Over the ridge, a gust hit them, throwing him into a sudden bank. Isodore gasped and swung sideways, but remained securely in his grasp. The turbulence continued to toss them, but his hold was strong and firm.

She was soon distracted from her fears. Belly down, with her forearms propped on his curled toes, she felt as though she herself were flying. Her hair streamed back with the wind. In spite of herself, she felt a sense of ecstasy as they floated away from the mountain and hung in the air while the strong, noisy wind blew past them. With sufficient speed, his wings beat shallow, unrushed strokes.

Relaxed at last, Isodore noticed the warmth on her fingers and the touch of his claw tips. It was a delicate touch, so conscientiously held that even when the wind jostled them, his talons didn't dig into her.

Knowing that this was her last chance for a broad view of God's magnificent creation, she looked around. As they descended, indigo lakes turned blue again and pebbles turned back to rocks. Stark crags and boulder fields gave way to meadows, then to woods. They passed a stream tumbling down the mountain and met an eagle at eye level. Pyramine stretched his wings wide and glided. She had to narrow her eyes and blink to keep them dry in the wind, but she wished they could fly on and on, just to fly. The strange sensation in her ears felt reminiscent of the day he carried her up the mountain. She jiggled her jaw and it disappeared.

When they approached the forest canopy, woods became trees, with distinct trunks and crowns. Out of the mountain's maze, she saw again the vast land of forested hills. He turned west and began beating his wings again.

By the woods, Pyramine's shadow joined them, rippling over the tree tops. There was more animal life. Birds with flashing wings, eagles, and hawks passed above and below them. Over the meadows, she looked for wolves and bears, but didn't see any. She listened to the whooshing wind and calling birds.

A raven called out in rapid succession. "Arkh arkh arkh! Arkh arkh arkh!" She looked for the bird but saw none nearby, though she heard it again. Three throaty caws, repeated. Yet still no bird.

There was something odd about the call. She listened. It came again, three uniform throaty caws. "Arkh! Arkh! Arkh!" Strangely even and repetitious. Twice more she heard it. She'd never before heard such repetitions. It came from behind now. She looked down but saw only crowns of trees crowded together with a dragon shadow rippling by. No raven. It had sounded to her like the ravens were talking to, or signaling to, each other. She looked far back to where she was when she first heard it, but nothing betrayed the makers of those sounds.

Something was signaling. Someone, perhaps. A woodland clan? A dragonslayer regiment? It wasn't the ghost whistle—that was clear. Galt's whistle made a sharp, high-pitched sound, barely audible even without the forest in the way or the wind rushing by. The raven call could certainly be heard by dragons, though Pyramine ignored it, as he ignored all birds.

She wanted to think the calls came from dragonslayers. Her stomach twisted into a knot and her heart quickened at the thought of being so close to her rescuers, close enough to run into their arms, to stand protected behind a line of tethered crossbows, shields, and dragon lances.

Then she went cold. She didn't want them to be dragonslayers. Pyramine wouldn't be a dragon for much longer. What would be the point of killing him? She wanted to warn him, *Fly on, Pyramine. Just fly. Far away. It's not safe for you in these woods.*

She wanted to save the dragonslayers as well. Pyramine had learned from the slaughter of the Deleret Expedition, but the dragonslayers never knew what happened. He could call on other dragons and lure the regiment to the same slaughter. If Galt had come for her, then died for her, she would have nothing. Every option was certain to doom them all.

Time and opportunity slipped away. The raven calls were gone. She listened and worried, telling herself it was just an excited band of woodlanders—or some peculiar ravens.

38

Yielding to Mercy

Miles from the ravens that may or may not have been dragonslayers, Pyramine dropped through the canopy where wind and disease had felled a tree, leaving a vertical tunnel. His wings beat furiously in the limited space. He dropped as much as flew. Isodore feared he might forget she was in his claws and crush her on landing. His wingtips hit the surrounding trees, snapping branches, liberating flurries of leaves and pine needles that struck her like leaves in an autumn windstorm. Isodore dashed away as soon as he released her so that he wouldn't land on top of her.

They made their way across the musty forest floor for a half hour, stepping on moldering leaves and over fallen branches, weaving around dense woods. Isodore spotted the decaying remains of a deer, but believed it to be the work of bears or wolves. Or dragons. Men would never leave a carcass in one piece like that. She scanned the forest for signs of dragonslayers, feeling simultaneously disappointed and relieved to see none.

The terrain rose steadily. The pair trudged up a moderate incline to a massive pile of shattered and tangled dry branches at the base of a cliff. Pyramine must have dropped the firewood from above rather than dragging it in the way they had come. Behind the pile was the cave, though not much more of one than the cave on the Ridge. It was a three-sided chamber at the bottom of a brownish rock cliff. The forest floor leading up to it had been trampled free of undergrowth. Inside, it wasn't a chamber as much as a shelter from rain. About thirty paces wide, ten deep and tall enough to stand in, it was cavernous compared to the narrow cave on the mountain. Bones, broken pottery, tattered animal skin, other refuse and a rock-rimmed fire pit indicated previous human habitation, perhaps by a family or small clan. She wondered what became of them.

Pyramine dragged the large pieces of firewood into the cave while Isodore gathered the fragments. He started a fire in the fire pit. Using the old helmet she had salvaged from the nest, Isodore melted a chunk of white rock from the shattered remains of a block that he had dropped earlier that morning.

She prepared the asterium paste and set it aside. She took a brief rest and found herself shaking in fear of what was next, acquiring the last ingredient for the transformation. Her blood. The spellbook stated that the human skull need not be fresh, but it had to be wet with blood. Asserting her spousal rights, she had for-bidden Pyramine from killing another person to obtain a skull in suitable condition. "We will wet it with my blood," she had said. It was time to show that she was as tough as those words.

Without a knife, they had planned to use Pyramine's sharp teeth. She was ready with the healing spell, but she feared the pain. Pyramine put the tip of his front teeth on her calf and eyed her. She took a breath and looked away. "Just do it. Fast! It'll hurt however you do it."

She felt the two rows of dragon teeth snap close. She screamed through clenched teeth and held her wound over the helmet. Dark blood dripped out. She breathed fast, but it took its time coming. "Come on, come on! Faster!" she urged the scarlet bite wound. After what felt like an hour, there was enough blood. She dipped her fingers into the gathered puddle and rubbed the sun-bleached bone until no white showed. There was even some blood left over.

She swung her bloody leg to the little fire ring Pyramine made earlier, scooped a handful of asterium paste, and pressed it into the row of tooth marks on her calf and began the healing chant. Though painful, the bite was very compact. The bleeding stopped within a minute. It was longer before the pain dulled.

Pyramine remained absolutely quiet, as usual. He looked from her pained face to her calf and back, occasionally toward the cave entrance, from whence an intruder might come. When she lifted her hands to look at her wound underneath, he was there, looking with great interest. The punctures had become a curved row of sealed cuts still bloody.

It was his turn.

He set a great heap of wood alight, then placed the burning pieces along the oval she had drawn in the dirt. His distaste for smoke was so strong that he had a constant grimace on his dragon face.

He lay down on his belly in the burning oval, facing the entrance of the cave. He tucked his hind legs under, and curled up his tail. His wings folded neatly on either side of him. He turned his crimson eyes to her.

"I am ready," he said.

I will never see those eyes again, she thought, trying to understand the unexpected feeling of loss.

THE SPELL HAD three phases: shrinking him to human size, dissolving the dragon form, then healing him into a man. She settled in for the lengthy process. Kneeling down, with her hands on his back, she began the first phase at midmorning.

The heat from Pyramine and the large fire ring felt like an oven. Sweat soaked through her dirty, ragged clothing. When she wiped sweat off her brows, it was mixed with soot. A mysterious breeze rose, cooling the cave. It carried an intense odor of oil, coal, and wine—the dragon scent, though far stronger. She felt the familiar tingles pulsing down her arms. Her hands felt as though they were reaching beneath his scales, into his flesh. The transformation was under way.

Something stirred and shifted under his scales. The scales began to fade, though he retained the same general form. Hours later, his body had shrunk noticeably from the fire ring. The strong dragon odor, she realized, was his horse-sized bulk, vaporizing like steam from a roiling kettle.

Shrinking him would take nearly a day. It was the longest, but least demanding phase, for the spell allowed brief periods of rest. She tracked progress by tallying chants in the dirt. She stopped as needed to feed the fire, and added logs to keep the fire ring burning. She stepped away from the heat and smoke of the large fire ring for fresh, cool forest air. Her hunger rose in the evening, and she ate the last of the preserved meat and figs.

She froze at the sound of wolves howling somewhere out in the forest. Of a distant origin, the howl blended with its own echoes. She felt alone. She missed the nest that had, while imprisoning her, kept her safe from all predators, except for the big, striped dragoness fed by men. She forgot to think about defense when they had left the nest behind. Instinctively, she looked to Pyramine. Defending her was his duty as her mate, but he appeared to be in a deep sleep. Even so, he provided a measure of protection. The strong smell of a dragon should send all other creatures that recognized it into retreat.

She worked through the night with little soreness; the healing spell she'd cast on her calf earlier alleviated it. But at times, she struggled to stay awake.

Pyramine's wing membranes thinned, became translucent, then dissolved, leaving behind long, bony fingers. His black scales lightened to a sapphire-blue. He shrank further, but still retained the general form of a dragon.

Each time Isodore replenished the fire ring, she moved it closer to the shrinking dragon form. When she moved it for the final time, she noted how vulnerable this man-sized dragon was.

Were she to kill him once he took human form, she need not wait. She could push the fire closer to him and let him burn when he became sufficiently human. He would then know what it was like to suffer at the hands of a dragon. She wouldn't be able to bear the sound, however. She could leave him, abandon the spell, deny him the asterium so critical to forging the human form. He'd said a dragon that couldn't fly couldn't defend itself, and his wing membrane was gone.

He would cry in rage over the betrayal. Betrayal was the one thing he had said would break his loyalty. It had chilled her when he told her, as though he was warning her. That same chill now crawled up her spine.

If she were to kill him, a quick death would be the least cruel, the kind of death she had asked him for, the beheading that noblemen insisted on, and the philanderer Armand had bargained for. She could grant him a quick death by smashing his head with a rock from the fire pit.

If she were to kill him ...

She carried on.

Light had returned to the forest when she began the second phase, dissolving the dragon form. His forelimbs, neck, and tail shortened. His scales softened and lost texture, reabsorbed into the underlying skin. His form gave way, but not to anything recognizable. Neither dragon nor man, but a wrinkled bag of soft gray meat, collapsing under its own weight. Strangely grotesque.

As hideous as he had once looked, she realized she had gotten used to his appearance. This intermediate form was disturbing to see. Neither man nor dragon, a creature that was never meant to be.

"We are creatures of magic," he had told her, "spirits forged into physical form. You, from blood, and I, from fire. We are magical. We have always been and will always be." Watching herself working in the fire ring, she no longer had any doubt of it. It was what her parents would have taught her, had they lived.

Soon, Pyramine, too, would be forged from blood—her own blood, given willingly to a beast who, on the day their paths crossed, would have eaten her. How ironic that, in the end, her blood would course inside him.

He would be her mate. The creature that had abducted her, intended to kill her, then forced himself into the remainder of her life, had now given himself over to her, to be transformed into a man—or murdered, if she chose.

How much loyalty did she owe him for his trust in her? She looked to the fire pit, with its blazing logs and heavy rocks. Tools of her betrayal, should she choose that course.

She eyed a rock from the fire pit, small enough to pick up but big enough to break his soft skull. She could use the surcoat to protect her hands from the heat. It would be simple. No witness except for God, and God loved a dragonslayer. She might even pay for her sins with this act.

Pyramine must understand why she had to kill him. He himself explained that the ash-winged dragon that razed her village was merely exacting revenge. She would be justified in murdering him. But justification wasn't the same as determination. She couldn't bring herself to murder a creature in its sleep, to betray a being that had put his life into her hands. Not at this point.

The howling of wolves startled her again. She realized that the smell of the dragon, which she had counted on to keep predators away, had dissipated when he stopped shrinking. The robust fire in the pit, especially the smoky new logs, and the fire ring might still keep predators out. Travelers, hunting parties and woodlanders built a fire each evening for warmth and noisily defended their camp from animal intruders. Some animals thus associated fires with aggressive men and avoided them. At least, that was what Sir Rowan had said. Regardless, delay couldn't be good.

She returned to her present task and resolved to keep her mind on her work. It wasn't the lips that cast the spell, her parents had taught her. It was the mind. She must keep her mind on the spell. She chanted, though her throat ached for rest. She labored to maintain the fire ring, though her belly growled for food. She spared Pyramine, though a part of her was sick of the injustice. She comforted herself with her imminent new life, though she wanted Galt.

When the last of the dissolution chants was complete, she picked up the human skull and gasped. The blood had dried. How foolish of her not to think of this. The leftover blood in the helmet had coagulated. She rushed to improvise a mixture of water and blood jelly to re-wet the skull before continuing. Her blood-red hands worked the reddened skull underneath him, close to his heart. It was the last she saw of the skull. His soft body swallowed it. She placed a scoop of asterium into his equally soft, shapeless mouth and found him awake enough to bring it into his throat.

It was time for the last phase, healing him into human form. He was at his most defenseless. The last phase would restore his strength and health. She took a deep breath and began the chant.

Beneath her fingertips, soft flesh began to grow firm. Its dull gray turned a tender pink and threaded with vessels of her scarlet blood. Wrinkled skin turned smooth. Hours later, an olive complexion masked over the color of human flesh.

Midday came and passed without notice. A kneeling, sleepy Isodore finished her last chant. The warm tingles in her arms faded away, and she felt herself disconnect from the naked body curled up before her. She stood and backed out of the wilting ring of embers.

His fetal position seemed appropriate for the re-birth into his new form. It was also a position of prayer. He pushed himself to his hands and knees, still dazed. He shifted back, sitting on his heels, casting wide, fearful eyes on the cave walls around him as if he had never seen them before, as if he didn't know where he was. But he was not alarmed.

With brows drawn together and jaw left slack, he turned his head in an arc, studying the ash and embers on the ground around him. He then took notice of his arms and legs, the hair on his skin and head. He turned his hands around to look at them, back and forth, back and forth. When he finally noticed Isodore watching, he tried to stand up, but he paused in a hunched position, as if afraid he would fall if he took his forelimbs off the ground to stand upright. He eased himself up slowly, watching his balance every second, and seemed surprised by how easy it was.

He stood more than a head taller than she, and solid. He was lean, not wiry like a farmer, but strong. A warrior in his prime. She wondered who this man had been before he died. Neither heathen nor Basque like her, nor Moor. He had skin the color of tanned leather with an olive hue, long black hair in curls tighter than hers. His eyes were deep blue, like the twilight sky. Perhaps he had been a Muslim knight before losing his life in battle with Pyramine. And he was handsome, as Pyramine had told her, the most beautiful man she had ever seen. It was hard to take her eyes off him. But she did, with a gasp, when he turned to her.

"What is it you see?" he asked, with Pyramine's words, but not in the dragon's voice.

"Nothing. I just don't want to see you like that."

"You don't want to see a man? Are there not men in your nests?"

"They wear clothes," she explained. "And you should, too."

"Why?"

"To cover that which I do not wish to look upon."

It was the first of many things she had to explain to him. "You should cover that part of your body—there. I shouldn't see that." She waved a hand at his waist while keeping her eyes averted.

"That is used for mating."

"I know! That is not what we're doing now. So cover it up." The heat of her own blood flushed over her, and she turned further away to protect her modesty. Where did he learn such things?

He stepped out of the fire ring and rummaged through the cave's refuse for leftover clothing, but the little rags and scraps of pelt he found were too small to wear. He managed instead to become preoccupied by the very anatomy she ordered him to cover, which he seemed to find both repulsive and distracting.

Realizing the task of clothing himself was too much for him, Isodore stepped in. She improvised a kilt from the torn surcoat, but there was barely enough cloth to encircle his waist. It was a struggle to tie the ends together.

The challenge to her modesty was greater than all previous combined, including Podlum's lewd suggestions. The whole side of Pyramine's body was in her face, yet she couldn't be expected to tie the knot with closed eyes. Enveloped by his masculine smell, she held her breath, but in the end, had to inhale so deeply and repeatedly that it rendered the effort to block him out entirely counterproductive. She had to pull the cloth's ends together so tightly that she might as well have had her arms around him. Her hands touched him at the waist. Her elbow braced against his thigh. By the time she finished, she remembered more of his body than she did of the knot she tied. A dragon no longer, he was a man many women couldn't help but notice, including, perhaps, proper lasses.

For her effort, she received complaints that the kilt was too confining. Against her admonition, he adjusted it repeatedly. Soon, there was a short rip. The cloth fell to his feet and a sheepish grin rose to his face.

"It broke," he said, as though it were the cloth's decision.

She tried again, this time with a long strip of cloth sacrificed from the bottom of her tunic. They had no knife, so she tried to tear it. The fabric was too tough. He helped. She told him where to tear, then watched in shock, not because he tore a sloppy, ragged line, but because he ripped the cloth with so little effort.

He appeared surprised too, but not at his strength. He dropped the fabric and studied his fingers, curling and uncurling them in raw fascination.

The cloth went around his waist twice, with enough length left to tie the ends together. He found his new kilt as confining as the old one.

"You'll get used to it. Don't touch it," Isodore ordered.

His attention returned to his hands. He spread his fingers, curled them and practiced grabbing things, like his wrist, with glee. After a while, he practiced throwing little rocks and litter he found on the ground. He brought a stone back to his ear and pushed it out without winding up or putting his body into it. The stone didn't go far.

She took in the childlike curiosity on his face. At last able to look at him without enduring a challenge to her Church-taught modesty, she allowed herself to admire his deep blue eyes and muscular frame. His skin was smooth, except over his arms and chest, which were a field of goosebumps.

He shivered.

"Are you cold?"

He hesitated, then inhaled and said with wide eyes, "Yes," as though he just found the name for his discomfort.

"You've never been cold before, have you? That's part of being human. We'll find more clothing to keep you warm."

"More clothing?" A look of dismay came over his face, mingled with uncertainty and a shade of regret.

"You'll get used to it. For now, we can just use this fire."

She sat him down by the fire pit. With a stick, she swept the embers from the fire ring into the pit. She dropped in kindling and small branches to revive the fire. When night fell, without a dragon next to her, she too could use the extra warmth. Her legs, exposed by the shortened tunic, reminded her of that.

Dying coals gave life to the new fuel. Wisps of smoke from the kindling were enough to make Pyramine flinch. Isodore arranged some small logs in the pit. He watched with confused wonder. It used to be his job to provide fire.

Until now, she had given much thought to betraying him and little to the alternative. She had mindlessly envisoned a life of mutual benefits, of working separate tasks but toward the same end, of sharing food and company, of gaining protection from men and beasts alike in return for her domestic contributions. The specifics were irrelevant at the time. She overlooked them.

In the back of her mind, she had used Sir Rowan and Galt as stand-ins for a husband who was beyond her ability to imagine. She had anticipated a life with Pyramine very similar to something she might have had with her knights, but without the wealth, status, or warrior livelihood. She was wrong. Life with the man she'd created would be unlike life with any normal man. She would have to adapt and help him with his adjustments, but she supposed that was better than having to fight for survival. Better than being an old maid pining for a long-lost knight. Far better than a lewd old carpenter or his underaged son. This new life was hers to choose, yet only now did she seriously consider it.

Pyramine's beauty certainly made him easier to want as a husband. She would be the envy of the lasses he was certain to attract. She wondered if she might become jealous, or if he would be faithful to her. It was so improbable for her to be with such a handsome man that she nearly forgot the improbability of the last two months of her life. The whims of fate were baffling.

The fire grew between them, casting light and warmth. The dancing flames gave her a sense of home and hearth, a promise of peace and ritual. Pyramine seemed to glow. She wondered if he saw the same effect on her. They glanced at each other, then shyly dropped their gaze. They watched the fire, the cave, the forest outside. They listened to the silence, occasionally broken by the hiss and pop of burning wood. Without a word, they awaited their mysterious future.

39

Animal Impulse

A growl gurgled in Pyramine's belly. He looked down, searching for the thing that caused the disturbance.

"It means you're hungry," said Isodore.

A look of comprehension came to him. His eyes brightened. He stood and strode out the cave, scanning the woods. "There is food."

"Where?"

"This way."

He turned and departed, leaving her stammering after him. She wanted to tell him to stop so they could discuss it first, but didn't know how to put it. Besides, she was hungry and he must be starving. It had been a day since Isodore finished the food she had brought down from the nest. Pyramine's fast was days longer. Flying the firewood down from the mountain had left him no time to hunt.

She ran after him. He strode on, seemingly confident in his heading. The branches and rocks on the ground apparently didn't bother his bare feet. She called to him to slow down. He did, for as long as his patience allowed. Then he resumed, with a pace set apparently to make up the lost time. He even ran, hesitantly at first, slowing down to examine his stride. Isodore gained on him, only to fall behind again when he restarted. His form was odd, unnaturally intentional but not fluid. What he lacked in grace, however, he made up in strength.

He descended to a narrow stream to drink, lapping at the water where it dropped off a stone step. Finished just as she arrived, he marched up the long ascent. She called to him, "Pyramine, wait. I can't keep up."

"Go back. I will bring you the food."

Flabbergasted, she stopped to gasp some breaths. Her legs burned and sweat moistened her face and neck. She scooped handfuls of water to drink.

Unable to see him afterward, she felt alone and vulnerable. It was one thing to live along a road's corridor, knowing someone would be by sooner or later. It was something else to be in the deep woods, far from fellow travelers. She found a branch to use for defense. It was just a stick, not a club, but it would do until she found something heftier. As a child in the woods, having a stick in hand had always made her feel less vulnerable. She trudged up the next hill after him, muttering, "I thought we were mates, dragon."

She feared she might be lost when the hill leveled out and she still couldn't see him. Then she rounded a tree and there he was, thirty paces away. He hadn't stopped, but he was barely moving. His back was turned to her as he peered around a tree.

He was stalking. She instinctively slowed down to avoid alarming whatever he was after. He left the tree and crouched toward a bush. She passed a few trees and stopped when she saw several puppies playing beyond the brush where he hid. Suddenly, he sprung forth and burst through the bush. Gray, black and brown shapes scattered, yelping.

Dogs. No, wolves! The pups scurried into an underground den. Pyramine dove after them, squirming into the entrance.

Two wolves immediately returned. They rushed to the den, their tails high. The hair stood up on Isodore's skin. "Pyramine!" she cried just as they clamped their jaws around his ankles. They twisted and pulled, dragging him out of the den. Roaring in pain, he twisted onto his back, flipping the wolves onto theirs. One wolf released him and jumped away. The other held on. Pyramine reached for its neck. The wolf released him. Its mouth opened to show curved bloody fangs. Its tongue stuck out, long and stiff. Its paws clawed at the air as its eyes opened wide. He was choking it. He stood and swung it over his head.

Isodore didn't see what he did next. She heard snarling from behind and turned. Three wolves faced her, hunched low, teeth bared. She screamed. The stick in her hand was pathetically inadequate. An electric tinge flashed through her body, and she fled.

They launched at her. One caught a mouthful of her tunic. One came away with a strip from the already torn hem. One missed. The first wolf pushed its paws into the dirt to prevent her escape. She grabbed her tunic, trying to yank it from the wolf's mouth, but its teeth held fast. She struck it with the stick, but that did nothing to encourage the animal to release her. She struck it on the head, then on the nose. That seemed to cause some pain, but no surrender.

One of the other wolves returned and attacked her from the side. She felt its teeth graze her thigh, but it caught just another mouthful of clothing. She screamed. The canine teeth stretched out the holes they made in her tunic.

Suddenly, Pyramine slammed into the two wolves. Arms out wide, he swept both animals off her and pulled them to the ground. One wolf twisted away. The other flailed violently as Pyramine fought to hold on. He had the wolf's back to his chest and tried to grab its throat. It snapped its jaws around his hand. He snarled with anger. The wolf shook its teeth to mangle the bitten hand. Pyramine took its jaw with his free hand and forced its mouth open.

The other two wolves came back for Isodore. Pyramine released his victim to come to her rescue again. The wolf slunk away, yelping.

The other wolves held back when Pyramine came between them and Isodore, neither charging nor fleeing. He shook his bitten hand and spat a furry ear at them. They kept their distance, their tails down.

"I don't think this is a good idea," Isodore said, but he wasn't paying attention to her. He charged the wolves. They kept a safe distance. He couldn't chase after them without leaving her undefended. Each time he tried, they circled back. They seemed to know this game and played him well. Time was on their side. Slowly, the pack reconstituted, except for one lying still, outside the den, and one that slunk away missing an ear. The wolves circled, their tails at a confident angle, and closed in.

"Come!" he shouted, and charged the wolves again. Frightened, Isodore kept right by his side.

"The plants!" he said, and they moved toward a waist-high spread of brambles. Once there, he stood between her and the wolves. She backed into the brush until its firm branches stopped her.

One wolf stood out as the leader. A large gray one. Bold and energetic, with its tail high, it charged and dodged as Pyramine grabbed at it. The others followed suit.

Pyramine sunk into his knees, ready to jump at the creatures he had viewed as prey all his life. He didn't fear them. But each time he charged one, others would come for Isodore, forcing him to abandon his attack before it began. He protected her, but as long as she was vulnerable, he couldn't save her. They had him.

She looked down at her hand, still clutching the stick that had been so useless. When Pyramine charged one wolf and another came, she tried to strike her attacker on the nose. It was difficult. The wolves were too quick. She gave Pyramine a few extra seconds before he had to return to guard her, but a few seconds made no difference.

As they worked, the pack grew more excited. They growled and barked louder, instilling fear in Isodore. Pyramine's growls did nothing to intimidate the wolves, though they sounded oddly comforting to Isodore. Her guardian seemed fearless.

Pyramine charged a pack member, and the leader slipped in. Isodore swung at a wolf's nose and it caught her stick in its teeth. She squealed and fought for control. A brown wolf came in. She swept the leader aside to block it.

Her stick snapped. The leader dropped its end and went for her leg. It yelped as it was yanked backward, its hind leg in Pyramine's grasp. As Pyramine swung it high and slammed it into the ground, Isodore shook her broken stick at the other wolf. It bared its curved teeth, close enough to bite her hand. She threw the stick at it. It launched at her but failed, struck down by the gray blur swinging in Pyramine's hand. Pyramine tossed the gray wolf aside and snatched up the brown, trying to subdue it. It squirmed until its jaw found his hand.

The wolf stopped thrashing to put all its strength into crushing his hand, giving Pyramine the chance to close his fingers around one of its front leg. Stretching the wolf out between his two hands, he brought it close, opened wide and bit the wolf's neck. It yelped and released his hand. But his hand did not release the wolf's mouth. His teeth pulled on the wolf's neck while he pushed away its mouth and leg. He shook under the strain. The wolf made a frightened, primal sound. The muscles in Pyramine's neck and arms tensed and shifted until suddenly, his arms pushed straight. A long red tear opened down the wolf's neck. Pyramine spat out a strip of brown fur.

Blood poured out of the wound. The brown wolf lost its strength and went limp in Pyramine's arms. The gray leader rolled on the ground, unable to stand due to some unseen injury. The wolves' attack faltered fast, their tails tightly tucked. There was horror in their eyes.

Pyramine raised the limp body in his arms and charged, roaring in wild supremacy. The pack scattered as he tossed their dead pack mate after them. Well away, they regrouped, but showed no will to try another attack. Tails between their legs, they returned to the den area, sniffed at the first wolf he'd killed, and watched from their safe distance.

The tension that had gripped Isodore's body flushed away, and let her think for the first time since she'd seen the pups. Pyramine had protected her. Whatever his flaws, he had put her safety first. She felt an immense sense of security watching her mate vanquish the wolves to defend her. Her gratitude wanted expression. She set herself to binding the wound he suffered to protect her. She would perform another healing spell, if needed; there was one asterium shoot left.

"No," he said. He wasn't bleeding, and the wounds already looked hours old. The spell that healed him into human form was still at work, as the one for Galt had for months after the incantation. If Pyramine still felt pain, it didn't bother him. Comfort was not what he wanted. "I am hungry." He passed her on his way to the suffering gray wolf and knelt down.

"Very well," she said. "Where is the food that you—" The gray wolf's body convulsed. Its limbs clawed at the air, like the first wolf did by the den. She watched from behind as he ended the wolf's misery. He then turned the corpse onto its belly, stood on its back and pulled up on its hind legs. She heard its spine break. Pyramine turned the wolf's back end around and around until it held on by a narrow twisted waist. He pulled the legs up, grunting heavily as the wolf's body stretched and then ripped in two. Cartilage cracked, sinew snapped, pelt tore, and blood was flung upward.

Meanwhile, it dawned on Isodore. "Were you after these wolves? How did you know they were here?"

Pulling the entrails from the hind quarters, he answered, "I hunt them. They always run to this hill, but the forest here is too dense for a dragon to run. Here." He handed the hind quarters to her with a bright nod, apparently pleased with his role as provider.

Her shock, which she didn't hide, failed to render any message to him. Where did this man's body come from? Pyramine had said that the man had nearly killed him, so perhaps he was a warrior of great strength. But how strong could a man be? Lord Edwin was renowned for his strength. As a young man, he could lift logs over his head and toss heavy hammers farther than any man. Could he have ripped a wolf in two? Or tear open its throat with his teeth?

While she tried to make sense of what she had seen, Pyramine dug into the wolf's abdominal cavity, flinging aside the viscera with blood-soaked hands. It was messy, but he had been so savage during the fight that she saw his rejection of unpalatable parts as a sign of refinement.

When he finished, he brought his head down and tore off a piece of rib meat with his teeth. Fascinated and repulsed, she resisted the urge to turn away. Pyramine worked the meat into his mouth, chewed sparingly, and swallowed.

He then gagged, spat, and sprung away from the jettisoned wad of meat as if it had attacked him instead of the other way around.

He looked from the dead wolf to Isodore, in childlike confusion. Blood dripped from his mouth as he muttered an explanation. "It tastes strange."

She explained as gently as she could, as she would to a child. "Perhaps it would taste better once cooked."

"Dragons don't eat cooked . . ." He had the sense to stop himself, so she didn't have to remind him of what he was, and was no longer.

PYRAMINE CARRIED TWO dead wolves back to the cave, leaving the one by the den. Isodore rushed to get to the fire before it went cold. She made it, but had to rebuild the fire from small embers, which meant more smoke. Pyramine sat apart, nibbling spitefully at a rack of raw wolf ribs, though he showed no enthusiasm for it. At least he wasn't choking on the small bites.

She roasted her share and began her bland meal, eating faster than he did. He watched her, holding his uncooked piece in hand while his stomach growled. She offered him a bite of the cooked meat, which he accepted. "Chew it first, like I do. It'll be easier to swallow."

He spent a long time chewing the small bite, moving it around in his mouth before swallowing. Apparently satisfied, he moved to the fire and held his rack of ribs over the flames. But he didn't first skewer it on a stick as she had. He held it in his hand.

Isodore watched aghast, wondering when he would withdraw his hand from the hungry flames. He clenched his teeth to bear the discomfort but kept his hand over the fire. It was not until the hair on his arm glowed orange and turned to smoke did she jump up, shouting. "Stop it! You'll get burned!"

He fell back, rubbing his singed skin, confusion on his face layered over pain.

"You're not a dragon. You can burn."

He nodded, then stared with fascination at the reddened skin from his wrist to his thumb. It was wrinkled and raw. He poked at it, but what pain there was must have been bearable to him. Later, she would have to teach him that men do not wrestle with wolves or hold their hands over flames. At present, other matters were more pressing.

"See how I did this?" She showed him her skewer.

He copied, selecting a crude stick and forcing it through the ribs. He held it over the fire, but he was impatient and inattentive. His piece caught fire and burned. She would have to cook for him, but that was expected.

He doesn't know how to be a man, she thought, watching him wait for his food. He's like a child. How can I kill a child?

While he ate, she set up another skewer, holding it in place with rocks while she melted a bit of ice for them to drink. She used the leftover water to clean the blood off him. He stared at her, mesmerized, as she rubbed blood off his hands. It made her feel an unexpected tenderness toward him. She cradled the back of his head with one hand while cleaning wolf blood from his face. He melted in her hands. His neck lost all stiffness, so she knelt behind him to brace him against her chest while she scrubbed. Bloody water dripped onto his chest. She wiped it off with a fistful of her tunic.

The warmth of his naked muscular back seeped into her belly and breasts, reminding her of the final hours of the spell, when the gray heap of soft flesh became a man at her hands. She had never laid her hands on a man's naked body before, and she found it distracting. During the spell, she had fought against the distraction by chanting louder, as though she were speaking to him. Now, she was overwhelmed.

She turned her eyes away, but couldn't turn her mind away. She studied the textures and scratch marks on the cave walls, the warm glow of the firelight on them, the soot stain on the ceiling over the fire pit. But it was no use. It was as if he were casting a spell on her, reaching inside her as she had done to him during the transformation spell. She was the subject, and he the sorcerer.

She looked at herself, sharply aware of her appearance. Embarrassed by it. Her tunic was filthy from two months of difficult life. Made of undyed wool, it was soiled through with the dirt that she sat, crawled, and slept on. There were grass stains over her elbows, knees, and buttocks. Blood had accumulated up and down the front from wrestling the skin off the meat that Pyramine gave her. Over her chest, the hole from his claw and a dark blood stain suggested a corpse long abandoned on the battlefield. Her tunic was too short and torn ragged. The roasting of meat had left a thin but stubborn layer of soot on her hands. Attempts to clean them only smeared black marks on her thighs and sleeves. Her nails were black around their perimeters. The dry mountain air left her skin cracked. She couldn't see much of her hair, but she could feel it, tangled like a rat's nest. Clumsy as Pyramine was in many ways, he was the most striking man she had ever seen. And she was a mess.

She crawled back to her side of the fire and rotated her skewer to turn the meat. Nursing a feeling of inadequacy, she stared into the fire, isolating herself with her thoughts. She wasn't sure they were hers, for she had never, in all her preparations toward a life with Pyramine, anticipated such ideas. Somehow, she had neglected to think of the essential sexual role of a mate. Not even with Sir Rowan, never in those years, had she dared acknowledge a truly carnal impulse. Now, denying it seemed pointless.

Pyramine got on his hands and knees and crawled around the fire to her. Her heart pounded at the sight of his approach. The condition that had afflicted her had a clear, noticeable effect on him. What she had worked to keep hidden was threatening to break its cover.

She tried to scoot backward, away from him, but her legs hesitated. Instead of backing up, her shoulders came down to the ground. He came up between her legs. Finally forced to look at him, she saw in his blue eyes a hint of desire, spinning in a powerful swirl of intrigue and fear that matched how she felt inside.

He positioned himself over her, then proceeded to try to reach her through her clothing. He hadn't learned everything he needed after all. She pulled up her tunic and slip so he could proceed, without passing judgment on his callowness, only grateful that he desired her despite her filthy appearance.

She wondered how much pain she would experience, how

much pleasure she would feel. She forgot to breathe until she had to gasp for air. Pyramine found his way into her and settled into his rhythm. To her relief, the pain subsided, and the discomfort was low compared with having her maidenhead checked.

Pyramine watched her at first. Then he was overcome by his own bodily experience. A spirit seemed to possess him. His rhythm quickened as if it was beyond his control. His back and neck arched. His eyes rolled toward the ceiling. He shuddered, then became still.

Pyramine waited, as if to see what would happen next. He regained his senses. Just as Isodore realized there could be pleasure for her, it was over. She looked at him for a long moment, wondering what he would do. She had never before thought this far, and he was even more lost. He got to his knees, but remained bent over, staring, not at her face, but where he had entered her. She found it rude and slapped her clothing back in place. Looking disappointed, he returned to his side of the fire.

She was left to contemplate, on her own, the brief exercise. They had consummated their marriage, but he had yet to kiss or embrace her. He hadn't said a word. Hadn't looked into her eyes the way she'd dreamed her husband would. It was an act of animal impulse, like fighting the wolves. He settled in beside the fire, distracted again by a still erect penis.

She felt foolish and discarded. Had he protected her from the wolves out of love, or had he merely been guarding his possession? She resented herself for desiring him, and her body for responding to him. But she was tired. Too tired to talk, too tired to move, and too tired to think. Too tired for anger or sadness, for wallowing in disappointment. Feeling his solitary dragon presence across the fire, she rolled away from him, curled up and closed her eyes, consoling herself with one final thought before she drifted off to much-needed sleep. He didn't know how to be a man. He was just a child.

40

Point of No Return

Isodore woke to find Pyramine throwing rocks at a tree outside the cave. No longer throwing like a child, he had the fluid form of a man launching a spear. She watched him learn to use his new body, until he noticed her. He came to her, lowered himself to his knees and handed her a piece of meat that was lying on the ground.

"Sorceress, I kept your food from burning!" The meat was still on its skewer. Even in her groggy state, she could tell it was cold and dry from overcooking. But he was right—it wasn't burned.

"I cooked food well. I shall need your service no longer."

She sat her tired body up, figuring that he wasn't speaking of leaving her but of his ability to cook his own food. She ran both hands through her hair, waiting for her circulation to wake as she squinted at the filtered light in the forest outside the cave. A new day was well under way, perhaps even past midday.

The uncooked head and neck of the gray wolf lay on one side of the fire pit, emitting a pungent odor. On the other side were the bones of the front legs. They had been picked clean, except for the feet and small morsels of cooked meat. Overnight, he had learned to roast meat without burning it or himself. Reason enough for his pride.

She went outside off to the side of the entrance, seeking privacy. While she squatted to urinate, she noticed that the second wolf carcass was missing. When she turned back toward the cave again, she called out, "What happened to the other—"

She never had her privacy, for he had positioned himself within view of her. This was worse than Trand spying on the girls bathing in the streams. She burned with indignation.

He remained cool with ignorance. "The other wolf was taken by a bear in the night. I couldn't catch it. But I have learned to run fast. Next time, I will catch it."

She hurried past the dense, ignorant man-child. Back in the cave, she paced, pondering the unexpected problem of how to live with this new Pyramine. He watched her, his head cocked at a lazy angle. She ignored him for as long as she could.

"I wish to mate again," he announced.

"No!" she snapped, reacting to memories of the night's event. "You can't. I don't want to."

"We are mates. You agreed to it."

"Well . . ." She made some sounds of objection before finding the right words. "I did not agree to be your servant. We can't mate whenever you wish to."

"Why not? We are mates. That did not end."

"That is the way of men. And you are a man."

His body tensed. Muscles hardened, reminding her of his extraordinary strength, and what it had done to the wolves. For an instant she feared he would attack her and take her against her will.

"How do men do this?"

Relieved that he didn't advance toward her, she gave herself a moment to consider. She was in no mood to explain, but he must learn to be a man somehow. And if she didn't teach him, who would? She resented the burden of this responsibility, but she saw no other way. She recalled once thinking that perhaps he could read her mind. That would prove useful right now.

"Well . . . both of us have to agree," she started with no enthusiasm.

"We have."

"Then, you have to wait for me to give myself to you. You can't simply take me. That's wrong."

He nodded. "Very well. Give yourself to me."

"You can't order me to do it! You must be kind and courteous. Then I'll give myself to you."

"Why is that necessary? We are already mates."

"It's the way of men. And you are a man."

"Men burn sorcerers. I don't."

The argument was simplistic and coarse, but strong, like him. It forced her to think.

"Fine. What about dragons? Do they mate any time the male wishes?"

"Yes, when the dragoness is receptive."

"Is that all the time?"

"In the spring."

"Women and sorceresses are different. We are receptive year round, but we require kindness and courtesy."

He thought for a moment, nodding to himself then straightened. "Very well. I will be kind and courteous. Let's proceed." He took a step toward her and reached out his hand.

She turned her shoulders. "No! You must show it through your actions, time and time again, not words in the moment. Then you must wait for me to give myself to you."

He sighed, still frowning. Instead of understanding, he became more frustrated.

"How long must I wait?"

"I don't know. I'll decide when the time comes."

"You will decide?"

"Yes." To ensure he didn't think she tricked him, she turned it around. "And should I wish to mate when you don't, I must wait until you give yourself to me. We can mate any time of year, not just spring. But only when we give ourselves to each other."

He gave it some thought, then shuffled away in a sullen mood, leaving her relieved but more irritated than before. She sat and stared into the cold fire pit, sulking.

Their relationship had been simpler when he was a dragon. She found herself seeking comfort in their past conversations, learning the nature of dragons and wondering where their places were in God's creation. She recalled his admiration of her spirit, and working together to understand the spellbook. The two of them, against the world of men, had bonded over those difficult weeks. Now, she had a man and all the trouble that came with men.

The unpleasant surprise of this day made her think whether it would have been any different had she become a dragon instead. She would have been scared to death of leaving the nest. Recalling her brief but that terrifying time on his back, she wondered if flying wasn't as simple as just flapping one's wings. Perhaps she should be more forgiving, but would have to wait until her resentment passed.

As the two sat in the cave, stilled by mutual resentment, a boy appeared outside the entrance and peered in. He was exceptionally quiet. Neither she nor Pyramine heard him before that point. He was perhaps ten years of age and carried a long, straight, sharpened branch for a spear. He wore an old sack with holes for his head and arms and a deerskin kilt. His hair was long and unkempt, his skin brown—a woodlander. He smiled at Isodore.

Pyramine stood and marched toward him. "This nest is mine!"

The declaration carried an unmistakable threat. The boy backed away.

"Go!" Pyramine ran at him, screaming.

The boy turned and dashed down the ramp. Isodore came out and watched his wiry legs carry him until he disappeared in the trees. She scanned the woods. No people, no wolves. She went back to sit by the fire. Pyramine returned to the entrance and stood guard.

She didn't think that he intended to be rude, but he must learn to deal with people properly. Dragons may be solitary creatures, but their lives now would be easier if they could befriend the woodlanders who inhabited this forest. Trade and mutual protection were a normal way of life for the woodlanders as much as for her people.

Pyramine was doing everything wrong, but it wasn't right to blame him. In the world of dragons, she had been the ignorant one, and he had patiently taught her. Now, in the world of men, how could she leave him to his ignorance? If he was ever to learn to be a man, it would take much teaching and patience.

She breathed deep and exhaled. "You must treat strangers with kindness and courtesy, as you would me."

"That man wanted to steal you."

"He was just a boy and he didn't want me. He has no use for me. He was only curious. Perhaps this was his cave, and we took it, as my people took the forest from his people."

Pyramine gave a hesitant nod. After some contemplation, he came to sit by her. "What must I do to be kind and courteous?"

She was taken aback to have a man ask such a question. Even her children, whom she had to teach to be kind and courteous, had never posed the question.

"You mustn't scream and threaten people without good cause. If they don't mean to harm you, you must treat them with courtesy."

"I didn't scream, or threaten you."

"That's good, but you must do more for me because I am your mate—your wife. You must listen to me, and talk with me, the way we talked when you were a dragon. You must protect me, like you did from the wolves. Help me when I need help. You have your duties to me, and I have my duties to you."

He was to bring food for her to cook. Be gentle with her, in word and in deed. Never use unkind words. Never threaten or frighten her. Be kind to their children. He must be loyal to her. In return, she would be loyal to him, cook for him and make clothes to keep him warm. She would be kind and courteous toward him and teach their children to do the same.

With each thing she asked for, she felt a rekindled hope for their future. To what degree he could live up to her wishes, she could only guess, but he listened as if he understood her requests, if not the rationale for men's customs.

Out of context, her long list must sound demanding to him. It did to her. She would never articulate such a list to a normal man. A normal man would take extreme exception to a woman telling him how he should behave, even if he agreed with her. Pyramine was better than a normal man that way.

She omitted the law of men that required a wife to obey her husband. She was in some ways grateful he didn't know about men's unfair laws. He could well reason that it was within his rights to order her to submit herself to mating any time he wished. In general, however, she thought men's laws were good, and she wanted him to follow them.

Of her omissions, she said, "I may think of more and tell you another time."

"It is very complicated," he observed gloomily.

"Perhaps men are more complicated than dragons. But you agreed to become a man, and you must be a good one. When I agreed to be your mate, I believed you to be a good dragon. Now, you must be a good man."

"A good—"

He stopped at the sound of footsteps and male voices outside the cave. She heard them too. They both held their breaths. Whoever were approaching didn't care for stealth. From the ramp up to the cave, two wicked iron spearheads rose into view atop long shafts.

"Be silent," Pyramine whispered. He pointed to an alcove along the cave wall and she tiptoed over. Though not hidden, she could squeeze herself into the alcove's shadow.

Two men, one tall and one shorter, walked up to the wide cave entrance. Dressed in tunics down to their knees, with boots on their feet, they were clearly not woodlanders. Nor were they Knights of the Cross. Or the Crown. Pyramine stood and approached them. They looked tired and weary, but upon finding him clothed with a dirty makeshift kilt, each man allowed himself a smirk.

Pyramine held up a hand to halt them. "Greetings, men. This nest belongs to me. You may leave unharmed."

It was a better treatment than the boy's, but not by much. The men glanced at each other, breaking their weariness with a snicker.

"If you leave, I will not hurt you. If you don't, I will kill you." Pyramine was bigger than both men, but they weren't intimidated.

"Don't give us orders," cautioned the tall man. "We come in the name of the duke, who rules this land. Tell us who you are, so that we may proceed."

"And where you came from," added the second man. He looked

past Pyramine and scanned the cave. His eyes lingered on Isodore before returning to Pyramine.

Pyramine stood with his fingers curled and stiff. "I am Pyramine. I came from the fire. Now, you must ..."

"Don't trifle with us, man. We're on an urgent task. Have you seen a dragon come this way?"

Isodore gasped.

"Many dragons come this way," replied Pyramine. "This land belongs to dragons. You must leave immediately."

"Answer our questions and we'll be on our way. We're looking for a black beast," said the tall man. "It has captured a woman."

Isodore's heart pounded. Each of the spearman's words brought them ever closer to her. They must be dragonslayers. Where were their wagons and hay-covered battle garments? How could they be here, so far past the frontier? How did they know to look for a black dragon with a woman captive? Unless, they were the ravens who had called when she passed overhead. Why didn't they recognize her?

Pyramine looked from one man to the other. "Do you intend to kill the dragon?"

"Of course."

"It's no longer here. It ended in the fire."

"A dragon. Ended in a fire." He shook his head. "Don't jest with us. We're on an urgent quest. We—"

"Your quest is futile. Leave now."

"He's hiding something," said the second man.

"We're placing you under arrest, on the authority of the duke. Yield immediately, to spare your life."

The men lowered their spears. Pyramine took a step back and sank into his legs, like a cat ready to spring. The men exchanged incredulous glances, and in doing so, they were a split second too slow to react.

Pyramine swatted the spears from his face and lunged for the short man's throat, coming so fast that the man backed away and fell. On top of him, Pyramine pushed his chin aside and bit down on his neck.

The tall man kicked Pyramine hard in the ribs. He regripped his spear and drove it into Pyramine's side, screaming a primal battle cry.

Pyramine arched upward under the pain. From beneath, his victim slammed a knee into his crotch. He howled and rolled off.

The tall man's spear struck him in the chest as he hit the ground. Pyramine grabbed the spear's neck, wrestling for control. It broke with Pyramine in possession of the spearhead.

The man swung the broken shaft madly. Pyramine held up an arm to shield himself. The beating had no effect. Pyramine even tried to grab the headless shaft. Seeing this, his attacker tossed it into the bushes between the trees, stepped back and drew his sword.

The shorter man, whom Pyramine had bitten, staggered to his feet. Blood leaked from the bite wound on his neck. He gripped his spear with both hands and moved in.

"Don't," cautioned the tall man, stepping forward and brandishing the sword. "He'll take it from you." When he swung his sword, Pyramine blocked it. The blade struck his forearm, and he grabbed it.

The tall man smiled. Everyone, even Isodore, knew what would happen next, except for Pyramine, who wrapped both hands around the blade. The sword drew back quickly.

Pyramine screamed.

Isodore wanted the savage fight to stop, but she had no time to think. The swordsman came swinging again. Pyramine took several cuts before learning to dodge and stay out of the sword's range. He didn't run, however. Urgent voices filtered up from below. More men were coming.

The shorter man didn't carry a sword. He used his spear to corner Pyramine but kept from attacking, as his partner had cautioned. Blood leaked from his neck. A dark red streak stretched down his body to his foot. He moved ever more slowly, as though he were falling asleep. Then, suddenly, his knee buckled and he collapsed.

Pyramine lunged for the fallen man's spear and retrieved it, taking a sword wound across his back before getting away. Armed, he turned to face his opponent.

Isodore jumped out of hiding and yelled, "Stop! Just stop! Please!"

"Stay back, sorceress! I will protect you!"

The words shocked her. The swordsman had heard. She saw it on his face. Panicked, she ran around him and put him between herself and Pyramine.

"I'm not with him. Help me! Please!"

The swordsman hesitated. Though confused, he wisely kept his eyes on his opponent.

"You're with me!" cried Pyramine, trying to get around the swordsman to reach her.

"Up there! Up there!" came voices from below.

Isodore backed away, down the ramp.

"No!" cried Pyramine. "Sorceress, they're coming!"

She turned away to hide from the horror of his words, just as two men emerged on the wood and charged past her. One wore a surcoat emblazoned with a familiar emblem, a golden cross over a suffering dragon. She looked to his face, but he'd passed her.

"Landis!" he called. Then seeing the short man's body on the ground, he added, "What happened?"

Isodore recognized his voice. She had conversed with that voice at the feast and for an hour, strolling around Auch's cathedral. Sir Wilfred.

Landis glanced quickly at the knight, then back to his adversary. His face gave a hint of relief. Sir Wilfred slowed to a walk; his sword was drawn, but he stayed out of reach of Pyramine's spear.

Pyramine looked past Sir Wilfred, at Isodore. A river of tears rose up in her. It blurred her vision and spilled down her cheeks. She wanted to look away, but it was already too late. She'd seen his eyes. She wanted to run, but she feared he'd call out to her again.

"He's very tough," Landis advised. "He killed Borbas with his bare hands." He, Sir Wilfred, and the third man took up positions surrounding Pyramine.

Sir Wilfred raised his sword, pointing it at Pyramine. "Drop the weapon and yield. Or forfeit your life."

Perhaps Pyramine sensed Sir Wilfred's confidence. Perhaps he recognized the emblem on the surcoat. His spear twitched, but he didn't attack.

"I've already given him that chance, Sir Wilfred. He will fight."

Pyramine suddenly turned and ran at the man who had come up with Sir Wilfred. Their spears clashed. Pyramine forced the other man's aside, knocking him off balance as he resisted. He stumbled backward as Pyramine rotated his spear to drive through him. Sir Wilfred dashed after, and stabbed his sword into Pyramine's back before veering to the side to avoid crashing into him. The confident grin on Sir Wilfred's face faded as he watched Pyramine recover.

"He's very tough, sir," Landis admonished again.

Sir Wilfred was collecting his wits when Pyramine turned the spear on him. Driven back by the spear's longer reach, Sir Wilfred exhibited surprising lightness as he danced and parried Pyramine's spear thrusts. His path swept out a gradual curve to position himself uphill on the ramp. The tall man tried to sneak a blow against Pyramine's back side, but Pyramine feigned charges to keep him back. Sir Wilfred swung hard at the thrusting spear and broke it behind the head, where it had been weakened from multiple meetings with the dragonslayer's renowned sharp blade.

Sir Wilfred pointed the sword at Pyramine's throat. "Drop the shaft," he ordered. Pyramine swung it instead. Sir Wilfred parried more thrusts, then knocked another foot off the spear shaft. He stabbed Pyramine in the lower chest, stopping him cold. Pyramine grimaced with pain and lunged for the knight's throat.

Sir Wilfred fell backward, with Pyramine on top of him. The sword burst out of Pyramine's back. The two wrestled before Landis stabbed Pyramine in the side.

Pyramine roared and leaped up, backing away. Seeing Sir Wilfred's sword in his chest, he slid it out and took it by the handle. Landis looked aghast and took a step back.

The healing spell! Isodore covered her mouth. *He can't be killed. What have I done?*

Pyramine came at Landis, sweeping Sir Wilfred's sword in wide but ineffective horizontal cuts. His adversary stayed out of range. Sir Wilfred sat up, blood spurting in pulses from the dark wound in his neck. He clasped a hand over it and tried to rise. He got to his knees, paused, then collapsed face down in the dirt.

"Sir Wilfred!" Isodore cried out.

Men ran up the ramp past her, swords and spears in hand. One had a tethered crossbow.

"Isodore?" someone called.

She turned around and immediately recognized the caller. "Galt!"

He stopped and placed a hand on her shoulder, as if to see if she were real. He scanned her face and her clothing, bewildered. She could read a hundred questions in his eyes, but the one he asked was "Where's the dragon?"

"Sorceress, come! I will protect you!" called Pyramine.

Galt turned uphill, frowning at the gathering dragonslayers. Isodore panicked.

"Sorcer—!"

"He's the dragon!" she blurted to drown out the awful words. Galt looked confused. "That man there!" she said, "He's the dragon!"

Galt took a few running steps up the hill but paused, staring in disbelief. He opened his mouth, but couldn't find his words.

"He's the dragon! You have to kill him!" Isodore screamed to drown out Pyramine's voice.

Galt's mouth closed. His face went from confusion to resolution. He turned toward the cave. As he ran up, Pyramine sent a roar echoing in the forest. He hurled down a boulder the size of a basket. Galt jumped aside and watched in shock as the object thumped past him, spinning.

The dragonslayers heeded the two bodies on the ground and the sword in Pyramine's hand. They formed a line but kept their distance. Landis warned them that he could take their spears. Those with swords shifted to the front. A crossbowman watched from the back.

Several men and two more knights in surcoats dashed past

Isodore. One stopped and looked back, cocking his head at a questioning angle. He looked her up and down and asked, "Isodore?"

"Sir Dalton!"

He didn't speak to her but pointed to a dragonslayer coming behind. "You! Take her to safety." Then he continued upward.

As Sir Dalton and Sir Gustav joined the line, Pyramine backed into the cave. He kept his eyes on the dragonslayers closing in, except when he looked past them, at her. Then the dragonslayers closed ranks and blocked her line of sight. She knew that he knew. She had betrayed him.

A hand grabbed her shoulder from behind. "Come with me, lass."

She stumbled as the dragonslayer tried to guide her. "What if he can't be killed?" she asked.

He looked up the ramp. "Don't worry. He has no chance."

Pyramine backed into the cave and the dragonslayer line followed him in. Why would he do that? To find a position protecting his back side? Or was he luring them into a trap? The crossbowman watched from the entrance.

The man guarding her attempted to bring her down the hill, but she fought him to stay. He managed to only pull her behind the wide trunk of an ancient pine. She kept looking around it toward the cave, where the sound of the fight was rising.

"Surround him!"

"Keep him in the cave!"

"Where's the dragon?"

"It's him."

"This man?"

"Good God!"

There were clangs of clashing swords then a scream she thought was Pyramine's. More swords clashed. Another scream.

"He's done that before."

"Woodness!"

"No spears! No spears! Back off! He'll take them from you!"

Landis's voice.

More swords clanged.

Sir Dalton yelled, "Move them! Now! Before they die there!"

Men were down, but the battle continued. Pyramine must still be standing. Two dragonslayers carried out a man in agony, a gushing cut across the side of his thigh. Another man was pulled out, his hand held against his abdomen and blood-soaked tunic. Yet another left the fight with a half a sword in his hands.

A second crossbowman came out of the trees and headed up the ramp. The first, who was watching the fight from the entrance, called into the cave. "Sir Dalton! Shall I use the crossbow?"

"No! He's just a man. But stay back. He's absolutely mad!"

Over the din of swords and screams, Sir Dalton tried to redirect the fight. "Back up! All of you, back up! Surround him. Two deep. Don't let him pass."

There was the sound of footsteps as men repositioned. A third crossbowman came up the ramp. The three positioned themselves at the center and on either side of the entrance. All pointed their weapons into the cave.

The sound of battle subsided.

"You," commanded Sir Dalton, "who are you?"

No answer.

"Where are your clothes?"

Still no answer.

"You're hurt, very badly. Yield, and we will help you. I will let you live."

Isodore gasped.

"Can you talk?" asked Sir Dalton.

"He can. He did," Landis answered for Pyramine.

"Does he . . . feel any pain?" asked Galt.

A deep growl rumbled.

"Look at him," said Sir Gustav. "He's hardly bleeding! Why haven't his entrails spilled?"

"Why's he not dead?" asked a nervous voice.

Isodore bit her lip. Pyramine was taking severe injuries but continued fighting? What if he killed Galt? What if he defeated the dragonslayers? Surely he would seek vengeance against her.

The long silence in the cave ended with the commander's voice.

"Sir Gustav. Sir Galt. Either side of him. Hornblum, guard his—"

A roar interrupted Sir Dalton, then screams and two clangs of striking swords.

"Stop him!" shouted Sir Dalton.

More swords clanged, but if anyone tried to stop him, they failed. There was a scream, but it wasn't Pyramine's.

The crossbowman at the entrance jumped back and turned away, barely managing to keep his weapon as Pyramine charged past him, hands reaching for the crossbow. Pyramine had lost the kilt she gave him. Red wounds covered him from head to ankles, from one arm to the other. He held a sword in one hand and a spear in the other.

Isodore wished she had not been looking, for he saw her immediately. His face was bloodied. He ran toward her, limping from the deep cut in his thigh, but he ran, his eyes wide, fixed on her. The dragonslayer guarding her pulled her back behind the tree and stepped forward, unsheathing his sword. But her guilt wouldn't let her hide. She stepped out to face him.

Pyramine alternated long and short steps on one weakened leg, yet he was still faster than the men pouring out of the cave. As he ran, a dark rod burst from his chest with a spray of blood and flew toward her. She flinched, but the rod suddenly stopped and fell to the ground. Two more rods crossed harmlessly in front of him, laying down their limp tethers.

The strike staggered Pyramine.

As he looked down at the first rod and the tether leading back through his chest, the limp rope came alive and pulled taut, dragging the blood-covered bolt across the forest duff, back toward him. He stared at it for a second before a look of recognition came to his eyes, which immediately turned to anger. He spun around and swung the sword at the tether reeling out of his back.

Just when the sharp blade would have sliced through the tether, another came between them, thrust there by the outstretched arm of a lunging Sir Gustav. The knight struck three times while returning to a fighting stance. He had little effect other than etching more wounds in Pyramine's lacerated body. Pyramine, on the other hand, had time for a single strike, a high chop, like an ax, down over Sir Gustav's shoulder.

The knight raised his sword over his head to protect himself. Pyramine's two-handed chop was powerful, smashing through Sir Gustav's sword, sending half of it spinning to the ground.

Sir Gustav dropped to one knee to buy a split second of time to dodge the deadly blade. He rolled onto his back. Pyramine wound up for the killing blow when Sir Dalton's blade plunged into his side. Pyramine staggered, then chopped at Sir Gustav's head anyway. Galt's blade parried.

Sir Gustav sprung away, yelling, "Sword!" One of the dragon-slayers turned over his blade, and backed out of the fight.

The knights circled Pyramine, moving in grimly, and the remaining dragonslayers surrounded them. No longer against the cave wall, anywhere Pyramine turned, he had a sword at his back. He cut long horizontal sweeps to keep his attackers at bay, but they were three swords and he had no help. They were trained, and he had had his weapon for only minutes.

Sir Dalton, Sir Gustav, and Galt took their openings. They sliced into his arms, legs, and his side. They respected his brute power. They didn't parry but shuffled back after each strike. The time for mercy was over. Pyramine screamed and tried to fend them off. Blood didn't pour out of him, but each cut seemed to weaken and slow him a bit more. At last, he dropped to his knees. The knights' swords rose and fell over him. Rose and fell, bloodier each time.

No longer a fight, it was an execution. Galt hacked muscle from Pyramine's shoulder, and Pyramine's sword arm went limp. He raised his other arm in a desperate bid to defend himself. Sir Dalton's sword sliced crosswise. Pyramine's hand fell to the ground, while his arm, with its red stump, remained to protect his head. Sir Gustav drove his blade into Pyramine's heart. The knight took his sword by the cross-guard and, with a wicked snarl on his face, cranked the weapon. The hole opened like an eye and erupted blood.

"Now, he bleeds," observed Gustav.

Isodore gasped and covered her mouth. The dragonslayer

guarding her put an arm around her shoulders and guided her behind the tree. But she kept watching. She wanted Pyramine to stand up and run for his life. But the cuts in his muscles left him little strength.

Sir Dalton put a sword on Pyramine's hand-less arm and pushed it out of the way. "Sir Galt," he commanded.

Galt stepped forward and braced himself on a wide stance. He wound his sword arm across his chest, took a breath, and unleashed the blade into the side of Pyramine's neck.

Isodore ducked, as she wanted Pyramine to do. Eyes closed, she heard something hit the ground, followed by something else. She listened for Pyramine's voice, even just a murmur. There was no sound other than the heavy breaths of those still standing. An eerie quiet fell over the forest. Each passing second of it brought certainty and dread.

A voice sounded, so subdued that it was hardly recognizable as the regiment commander. "Who in God's name? What in God's name?"

Isodore collapsed at the foot of the ancient pine, weeping.

41

The Dragon's Curse

Galt knelt and placed a hand on Isodore's back. She wept and trembled, unable to say anything. He walked her down the slope, away from the dead man, holding her hand and clasping her shoulder. She looked back toward Pyramine's body, but it was blocked by the gathered dragonslayers.

Galt guided her toward level ground at the bottom of the hill. Her legs buckled, and he lowered her down. He sent a young squire for water and a towel. She and Galt sat, waiting. She wanted to be alone, to curl up and cry, perhaps says some final words to Pyramine. To do anything but be in the company of people. Galt kept his arm around her as she sat curled up. Long moments passed, but it wasn't enough time for her and would never be.

The squire returned with a full skin of water. "I can't find a towel, Sir Galt. The carts are still far behind."

Isodore drank. Galt gave her his surcoat to use as a towel and poured water for her to wash the tears from her face. She looked in puzzlement at the black stains her face left on the golden cross.

"There's soot all over your face," Galt said. "What happened?"

"I . . ." she struggled through her first coherent sentence since the battle. How could she begin to describe what had happened to her over the past two months? "Wood fires. I had to . . . cook . . . and keep warm . . ."

Soot. That was why the men hadn't immediately recognized her. In her disheveled state, in torn, filthy clothing, she must look like a woodlander to them.

"You were injured?" Galt said of the bloodstain on her tunic.

"Yes, but it's . . . not as bad as it appears," she said of the wound that had nearly killed her.

Dragonslayers, spread out afar, gathered and made their way up the ramp in ones and twos. Relief and triumph filled their voices when they saw Galt with Isodore. Some cheered, some roared, though each man quickly ceased his noise and passed quietly to give the two space. The latecomers headed up the hill, eager to hear details of the battle.

Isodore expended all the water. She stalled, afraid to rejoin the dragonslayers. Galt awaited her. She felt a need to talk with him, explain away the things he had heard and seen. Voices up the hill were asking questions about what had transpired. "How could he be so strong?" "Why didn't he die?" "Who did he call 'sorceress'?" "Who was he?"

How could Galt not have those same questions?

She didn't know how much time had passed before someone downstream called out, "All men, if you are not injured, down here! We have to clear a path for the carts." Dragonslayers stood their sluggish bodies to answer the call. The men headed down, giving Galt and Isodore a wide berth. After they passed, she stood, and Galt walked her up the hill.

The wounded dragonslayers were being moved from the cave entrance into the cave. Branches had been laid over the faces of the dead dragonslayers. Nearby, Sir Dalton and Sir Gustav stood talking with Landis. Isodore felt weak again, and sat down at the tree where she had waited out the fight. Galt stayed with her.

Eventually, Landis and the two knights left. When they passed, Isodore kept her eyes on the ground. She shivered. Galt's hand on her far shoulder pulled her close to him.

"Are you cold?" he asked.

"I have to see his body."

"Of course."

He walked with her, but as they approached the body, he tried to hold her back. "I don't advise this, Isodore. It's horrific."

"I must," she said, almost to herself. She didn't quite know why she had to. To face him, perhaps. To accept his hated. To make sure he was dead, she could say if Galt asked. He didn't.

Pyramine's naked body lay on its back, with his knees bent and his feet under him. His severed hand was next to him, but his head was two steps away. Blood painted his body in long thin streaks. He had, just as Sir Gustav had said, hardly bled, despite the countless wounds, big and small. Except for the gaping hole that Gustav's sword pried open in Pyramine's heart, and the open vessels in his neck, blood seemed to have only trickled out.

His face was frozen on the severed head, not in anger, but in fear. It wasn't the face she'd thought she saw when he'd charged down the ramp toward her. The blood on his mouth, from the men he'd bitten, made him look like a victim. He was just a child. Could he have been afraid? Afraid of dying? Of dying betrayed and abandoned?

A wave of sadness and guilt washed over her, heavy in its finality. She wanted to mourn, as if she had lost an acquaintance she had just begun to know. She felt responsible for bringing this man into the world, only to be violently destroyed for the crime of knowing her secret.

He had been a dragon, beautiful from above, terrifying from below and hideous up close. Now, beyond hideous, reduced to a butchered body resembling meat more than corpse. She had done this to him. She had calculated and schemed, lied to a creature too naive to appreciate the depth of human deception. A creature who had looked through her soot-covered face and saw her beautiful spirit. Some people were kind and courteous, she had told him, as if men were better than dragons. What must he think of her now? Of her beautiful spirit?

She turned away from his body and, step by hesitant step, picked her way down the hill, so absorbed in her own thoughts that she had forgotten that Galt was with her. When she became aware of it, she was all alone.

FOUR DRAGONSLAYERS HAD perished, including Sir Wilfred and Borbas. Two had died in the cave for failing to heed Landis's warnings about the strength and resilience of their deceptively vulnerable-looking adversary. Others suffered injuries of varying degrees, one very severe.

A dragonslayer and a woodlander guide were sent ahead to inform the archbishop of the regiment's success and casualties.

A dozen men were sent back to find the carts they had not seen since they rushed ahead to find Isodore. They would bring equipment by hand if the cart couldn't reach them. They had to dig graves in dirt crisscrossed by age-old roots.

The regiment was hungry. Sir Gustav led a group on a hunt. Fires were built in preparation. Men found enough level ground a ways down the hillside and set up camp there. Many quickly fell asleep. Galt built a smaller fire for himself and Isodore, away from the men's camp.

The hunting party returned with a deer, and the men skinned and roasted it over their fire. Despite the activity, the camp remained quiet, something she hadn't expected. After questions had been answered for the men who'd missed the battle, there was little conversation for hours, save some whispering. It was eerie. Isodore thought the men were simply tired, but that wasn't it. The camp was so quiet because Sir Wilfred, the talkative knight, who had always made her feel welcome when she needed it the most, was dead. Her eyes filled up and she cried quietly.

When the deer was cooked, Galt brought her a piece and ate with her.

"I'm sorry so many men died to save me," she told him.

Galt nodded.

"Why did you come?" she asked.

"What?"

Realizing that the context for her question had been private, Isodore added, "That is, how did you know I was alive? I was certain everyone thought I was dead."

"We did, too, for a time."

He told her of the afternoon he put it together with Sir Gustav, of the reports of an odd young dragon stealing bags of fruit.

He wasn't a young dragon, thought Isodore so distinctly that she felt her tongue move.

"Sir Dalton and Sir Wilfred were just as skeptical when I told them. But they could no better accept the reports as coincidental. We dispatched messengers to verify the claims, and the witnesses stood by their accounts. Our messengers even found corroborators for the stories."

"I made my case to the archbishop. My special status was useful after all. I told him this was a test of my worthiness. You were alive and I could abandon you no more than I could disregard signs from God."

From villager accounts of Isodore's capture, the knights determined the dragon's heading. They reasoned that a dragon that small, so far from Dragon's Ridge, and carrying a full-grown adult had to take the most direct path possible back to its home. They proceeded in that direction. Eight days later, they entered the valley that penetrated Dragon's Ridge, but from there, they were confounded.

Confronted with a convoluted terrain, it was hard enough to decide where to go on the ground, let alone guess where Isodore's captor had carried her. "We camped and posted sentries to search the sky. We saw many small beasts, dark and possibly black in color. On the frontier, these little dragons are rare, but here, they're all small. It was impossible to know which one to follow."

Isodore reeled inside each time he referred to dragons a "small" or "beasts."

Oblivious, he continued with modest excitement. "Then we noticed one peculiar dragon. It was carrying, of all things, tree branches. Leafless, dead branches. We thought perhaps it was building a nest, like birds do. But it was the only dragon doing this. It took the branches up the mountain then came down and took more up, again and again. It was a peculiar behavior, but then, so was taking fruit.

"We followed it up the mountain. We couldn't move as fast, but God helped us. The dragon returned. It flew back and forth the same way, carrying dead branches up the mountain. It was telling us where to go. It turned into corridors we could never have guessed."

Isodore kept still and quiet. She allowed herself a look of surprise, which Galt could expect, to conceal her shock as she recalled the many trips Pyramine made to bring firewood for the transformation spell. While she had sat on that ledge studying the spell, Pyramine was leading the regiment to his nest. The sentries were already turning the tables on him, watching him from the concealment in the forest as dragons often watched men from fog banks.

"We had no idea how high we had to go, or what obstacles we'd face. Or what we'd do once we left the forest. But I knew it would be revealed to us. Then one day, the dragon reversed direction. It brought the branches back *down* the mountain! We turned and followed it.

"We rushed down the mountain as fast as we could. Again, it showed us the way. It turned north and we followed. We were strung out for miles because we had to move so fast. There was something about those branches. Wherever it was taking them, that was where we had to be.

"And, by God, that was it! Two days ago, when our scouts signaled us that the dragon was overhead, we looked. We saw it flying, not with a branch in its clutch, but a woman! It was moving too fast for us to see you, but I knew it was you. We raced after you with no more than our weapons, bedrolls and food ration!"

"I heard your calls! Galt, I heard you! You sounded like ravens."

Galt smiled brightly, a disconcerting sight to her, as he had no idea she was still in disbelief. What would he have thought had he seen her riding on Pyramine's back?

"You didn't use the ghost whistle?"

"No. I couldn't make it loud enough. But the woodlander scouts have their own way of signaling. They mimic animals. We made all haste to find you. We walked through two nights with almost no sleep."

Isodore was suddenly and profoundly saddened that the ghost whistle didn't work. Had it worked, she would have known for certain it was Galt. Oh, the things she had done for want of that certainty. While he was rushing to her, she had lain with Pyramine. Galt smiled at her and she returned a false smile of her own. He was so naive, so blissfully oblivious, so easily fooled.

She felt on the verge of bursting and had to end the conversation before she broke down. "Well, that explains why the men are so exhausted. You must be tired, too."

"Yes, but it's the greatest day of my life."

She couldn't bear to look at the joy her false smile gave him. "Some of the men are sleeping. And it will be dark soon. Why don't you sleep too? I'll wait here until you wake."

Galt lay down, still too excited to close his eyes, but soon enough, exhaustion caught up to him, as it did many of his men, and he fell sound asleep. Isodore sat by him, crying softly.

THE CARTS DIDN'T arrive the next day, and the men didn't break camp. It was midday before all of them were rested enough to become their usual selves. Playing, practicing, hunting, more sleeping, and figuring exactly what happened and who said what during the battle. Conversations restarted each time a new dragonslayer arrived. Tidbits circulated of the person now known as "the madman," what he was, what he did, what he said, how he had killed Sir Wilfred, why he hadn't died sooner.

Isodore stayed apart from them so they wouldn't ask her. Unable to hear their hushed conversations however, she feared even more what they might be saying about her. So she snatched bits of their conversations when it was quiet enough for her to listen in.

"How did one naked man kill four of us?"

"He was far stronger than he looked."

"He broke two of our swords, though he had no sword skill himself."

"Someone said Isodore told Sir Galt that he was the dragon."

"Sir Galt?"

"No, the madman."

"How's that?"

"Who did he call a sorceress?"

"What happened to her?"

Confused chatter eventually converged on one conclusion. Somehow, the madman had indeed been the dragon. As for the sorceress, some men shrugged. Others carried puzzled looks long after the conversation.

Whenever they met her eyes, the men would nod and greet Isodore. Whether they were polite or they were ordered not to, she wasn't sure, but they didn't ask her the questions they asked each other. She avoided their eyes when she could, so they wouldn't be encouraged to.

Pockets of dragonslayers continued their discussions in low voices. Sometimes, they glanced at her. Which of them, she wondered, had heard Pyramine's awful words? Which had seen where the madman had been looking?

Strangely, it was the woodlander boys who seemed unaware of the growing rumors and suspicion in the camp. They still smiled at her. She couldn't tell if they talked about the madman or the sorceress, for they spoke a slightly different dialect, and too fast.

A nauseating smell drifted into camp, a smell that, under normal circumstances, would have told her that a rat had died in the cottage thatch.

Sir Gustav and three men walked up the ramp carrying a body up to the other four. Pyramine's last kill. A voice shouted, "I want men up here!" The men trudged up, sensing no urgency.

They foraged and cut branches to cover the five corpses awaiting burial. The thick layers of branches kept the some of the dead's odor from stirring into the breeze. They also kept the ravens from pecking at the dead.

Pyramine wouldn't be buried. They dragged his body by the tether and carried his head and hand on the ends of spears. At a clearing that they swept free of dry detritus, they burned him. His fire was bright.

The men returned, but the knights remained atop the ramp, talking.

Isodore's insides knotted up. The spellbook! The asterium and jewelry left over from the transformation. She couldn't hide her look of distress, so she turned away when they came down. Two knights passed her and blended into camp with no word of anything unusual. Galt stopped to tell her that the equipment should arrive in another day. They could leave after burying their dead.

"I'm so sorry you've lost good men trying to save me." It sounded ironic, for it was her actions that had given Pyramine the strength and resilience to kill them.

"Tell me of your captivity," Galt said, sitting down.

It was an unexpected request, but of course he was curious. She was glad it wasn't one of the questions the men whispered among themselves.

"I . . . was kept in a cave. We stopped at the . . . foot of the mountains, before going to the cave. I tried to escape . . . but I couldn't." She picked what to tell him and what to omit. Her account of the past two months weaved around unspeakable things: spells, a bargain to stay alive, faith she had lost in God and humanity, the carnal union with the madman.

"Why did you say he was the dragon?" Galt asked.

"He . . . he was."

Galt looked at her, waiting, expecting more explanations.

"He changed. And he said he was. One day, I was the dragon's captive. The next, I was his."

Galt frowned. "Isodore, this . . . man, he called out to a . . . sorceress. Do you know whom he referred to?"

"No. I heard him, too. But I don't know who. He . . . seemed to have lost his mind."

"Yes, that is true," said Galt. "No doubt. I've never seen anyone like that."

Guilt weighed on Isodore. She had deceived Pyramine, and now, she was lying to Galt. She had lied all her life to protect herself, but it had always been a necessity. It had never felt like a betrayal until now. She felt tears well up and turned away so Galt wouldn't see. After a moment of her silence, he left.

Later that day, she wandered up the ramp to see if she could find the spellbook. The two men guarding the pile of branches nodded at her, and she veered away.

THERE WAS NO point bringing the carts any closer, given the dense woods. The necessary equipment arrived on the backs of mules and men. Dragonslayers trudged up the ramp for their grim work, taking turns close to the nauseating smell. The men dug five graves and spoke a brief prayer for each fallen dragonslayer. Sir Dalton asked the Lord to look after Sir Wilfred's wife and children. Isodore felt sorry for them, robbed of husband and father by a sorceress.

After the ceremony, Isodore waited for the last man to leave so she could wander into the cave to destroy whatever evidence might incriminate her. But Galt found her.

"It's time to go," he said. "We should get a head start. The men will catch up."

Walking her away, he reached around her back to put a hand on her shoulder. His fingertips came down on the dark red blotch where Pyramine had pierced her, over the old wound that nearly took her life. His hold was courteous. It should have been a comfort, but it felt like new claws closing around her.

42

Rumors of the Damned

A dragonslayer sent ahead with news of Isodore's rescue reached Auch days ahead of the regiment. A party rode out under the banner of the Church to greet the triumphant men the moment they arrived at the first frontier village.

Isodore was whisked away and made presentable with a long bath and clean clothes. The men cleaned up, too, but no clean clothes were brought for them. They arrived in Auch in their muddy, sweat-soaked, bloodstained clothes.

A grand welcome awaited them in Auch. Trumpets blew. Auch's banners flew tall and proud. Crowds waved. Young lasses blew kisses. One by one, and despite their somber mood, the men allowed themselves to be swept up by the cheers. The madman and the events surrounding his death were, for the moment, forgotten.

A host of noblemen received the regiment. The Frankish king even sent his own son, the crown prince, as representative.

The archbishop held Mass, and a grand feast began the celebration. His dragonslayers had accomplished a feat none believed possible. "This is the first time, in the history of heaven and earth, that anyone has been rescued from Dragon's Ridge!" he announced. "By the Knight of God's Miracle!" Not even al-Andalus could make such a boast.

In his sermon, the archbishop heaped praise on the regiment, especially his exemplary chivalrous knights and, in particular, Galt. "The Dragonslayers worked hard," he said, "honed their battle lived honorable, spartan lives for the sake of Christianity." The families of the dragonslayers slain by Pyramine were recognized. The late Sir Wilfred's sword was presented to his eldest son, who the archbishop announced would be joining the dragonslayer corps. The crowd nodded and lifted their chins in pride, for it was they, after all, who had supported the dragonslayers in the face of naysayers.

This was truly the beginning of the end of the dragon scourge. Dragonslayers would no longer hesitate to pursue a beast into Dragon's Ridge, no longer wait while good Christians were carried away in evil claws. To fulfill God's will, a new regiment would be added to the dragonslayer corps, to be led by the Knight of God's Miracle himself. This announcement drew fewer cheers than the others and a few grumbles of more taxes.

At the feast, it seemed the world had gathered to hear all about the unprecedented rescue, the stories of the Knight of God's Miracle and the maiden of Savelle.

Only she was a maiden no longer. And the stories she recounted for the people were simple embellishments of the lies she had told Galt. She hadn't been injured, nor had she cast a spell to heal her wound. She hadn't spoken with the dragon. She had made no bargain. She'd neither sympathized with it nor changed it into the madman. She hadn't given up her maidenhood. All she had done was pray for rescue. She even lied about the location of Pyramine's nest. She didn't know why, though it mattered not, for no one would dare climb those heights.

Isodore hid beneath layers of polite manners and peasant humility, steeled, offering nothing when the dignitaries speculated on the mysterious transformation of the dragon into the madman. They debated over why a dragon would choose to become a man.

"It's the only way they'll carry on. Their days are coming to an end!" said one.

Isodore nodded, her lips closed in thoughtful consideration.

"Easier for them to kill people without having to face the

317

dragonslayers," said another.

"Hmm," she mused.

"The ugly beast saw its reflection in the water and was repulsed," laughed a third.

She mourned the death of her naive dream. She had once thought she could be the emissary between dragons and men. Now, she nodded along as men mocked dragons.

When asked, "How do you think the dragon became the madman?" she did her best to look as puzzled as the questioner.

She cared little that she was deceiving the dignitaries, fearing only that she might be found out. But for others, her deception brought her a heavy guilt: the knights she had come to regard as friends, the dragonslayers, Lord Corvin, his family, his servants, Sir Wilfred's widow and children. But not Mereine and her daughters, who were present but in no celebratory mood.

Isodore could no longer look at Mereine or be close to her after the only time their eyes met. Those green eyes stared in silent rage. Isodore imagined what Galt's mother might have said when she learned that he had chosen to risk the lives of the regiment to pursue a woman who should have been dead. It would have been poison to Isodore's ears.

After the celebrations, she expected to return to Savelle, but Galt couldn't arrange for her journey. "I would like to accompany you, but there are other matters that require my presence here. The region's lords have come for the festivities, and the duke thought it timely to hold a council. My uncle wishes for me to stay close to him. I'll bring you to Savelle soon. Meanwhile, if you wish, you can lodge in Uncle Corvin's home. But . . . mother is there as well."

She declined. Galt agreed that it was best and departed. Oddly, she wondered if he were being entirely forthcoming. Lord Corvin wasn't the kind of man with a taste for things such as the duke's council. Nevertheless, she was in no position to question Galt's truthfulness, after lying to him.

She remained at Auch's abbey, where she had been housed since her return. It was next to the orphanage; both were across the road from the cathedral. She earned her meals by helping with the chores and caring for the orphans.

Little changed at first. Few who hadn't attended the celebration recognized her. Visitors didn't know her name. The monks and nuns spoke little and never deviated from their routines. The orphans were meek. But outside the enclave, she began receiving glances in place of greetings. Furtive, lingering glances, from heads held close in hushed conversations.

Speculation swept through the town about the dragon who had become a man. When that mystery resisted resolution, they chased after another: that of the woman whom the madman had called "sorceress."

Isodore was tied to the madman, of course. She'd said that he was the dragon who'd captured her. But being tied to the madman meant that she was also tied to the unseen sorceress. And speculations about the sorceress had to consider the woman found with the madman.

No longer stopping just to see what the rescued maiden looked like, passersby studied her with fear and fascination in their eyes, as if she had horns on her head. Church visitors came to pray, ostensibly, but their prayers were short and their loitering long.

The attention annoyed even the priest, Father Vernon. "I have trouble going from here to there without commoners pestering me with questions about you," he complained. "Do keep yourself out of sight." It was more of a demand than advice.

Galt came to see her. His status allowed him to make use of Father Vernon's study, where they could talk in private. He brought her a change of clothes and suggested she wear her hair up. "The archbishop is quite concerned about the attention you're receiving," he explained. "But we can use that to get you out of here. Some place safer. Uncle Corvin suggested you lodge in his home, and the archbishop and the council agreed. Mother will leave soon. You can come then."

"I would rather return to Savelle."

Galt hung his head, exhaling. "I know. They would rather that, too. But the duke and his allies, they won't allow it."

"Won't allow? Am I being held?"

"No," he said, before adding, "not quite. But don't try to leave. It will look . . . very bad." He looked outside and around before continuing, in a whisper.

"You're being watched. The duke posted men outside the abbey."

The implications boggled her. "Why? Isn't this a matter for the archdiocese?"

"They're for your protection. So he claims, but . . . He's up to something. He and the archbishop are at odds, despite their public solidarity. That's not unusual. Archbishops and dukes have often been at odds, even before the dragonslayers. The Church and the Crown have always competed with each other. Auch's influence rose and fell with the dragonslayers' success. It had never recovered from the Deleret Expedition . . . until recently. With my healing and your rescue, the archbishop now holds far more sway with the populace. My uncle believes the duke aims to undo that. And he thinks he can do it by reminding everyone of the archbishop's fallibility. To do that, the duke wants a forum where his allies can publicly question the archbishop's wisdom."

Galt had slowed as he explained, then stopped. He continued only after Isodore urged him to.

"The archbishop had taken all the credit for sponsoring your rescue, so he could be discredited by . . . by maligning you. You're . . . under suspicion. Of practicing witchcraft. The duke wants a public trial."

She wasn't surprised, but his statement knocked the wind out of her.

She asked, "Can the archbishop prevent that?"

Isodore had watched Galt struggle to tell her the duke's plan, but it was nothing compared to his struggle with the next answer.

"Isodore, the archbishop already believes you're guilty. He just wants to avoid the attention a public trial would bring."

"Oh . . ." Tears filled her eyes faster than she thought could be possible. "What . . . What am I to do?"

"The archbishop won't risk his new popularity by letting himself be accused of making a special case for you. The duke and his allies have promised to expose the double standard, should any leniency be given to an associate of the Church. But if we show the archbishop enough voices asking him to show leniency, we could perhaps change his mind."

Galt took a breath. "The council and the Church have agreed to formally hear what happened when we found you. They'll question everyone who was there. Is there anyone we can bring to testify on behalf of your character?"

Isodore asked for Father Julian and Father Serafin. But requesting them left her feeling guilty and undeserving.

ON THE DAY of the council meeting, Isodore looked for the priests. People on the road parted to make way for an entourage of armed men arriving on horseback. Corvin's black-bird banner flew next to one that depicted three hunting dogs. She had seen those banners together before. At the center of the group was Lord Corvin, accompanied by Mereine and a dignified knight somewhat older than Lord Corvin. They rode past the cathedral, surrounded by six younger knights. One was Galt. Two were Corvin's sons. Two she didn't recognize. The last was the handsome knight she had seen talking to Corvin and Mereine at Galt's dubbing ceremony, Sir Reginald, brother to the brown-haired lass Aida who had stared at Isodore during Mass that day. The older knight must be Lord Harold, their father. Sir Wilfred had told her that Lord Harold was Corvin's first backer in his rebellion. The entourage turned into the cathedral grounds and out of her sight, perhaps to attend the council meetings that she thought Corvin had little taste for.

Isodore thought of Sir Wilfred's sober advice at Galt's dubbing ceremony: "Inquire no further about Aida. It can do you no good and quite possibly make you more enemies than you already have." Galt's mother and sisters must be the enemies she already had, and she couldn't help but wonder if somewhere under the hunting-dog banner were the enemies Sir Wilfred warned about. She retreated into the nunnery and further into despair.

In the afternoon, a page delivered to her an unassigned

message. "Mother has departed, and you've been granted leave to lodge in my uncle's home. I will send for you tomorrow morning."

Afterward, Fathers Julian and Serafin came to see her. The elder priest was more rotund than before and was virtually bald, but he was still authoritative, while Father Serafin squirmed nervously next to him. Father Julian introduced himself to Father Vernon. He asked for a place to sit with Isodore and was shown to the unoccupied kitchen. They sat on benches at a trestle table. It soothed her to be in the company of those who were concerned about her. Father Serafin delivered a message from Savelle's orphans. They liked their new headmistress, but missed her. Both men assured her that they told the council that they thought she was a good Christian.

"I said that you were modest and wanted only to care for the orphans. Not at all ambitious or opportunistic. Not at all!" He was so emphatic that she wondered what prompted his defense. She recalled seeing Mereine on the road that morning. The woman must have come to testify. If she had given her opinion of Isodore, that would explain why she was only departing today. She wanted to give her testimony to the council. Isodore suppressed a cold rage.

Father Julian asked for her account of events. She told them what she had told everyone. She had grown used to talking right past her omissions, hoping that a quiet repentance for what she had to do, and a vow to never do it again, might be sufficient for God.

At the end of her abbreviated account, Father Julian looked puzzled. "The witnesses talked of a sorceress."

"Oh, the madman called out for someone. But he was mad. The regiment never found that person."

Julian shook his head. "Some of the men thought it was you, child." He said it as though warning her of something she didn't know.

"I don't think the madman should be believed."

"But there must have been a sorceress. How did the dragon become a man otherwise? If there were such a person—if we're to believe a madman—what happened to her?"

Isodore hardly breathed as Father Julian spoke in low tones.

She kept silent while he considered various explanations. The sorceress escaped during the fight. The madman was deluded. There was a mistaken identity. He circled but did not touch the one explanation that could tie it all together: that the sorceress and the rescued maiden were one and the same. Father Julian did most of the talking. Father Serafin listened with a deepening worry on his face.

"I fear for you, child," said the elder priest after the speculations. "The evidence and testimony, they are all against you. All the dragonslayers who heard the madman call to the sorceress thought he was addressing you."

Everyone? Surely not Galt, she thought. He was trying to help her. Wasn't he? His mother had spoken against her, and he said nothing? She looked to Father Serafin, to see what he had to say, but the young priest looked too frightened to speak. Somehow, Isodore found enough strength not to cry.

"I think if he had been addressing me, he would have said 'Isodore.' Wouldn't he?"

Father Serafin nodded, dropping his eyes, appearing to consider it.

Father Julian looked at her. "Then you say that you didn't change the dragon into the man?"

"Me? How could I? How could anyone?"

"There was a book of spells," explained Father Julian.

"Was there?" Isodore swallowed.

"Yes. They said that a spell to transform a dragon into a man was in it, and you could have easily done it."

"Just because there was a book doesn't mean I did. Why would the dragon allow me?" It was her strongest defense.

"One of the men said the madman shouted to you, 'I will protect you.' Did you make some kind of bargain with that beast?"

She could challenge the idea of the bargain, but the more she spoke, the more she had to stand by her lies. And the more she stood by them, the shakier she felt. She gave no answer.

To the priest who had been her childhood guardian, her silence might well have been an admission of guilt.

Isodore felt helpless watching the man who had sheltered her, fed her, and taught her now lose faith in her.

Father Julian bowed his bald head in silence, his fingers interlaced. He shook his head. "You went through a terrible ordeal, child, but it was for a purpose. You have to know that. It was a test of your faith, just like Abraham's. You remember Abraham, don't you, dear child? He didn't lose faith in God when the Lord commanded him to sacrifice his son Isaac. That was the test of his faith. And the Lord saved Isaac at the last moment. We all have our tests. Rescuing you was Sir Galt's. And the dragon was yours. You needn't have resorted to the tool of Satan, Isodore, because you had the tools of God. The dragonslayers!

"You faced a terrible fright, child, and perhaps . . . it was too much for you. You found your own way out, but it was not the way the Lord showed you. You have sinned, as Rowan sinned. But he ran from God. Now, you must do better. Do what he couldn't, Isodore. Face what you've done. You must repent. Put yourself at the mercy of God. He will pass final judgment. Don't run away. You will spend all of eternity in Hell. We've already lost Rowan. He can't protect you now, so I must. I will pray for you, but only you can show God your repentance." Tears glistened in Father Julian's eyes.

Father Julian bade farewell to Father Vernon before leaving. He defended Isodore, but she couldn't help believing she had lost him as an ally.

"She had been a good Christian, but the ordeal of the dragon would be too much for all but the most devout of us."

Father Vernon agreed. After Father Julian left, he told her, "Father Julian is right. It was a test of your faith, and you failed. It would serve the Church well to make an example of you."

The priest had never been particularly kind to her, but his cold opinion shook her, awakened her to the knowledge of her misguided belief. Until now, she thought that she could live among men. She wanted to run. She would have, if Galt hadn't warned her that she was being watched.

She went to bed in despair and dreamed she was back at the nest. She stepped to the precipice, looking across the mountain tops. Dusk. The valley below sank into darkness. Rocks and grass, near and far, shifted to black, blending together in the murky shadows of Dragon's Ridge. Gascony was a fathomless sea, ringed by mountains on her side and twilight afar. Gazing at the fading details below the cliff, she felt dizzy and confused, yet calm, without the anger she once had when she stood there as a captive. Something beckoned her, floating out of the valley on a dying breeze. Invisible yet insistent. A ghostly spirit, felt but not heard. A warmth penetrated deep inside her to counter the cold. She leaned out, into it, farther and farther, heedless of the sheer cliff, until she toppled. The wind rushed by. Faster and faster she plunged. Skulls in the pile of sun-bleached bones came forward from shadow to welcome her into their eternal silence.

43

Desolation Dreams

The morning after Isodore's dream, one of Lord Corvin's sons and four of his guards came to the abbey to escort Isodore to Laronde. They didn't bring Winter, the horse that she had ridden and raced that fine spring day earlier in the year, when her life had looked so promising. She rode a lethargic palfrey, next to a sheriff with the crest of Gascony on his vest. He had a stern, pockmarked face and a proud smirk. No one introduced the man, but Isodore didn't need an introduction to know that he had been sent by the duke to make sure she didn't escape.

The guards' arrival drew some gawkers to the abbey. Seeing her being whisked away, the gawkers followed, throwing accusations, insults and threats.

"How could ye resort to the tool o' the devil?"

"Don't ye know it'd bring more dragons?"

Some on horseback rode after the party, stretching to look at her, but the guards drew their swords and put an end to it. The sheriff watched with amusement.

Laronde's gawkers were tamer or unable to recognize the notorious suspect. The party passed through the gates into the protective embrace of the palisades, the sheriff included.

In Corvin's hall, Glennis greeted them with her characteristic brevity and directness. "Welcome, Sheriff Edmer, Isodore," she said, nodding at each of them.

Isodore remembered Glennis for the casual way she'd cut down Galt's mother when the latter had demeaned lowborns. But she suspected that Glennis was motivated more by dislike for Mereine than affinity toward lowborns.

Edmer took a seat at the table, where the servants brought him a cup of mead. Apparently he knew about the arrangements. Isodore stood, waiting for instructions from Glennis.

"You are welcome to rest, play, bathe, or eat as you wish. The servants are at your disposal. No one will harm you. Sheriff Edmer may demand to see you any time he chooses, without notice. Just answer him when he calls." To her grandchildren she announced, "Children, these are our guests, Sheriff Edmer and Isodore." The children bade them formal greetings. The boys nodded and the girls curtsied. Some left for riding lessons. Others gathered at one of the tables where a young man taught them reading and writing.

"I will speak with your palisade guards, to ensure that they understand the rules," said Edmer.

"Of course," said Glennis.

Edmer refilled his mead cup and walked out, while Glennis and her sons pored over the details of a message Edmer had brought from Lord Corvin. Something about masons for constructing a second keep.

Isodore watched the servants tend to the needs of the family. Eventually, they prepared the hall for dinner. No further instructions came from Glennis. Feeling out of place and useless, Isodore stopped Margot to ask what she should do. To her dismay, Margot called out, "Dame Glennis, what shall Isodore do?"

Glennis's head rose from the huddle with her children. "Whatever she likes. Didn't you hear me, lass?"

"I did, but—"

"Well then. What shall you do?"

Isodore stammered then stopped herself. She must be a proper lass, and fast. "I would like to be outside. To see the garden."

Glennis shrugged. "Then do so."

Her sons glanced at Isodore but said nothing.

"Thank you." Isodore curtsied and backed out of the great hall.

The bright sun, blue sky and a breeze soothed her with a sense of freedom. Her respite in the garden was short-lived, however. After she'd calmed down, out stepped Glennis, followed by the sheriff.

The two walked past Isodore without a word, heading to the palisade at the base of the motte.

Isodore thought there was something different about Glennis. The woman was more beautiful when she smiled. She had a graceful, elegant walk that Isodore hadn't notice before. Isodore observed them from a discreet distance. The sheriff stopped at a section with a different color than the rest.

"This section is new," explained the mistress. "This was where Corvin burned the palisade during the siege. It was replaced, of course. Have a closer look." She went on to tell him about the final battle of Corvin's rebellion. She spoke of the duke's assistance and talked at length about their familial relationship. She mentioned neither that the relationship was only through marriage nor of Corvin's scornful attitude toward the monarch. Isodore wasn't the only one omitting inconvenient facts.

The smell of roasting meat and cooking herbs wafted out of the kitchen, making Isodore a little hungry. She absentmindedly pulled weeds from the vegetable garden while Glennis and Edmer traced the perimeter of the bailey and returned. It was the most talking she'd ever heard from the stern mistress.

"Sheriff Edmer, if you're satisfied with the execution of our custodial obligations, you're welcome to join us for dinner. That is, if you haven't tired of the dried beef endured on your journey from Toulouse."

He accepted.

"Dame Glennis," Isodore said. "I am not at all hungry. May I remain here?"

"That's up to the sheriff. Edmer?"

The sheriff looked Isodore up and down. "If she's not hungry, I see no point in feeding her."

Glennis smiled again and led him inside without a look back. Isodore walked the rows of the vegetable garden. She fixed up the mound where it was needed and removed caterpillars and snails.

The servants passed back and forth between the kitchen and the great hall, bringing food and mead.

Physically, Isodore knew she was safe. She wasn't permitted to leave the bailey, but she was free inside it. Free, like Armand had been at Lord Edwin's home before the Sheriff of Belmont had come for him. She stayed out of Edmer's sight, coming only when he commanded her to, which was less often each day. She rarely ate with the family, and when she did, she sat apart. Edmer always sat with Glennis and her children. They talked of horses, land disputes, the reliability of merchants, plans for a stonework keep, interests of the noble aristocracy. Isodore tried not to listen, for it reminded her of how little she fit in.

She busied herself helping the servants in the kitchen and stables, washing and drying clothes, planting vegetables, removing garden pests, grinding flour, brewing mead and ale. Margot thought it improper for a guest to be put to work, but Glennis ordered her to let Isodore help. No more fancy outfits, she was given a nondescript tunic of undyed wool, a house servant's outfit. She slept on the family's end of the great hall, but her cot was the last one, closest to the servant's end. Edmer slept closest to the loft, a place of honor.

Three days after her arrival, Isodore had the dream again. She stepped onto the precipice of the dragon's nest at dusk. Something beckoned on the breeze, she leaned out and plunged down toward the graveyard of Pyramine's long-forgotten victims. She woke with a start.

She looked around the dark hall, shaking. Corvin's grandchildren were next to her and his servants on the other side. No Mereine, no Sevina, no Christiana. Glennis was in the loft. Edmer lay somewhere in that direction. Light snoring drifted throughout the great hall, peaceful and calm. Yet there was a cold hostility that she had never before felt, not even as a prisoner on Pyramine's nest.

GALT AND CORVIN came home on Isodore's fourth day. While the lord reviewed the domain's affairs with his wife, sons, and steward, Galt and Isodore went to the stables to talk. He was apologetic.

She was glad they could talk without the need to evade strangers on the cathedral grounds. But the talk wasn't comforting.

"I'm sorry that you're made a prisoner in my uncle's home. The duke wanted you in his dungeon. This is the best that we could do."

She stood in the shadow as Galt paced down the row of stalls, peering in each one. Then he looked outside, checking for eavesdroppers.

His voice was low. "There's something I must ask you. I didn't want to risk being overheard in Auch, or appearing subversive, but . . . our men searched the madman's cave. They found some jewelry and . . . and a large book." He paused to watch her reaction. "It's said to be a book of spells. Do you know anything about it?"

She shook her head. Another lie, another betrayal. Father Julian didn't believe her. Why should Galt? The lonely well of her anguish deepened.

"It described the steps for turning a dragon into a man. There was jewelry in the cave, and the spell called for gold and silver. You said that the madman was the dragon. We know how it could happen, but not who cast that spell. It couldn't have been the madman, because he didn't exist before it was cast."

"Perhaps the dragon itself cast the spell."

"Impossible. Dragons can't read or voice the words of the spellEven dragonslayers knew so little about the beasts they were exterminating. Her admiration for them, and for Galt in particular, dropped a bit. Clever and brave, they were, but knowledgeable? No. Two months of talking with a dragon had taught her more about dragons than the dragonslayers had learned in two hundred years of fighting.

"Was anyone else there with you, or nearby, who could have sneaked in? Anyone else who could have cast the spell, perhaps while you slept? You must've been tired from your ordeal." Galt was desperately looking for a reason to reject the easy speculations.

She wanted to say yes, but she couldn't bear to tell him another lie.

"It would have taken more than a day. If the dragon had cast the spell, where were you when he did this?"

She could think of nothing to say.

"Did you try to escape?"

She stared at the suffering dragon on Galt's surcoat and counted breaths from his chest movements. He ended with a sigh of frustration. "You have to say something in your own defense, Isodore."

Why? she thought. *You said nothing in my defense.* It wasn't entirely fair, but she couldn't help her resentment. She felt ashamed.

"The spell's instructions were translated into Gascon. I didn't mention to them that you could read and write, but they know. Father Julian said he taught you, so you could help run his orphanage."

She felt her world collapse. Her last ally in this world was desperate for an explanation, and all she had for him were silence and lies. She shrank further into isolation, even from him.

Galt and Corvin left the next day without a word to Isodore. She wondered if they went to testify about her explanation for the spellbook. Perhaps she should have given Galt a better story to tell them.

Corvin's brief time at home did nothing to hinder the relationship developing between his wife and the sheriff. The lord knight was either completely oblivious to it or didn't care. Corvin, Glennis and Edmer laughed and drank together. They spoke of Corvin's finding a squireship for Edmer's son. Either Glennis was a very daring woman, or Corvin was a very understanding man. Isodore kept quiet. It wasn't her concern if Glennis was playing Corvin for a fool. In some ways, she feared the mistress more than she did her husband.

Isodore's only friend in the family was Corvin's grandson Zephir, who had a curious mind and wandering feet. One day, he wandered over to the stable, where Isodore was brushing down a horse. She let him take handfuls of hay to the horse stalls. He reminded her of Xabi. She thought he liked talking to her because, due to her redundant status, she had time to answer his inexhaustible stream of childish questions. She enjoyed his company, but she tried not to encourage him, sensing it would get him into trouble.

Too late.

"Zephir!"

He dropped the hay. "Yes, Grandmother?"

"This is your study time."

"Yes, Grandmother." As Zephir shuffled across the grounds to the great hall, Glennis crossed toward the stable. "Posture," said Glennis, and Zephir's back snapped straight.

Isodore braced herself for a crushing reprimand.

Face to face with Isodore, Glennis said in a soft tone—at least, it was soft for the mistress—"I must ask something of you."

"Yes, of course. Please. I am at your service."

"You must not let the little children become too attached to you. It will only make things difficult for them."

"Yes, Dame Glennis." Isodore thought better of asking why.

Glennis turned and walked away, then stopped and looked back. "Do you ... have everything you need here?"

"Yes," said Isodore, thinking, it an odd question.

"Good," said Glennis. "If there is anything else, you are to talk to Margot or me. Not the children." She looked into Isodore's eyes for the briefest instant, before resuming her exit. Perhaps the mistress found her obligation to treat Isodore as a guest distasteful.

When Zephir made his way to Isodore again, she made up an excuse to send him away, even though she very much wanted a friend. She could think of only two reasons why Zephir's grandmother didn't want him attached to her. Glennis didn't like her house guest. Or she didn't want to explain to a child why his new friend had been turned over for execution.

That night, the strange dream returned. Isodore stepped to the precipice, leaned into the whispering breeze, and plunged into the bone pile, waking just before smashing into it. She stayed up, thinking of her time on that ledge, remembering how strangely calm and protected she'd felt up there after she'd learned to trust Pyramine. She didn't have to defend herself. There was no specter of a trial or of an execution. She had something to live for: escape and return to her people. Now, she had nothing to escape to.

Adding to her anxiety was her private watch for the assuring sign of menstrual blood. It had come twice when she was up on the mountain. She remembered how she couldn't rid her slip of the stain. All the clothing she wore when she was rescued had been destroyed, but her memory was clear. She hadn't bled since she came down from the mountain, more than a month ago. She checked herself every morning for any sign of the blood, but it only brought her worry.

She thought she hid her worry well. Her whole life, she had to hide her fears and secrets. She thought herself good at it. But the woman watching her wasn't fooled. "Something has been troubling you the past three days," Glennis asked. "What is it?"

Three days? Glennis was keeping track. Afraid that she couldn't hide from the woman's scrutiny, Isodore admitted that she felt ill.

The servants reported that Isodore woke some nights, gasping. Glennis's eyes pierced her as if reading every corner of her mind, but she said nothing further. When Galt heard the news, he thought Isodore was still suffering from the dragon's torment, and she accepted that explanation even though she knew it was false. She wanted to stop lying to him, but she couldn't bear the truth herself.

The servant girl Sorrel came to Isodore while she rested in a shady corner behind the kitchen. "I've a gift for ye. I received this when I was ill. It helped me return to health. I think it will make ye feel better as well," she said, kneeling down. She dropped into Isodore's hand a strip of lace made from dark green thread. Recalling how out of place she felt wearing the previous lace, Isodore tried to refuse it.

"I can't take this. It is so beautiful and special. You should keep it for that."

"It's all right," whispered Sorrel. "I've many."

Wishing not to draw attention to herself, Isodore wound the lace around her wrist to make a set of connected bracelets. Sorrel tied the ends together for her. The girl watched Isodore admire the intricate network of knots and loops before shyly backing away, gratified to be the giver of such a prized gift.

Isodore's dream came every night. She thought it might be an omen, but the events in it had taken place in the past. It felt like a memory. She could recall her real temptation to let herself fall off the precipice to her death. Had she done it, it would have saved so much misery. And the misery that was surely to come.

She wondered what would happen if she didn't wake at the end of her plunge. That night, she found out. As she dove toward the bone pile, she was determined to crash into it, but she was pulled away by giant claws holding her around the chest and thighs; they kept her an arm's reach from smashing into the rocks, and she skimmed over the escarpment in the shadow of enormous wings. The rocks blurred by until she was lifted away. Dusk somehow became day. Pyramine carried her along the north-running ridge to the notch. They went through the notch, across the three-sided chasm, over lakes, boulders and finally trees in a familiar flight path. A pleasant wind rushed by. They shared the sky with eagles. At the foothills, they turned north, heading for the cave where she would transform him into a man.

"Arkh arkh arkh!" called the unseen ravens.

Galt! This time she knew. She struggled in Pyramine's claws to look for the regiment.

"Go back! Please, go back!" she whimpered in futility, afraid Pyramine would hear her. "Don't come for me! Go back! Go back. Go back."

At breakfast the next morning, Glennis questioned Isodore, out of the blue and with the woman's typical directness. "Who were you talking to last night?"

Confused by the sudden question, Isodore made the connection after noticing that the servants in the room all stopped, waiting for her answer. They all knew what Glennis was speaking of. "Uh, no one," Isodore said.

Glennis ignored the servants. "You said, 'Go back. Go back.' What were you doing up?"

"Oh, that. I was . . . um, dreaming. One of my orphans was outside when a dragon was seen in the sky. I wanted him to go back into the cottage."

Glennis stopped the questioning and dropped the subject, giving no indication whether she believed Isodore's explanation.

The servants exchanged quick glances, then followed her lead. No one spoke of it again.

LORD CORVIN WAS rarely home. Isodore couldn't imagine the council meetings going on for so long, but perhaps he had other business to attend to, planning his stone keep perhaps. When he returned, he called her into the great hall to ask about her illness. Afterward, she asked when she might return to Savelle.

"There's no need for you there. Your orphanage has a new headmistress. But I will see if we can arrange for you to visit your children. You can't live there, however. I've learned that the people of Savelle oppose your return. Lord Edwin can't protect you from all of them if they fear you would bring God's wrath."

It wasn't what she wanted to hear, but it provided her with certainty that, until then, no one else had. "Lord Corvin, I know I will stand accused. Sir Galt said that you have seen the archbishop and representatives of the duke. Will you please tell me what will happen to me?"

Corvin sighed. "It depends on which man has his way. The archbishop prefers to treat your situation as a matter internal to his archdiocese, but the duke insists that you be treated no differently than any others. Alas, you, too, have become a pawn in their game."

Galt had explained that the duke was trying to undermine the archbishop's popularity with Isodore's public trial. She was hoping Corvin would present a less bleak interpretation of the situation. But not only did Corvin confirm this situation, he went further. Whereas Galt said that the duke wanted a public trial, Corvin told her the monarch was pushing for a public trial and execution.

"Do they want me burned?" She asked, trying to disguise a paralyzing fear.

"The Duke's allies advocate that. The Church forbids witch burning, Isodore, but one wouldn't know it, looking at the frontier. More heretics are burned on the frontier, and I don't believe there are more heretics out there than elsewhere. I wouldn't be surprised to see them add heresy to their list of accusations."

She found the lord knight unusually patient with her questions.

His tired, dejected tone belied his indifference toward her earlier, at the feast. Isodore once feared death at his hands, and hated him too. But she had come to respect him. Perhaps because she understood his motivation. Perhaps merely because he was here, talking with her, the way neither Galt nor Glennis were. He had even gotten rid of Sheriff Edmer for a few days.

"Do you think my rescue was a mistake?"

Corvin sighed again and thought it over. "Too many have passed judgment on you, lass, judgment that is best left to God. If you've done what your accusers say, then God help you. You have my prayers, regardless. If you are innocent, I pray the trial will acquit you. But I've seen the evidence they have against you, lass, and . . ." He shook his head. "I'm sorry."

Corvin sent for a physician before leaving again. Days later, Ilsa brought a scholarly man to the great hall. He felt for Isodore's temperature and checked her eyes, mouth and ears. He moved her joints and palpated her chest, abdomen and back. He made notes. While he worked, a group of curious servants gathered, supposedly to help but mainly to watch. He asked Isodore a lot of questions and received mostly truthful answers in return. He sent her out to fill a ceramic bottle with her urine. She went to the waste pit enclosure for privacy. The bottle was messy to fill for a woman. After corking it, she stopped at the basin to rinse her hands. When she returned, she overheard the group in a lively chat.

"What ailed her?"

"Well, we never did find out, but it came and went like spring storms," said the physician.

"We thought she was better months ago. What 'appened?"

"She recovered slowly, but then she suddenly plunged into the depths of despair. I tried everything. She refused to eat or drink. I think she was terribly fearful for Sir Galt on his expedition."

Sorrel moaned with compassion.

Margot commented, "And after all the worry, she missed the festivities. In Auch and 'ere. What a shame. Terrible shame."

"Well, she seems to be doing very well now, I can tell you. She's regaining her weight. She's returned to her painting and embroidery. And she talks of learning to play the vielle. Ah, that reminds me . . ."

The physician reached into his bag, shuffling through things and drew out a stretch of tri-colored lace, green, yellow and orange, longer than his arm. Sorrel's face lit up, her eyes wide as the man presented the elegant strip of needlework to her. She received it draped over her open hands with great awe.

"Your pastries arrived just in time. Aida said they were exquisite! That's what's helping her gain weight." He winked.

Sorrel clutched the lace to her chest, a wide smile stretching across her face. Isodore fingered the lace bracelet on her wrist, feeling suddenly as if it were a stranger's hand gently holding her. Aida's hand. Aida, about whom Sir Wilfred had cautioned Isodore not to inquire, because "It can do you no good and quite possibly make you more enemies than you already have."

"When did 'er condition turn?" someone asked.

"She started to improve a fortnight ago. Yes, when Lord Corvin and Sir Galt paid her father a visit. Her dear mother refused to let her hide. She insisted that Aida present herself to share wine with their old friends."

"'Twas Sir Galt who did it! 'E's the Knight of God's Miracle after all!" The group chuckled good naturedly.

Isodore listened, engrossed. Aida seemed loved by the servants, in a way that Isodore could never hope to be. How ironic.

Margot saw Isodore standing by the doorway. "Isodore, come, come!" laughed the old servant.

"Perhaps she can spend a few days with Master Galt too," someone said. "'E might just cure her ailment as well!"

"Who did he cure?" Isodore asked, pretending she had not been listening long.

Margot answered, "Aida. Lord 'arold's daughter. They've known each other since Master Galt was a child livin' 'ere. She used te come when 'er father 'ad business with m' lord. Lovely lass."

"She was teaching me embroidery before she fell ill. Look what she just gave me!" Sorrel chimed in, showing Isodore the tri-colored lace.

By now, Isodore was used to smiling when she didn't mean it, to hide the turmoil inside.

She couldn't tear her mind from the bonds that connected her to Aida, real and imagined. Both of them had some sort of special place in Galt's heart. Aida's lacework had once crowned Isodore's head and was now wound around her wrist. At Galt's dubbing ceremony, Aida looked so forlorn, while Isodore's life was on the cusp of a promising future. But Aida was no longer a sad lass. It was Isodore. The tables had turned. One lass's blessing was the other's misfortune. One's illness was the other's well-being. Their outlooks rose and fell like the two sides of a balance. A balance that favored Aida now and forevermore.

The dream came again. Isodore neither hesitated nor waited for the wind to beckon. She simply walked to the edge of the precipice and toppled with the full intention of discarding the last four months of her life. The bone pile was so familiar that she recognized the skulls staring up at her. As Pyramine's claws kept her from plunging into the escarpment, she tried to struggle out of his grip. The struggle woke her. She spent the rest of the night thinking about Galt and Aida, about herself and Pyramine. About Sir Rowan and how she might soon be with him again, for all eternity.

CHANGES STIRRED THROUGH Isodore's body. Nausea and fatigue rendered her even more private and isolated. Soon, there would be no hiding her pregnancy. Perhaps the physician had already discovered her condition.

She couldn't escape the disturbing thoughts. For all Galt's stubborn defense of her, he'd have to accept that the maiden he had chosen, for whom he had exchanged precious tax revenue and five dragonslayer lives, was not what he thought she was. On top of all other things troubling him—the rumors and suspicions, the impending trial, his family's opposition, her silence—the scandal would crush his terribly naive heart. All the scrutiny his uncle had warned about would come down. A strengthened Mereine could fight their union, unfettered. A peasant with no family, accused of witchcraft, soiled before marriage, and pregnant with a madman's bastard child. Isodore couldn't imagine anyone wanting to wed her.

When Galt spoke with her in the privacy of the stable again, she knew it was over for them. "For your sake, you must forget about me."

Isodore sat on a stool just inside the stable's wide doors while Galt paced, occasionally looking out into the light. He dismissed her idea simply by turning away from her without a word. Isodore begged him to return her to Savelle.

"You're safer here," he said forcefully, as though force itself were reason. The prospect of Glennis discovering her pregnancy would only increase until it became assured. Galt's regiment would leave Auch soon, and her pregnancy would show before he returned. How would she hide from the astute mistress? Or explain to Galt's uncle? What would be the point? Her own thoughts gave her all the reasons to be terrified.

"Galt, I'm under suspicion. You don't have to wed me. I know what your family thinks of me. You can simply send me back to Savelle. No one would have to know what we had planned."

He considered her words and remained eerily calm. The idea was obviously not new to him. "Do you no longer wish to be my wife?"

"I . . . I don't think it is wise. I believe Lord Corvin is right. It'll be . . . much too difficult. Especially now."

With his back to her, he nodded. "So you have changed your mind."

"It's not that I refuse you. If you wish to go through with it, then I will do it. But you don't . . . I think you won't want to wed me."

He remained dead calm, looking away, his hands together behind his back. "Why?"

Something blocked her words. The silence stretched out. Galt stood in the hazy light of the late afternoon, in the sunbeam angling beneath the eaves of the stable. There was no sound but the slight movement of horses and the buzzing of flies. Something told her Galt knew. Perhaps, he didn't know the exact details, but he knew a lot more than he told her. He knew about the spellbook and the jewelry but didn't tell her until she'd come here. She was doomed. She might as well be brave, though her head bowed.

"I'm not a maiden," she whispered, unsure whether he heard her.

"I told my family you were. Have you made a liar of me?"

"No. I was a maiden when I told you I was. I am no longer."

He stopped cold. His hands balled into fists. She counted his breaths.

He left the dusty sun beam and walked into the shadow of the stable's interior. He crossed in front of her and paced back and forth, taking deep audible breaths. "We don't have to tell anyone," he said, not looking at her.

"I don't think that will work. People will know before your regiment returns. I . . . I believe I'm with child."

Galt stopped pacing. He stopped breathing. Finally, he looked at her, and she realized. He hadn't known everything. He hadn't known this. She had seen him in pain and in joy, with pride and with reserve, but she hadn't seen him in utter shock until now. He was searching for a reaction.

"What? Why haven't you told me before?"

"I . . ." An overwhelming sense of fear shot up her back and disabled her speech.

"You are pregnant? Pregnant?" His face and neck turned red. "By whom?"

She couldn't answer. A vein swelled over his temple. Cords of tendons lifted from his neck. Tears blurred her vision.

"The madman!" Galt whispered in a tone unmistakably pinpointing the blame. "Did he take you against your will?"

It wasn't the question Isodore expected, but one she could benefit from. Yes, blame it on Pyramine. She'd already betrayed him. What worse could she do? Galt showed her the way out. He was a man of tremendous faith. Somehow, through all that had happened, his faith had not completely vanished. She had only to give him a reason to believe.

"No," she said, determined to stop lying to her last ally. She waited for the consequences.

Galt's arms tensed up, down to the fists. He shook his head. "No, no. No!"

Isodore dropped her head into her hands. She heard him roar. The all-too-familiar cry of a man betrayed.

He grabbed a handful of tack from the wall behind her and threw it across the stable, where it crashed with a shattering sound. Horses whinnied. Galt kicked the wall and pounded his fist against it. He kicked the pile of hay next to her, sending it into the air and swirling all around. He sent a pail flying. More bridles sailed across the stall. Too late, she realized. He might have been kind and gentle to her until now, but he was still a warrior, no less than his uncle. As he raged against everything in his reach, she sat shrinking, wondering when his hand would find its way to her, or to his sword.

He pounded and kicked, lifted and tossed, ripped and tore. When he was done, buckets were spilled, a pitchfork lay broken and brooms had scattered on the ground. A shelf was torn off the wall. The hay pile was scattered all around, floating in the musty air and drifting into the adjacent stalls. Even the horses feared him, each cowering at the far side of its stall.

Isodore sat, curled into her knees, hands covering her ears, trembling. Except for slivers of hay that drifted down on her, she was untouched. Galt leaned against the stable's center post and slid down, curling up across from Isodore. His rage had been freed like blood from a wound, but something remained trapped inside. He sat on the ground, his arms on his knees, wrapped around his head.

There was nothing left to say. Not about that. They must move on.

"Please, Galt. You owe me nothing. I know that you're in a terrible position. But no one outside your family knows of our plans. You don't have to tell anyone. You can choose another lass. Just send me back to Savelle, please. Turn me over to the duke. Or whatever you want. But please don't be angry at me for long."

Galt shook his head, his face red and bitter. The rude awakening she had given him had shattered his illusions.

"You're releasing me," he said.

She nodded, biting her lips so she wouldn't cry out loud.

He struggled to his feet and wandered haplessly into the harsh light at the doorway. He reached up and held the header as if to keep himself from falling. She dried her tears on her sleeve and heard a sardonic mutter.

"How very convenient."

She turned to see what he meant, but he disappeared from her view.

It took her the rest of the day to clean and fix the stable. Sorrel came out to help. Both of them worked in silence. When Zephir wandered over, she asked Sorrel to send him away, so he wouldn't have to see her cry.

She didn't know where Galt had gone. Perhaps to pray, as Sir Rowan often did in times of loneliness. Perhaps he consulted with his mother. Perhaps he sought comfort in what was familiar, perhaps in Aida's arms.

In the nights that followed, Isodore sought out the recurring dream for the unexpected comfort it brought. In those dreams, Pyramine was still a dragon, she had betrayed no one, and her insurmountable troubles had not yet begun.

44

Last Ally

Two days after Galt walked out of the stable, Glennis called Isodore into the great hall. She found the mistress with Edmer and waited for them to address her.

"I received a message from my lord husband. You've been given permission to visit your children in Savelle. The duke is allowing it while the bishops investigate allegations of heresy. My son will send guards to escort you. You will depart after breakfast tomorrow.

"Thank you."

Glennis nodded to the sheriff. "Sheriff Edmer will come along, of course. I trust that you won't give him any trouble on the trip."

"No, Dame Glennis."

"Margot will prepare your travel clothes. You may help the servants prepare the trip provisions."

That night, neither Corvin nor Galt came home. Isodore had her strange dream. In the morning, she was given clean clothes for her trip.

In the bailey, Glennis ordered the stable hand to give her Winter and he did. Isodore thought there was a smile on the mistress's lips just before the woman turned away.

Isodore fished out two apples from the food that Sorrel had packed for her and gave them to the stallion, petting his neck. "I will ride as well as I can. You'll be rid of me soon enough." Sounds of fighting rang over the palisade from outside, but no one was concerned, not even the guards peering out from their catwalks.

Glennis exchanged farewells with Sheriff Edmer, as pleasant as two old friends. A servant brought the man four bulging skins, for which he appeared pleasantly surprised. "Margot said that all we have for your journey is hard, dried salami and bread. I told her to give you something extra to wash it down. We shall have a little feast when you return."

Isodore thought the reason supplies were low was that Edmer had been feasting ever since he arrived. He stuffed the skins into his saddle bag with a big grin. He had become great friends with Glennis since he'd arrived. He'd paid more attention to her than he did to Isodore.

Isodore, Sheriff Edmer, and three guards rode through the gate. On the grounds outside, Corvin's black-bird banner flew alongside Lord Harold's hunting-dogs banner. Scores of armed men fought in a well-organized mock battle. No shouting or screaming, just the dull knocking of wooden swords. But each side seemed intent on battering the other.

Lord Corvin stood apart, talking with Galt. Isodore thought it odd that they had been away that night only to be here in the morning. The lord knight wore chain armor and held his helmet in one hand. His graying auburn hair was slick with sweat, his surcoat and trousers mud stained. He acknowledged Isodore with a nod and sent Galt off with a hard slap on the shoulder. Donning his helmet, he marched back to the fight. Galt mounted his horse and joined Isodore's party. No one told her that he was to come along, and she wondered whether it was deliberate or an oversight.

The party set out for Savelle under cool autumn skies. They rode fast and soon came to the woods, where the road narrowed and wound through thick tree cover. Dragon territory.

Galt bantered with the guards, leaving Isodore to the side. She tried to get used to it. She had gravely disappointed him and couldn't expect him to care about her as he once had. Her only friend was Winter. The horse seemed to sense her despair and gave her little trouble. In return, she was gentle with her signals and sat straight in the saddle. What bothered her were the men's grating complaints about things that, for all her life, she only wished she had. Someone complained about the salami, and the rest joined in, as though they had never known what it was like to be hungry for days.

"Sir Galt can bring us fresh meat," said one of the guards. "We're in a frontier county now." The men cheered the suggestion.

Though it wasn't Galt's land, knights of the dragonslayer corps had the privilege of hunting anywhere in the frontier counties. Years before, an archbishop bought that privilege with a modest reduction in Auch's tax. With rising encouragement from the rest of the party, Galt agreed. They stopped well before sunset to give him time to hunt.

While Galt was away, the guards took turns watching Isodore. She wasn't foolish enough to try an escape, so she found it insulting. One guard was bolder than the rest, or less courteous. He glowered at her and didn't bother with discreetness. Even Sheriff Edmer was more relaxed. The guard was about Galt's age, tall and built like a warrior, strong but not bulky, more formidable than the rest of the men in her party.

The others gathered firewood, then sat to enjoy their rest, drinking away the time. The glowering man kept watch. Isodore thought he looked familiar. She turned away to think. Sir Reginald—that was who he reminded her of. But younger. She had seen him the day the council had taken testimonies regarding her. He had ridden with Sir Reginald, Lord Harold, Lord Corvin, and some of Corvin's sons. Perhaps he was Harold's son, working as Lord Corvin's guard in the name of their alliance. However, it wasn't Lord Harold's name that ran through in Isodore's mind. Neither was it his son Reginald. The person Isodore kept returning to was Harold's daughter, Sir Reginald's sister—the brown-haired lass, Aida.

Hours later, Galt returned with a small feral pig over his shoulder. He'd cleaned and gutted it. The group greeted Galt with smiles and congratulatory remarks. The glowerer smiled for the first time since Galt had left. He went out to take the pig that would provide enough meat to last most of the journey. The men shuffled away to prepare the meal, all except for the guard watching her.

She turned away, glanced around, and longed for a view from the mountain top and a good breeze. The forest canopy was so stifling, the sound of excited men so shrill and irritating. She began to feel a sudden dislike toward the glowerer. Was he the enemy Sir Wilfred had left unnamed?

After some time, Galt relieved the guard watching her. He had donned his long surcoat and brought her coat as well. "Let's take a walk," he said, handing it to her.

She took it without question. She had lost her appetite due to constant worrying. Perhaps Galt had as well.

He grabbed a torch from one of the supply bags, and they headed into the woods, alone together for the first time since she'd told him of her pregnancy. Her mind was a flurry of thoughts, none coherent, none pleasant. A part of her had ceased to care what fate intended for her.

They were far from settlements, so the forest was dominated by old trees with high, dense crowns. The forest floor, where sunlight had not reached in ages, supported mostly ferns and some wiry brush. There wasn't much obstructing their way. Galt talked only to point out obstacles. The silence suited Isodore.

She followed him, not paying much attention until they began weaving around increasingly difficult tangles of drooping and downed tree limbs, screens of broken branches. At times, he drew his sword to hack through brush. She had not encountered such obstructions since her years living in the woods. They had gone far from the road where dead wood was constantly cleared by travelers collecting fuel for campfires.

The sky had dimmed by the time Galt came to a tree where his hunting bow and quiver of arrows leaned, hidden by the surrounding ferns. The quiver's belt had been removed and used to secure a black boar piglet to an overhead branch. An arrow had struck it behind its front leg and lay lodged in its chest. The piglet had been cleaned and gutted. Two ravens were pecking at the exposed cavity.

"You killed another?" she asked.

He nodded. "Our supper."

Isodore relaxed a little. Her appetite returned.

Galt crouched down and leaped to catch the branch with both hands. The ravens fluttered away but circled back and landed further up the branch, watching. He threw his legs around the branch and crawled upside down to the piglet. He hooked an elbow around the branch and proceeded to unbuckle the belt with one hand.

Recognizing that they were about to lose their meal, the ravens moved back in. They squawked and pecked Galt's hand. He jerked back and waved them away, but each time he tried to work, the brazen birds moved in and pecked him. Finally, he drew the arrow from the piglet and used it to swat them away before they got close enough to peck. They gave up the fight but remained just out of reach, scolding in loud squawks, as though insisting that because the arrow was fletched with raven feathers, they deserved the kill and he was the thief.

After unbuckling the belt, Galt took it and the piglet in one hand and dropped to the ground. Glaring up at the two birds, he huffed. Nearby, he and Isodore found a tree that had fallen and now lay decaying. They cleared away the ferns and forest duff. He used a rock to scrape a shallow fire pit by the tree. Isodore broke off its crumbling branches for firewood while he started the fire with flint, striker, char cloth, and tinder. In a waist pouch he had brought all they needed, even salt and pepper. Except for the ravens, this meal had been planned.

After building the fire, Galt gave Isodore his dagger to whittle skewers and construct a spit. He flayed, then butchered the piglet. Because swords were of little use against dragons, the blades of dragonslayers often had fresh, sharp edges. Galt chopped off the feet and deeply scored the flesh to hasten the cooking. He tossed the discards to the ravens, which carried off each donation and returned to wait for more.

Isodore sprinkled salt and pepper from the small ceramic bottles as Galt rubbed the mixture into the meat. She held the skewer while he slid the pig on and splayed it with cross sticks. While she tended to the cooking, he left to clean his bloodstained hands. Winding through the trees, he went in and out of view before reaching the lush undergrowth at the river's edge where, with careful steps, he disappeared down the steep bank, leaving her in the company of the ravens.

Under the birds' watch, she monitored the meat and the fire. The smell of smoke mixed with damp earth brought back memories of Pyramine's nest. She recalled with unexpected longing the meals she'd cooked on the ledge. She noted the smoke, surprised by her sentimentality. Dragons disliked smoke. They relished fire, as she did at this moment, staring at the dancing flames.

"You are like a dragon," Pyramine had told her when she declined to eat the crows he burned alive.

Watching the fire, she turned these words over and over in her head. Perhaps she was like a dragon. She no longer had any place among men.

Her eyes had adjusted to the firelight so much that the forest appeared much darker when she heard Galt return. He didn't sit with her against the dead tree but stopped at a large standing oak several paces to her left. He unbuckled his sword belt and lowered himself to the ground, facing her and the fire, watching. His hands were clean, but blood was smeared across the front of his surcoat. She wondered if he was still angry, and whether he was angry with her.

They watched the fire and the roasting meat, without talking. Isodore cut off a hind quarter each for her and for Galt. They ate with no more than brief words of courtesy. It was a filling yet somehow incomplete meal. She missed the conversations with Pyramine at the end of the day on the mountain. They had talked of sorcery and questioned their places in God's world, things she could never do with Galt.

After eating, Galt broke the sad silence with even sadder words. "The duke, he . . . Do you know what he found out?"

She shook her head, mouthing the word "no" without the strength for even a whisper.

"He said that your parents were spared by the dragon that razed their village. And they were burned for practicing witchcraft."

Isodore nodded. The burden of hiding that truth was lifted from her shoulders but left her no happier.

"He acquired the record of their conviction. He said you were placed in an orphanage, but the orphanage lost track of you."

"I ran away."

"Why?"

She didn't answer. There was too much to explain and too little will left in her. It didn't matter anyway. It would change nothing.

"The officials are speculating that you, too, are a witch. Many are convinced."

"Are you, as well?"

He didn't answer, and that was only fair. So many of his questions to her had gone unanswered.

But he was the only friend she had left. She didn't care whether the duke or the archbishop or the king believed she had fallen to Satan. She could face death again, but she wasn't prepared to see Galt abandon her, not yet. He might be powerless to persuade the council, but he was all she had left, and she didn't want to die forsaken by her last ally.

"They will kill me, won't they?"

"You know what you did was criminal and forbidden."

"I know it was forbidden, yes. But it was not wrong. It wasn't evil."

She had wanted to tell him that for some time. She watched for his reaction. He looked at her as though she were a stranger from a faraway land, who had misspoken horribly.

"I am not evil, Galt. I did what I had to do to survive. And I hurt no one."

"Are you a witch?"

Her reply stuck in her throat for a second, and she feared losing the courage to give him the truth he deserved. She nodded. "I cast the spell to change the dragon. But that wasn't the only one. I also cast the spell that brought you back from the brink of death and healed your scars. And another, when I was on the dragon's nest, to save my own life." She pulled aside the neck of her tunic to reveal the half-faded scar below her clavicle. "This was a festering wound from the dragon's claw. It was killing me. I cast these spells Galt, because if I didn't, I would have died. And your mission would have come to nothing."

He wasn't as shocked as she had expected. He was silent, but his eyes took in every part of her, perhaps awaiting his rage to build. It didn't, not yet.

"You can't know fate. God kept you alive after the dragon took you. You should have let Him finish His work."

"I didn't know God was on my side."

"So you accepted Satan's hand?"

"That wasn't what I said."

"Witchcraft is a tool of Satan. That book was the temptation of the devil. How could you possibly have considered it?"

She grew weary of defending herself, of his unshakable faith. "I am not evil. I did what I had to do. I'm not a knight. Not a dragonslayer. I couldn't buy my freedom. I am a sorceress!"

At that proclamation, Galt leaned away from her, as though she'd grown horns.

"I didn't choose sorcery, Galt. I am a sorceress by birth. If that makes me evil, then I was evil before I did a thing in this world."

He stared at her, confused. So she explained.

"Sorcery isn't something one simply decides to practice, Galt. It isn't like changing your religion. If you or your men tried the spells in that book, it wouldn't work. You have to be born a sorcerer."

"So that is your defense? You were born a sorceress? They'll gleefully make an example of—"

"I don't care!" She took some deep breaths to calm herself as tears blurred the face before her. "My parents were sorcerers. I was born a sorceress."

He turned his head and looked into the dark forest, unmoved by her explanation.

"Do you know what a sorceress is, Galt? I am not even a woman! A sorceress is a spirit forged into physical form by magic. That was what the dragon said." She added the final statement to mitigate the preposterousness of her claim, but it sounded only more preposterous.

"The dragon?"

"Yes."

"It could speak?"

"Yes. It knew what I was. I was afraid it would expose me as a sorceress. So . . . I tried to kill it."

"By changing it into a man?"

"Yes! How could I kill a dragon? I thought a man would be easier—"

"And it simply agreed to your plan?" His voice was incredulous, his face redder than she'd ever seen.

"No! First, it wanted me to change myself into a dragon, but I—"

"What? Why?" He almost laughed but it came out as a pleading cry.

"To be its mate. But I refused! Then it said I must change it into a man—"

"To be its mate? That madman's mate? That was your escape plan?"

In the time it took Galt to express his incredulity, it had spun into anger. Isodore dropped her head to her knees and wrapped her arms around it. Put into spoken words, her plan sounded so ridiculous.

"You lay with him! Have you truly escaped if you are carrying his child?"

"You don't have to wed me," she reminded him. "You're free to do whatever you wish."

"That doesn't excuse what you did!" He kicked the dirt and sent some flying toward her, where it settled in the creases of her tunic. He was acting like a child. Perhaps his uncle was right. He was just a boy.

She felt his anger as she had his uncle's. But while Corvin's threats were like a hammer, Galt's words were like a knife. She wanted to cry. She wanted to ask if he really thought she deserved to die for what she'd done. If so, he should take her life right now. But the words didn't come.

There they sat, stewing in anger and reproach.

Out of the trees swept a blur that looked like a mottled brown cape carried on the wind. But there was no wind, and the cape was silent as a ghost. It cut a diagonal path from the branches. Isodore barely saw it pass at the top periphery of her vision. When she turned her eyes toward it, a raven was scrambling away, squawking. A puff of black feathers floated down from the branch where the birds had perched to wait for scraps.

Galt picked up his sword and stood to look around the thick oak he had been leaning against, in the direction the blur had gone. He shielded his eyes from the bright flames and peered into the darkness. "An owl," he said, anticipating her question. "It has the other raven." He turned and paced back and forth on the far side of the fire from Isodore, holding the sheathed sword in his hand. That was the end of his concern over the disturbance.

Not so for Isodore. The owl was a herald of death, and death it was, for the raven. The sound of a wing slapping pitifully against the ground seemed to call to her. The sound of her own fate. Unable to contain herself, she sobbed. Death was everywhere. It was coming for her. She cried for the raven that had escaped, mourning for its lost mate, fearing for her own horrific execution.

Galt only paced, perhaps silenced by the shame of what he had said earlier, but unmoved by the death of a bird. He waited for her to stop crying. She watched him pace. It was up to her to salvage their rapidly fraying bond.

"I am sorry that I agreed to be the dragon's mate, Galt. I was certain you believed me dead and there was no other way to escape. If I hadn't done it, he would have killed me."

"If you hadn't resorted to sorcery, this ordeal would have been over long ago," Galt said gently but firmly. "You said you heard our signals. Why didn't you leave it to us? We could have killed the beast."

"How could I have known you were coming?"

Galt glanced toward her, then out to the dark forest, shaking his head. "How could you have not known?"

"What?" She couldn't believe she'd heard him correctly.

"How couldn't you have known? I knew! I knew you were aliveShe opened her mouth but had no reply.

"There were signs, Isodore. From God! They led me to you! Didn't you see? The dragon kept you fed. It kept you alive!"

She wanted to scream. She was alive because she had mastered the healing spell, because she let Pyramine believe she considered becoming his mate, and because a beast thought she had a beautiful spirit. How could she explain it? How could she even begin?

"We came to you, Isodore. All you had to do was wait. We would have easily disposed of that juvenile creature. We have killed far greater dragons."

The assertion was insulting. When she had suspected the raven calls were signals, what she'd feared most was a confrontation between Pyramine and the regiment, and the guilt she'd feel should Pyramine kill Galt. The fear she had of becoming a dragon that knew all the dragonslayer secrets was so great that she'd chosen to die instead. How could he know so little about the enemies he had to out-think? His ignorance could cost him his life one day.

Isodore's contempt for him at that moment must have been palpable, by the way he looked at her. "What?" he demanded.

"He was not a juvenile. He was a full-grown, mature dragon. I saw him kill another beast twice his size! And you saw the surcoat I had with me. He had killed a dragonslayer as well. That made him a dangerous beast. You said so yourself. He was older than Savelle and learned many things about men. He was very intelligent!"

Galt eyed her coldly, saying nothing. She'd meant to educate him, but it came out wrong, like she was defending Pyramine's honor. She was trying to find another explanation when she sensed the wheels in his mind turning, calculating.

"According to the book, the spell would have taken more than a day. You could have run away."

"Away to what? Back to Auch to be burned?"

"Back to me! You heard our signals!"

"I heard ravens!"

"That was us! You suspected so! Did you even think to look?"

"What reason did I have to believe you or any dragonslayer would come for me? Dragonslayers would never again come to Dragon's Ridge. You told me so, yourself. Sir Dalton, Sir Wilfred, everyone believed that. Do you think I wanted to be forsaken? I wanted you to come, of course I did. But I was supposed to be dead! Why should anyone come for a dead woman?"

"Yes! Why? Why didn't it kill you? Why did it steal fruits to feed you? Because everything was different! Nothing turned out the way we expected. Nothing, for that was God's will. Time and time again. All you had to do was stop. You could have left him to look for us. You had hours to consider it. We gave up sleep to chase after you. But you chose the dragon! Why, Isodore? Why?" He turned and kicked the tree, roaring a curse.

"No, I didn't choose him. I meant to kill him and escape."

He took an endless look into her eyes, then down and up her body. His jaws clenched.

"Don't you believe me?"

He gave an anguished grunt. "I want to believe you. But my men—and my scout—gave testimony that you did not appear to be the madman's captive. They even thought you were his companion when they saw you. And . . . and I . . . saw your loyalty to him. I know you tried to hide it. Even now, you admire that beast." He turned from her and looked into the darkness beyond the fire's glow, as though unable to bear the sight of her.

"I feared for my life, Galt. I had to feign loyalty to him. I ran from him, Galt. To you! I am loyal to you! You are my knight!"

"No!" Galt snapped, slamming a fist into the tree beside him, then spun around and pointed an accusing finger at her. "You turned on him after we found you. Not before! Your loyalty was with him. The man you claimed you would kill! The man whose child you carry! Why, Isodore? I have stood by you, against my own family!"

He kicked the oak again as he finished, but his will was draining fast. He put a hand on the trunk to steady himself and fumed. Without looking at her, he turned and slumped down to sit on the ground with his knees drawn up, sulking at the foot of the great oak with his sword beside him.

Isodore was in tears. "I saw no choice, Galt. My heart was still yours, even as I believed you had given me up for dead."

"I never gave up on you. Never. You didn't want to be forsaken, but you forsook me. You didn't trust that I'd come for you, even after hearing our signals. Who would be out here, but our regiment? Why would we come, except for you?" He brought his sword around his legs, planting the scabbard's tip in the ground between his feet. Gripping it in both hands, he curled forward and pressed his forehead into the cruciform weapon as though praying. Or pleading.

"I'm sorry, Galt." She would have done differently in hindsight. Looking back, everything was so easy. Leave Pyramine in a vulnerable state and run back to where she'd heard the raven calls. Even if it hadn't been Galt, even if it wasn't another regiment, it would have been a heathen clan who might have helped her. "I've destroyed it all. If I could have those hours over, I would never have cast that spell. I could have found an excuse . . . to delay the spell, at least."

Galt's fingers tightened around the scabbard, turning his knuckles white. "I would gladly choose to face the dragon rather than this."

Coincidentally, Isodore thought the same, certain somehow that Pyramine would have granted her the quick death she'd asked for rather than the barbaric one her people had devised for the likes of her.

"They will burn me, won't they?" she said, hoping for some words of comfort from him.

Galt said nothing. He smirked and rotated the sword in one hand until the grip came to his other.

"They burned my parents, Galt," she said. "I heard them scream. It sounded so horrible. I am so afraid of that pain." She stared into the fire, imagining herself a small figure crumpling at the center. won't let you die like that," he said. "I won't let anyone hurt you, Isodore. Never."

She heard the hiss of the blade along a scabbard's interior. She looked toward Galt. His right hand was on the grip, slowly drawing the blade. Halfway out, the polished steel glistened in the firelight under jagged red streaks still wet from butchering the pig.

She had prepared for death so many times that it had become just a sad routine. It had been difficult for her to ask Pyramine for the mercy of a quick death, so she was thankful she wouldn't have to ask Galt. The sharp-edged dragonslayer's sword flashed the promise of a clean, fast death. The least painful, the most dignified. It was why the noblemen insisted on their right to be beheaded. Not hanged, not stoned, not burned. No screaming. No mockery. How fitting to be killed by the same blade that had ended Pyramine's pain. She closed her eyes and waited for Galt to rise to his feet.

What she heard instead was, "Make no further move, Sir Galt."

45

The Owl and the Raven

Isodore opened her eyes to see Galt spring to his feet, whirling to face the fallen tree behind her. His sword whipped out, sending into the dark forest a high-pitched ring of steel scraping past the scabbard's bronze throat. Behind the fallen tree stood a figure in a filthy, raggedly torn brown robe, with tangled, gray-streaked hair and a bushy beard. He had a sword, lowered by his side, relaxed.

He held up his free hand. "I wish you no harm, Knight of the Cross," he said in a hoarse rasp. "I'm here for the lass. Leave her with me and be on your way. I beg you. Please. I shall tell no one of this meeting."

The fire shone a harsh light on the stranger, deepening the irregularities on his face. Gruesome scars cut across his cheeks and neck—and the bruises that covered them. Even his ear was bruised purple. It was an awful face to behold, striking Isodore simultaneously with pity for what had happened to him and fear for what he could do to her. With uneven eyes and a crooked nose, he appeared to have been cruelly beaten, yet he showed no fear facing the famous knight.

Galt collected his wits and straightened from his fighting stance. "Who the hell are you?" he asked, his tone irritated.

"No one," replied the stranger. "I am nothing to you. I only want the lass. And I beg you, leave her here and be on your way." He lowered his head respectfully as he spoke but kept his eyes on Galt.

Galt relaxed, lowering his weapon and appearing unconcerned. "What sort of man makes such a demand of a Knight of the Cross? You will leave us. Now."

"I will leave you, certainly. But the lass will come with me."

Something seemed to change in Galt's eyes. "Who sent you?"

"No one, great Knight of God's Miracle. I serve no one."

Galt glanced quickly at Isodore then back to his adversary. "I've no time for this game. Tell me who you are!"

The stranger smiled, revealing missing teeth. "Just a passerby who has seen and heard much this evening. But I will forget everything. Yes, everything—if you give me the lass. I only want the lass. I have no wish to do you harm. You will not see either of us again. No one will. If you're as wise as you are brave, Knight of God's Miracle, you will agree."

Isodore scooted away, eyeing the stranger. Something about the man, his command of the potentially deadly situation, belied his indigence. It was as if he were two men, a beggar and a killer, bowing his head to Galt yet watching his every move. He was ashamed one second and confident the next.

Like the owl upon the ravens, he came upon them in perfect stealth. He gave away the element of surprise when he could have killed Galt and taken her by force. She shivered as she realized that no matter the confidence Galt projected, the stranger was not afraid of her fresh-faced young knight.

Galt's eyes darted between him and Isodore. He was searching for a connection between the intruder and her, waiting for a cue. She was unsure what she wanted, but she certainly didn't want to be simply handed over like a possession, as the stranger wanted.

Her hesitance was enough for Galt. He launched forward, jumping onto the log and swinging his sword in a flurry of strikes, left and right, high and low. His sword came close, but the stranger successfully defended himself, backing up through soft ferns. Galt dropped off the log and advanced. Isodore thought he would drive the intruder away, but the robed man held his position and continued to deflect Galt's blade. Galt seemed surprised and paused to examine the beggar. The men's eyes locked on each other before Galt swung again. This time, the stranger counterattacked. He advanced, keeping Galt on the defensive while walking back his lost ground. His sword swung from one move to the next, as if they were all part of the same choreography, fast and graceful. They made Galt's defense seem awkward. He pressed Galt back to where he had started, then further, before stopping to offer a warning.

"You're a dragonslayer, Sir Galt," he said in the quick, confident voice. "How many men have you killed with that sword?" He motioned to Galt's sword with his own, flicking his weapon as if it were an extension of his own arm. "This," he raised his blade, "has killed countless."

His sleeve slid back when his sword hand came up, exposing burn scars on his arm—not the formless burns of dragon fire but sharp imprints of hot iron. Torture burns.

"Save your bravery for the dragons, Sir Galt. You're not trained for this. You and your Church have no use for this woman but to put her to death. Give her to me." And there it went. His voice changed from commanding to pleading, ashamed. "Give her to me, and neither you nor the Church will ever see us again. You needn't defend yourself. I have no grudge with you. Just give Isodore to me."

The stranger's eyes fixed on Galt. Isodore's darted between them. Though he seemed to have shrunk when his voice changed, his bold claim rang true. Sir Rowan had always said that dragonslayers were generally not remarkable swordsmen because the sword wasn't their primary weapon against the beasts. This beggar fought like a remarkable swordsman.

At that instant, she saw through his bushy hair, his thick beard and shabby clothing, through the scars, swollen eye, and crooked nose. One by one, his wounds gave way, revealing to her the face beneath. Galt was facing a warrior with a lifetime of training, a veteran of men's battlefields, many times a victorious killer. She knew this killer only through stories, because toward her, he had been nothing but kind. He was a knight who knew forests well enough to follow and sneak up on them undetected, well enough to escape bands of pursuing Normans—in the stories he himself had told her, long ago.

"Sir Rowan?"

He seemed to barely hear her. His eyes still on Galt.

"What has become of you?" she whispered.

"Sir Rowan," Galt echoed. "You're Isodore's friend. A Knight of the Cross? What . . . happened to you?" He cocked his head and lowered his weapon.

The stranger's lips trembled wordlessly for a second. In a raspy voice, he blurted, "I need the girl. She has something I want. That's all I want. Give her to me, and I won't harm you." It was half an order, half a plea. Isodore wasn't certain he was Sir Rowan. Only part of him was. But the knight she thought she'd never see again in this life was perhaps somewhere within.

"I fear no harm from you. Who sent you?" said Galt, pointing his sword.

"No one. I have told you."

"What do you want with her?"

"That does not matter for you."

"You will not have her. Leave now, or forfeit your life."

Sir Rowan, or whoever he was, breathed deeply, sadly. "Very well, Knight of God's Miracle. May God have greater mercy on your soul than He has had on me." He stepped forward and attacked. His sword moved so fast that Galt barely had time to defend himself. He slipped behind a tree for a second to take a measure of his foe, then charged out with his own attack. The striking swords sounded louder than before. Murderous. But within a few strikes, Sir Rowan had him on the defensive again, retreating behind another tree. He didn't give up, but his sword no longer came close. At least he can defend himself, thought Isodore.

On the next bout, Sir Rowan's blade came under Galt's sword arm and bit into his side, sending him lunging awkwardly behind another tree.

"No!" cried Isodore.

The men ignored her. Galt, frustrated but unhurt, was saved by the light leather armor worn by dragonslayers when they traveled. It was clear that he was the lesser swordsman, and his advantage of armor didn't seem enough.

Sir Rowan flushed him from one tree to the next, appearing stronger and more proficient the longer he fought. No longer gauging his adversary, he was out to kill, the stronger combatant in an utterly one-sided duel.

What disturbed Isodore most was the sight of Galt trying to keep a tree between him and his attacker. The woods had always been used against dragons, by peasants and dragonslayers alike. It was a common defensive strategy against creatures with so much more strength and power. That was now Galt's strategy, moving from one tree to the next to put off a humiliating defeat. He couldn't face Sir Rowan in the clear. Her heart went out to him, the young dragon-slayer against a far more experienced warrior. What chance did a knight who killed dragons have against one who killed other knights?

What was she to do? Isodore's confusion turned to panic, then back to confusion, spinning like a whirlwind in her head. She opened her mouth but didn't know what to say, averted her eyes but didn't know what to pray for. Not for Galt to give his life defending her. Not for Sir Rowan to die trying to save her from the Church, if that was his intention. She feared losing Galt and falling into an uncertain fate with this new version of Sir Rowan.

She wanted to run, but there was no escape she knew now. She had tried to escape from Pyramine but only managed to betray him. Now, he haunted her conscience and her dreams. There was no way to detach herself from these men. Either Galt or Sir Rowan would fall in this battle, and she couldn't let either of them take his last breath having been abandoned by her the way she had abandoned Pyramine.

Galt had been driven so far from the fire that he disappeared into the darkness, and even Sir Rowan was barely visible. Suddenly, Sir Rowan turned and dashed back to Isodore.

"Isodore, run!" Galt yelled, giving chase.

She jumped up and ran, but it became immediately clear she would not get far, for as soon as she left the light of the fire, she faced a pitch-dark forest and had to slow down for fear of running headlong into a tree or being brought down by a blind step. She turned to look for her pursuer and saw him spin around at the fire. He skidded backward and stopped with one knee touching down in a deep lunge, eyes and sword raised back toward Galt.

Suddenly facing not Sir Rowan's back but the tip of his sword, Galt lurched to a stop. Sir Rowan wasn't after her at all. As he knelt, shaped like a thunderbolt ready to strike Galt down, Sir Rowan reached a hand behind and found the unlit torch on the ground. He rose, victorious, touching the torch head to the hot coals without taking his eyes off Galt. Flames attached to the dry wrap around the torch head. Galt could only watch. Taking the torch was what he should have done. Inexperienced, under-trained, and now, he had lost the only thing that could possibly save him in this hopeless fight, the cover of darkness.

Sir Rowan let forth a roar as he launched himself—blade, light and fire—at Galt. Galt retreated faster than before. Isodore followed the light of the torch as the fight wove between the trees. Soon, the torchlight dimmed. Its dry wrap burned out, but not before igniting the roll of tallow cloth beneath. A small flame clung to the torch head, gaining brightness as it fed on new fuel. Sir Rowan held the torch head above and behind his own head, forcing Galt to look at it while he fought. Against the darkness, the yellow flame was blinding.

Galt shuffled behind a tree and tripped. Sir Rowan rounded the tree and struck as Galt rolled away. The sword tip ripped through a flap of his surcoat. He stumbled to his feet in time to get behind another tree. At least he was fast. Once again, his armor had saved him.

It was clear to Isodore that this was Sir Rowan's element. He had sneaked in and surprised her and Galt the way that owl had swooped, silent and unseen, out of the trees to take that raven. That battle had been one-sided too. The owl wasn't just the harbinger of death. It was death's agent, a natural predator in its element, a creature of the night. Like Sir Rowan, it had the advantage of sight, while Galt and the poor ravens had lost theirs to the darkness. The outcome was bleak for her young knight.

"Sir Rowan?" she called. "Sir Rowan, please stop. I'll . . . I'll do whatever you wish."

The attack stopped, but not the frenzy in Sir Rowan's hoarse voice.

"Whatever I wish? Whatever I wish!"

"Yes!" When the echoes of her voice faded, she could hear the men's heavy breathing. "Yes, Sir Rowan. Just say it."

"Start," he roared without taking his eyes from Galt, "by telling Sir Galt to leave us. Tell him to spare himself and return to his camp. I have no wish to kill a Knight of the Cross. He is trained to kill dragons. He will not best me."

"Galt, please do as he says. Please just do it."

"Are you working for the duke?" Galt demanded.

"No."

"What do you want from Isodore?"

"Only that which she gave you. Nothing more."

There was silence, but in the time needed for a man to come to a conclusion, the blades whirled again, and everything else Isodore said was drowned by the clash of swords or ignored. Galt seemed strengthened, enraged, growling and grunting as he fought. But it did him little good.

Isodore tried to come to them, making her way slowly through the dark woods away from the fire. Galt seemed to have worn himself out with his rage. He grunted more than growled as he swung his weapon.

A different sound suddenly ended the clanging of blades. Galt's sword, swinging toward Sir Rowan's leg, stopped with a distinct thunk as his sharp blade bit deep into hardened leather.

Did the beggar have armor under his cloak?

No. Galt's blade had struck the side of a tree. Sir Rowan's boot was upon it in an instant, trapping the sword where it lodged. Sir Rowan barked a satisfied laugh. Unable to lift his weapon out of the cut it had made, Galt grabbed the cross-guard with both hands to yank it back. Sir Rowan gave him no time. His decisive slash would have severed Galt's hands had he not released his weapon.

Sir Rowan came forward, forcing Galt back by the point of his sword. He freed Galt's sword with his torch hand. The weapon dangled from his fingers by its cross-guard. Sir Rowan tempted Galt for a second before heaving it into the air. It spun into the darkness and fell with a swish of disturbed brush.

Galt drew his dagger, to which his adversary mocked, "A kitchen knife!" Sir Rowan moved forward, and Galt retreated, moving just fast enough to keep a tree between himself and the slashing blade. Sir Rowan drove him further away. It was hard to see the men through the trees, but Isodore could follow the torch flame and the trees lit by its orange glow.

And then, even the trees disappeared.

The torchlight stopped moving. Isodore found a line of sight to the men. Sir Rowan had his back to her, but she could see Galt's face, and the faltering remnants of his resolve. Sir Rowan advanced, forcing Galt backward over lush undergrowth. He backed up against a wall of darkness. There were no trees behind him.

No. Not a wall of darkness. The river!

Sir Rowan swung his blade across Galt's neckline. Galt jerked back, whirled his arms and dropped. Isodore heard a crash.

"Galt!" she screamed.

Sir Rowan looked back over his shoulder, and she realized what a madman truly was. It wasn't Pyramine. Pyramine she could understand. Madness was a man of two minds, two voices, tortured within and without. She feared him in a way she had never feared the dragon. More than death. She feared the scars on his face, the wild look in his eyes. The owl that rules the night.

But hadn't the owl taken only one raven while the other fled unharmed? One died while the other escaped.

Sir Rowan stepped to the river bank, holding the torch high, and looked down. Isodore turned and fled.

She knew she couldn't get far without a torch, but she could perhaps move through enough unlit forest that Sir Rowan couldn't guess where she went. She reached out her arms blindly to feel for the trees she might crash into. She heard him coming, breaking through brush and sweeping away ferns. She changed her direction to fool him, but it didn't work.

"Isodore, wait!"

An orange glow illuminated the forest for her, but it was no light of hope, for with the torchlight came Sir Rowan. He grabbed her shoulder. She twisted away and fell into the ferns. He turned her onto her back and struck aside a fern leaf to look at her. The stench of his breath came down on her, hard and heavy and awful. His eyes bulged above the marred face, glistening in the torchlight.

He straddled her. "Isodore! It's me! It's me! Sir Rowan! Oh, dear lass! It has been so long!"

It was him, yet she couldn't find it in her to greet him the way she had always imagined she would. His voice was full of joy, but not the joy of reunion. It was the joy of possession.

"You do remember me, don't you? I know you do. You called my name!" There was a faint laugh in his voice, but not an infectious laugh. A greedy laugh. She tried to wriggle free, but he had her pinned down.

"Sir Rowan . . ." She tried to look past the heavy beard and scars, the swollen eyes and crooked nose. "Sir Rowan, what happened to you?"

"What?" He asked as though he had no idea.

"You're hurt. Your face is . . . Who did this to you?" Despite her revulsion, tears filled her eyes. She felt an instinct to reach a part him somewhere behind those greedy eyes.

"This? It was . . . It was nothing. My . . . penance. I finally . . . finally . . ." He trailed off. A spark of hope came to his eyes, then it seemed to pull him away. Far away.

"Your penance?" she called, and he returned. "I thought you escaped. Who did this to you?"

"No one. I repented, you see, I repented. Oh God, I . . . I knew I was committing crimes against my Lord. But I repented. I'm not evil. I know I've sinned. And I've repented. You see it, don't you? I've repented. God must take me back. I'll change . . . You'll help me. I'll be normal at last. Normal."

"Sir Rowan!" He looked down at her, returning again from afar. Afar, where the madman was. She had to keep the madman away. "Why? Why so much? Your face. Your arms. Your teeth. You did all this to yourself?"

"I had to, Isodore. It was . . . a training of sorts. I trained hard, you see. I trained myself to stop. Because nothing worked. Nothing could cure me of the perverse forbidden lust. For men! I lusted for men! No, no. Please tell no one. I'll never do it again. Never, because you'll help me. I've tried everything to stop. I've even visited the pagan healers. God forgive me. I learned to make myself stop. But it was painful. So painful."

"You did this to yourself? Your scars? Your burns?" She cried, knowing he had.

"Yes, of course. I had to repent, you see, each time I gave in to the perverse lust. Else God would bar me from His kingdom, don't you think?"

"It's so awful."

"It's painful. I can't go on like this. You will help me, won't you?" He nodded, shaking the strand of drool hanging from his lower lip. "I heard the Knight of God's Miracle had rescued you. The first ever to be saved from a dragon! I came to Auch, just to look upon you again. I have missed you so. Won't you help me?"

"H–How?"

"They said you're a sorceress! I couldn't believe it, but I heard you tell Sir Galt. You're a sorceress! You are! You healed him! You're a healer!"

She nodded, despite her revulsion. The utter disappointment of this reunion!

"You can cure me of the perverse lust. Won't you do it, Isodore? Save me from my suffering. Please!"

"N–N–" The word "No" wouldn't come. "I can't, Sir Rowan."

"Yes, you can. Yes, you can!" He stabbed the sharp end of the torch into the ground so it stood on its own, took both of her shoulders in his hands, and shook her. "You can! You must! Don't let me go on like this!"

"I can't, Sir Rowan. It . . . it's not an illness. Is it?"

"It is!" he insisted, shaking her shoulders. "I'm ill! Don't you see? Madness for a man to lust for another man."

"I don't have the materials anymore. They're very hard to find."

Though she argued, her mind was on his hands tightening on her shoulders. Both hands. No sword. He must have dropped it to grab her. He was right-handed, so the sword must be on her left.

"I'll find you the materials. What do you need? Gold? Silver? I'll get it."

"No. I'm afraid to foul it up. My parents never taught me. I'm not good. I'm afraid something would go terribly wrong."

"I don't care! I'd rather die. I must be cured! Nothing has worked. Do you hear me? Nothing! Just do what you did for Sir Galt."

"But it's forbidden. They'll burn me. You know they will."

"No one will know!"

"God will."

Sir Rowan stopped shaking her. She moved her hands slowly to the ground, feeling for the sword. He began to cry. "God. My Lord. My Lord." Little snuffles turned into sobs. "It's wrong, it's wrong. Yes, I know. I'm sorry, Isodore. Sorry I asked you to commit such a sin. It's wrong."

"It's all right," she said, walking her fingers through the forest litter by his leg, searching for the sword.

His face winced, just as a fist slammed into the side of his head.

"Sir Ro—"

The fist came again, slamming into his bruised eye. She looked for Galt but already knew it wasn't Galt. The fist belonged to Sir Rowan himself, slamming into his own face with sickening thuds. She grabbed his arm as he tried to throw another punch.

"Sir Rowan! No! Stop it! Please!" She wrapped both her arms around his and pulled herself against it, using her own weight to restrain him. He switched arms.

"Bad. Dirty, Rowan," he scolded as he brought his head into each blow.

Isodore swung her arms around his neck and pulled herself against him. "Stop it, please," she begged, whispering into his ear, trying to soothe the madness in him. "Please stop. Please stop. Don't go away. Come back to me. Come back."

He stopped. She felt his muscular back soften. She released her arms and lowered herself back to the ground, still pinned under him. Her hands slipped down his arms and held them until he loosened his fists.

"Please, Sir Rowan. Don't do this to yourself."

"I must repent. It's the only way."

"There must be another."

"There is no other."

"There must be, Sir Rowan. What have you tried?" While she spoke to keep him present, her hand went back searching for the sword.

"Medicine. Potions. Isolation. Celibacy. Punishment. Only punishment works. The pain prevents me from giving in to my temptations. But the awful desire still plagues me."

"Perhaps God made you that way, like He made me a sorceress. I've often wondered where sorcerers came—"

"No! It's disgusting." He looked at her as if she had done something wrong. "Very un-God-like."

"Well, then can you, perhaps, take a woman to bed to satiate your desire? Can you . . . desire women?"

He shook his head, his eyes looking into the darkness in front of him as though he could see through it, to the other side where his sanity lay. Stay with me, Sir Rowan, she thought. Stay with me. Her fingertips, patting the damp forest detritus, touched something hard and smooth by his leg.

The pommel.

She smiled at him, willing him to keep his eyes on her face, away from her hand. She wasn't sure what she would do with the sword. Perhaps ward him away. She doubted that she would or could attack him, and he likely had a dozen ways to disarm her, but perhaps she could keep him at bay while she figured something else out.

"No," answered Sir Rowan. "I have yet to find a woman who could inspire in me the slightest lust."

She tried to pull the sword into her grip, but it was stuck. He looked down at her hand. She realized that it wasn't the sword she found, but something firm and stiff, perhaps the buckle on his boot, and in grabbing it, she'd pushed her fingers into his leg, and he felt it. He studied her fingers then back to her face. To hide her intention, she smiled wider, though there was no hiding her nervousness. He smiled back a bruised, swollen-lipped smile. "Isodore?"

An awkward silence passed as his eyes scanned her face and shoulder in the torchlight. He looked down on her chest, still heaving from the run and the struggle to make him stop hitting himself. His hand hovered above her breasts while a stunned grin came across his face.

She felt sick with the realization that she had given him the wrong impression by fingering his boot while suggesting he take a woman to bed. She wanted to tell him it wasn't what she meant, but something stole her voice. She feared what he might do if she resisted. The man she knew had sunk back into the huge robe and the madman peered out. The words "No, no" formed on her still soundless lips as she shook her head. It wasn't until his hands were right over her breasts that a self-preserving instinct brought her arms across them and she suddenly found her voice. "No!"

It startled him and he withdrew his hands as if from hot coals. His eyes found the fear and disgust in hers, and soon she saw the guilt in his face. He stammered an apology. "I . . . I'm sorry. I thought . . ."

"You frighten me."

"I know. I'm sorry. I . . ." He squeezed his eyes and lips shut, whimpering.

"What is it? Sir Rowan, what is it?"

He straightened his back and shook his head, his eyes unfocused. "I am so vile. You are so pure, and I am so vile."

Crack! A fist slammed into his face.

"No!" she screamed, but fists wound up and struck from both sides.

"Vile, Rowan. Vile." With each word, a fist came up and his head bowed down to meet it.

Isodore tried to grab his arms but they moved too fast. She grabbed his shoulders and shook. "No, Sir Rowan. Stop it! No more! Please!" Her effort did no good, and she was left crying and whimpering. "Stop. Please don't!"

To her surprise, he did. Abruptly. Mouth agape, he stared out into the forest in front of him.

"Oh," he said. "Oh, dear." His lips peeled back, his teeth clenched and his eyes squeezed shut. A pained expression passed over his face as he let out a low and intense grunt.

When his eyes opened again, they were clear and alert. Sir Rowan's eyes. The madman was gone. The knight turned and lunged behind. He crawled on his hands and feet away from her, sweeping aside fern leaves to search the ground.

The torch lit his back, from whence protruded a thin shaft. Straight, smooth, and fletched with black feathers. The raven had returned.

46

Double Defeat

The arrow stood tall on Sir Rowan's back as he scurried on the forest floor, peering through the undergrowth. His breaths were rapid. His hands struck aside fern leaves. Watching in disbelief, Isodore missed the chance to escape.

At last, Sir Rowan stopped. He rose to his knees then his feet, holding the object she had hoped to retrieve earlier. His sword.

He stumbled toward a tree to shield himself from the direction of the arrow. A painful grimace passed across his face.

"Sir Rowan, you're hurt."

Isodore began to stand, but he hissed, "Stay back! Stay down. Hide!"

She remained on her knees but strained to look for Galt. In the darkness she heard the sound of footsteps and disturbed brush, like a wild animal approaching. And it didn't care for caution. Galt burst into the orange glow with a bow in his hand and vengeance in his eyes. He headed straight for the tree shielding Sir Rowan but spotted her.

"Isodore! Are you all right?"

Realizing she had not hidden as Sir Rowan instructed, she stammered. Two opposing instincts wrestled in her mind. To warn Galt that Sir Rowan was hiding behind the tree, and to warn Sir Rowan of the murder in Galt's eyes.

"What was he doing to you?" Galt demanded.

"He was . . . He wanted me to . . ."

"You were screaming. Was he raping you?"

"N–No!"

"Did he attack you?"

An old sense of loyalty, not completely extinguished by Sir Rowan's behavior, kept her from sending Galt after him.

Galt assessed her for a second, then scanned the surrounding trees. He held the bow and a clutch of arrows in one hand, and in the other, a single shaft, nocked but not yet drawn.

"Step out of hiding, Sir Rowan. You can face me like a knight or die like a coward. I know my arrow found you."

Sir Rowan glanced back at Isodore, mouthing "Hide!" then stepped out from behind the tree. Incredibly, he sounded even calmer than he had earlier, when he'd had the upper hand. "I am not hurt as badly as you think."

"What were you doing with Isodore?"

Sir Rowan sighed. "That is between her and me."

"Don't toy with me!" Galt lifted the bow enough for Sir Rowan to take note.

"Loose that arrow, and I'll cut you down before you nock another." Sir Rowan spun his sword in a loose grip and brought the weapon forward as a reminder to Galt.

"Is that so?" Galt mocked. "You are a formidable swordsman. But this is no longer a duel of blades, is it?" He drew back the bowstring.

Sir Rowan looked around. Several long strides separated the two men, unobstructed save for some dropped branches. Isodore thought he might dart back to the tree, but he again mouthed to her, "Run!" He took a step, positioning himself to block her from Galt.

Galt remained calm. "I'm tired of your game. I struck you with a slow arrow, so it wouldn't pass through you and hit Isodore. This one will not be so kind." He finished drawing and took aim at Sir Rowan's head.

"What I wanted with Isodore, I . . . I'm ashamed to admit. But now, my intention is to save her, with all the strength I have left.

And I swear to that."

"Save her? From whom?"

"From you! And the trial! And the Church!"

"A Knight of the Cross betraying the Church? You'll burn in Hell."

"Oh, I'll burn in Hell for far more than you know, but until I do, she is under my protection."

"Your protection? You're in no position to protect anyone."

"I've killed far better knights than you."

"And I will send you to them, so you can brag."

"Sir Rowan . . ." Isodore began.

"Why are you still here, lass? I told you to run!" A string of coughs followed his words.

Galt gave a scoffing laugh. He relaxed his draw and cocked his head, studying Sir Rowan. "Blood in your throat, is it? You'll be dead by morning if you fight. Tell me why you came and who sent you. My men will care for you—you have my word as a Knight of the Cross. You might survive if we help you before you drown in that blood."

Sir Rowan spat.

"Very well. You leave me with only one way to ensure the duke never hears from you." He re-drew and aimed again at Sir Rowan's head.

"I'm not an agent of the duke. I give you my word as a Knight of the Cross."

"Who hired you?" Galt's words simultaneously commanded and threatened. He kept the arrow aimed at Sir Rowan's head.

"No one. Would you hire a beggar like me? No. I came for myself."

"Why?"

"To . . . seek Isodore's help." He lowered his head and his shoulders drooped. He lost his confrontational tone, perhaps convinced at last that Galt was ready to kill him. Isodore was glad to see them talking, but feared that at any instant, the arrow would fly into Sir Rowan's skull.

Galt continued the interrogation. "How would she help you?"

"It matters not. She refused me. And rightly so."

"She screamed for you to stop. What were you doing?"

"What, indeed. I . . . I was . . ."

A profound sympathy for Sir Rowan's shame moved Isodore. "You don't have to say, Sir Rowan. Don't make him say it, Galt. It's between him and me."

It was his secret, as sorcery was hers. And she had grown tired of being villainized. Galt looked to Isodore, clearly not having expected her defense. Sir Rowan lowered his sword and looked over his shoulder at her.

But that was a trick. He was just winding up. In a blink, the sword came back up, hurling from his hand, point first, at Galt's chest.

Galt turned aside and raised the bow out of the way. The sword passed under his armpit. Its cross-guard glanced off his ribs, but it wobbled on. Sir Rowan leaped over the fallen branches, charging at Galt. Galt brought the bow down and loosed the arrow. It flew past Isodore with a treacherous whipping sound.

Galt went down on his back with Sir Rowan atop him and the bow trapped between. Sir Rowan pinned Galt down. Each man had a hand on the other's throat. Galt reached for the dagger on his belt, but Sir Rowan seized his wrist and pinned it down as well. Galt released Sir Rowan's throat to reach around for the arrow, but Sir Rowan pushed himself away. Galt only managed to grab the robe, but it was enough. He yanked on the cloth. Sir Rowan roared, but didn't let go. Galt wrenched his fistful of cloth, and the arrow leaned to one side. Sir Rowan gasped between cries of pain. He shook as he tried to choke the life out of Galt. Isodore screamed for them to stop. But they were too preoccupied with killing.

She plucked the torch from where it stood and ran around the tree. She ran past the men and scanned the ground. A short distance further was Sir Rowan's sword.

She ran back to them, brandishing the weapon. "Enough! That's enough!"

"Isodore, run!" they yelled, still snarling at each other. No pause in the brawl.

Without thinking, she raised the sword and brought it down,

slapping the flat of the blade hard on Galt's wrist. "Stop!" she yelled. He released Sir Rowan's robe. She struck again, on the back of Sir Rowan's head. "I said, stop!" Both men turned to her.

"Stop tellin' me te run!" she scolded. "I'm not the one in mortal danger 'ere. You are! Both of ye. Stop fightin'!" She thrust the sword between their faces to show she was serious. They looked at the blade then back up to her, more surprised than afraid.

"Get up," she ordered, shaking the sword.

Somewhat stunned, they obeyed. They rose slowly, each taking an arm of the bow. Neither wished to be the first to loosen his grip. She confiscated it with two fingers of the hand holding the torch.

"His dagger?" Sir Rowan said.

Galt rolled his eyes and daintily handed over the weapon he was trying to conceal.

"His is in his belt," Galt said.

Sir Rowan reached into his robe for the short blade and turned it over to Isodore.

The warriors brushed bits of forest floor off themselves. Galt gathered the dropped arrows, whole and broken, and handed the clutch to Isodore, leering at Sir Rowan, who followed his movements with suspicion.

They were trained to fight, and that was how they solved their disputes. She was tired of the distrust and shouting and combat. She wanted to sit and sort things out. There was no space where they stood, so it was back to the fire they went. "No more fighting," she ordered. "And stay on your own side."

They walked, but the two men immediately closed in on her. "Keep your distance," Sir Rowan barked.

"I'm only making sure she doesn't end up a hostage."

They argued, neither trusting the other to stay a safe distance away.

"Fine," said Isodore. "I'm going ahead. You two figure it out."

She led the way for a few paces.

"That's close enough. Back off," Galt ordered.

"Don't give me orders."

"Then keep your—"

She heard the sound of scuffling and turned around. "Will you two stop squabbling?"

"He wants that sword," Galt said.

"I don't need a sword to take care of you."

Galt turned to Isodore. "He'll take that sword from you, and we'll be right back where we were before."

"Bah!"

"He's a trickster and a madman. He's taken you by force. He doesn't care what you think of him."

Isodore looked from one man to the other, each seething with distrust. "Woodness, can't you two just walk without fighting?"

"I'll walk if he walks. If he fights, I'll fight."

Isodore rolled her eyes. "Can't you trust each other for just one minute? You're both Knights of the Cross, for heaven's sake!"

They glared at each other.

She sighed. "All right. I'll watch to see who can be trusted and who's playing tricks, all right? Walk ahead of me, both of you. To the fire. Go!"

They shuffled past her.

She marched them forward, her arms full with torch, sword, daggers, bow and arrows, while their hands were empty and their chins down, warriors bereft of weapons and hubris.

47

The Price of Wisdom

Galt snuffed out the torch in the soil mound by the fire pit. Sir Rowan lowered himself to the ground, gritting his teeth. He leaned his shoulder against the downed log. Because of the protruding arrow, he couldn't lean his back. Isodore watched his eyes for the crazed look of the madman, but she saw only a grim inward focus. Perhaps it was the pain, or the mortal wound, or being bested by a lesser knight, but he remained somber. No room left in his head for the madman. Or perhaps he had lost hope. The madman was high on hope, if nothing else.

She wanted to ask if he could keep the madman from returning, but she thought it better to let him deal with it his own way. Talk of the madman might agitate him. Keeping him calm would be best. Her sympathy for him grew, the longer the madman stayed away. His lips were red from the blood he coughed up, but when she tried to comfort him, he waved her off.

"It's a minor wound."

She exchanged a glance with Galt, but neither said a word.

Galt fed the fire more wood and took a seat on the ground, facing Sir Rowan across the fire. Isodore sat by the log, next to Sir Rowan, leaving the weapons out of his reach. The three sat for a moment, their breaths calm, soothed by the flames.

Sir Rowan stared into the fire and Galt stared into the night. They were more likely to argue than talk. Isodore had to speak first.

"I don't think either of you wishes me harm," she said.

"Right. He was going to show you mercy," Sir Rowan said, "with a gentle beheading."

Isodore followed Sir Rowan's gaze toward Galt, who avoided their eyes. She recalled where they had left off. So much had happened so fast that only now could she give it thought. Galt did draw his sword. Blood-red streaks on the polished blade remained vivid in her mind. Given the certainty of her conviction and barbaric execution, she had thought a quick death was more merciful, and that Galt had been prepared to give it to her.

Galt looked worried. Resentful, but not remorseful. Isodore waited for his explanation. The struggle to escape during the fight had revived her will to live, and with that, the fear that she might not do so for long.

Galt scanned the woods beyond their sphere of firelight. "If there's an agent of the duke here, then this will doom us."

"There's no such person!" Sir Rowan coughed blood again.

Galt ignored him, directing his words to Isodore. "If he had not interrupted us, you would have known by now. I would return to tell the sheriff that you confessed your crime. You knew you would be burned and begged me to spare you the pain. You asked for a merciful death, and I granted it. Blood on my sword would have been proof. He wouldn't have known it was the piglets."

"The sheriff is not a fool," Sir Rowan put in. "And neither am I."

"I intended to let you go, Isodore."

"Oh my, what generosity!"

"And your intentions were so honorable, you couldn't even admit to them! What were you doing to Isodore?"

"He admitted to me," said Isodore. "That's enough for me."

"So he deigns to save you. Why, then, didn't he give you to me?" Sir Rowan asked.

"Because I've had enough of madmen!" snapped Galt.

"Enough. Both of you." Isodore took a deep breath, then another. "Galt, you would lie to the sheriff? You'd have to deceive the archbishop and the council as well."

"I know."

"What if they don't believe you?"

Galt took another look around. "I'll have a corroborator to affirm my story. And they'll want to believe that you have been . . . disposed of. The prince himself suggested as much. He said that the sooner God could pass judgment on you, the better. If I dispose of you, the council can put all of this behind it. They won't have to decide between the duke and the archbishop, which makes it easy for them. Many of them agreed with the prince, so I think they'll be relieved to hear that I took his advice. He'll deny any talk of it, of course, but the council knows."

"What about the archbishop? If you anger him, he'll remove you from the Dragonslayer Corps."

"Have no concern about me. I can serve my uncle. You said you lived in the forest when you were a child. Can you manage it again with some resources? At least for a while?"

Isodore nodded without really thinking. The idea of living away from her persecutors brought her new hope. Galt pointed to the waist bag of provisions that they had left forgotten on the ground when Sir Rowan had suddenly appeared. He had carried in it the salt and pepper for the pig, and the tinder and char cloth for the fire. "That's for you. Take it."

Isodore picked it up. It weighed more than she expected. She felt a bulky, heavy lump inside.

"There are fifty silver pieces in there. It may be enough for two years."

"So you're buying her—"

"Hush, Sir Rowan! You can't give me this, Galt. It's too much. You're already putting yourself at risk."

"It's not all from me. Half is a gift from my uncle. And don't be concerned about our risks."

"Lord Corvin is part of this scheme?" Immediately, she regretted nicknaming him Corvin the Schemer after he tried to intimidate her out of marrying Galt.

"Yes. This was his plan. He devised it when I asked for his help."

"The duke will be furious. Your uncle can't afford to make an enemy of him."

"We've taken measures. He renewed a pact with a powerful ally. It won't be worthwhile for the duke to trouble us over this."

"I hope you're right. Lord Corvin is taking a great risk for me. I didn't thank him when we left, because I thought I would be back."

"He'll understand. Do you believe me now? I never had any intention of executing you. I only wanted the appearance of it."

Isodore nodded.

Galt glanced at Sir Rowan, addressing him with mock formality. "Then if you will excuse me, I must go find my sword and return to camp before the sheriff comes looking."

It was Sir Rowan's turn to stare in silence at the fire. Isodore checked his eyes. No madness. Only contemplation, like the old Sir Rowan who could sit for hours in Father Julian's garden.

Galt held the torch's head in the flames and waited for it to relight. The red glow softened his face. Though he had gloated briefly over Sir Rowan, he looked defeated. When he stood and walked off, the dejected mood was in his posture. He had worked with his uncle for a month to let her live. She had already lost her opportunity to show her gratitude toward Lord Corvin. And she was running out of time with Galt.

Isodore sprang to her feet, headed after Galt, then turned around. "Sir Rowan, I'll be back. Will you be all right?"

He nodded, but it did little to ease her guilt for leaving him injured and alone.

"Can I make you more comfortable somehow?"

"No. You go on. The less I move, the better."

She caught up to Galt as he examined at the trees and the ground, trying to retrace the steps of the fight. He walked from one tree to the next, checking their trunks.

"What are you looking for?"

"The place where he took my sword. It has a fresh cut."

She helped him look, but it wasn't easy to find a single sharp cut among the many trees around.

"It may take long to find your sword. Will the sheriff not be suspicious?"

"We've been long. But he may be too incapacitated to look for me right now, if he's the kind of man we think he is."

"What kind of man is that?"

"The kind who takes to ale, mead, and flattery."

Ale, mead, and flattery. Now Isodore understood what went on in the great hall between the sheriff and Corvin's wife. She was glad she didn't bring it up to Lord Corvin. "Your aunt, she plied him with drinks, didn't she?"

"We had to see how much mead it took and what we could count on when that happened. She's more charming than many people know." A bit of pride showed in Galt's smile. When it faded, he looked as though he still had something on his mind. He also looked like he didn't want to talk about it.

"Why didn't you tell me about this plan?"

"There were several plans, and we didn't know which could work. We weren't certain we could go through with this one until yesterday."

"What happened?"

Galt shone the torchlight on a tree and found the deep, fresh cut where his sword struck, before Sir Rowan disarmed him. From there, Galt turned to look in the direction Sir Rowan had heaved the sword—a discouraging amount of ferns and brush covered the ground.

"He was right here when he tossed it. I didn't hear it hit a tree. So it must have gone somewhere in here." He held his arms out in front of himself, along two imaginary lines that marked a wedge of ground not blocked by trees. "Or there. Or there."

Having identified three sections to cover, Isodore held the torch while he moved the leaves aside to look. His few words masked a palpable anger. With passing time, the urgency to explain her behavior increased.

"Galt, what you said earlier—that I was loyal to the dragon. That wasn't true. I wanted you."

He remained silent, scanning dirt and vegetation instead of looking at her. They searched the first wedge of ground, as far as a man could toss a sword. Galt returned to the spot where the sword was tossed, eyed the next section, and began searching it.

"Galt, did you hear what I said?"

He looked at her with a piercing intensity but ignored her question.

"Please, you must believe me."

"It doesn't matter if I do. You won't be tried. You'll be free."

"It matters to me Galt. I feigned loyalty to him because I had to."

"Are you feigning the child in your womb as well?"

Isodore froze. This was Lord Corvin's insult the evening of the feast, only sharper and deeper. How many times must she bear it?

"I'm sorry," Galt said, but for Isodore it was too late.

"Take me back to the sheriff."

"Isodore —"

"No! Take me back. Turn me over to the duke if ye want. I don't need yer help!" She turned to leave, but he grabbed her wrist. She couldn't wrench herself free.

"Listen—"

"Save yer sympathy! It's meaningless."

"Listen to me," he said. "Then I will listen to you. You wanted to tell me something. I swear, I'll hear you."

She stopped struggling, and he released her.

"I know you had to feign. I did the same. This whole scheme was a lot of feigning. I wanted to take you on a pilgrimage so you could beg forgiveness your sins, but my uncle said no, and he was right. He knew the men in power. What they want wouldn't change because of your repentance. If I had shown any inclination to intervene on your behalf, they wouldn't have let you stay in Laronde. They would never have let us escort you here. We had to feign dispassion toward you. As far they were concerned, there was nothing for us to gain by saving you. You're a pawn to them, and they expect you to be a pawn to us, too. We knew that, and gave them what they expected to see. We even had my mother speak for our family against you, because that gained us their trust, and because nothing we can say would change their minds. So do not think I don't understand about feigning."

He took a breath to rein in his passion, which threatened to overcome him.

"But there is a difference. We didn't carry on our acts in their absence. You were treated hospitably. Isodore, I understand why you had to feign loyalty to the dragon, and then the madman. But your affinity toward him continued after he had died. Your loyalty to him was real. I saw it with my own eyes. You were so distraught beholding his dead body that you didn't even see me standing by your side. I risked everything to rescue you, and you didn't even see me!"

His passion won, filling his voice with rage. "You said you wanted to see his body. I thought you meant Sir Wilfred's! My regiment was mourning his death, and you were mourning the madman's! The beast who would have killed you!"

He took deliberate breaths to calm himself and turned away, leaving her to deal with his disgust.

Isodore could deny nothing. All of it was true. But she had to make him understand somehow. She couldn't let her last ally believe she had chosen the dragon over him. Even though it'd make no difference in their destinies, it would change what he thought of her. And that was vital to her.

He'd calmed down and returned to his search, and she came to him, lowering the torch to ground level where he was looking under the ferns. "I see it," he said and marched through the soft leaves to a stiff bramble. She breathed a sigh of relief. He was still talking to her. She sat down to bring the torch light under the brush's leaves. He slithered in. When he backed out, he sat up and laid the blade across his lap. The sword fight had knocked off most of the blood. What remained was coated with forest debris. Despite that, he gave her a wry smile. A hesitant peace offering.

"Please believe me, Galt. I was loyal to you. I . . . I even tried to learn as much as I could about dragons, so I could tell you. Sir Wilfred was right. They are learning, and they're intelligent. Some of them do understand our language. That's why his Latin worked. You have to carry on his plan. And vary your tactics. They are born with memories from their parents. That's how they know. You said that Sir Gustav speaks Latin. Let him carry on Sir Wilfred's plan. The dragons are dying out. The end is near for them."

He looked at her, astonished, not suspicious.

"And the large dragons, they can't fly far, and they don't live in the mountains. Perhaps you can track them back to their nest and ambush them in their sleep. Perhaps you won't lose so many men.

"I wanted to tell you these things if I ever returned alive. I knew that you believed me dead—at least, you should have—and you would choose another lass to marry. But I wanted just to tell you. I was loyal to you, even though I believed you had moved on. When you came to me, I hadn't expected you, and I had no time to think. But I understand now the immensity of the struggle you had to go through to save me, not only from the dragon but from the trial, too. I swear, I remained loyal to you even though I never expected to see you again."

She waited to see if he'd call her a liar, then gave the confession he'd suspected. "But you're right. I was loyal to the dragon, too. He offered me the only life where I wasn't afraid to be what I am, a sorceress. Yes, he had intended to kill me, but he didn't. And he was the only being who didn't want me dead because of what I was. The only one."

Galt's mind drifted somewhere, perhaps to some other time. She was thankful that he was thinking, not angry or disappointed. It was long before he spoke. "After the dragon burned me," he said, his mind still off somewhere, "I wondered why God had put me in so much pain when I had served him well my whole life.

"I had a lass then. We'd known each other since I'd come to live with my uncle. She was daughter to a close ally of his, and my family adored her. We were betrothed, and she had accepted me without reservation. We were to wed when I became a knight. But when I returned to Auch with my hands and face burned, she could no longer bear to look at me. The mask I wore, I wore for her. I became a Knight of the Crown, but we didn't wed. I released her from her promise, because I couldn't stand to be the object of her fear and revulsion. But then, my scars faded, and I was declared the Knight of God's Miracle."

He huffed a laugh, while two streams of tears inched down his face.

"She came back to me and wished to be my wife again. At last I thought I knew why God had let the dragon burn me. It was to help me see clearly. Aida couldn't bear the way I looked. But you, Isodore, you looked upon the horrible sight of my burns for days, and you wished to see me again before you knew they had healed—before you knew you were talking to me! I believed God had sent you to me. And when the dragon took you, I believed He wanted to see if I had learned my lesson, if I deserved you. Why else would God do that to you? I pleaded with the archbishop to send me to find you and convinced him that it was an affront to God's wish that you were taken, so he agreed. Then we found you alive, against all odds, all logic. I had believed that God had looked after you, the way He looked after me. But now, I don't know what to believe."

Galt looked into her eyes. "I had my suspicions about you. I suspected you engaged in sorcery. Not because of what the madman called you, but because my pain disappeared overnight and my scars faded without a trace. When I woke for the first time without any pain, you asked how I felt, as though you knew. You knew something happened, though you said nothing had. I recalled hearing a voice chanting when I slept that night. I thought I was dreaming. Or that it was angels. Sir Gustav looked through that spellbook. He said it was full of chants. It was you I heard, wasn't it?" She nodded.

"I went against my Lord for you, Isodore. I knew you were a sorceress. But I didn't want you dead. I never have, and never will."

WHEN THEY RETURNED to the fire, Sir Rowan was on his feet. He wasn't by the fire but next to a tree, hiding from the light. He looked at them, his sword in hand. Galt stopped Isodore and took a few steps forward with his own sword. Isodore couldn't tell if the madman was back, for Sir Rowan was in shadow. But he was calm. He raised a finger to his lips and mouthed, "Someone's coming." He pointed across the fire. In the darkness of the forest beyond, deep in the trees, moved the orange glow of another torch.

Galt snuffed out his torch, handed it to Isodore and nudged her toward a tree. She hid behind it while he continued to Sir Rowan's side. Isodore's heart beat faster. The sheriff, she thought.

Galt whispered, "Sir Rowan, do you truly intend to help Isodore?"

"I swear it." Sir Rowan handed Galt his bow, quiver and dagger.

"Then I will take her to hide. Don't let him find us. If it's the sheriff, our plan is compromised. He doesn't know you. Tell him this camp is yours and convince him to leave without looking further. If he seems suspicious, he must be killed."

Sir Rowan wiped the blood from his mouth with his sleeve. "Leave it to me. He won't find you."

Galt took Isodore into the cover of a bush hidden by trees and darkness. They listened to the confrontation at the fire, though the men's voices were muffled by the intervening trees and brush. The newcomer arrived and proceeded to treat Sir Rowan with great suspicion, interrogating him roughly, even drawing his sword. He demanded to know what Sir Rowan was doing so far off the road. Sir Rowan claimed to be a passing vagabond who would clear out in the morning.

"Not just a vagabond," said the newcomer. "I see you were hunting. Have you permission to hunt on this land?"

Sir Rowan responded, but Isodore couldn't hear him over Galt's voice.

"It's not the sheriff," Galt said and headed back to the fire. Isodore followed.

"Galt?" called the newcomer.

"Haron," Galt answered back. Isodore recognized Haron as the guard who glowered at her in camp.

"What has taken so long here?" Haron demanded.

"I had unexpected problems."

Haron cocked his head toward Sir Rowan. "Who is this?"

"He— Nobody."

"What's he doing here?" Haron marched toward Sir Rowan, his sword still in hand.

Sir Rowan whirled his weapon in response.

Galt stepped between them with his own weapon. "He won't give us any trouble."

"How do you know? He could be one of the duke's men, or the archbishop's."

"He isn't. And in any case, he won't survive long. He's taken an arrow and is coughing blood."

Haron took some steps aside to assess Sir Rowan.

"Where's the sheriff?" Galt asked.

"Camp. Resting off his mead. He looked for you, you know, when he saw that you weren't there."

"What happened?"

"I let him try for a while. He was drunk enough to lose his way. I brought him back and said I'd find you for him." Haron continued around Sir Rowan, from several paces away, until he saw the protruding arrow. "Let's put this man out of his misery."

"No," said Galt.

Sir Rowan lowered his sword and cocked his head. "Is this your corroborator, Sir Galt?"

"He is."

"Then he's lucky. Otherwise, I would put him out of my misery."

Haron turned to Galt. "You told him our plan?"

Isodore rushed to Sir Rowan's side. "He has sworn to protect me."

"Has he? Then find someone else. This man won't serve you long."

"We don't have time for this, Haron," Galt said. "Put your sword away. You too, Sir Rowan."

"Sir Rowan, is it?" Haron looked over the disheveled warrior.

"Yes," said Isodore. "He's a Knight of the Cross." She couldn't stand seeing him insulted. "He saved me when I was a child, and I trust him."

Galt picked up his scabbard to stash his sword.

"Where's the blood?" asked Haron. "You're supposed to have blood on that blade."

"I told you. I had some problems. I'll say that I cleaned it."

"No blood and no head. That is a big problem, my friend. I say we cut off this man's head."

"How about we duel, master Haron," Sir Rowan proposed. "The

loser will provide the blood."

"Enough," said Galt. "I have instructions for Isodore before we leave."

Sir Rowan tossed his sword on the ground. "I have a solution for your problem, Sir Galt. And we need not cut off Haron's head for it. He can thank me later." He began to remove his robe, and Isodore helped him, supporting the heavy garment as she slid it off the arrow shaft. "Clean your blade, Sir Galt." He took his robe from Isodore and tossed it to Galt.

Sir Rowan wore not armor. His shirt was soaked red below the wound. He lifted it. The entry wound, mangled in the fight, was dripping fresh blood. Galt wiped both sides of his sword across Sir Rowan's robe then scraped the blade up the red swath of Sir Rowan's back. He gathered enough blood to coat a section of the blade on both sides. As Haron watched, the cocky smirk melted from his face.

LEAVING SIR ROWAN and Haron, Galt took Isodore back to the bush, where he had left the bow and quiver of arrows.

"I'll leave these with you. Do you remember what we taught you at Beardsley's Den?"

Remember was an overstatement, but she nodded, thinking back to her brief archery lesson, given that day solely for amusement.

"I intended to leave these for you to protect yourself. You can also find safety traveling with the woodlanders. They can be friendly, some of them, unlike what many say. Be generous with the silver, but never show how much you have. They have no loyalty to Church or Crown, so you could be safe with them even if they know who you are. Just beware in case the duke offers a reward for you. It's unlikely, though."

They walked slowly back to the fire.

"If the sheriff doesn't believe what Haron and I tell him, he may ask to see your body. He won't bother to search in the dark, so you may stay here, but leave as soon as you can see your way. Restore this area. Make it look like no one was ever here. Go south or southwest, away from the frontier. Don't go east. Haron's brothers are there tonight. They have a slaughtered pig. They'll put it in your old tunic and have their hounds tear it apart. I'll take the sheriff there if he demands to see your body. When we find the remains of the tunic, it'll look like wolves found you first."

"It's risky, Galt. What if he doesn't believe you?"

"He'll have a choice. He can be faulted for letting you die, or for letting you escape. He may be angry, but I am certain he would rather admit that he let me behead you."

So much planning and risks, just to save a peasant's life. So many people involved. Isodore wanted to throw her arms around him but feared it would be misunderstood if Haron happened to see.

"Your corroborator, Haron, he's Aida's brother, is he not?"

"How did you know?"

"He bears a resemblance to Sir Reginald."

"You know Sir Reginald?"

"He accompanied Aida at your dubbing ceremony. Please forgive my curiosity, but she was looking at me that day. I asked Sir Wilfred. He said that their father was Lord Harold, who supported your uncle during his rebellion. Lord Harold is party to this scheme too, isn't he? He's the ally your uncle sought to deter the duke's wrath."

Galt nodded almost imperceptibly.

"Is that why you didn't tell me of this plan? You had to secure Lord Harold's support first."

Galt turned away.

"Were you the price for his support, Galt?"

He looked up at the trees.

"Galt, I know about Aida. She fell very ill when you left to find me. And I know she recovered only recently. That was when your uncle and her father renewed their alliance, wasn't it? She was heartsick. Their pact requires you to marry her, doesn't it?"

Galt's stoicism neared its cracking point.

Isodore let the irony roll softly off her tongue. "You will wed Aida to save me."

"I," he corrected her in the soft tone of a man condemned, "was married yesterday."

BACK AT THE fire, they found Haron and Sir Rowan settled against the log. Haron had somehow cut off the shaft protruding from Sir Rowan's back. Able to turn his back to the log, Sir Rowan positioned himself more comfortably. The young warrior listened, engrossed in Sir Rowan's account of battles in England against William's men, the way Isodore had been as a girl. She was sorry the night couldn't go on longer, but Galt and Haron had to leave.

Galt knelt beside Sir Rowan. The men stared into each other's eyes, absent hostilities. Gradually, their lips curled, subtle but esteemed. The young knight offered his hand, and the old scarred warrior shook it.

"I have misjudged you, Sir Galt."

"I did you no better. Let us forgive each other and think of it no more."

"May the sheriff believe your story and the duke leave your uncle in peace."

"Thank you. Sir Rowan, it will be a long walk before you can find—"

"I will not be a burden to Isodore. I can assure you of that."

If Galt had a response, he decided against it. He nodded, stood, and went to Isodore.

"In time, this argument between the duke and the archbishop may be forgotten. People won't remember what you look like, and it will be safe for you to return under another name. When that day comes, you are welcome wherever I make my home. Thank you for staying by my side when I was in pain and dying. And for the lesson you taught me."

In a long embrace, she recalled when they had stolen away in Laronde, his anger toward some unnamed person. She now understood that she wasn't the subject of that resentment, but having been on the receiving end of his resentment earlier, she could imagine how a young lass might take it. His uncle has said that Galt had little patience for human failings. She wasn't certain it would be wise for her to speak up or how Galt would receive her words, but something compelled her. She looked into his eyes and decided.

"Galt, Aida was young and frightened. That was why she couldn't bear your scars. We all have lessons to learn. Perhaps that was hers. She's a kindhearted lass. I could tell, because Lord Corvin's servants love her. She must treat them well. A highborn lass who treats servants so well must have a kind heart. I think she will make a good wife for you, and I hope she will give you many loving children." Isodore fought back tears to say those words. Galt remained silent as he turned away. She hoped that, in time, he could forgive Aida her rejection and the difficult circumstances that killed—then resurrected—their betrothal.

She didn't expect a farewell from Haron, but he hesitated when Galt walked past. Haron stepped before her and dropped to one knee. He quickly kissed her hand, then rose. She froze when he stepped forward, as if he would kiss her cheek, but he only whispered. "Thank you for those words. My sister is a kindhearted lass. As are you." He turned away before she could respond.

She watched the two young warriors depart with Haron's torch. Galt turned one last time to look at her. "Sir Rowan has sworn to protect you. The two of you will be stronger together. You should help him as much as you can."

True, but an odd thing to say, thought Isodore.

"The less blood he loses, the longer he'll last. In what I left you, you can find some cloth to dress his wound." With that, he turned and walked out of view.

"What is he talking about?" grumbled Sir Rowan. "Haron already cut the arrow. Don't remove the rest of it. That will only unplug the wound."

Isodore agreed, except with his stubborn denial that he was mortally wounded. She didn't think he was losing all that much blood from his back. It was the blood he coughed up that worried her, for it meant he was bleeding inside. But she wasn't a warrior and hadn't seen many men die of battle wounds. Regardless, she found the advice odd.

She opened the pouch Galt left her. Along with the salt, pepper, char cloth, and tinder, she found a tightly tied inner sack. Untying that, she found the silver pieces but no cloth to dress the wound. She felt around the bottom and pulled out a segment of dried shoot attached to a small bulb. She stared at it, her mouth agape.

"What is that?" Sir Rowan asked.

"Something I lost when I was rescued. Asterium."

48

Salvation

Firewood for the healing spell came from the fallen tree they had used for a backrest. Isodore broke off its decaying branches. Sir Rowan wanted to help but spat up more blood each time he exerted himself, so she made him sit still.

"Have you pure water with you? The spell requires exceptionally pure water. Rain would serve, but we don't have time to wait."

"Water from the river is clean. Just take what is clear and running fast. Moving water in the frontier is clean. It's only in settled land that streams sicken."

She chewed the asterium and went to the river to soak it, lighting her way with the torch. At the bottom of the steep bank, she found footprints next to a crushed bush. This was where Galt went to clean his hands after butchering the pig and where he fell off the ledge fighting Sir Rowan. He knew the bank was steep. Why did he retreat here? Had he staged the fall to buy time to turn his hopeless fight around? He was as good a trickster as Sir Rowan. Her pride swelled. His uncle was right. "You'll make a good knight, Galt," she whispered.

Sir Rowan had built up the fire. Isodore started arranging the burning logs into a ring. He stared at the asterium she left on the log like it was a gleaming gem, though he was careful not to touch it.

"You say this is the same spell that saved Sir Galt?"

"Yes."

"It reversed his scars?"

"Yes, but that took months."

"But it worked," he whispered. "It worked. This will cure me!"

His excitement changed the tenor of his speech. She disliked the greedy tone of his voice, the wild look returning to his eyes.

"I'll be free. At last!" His breaths quickened. "Isodore, you will be my salvation! At last, my—"

"No!" Isodore sprang up and backed away, putting the blazing fire between her and the crazed eyes. "No, Sir Rowan. Don't talk like that."

"But you ... you will help me, won't you? You said you would. Please!" He choked through a long series of coughs, spraying dark droplets of blood into the fire. "You must. I beg you." His eyes pleaded with her, their glint of wild greed turning to desperation. He reached out to her.

She couldn't abandon him, not like she had Pyramine. Unable to turn away, she stood there with the fire between them.

"Please don't beg. Don't talk like that. You frighten me."

"I didn't mean to. I'm frightened, too. I don't like what I've become."

"You weren't like this before."

"No. I think it was a potion I bought from a shaman. He said it would fix me, but it failed. It made me so ill. Burned me from within. It scorched my throat and changed my voice. It gave me head pains and made me unpleasant, like you have seen. I tried to reverse it. I tried so many things, but nothing worked. I have changed so much. And none of it is good, Isodore. I am sorry to burden you with my condition. Please forgive me. Please—"

"Stop it! Don't beg. I don't want to see you beg. You were a proud man."

He stared into the fire. "Yes," he said, to himself as much as to her.

"What will you do, if I can't change your desires?"

"You will still save me? Even after what I've become?"

She knew the answer, but she had to think about the reason. "Do you know what the dragon said to me? It said that dragons and sorceresses are the same spirit in different forms, both magical, both persecuted by men. You're persecuted, too, Sir Rowan. Can't you see? They are so close to wiping out the dragons. They burned my parents alive. Yet we are the ones out of God's grace. They see no crime in what they do, only in what we are. Far more men die at the hands of other men than in the teeth of dragons, yet it's the dragons that are evil. It is the sorcerers. I have done no evil. My parents had done no evil. And neither have you. But they've destroyed us! They destroyed you, Sir Rowan. And I can't bear to see you a destroyed man. I don't know why you let them do this to you, why you beat yourself senseless. You've committed no crime in my eyes."

"It is a crime against God," he whispered.

"On the eve of our conversion, my mother asked why we should worship a God who hates us so. My father said that he believed God was good. But he didn't believe what the Christians said about God. Sir Rowan, I don't believe what they say either. The dragon knew I was a sorceress but didn't harm me, even when I gave him reason to. The dragon—God's retribution for the sins of men—refused to harm me! Men burned my parents because of a dragon! And yet the instrument of God's retribution refused to harm me."

Sir Rowan stared into the fire. She could see him struggling, not with his madness but with her logic.

"Was it God who told you what a crime is and what it isn't? No, it was men. Men as fallible as you or I. If you think what you did was a crime, then you must also believe my sorcery is a crime. I am through being treated like a criminal."

Sir Rowan bowed his head. She didn't know if his silence meant he agreed with her or if he sought only to appease her.

"The spell will take all night. I will cast it, but on one condition. You must decide between being with me and trying to change yourself. As long as you hurt no one, it's enough for me. But I will not watch you beat yourself and call yourself vile. And I will not have you drink poison that burns you up inside. You must swear to abandon your attempts to change yourself, othwise leave me. You have until morning to decide."

She began the spell. Throughout the night, she chanted and replenished the fire ring, held the asterium against his wounds and felt the warm pulse traveling down her arms. He watched her intensely at first, then a calm came over him, carrying him farther and farther away from what was happening. When she felt confident he would bleed no further, she removed the remaining bit of arrow so he could lie on his back.

She chanted until first light. Though still horribly scarred, he had visibly changed. Confident and in control of his mind, he moved with purpose as they cleaned and restored the site.

He had lost weight but not strength. He removed his robe and ran back and forth to the river, soaking up water in the robe to wring over the fire pit. He carried steaming logs in the dripping garment to dispose of in the river.

Isodore dispersed the unburned wood. He swept away bits of ash left in the dirt and gathered material from nearby, meticulously covering what they had disturbed. They spoke little, but it pleased Isodore to see the vigor in his steps. He was growing on her again, as he had done so many years ago. Her heart softened, though she was determined to reject him if he couldn't accept her demand.

When finished, they took a final scan of the area.

"That should do," he said.

"Yes."

He turned and met her eyes. She was anxious to leave before someone showed up, but she waited. His eyes turned steely and his lips closed as a breath sighed out of him. He straightened, drew his sword, looking at the blade with reverence before handing it to her. He lowered himself to one knee and put an elbow on his other knee, bowing.

Suddenly uncomfortable, she wanted him to stop. She wanted to give back his sword and tell him he didn't have to supplicate himself, but she let him proceed, knowing the importance his actions had for him.

"Isodore," he spoke to her feet, "I accept your condition and will devote myself to you completely. My sword and my life are yours. By your wish, I vow not to beat or try to change myself. I offer to serve you above all others and do as you command. I will be your knight and protector. If you accept me, then command me to rise and give the sword back to me. If not, toss it aside."

She wanted him to stop the formality. He had been her hero, her protector and advocate, and she had dreamed of his love. What she had gained instead was his obedience and his service.

"Rise, Sir Rowan," she said, and gave him his sword without ceremony.

THEY HEADED SOUTH until well away from the frontier, then west, away from Auch.

SURVIVAL IN THE forest far from roads and villages proved to be a new ordeal. Sir Rowan might have been a superior swordsman, but he was neither the archer nor tracker that Galt was. He lost much time and too many arrows for the few pheasants he killed. Pigs and deer escaped, taking more arrows with them. Were it not for encounters with woodlander clans willing to trade food and arrows for coins, they would've had to return to civilization. He vowed that Isodore wouldn't die of hunger, but they were hungry most of the time.

The desolation dreams visited with enough regularity that she no longer feared them. She began to anticipate and even take comfort in them. She would dive off the cliff knowing she'd be taken into the air. She took pleasure in riding the wind down the mountain. When she heard Galt's raven calls, she neither worried nor struggled in Pyramine's claws. She simply repeated her well-wishes and flew on.

Sir Rowan merrily learned as much as he could to survive like a woodlander. He learned how to find edible leaves and berries. He hunted with the woodlanders, acquiring their tracking skills. He even learned from the women how to braid a rope from the available plants. He traded for a large deerskin cloak to keep the cold and rain away. He set up and packed away their shelter and carried their worldly possessions on his shoulders so she had little on hers.

The woodlanders whom they encountered were wary of strangers, but not hostile. They spoke a variation of Gascon that was difficult for Isodore to understand, but Sir Rowan spoke for the both of them. It was just as well. He kept Isodore out of sight when he could, in case the duke sent men to inquire about her. He learned their dialect. After his endless attempts, they warmed to him, just as Isodore had warmed to Pyramine after the hours talking to him. Sir Rowan thrived on meeting and learning about new people. What he learned helped him befriend the next group.

Despite his improved communication, he never found the words to explain the peculiar relationship between him and Isodore. It was easier to let them believe she was his wife. For all practical purposes, she was.

His scars faded through the months of autumn. He planned to head west, then up the coast to the Duchy of Bordeaux, where he was certain he could find work for himself and eventually a home for them. But it was the wrong season for long journeys through the woods. Each time a storm rolled in, they stopped at the next place they could use as a shelter.

Because all the good shelters were occupied by woodlanders, they often ended up in their company. In early winter, they were sheltering with a four-family clan, during what turned out to be a series of major storms. They sheltered under a rocky overhang that protected them from the driving rain of a northwest wind. Pinned down by the storms, Sir Rowan and Isodore's food supply dwindled quickly. They hadn't prepared as well as the woodlanders, a mistake Sir Rowan swore never to make again. Because of winter, the clans were unwilling to sell their limited food reserves.

The storms brought relentless driving rain. Forest creatures went into hiding and searching for them would be a cold, wet, miserable experience with little chance of profit. The storm abated at times, unfortunately at night, when hunting was impossible. There were birds to be had in meadows and rivers, but no one dared to go there in foul weather. Dragons dropped out of the low clouds and fog, giving their prey little time to flee. The sound of enormous wings over the canopy was a regular reminder of this danger.

Isodore's pregnancy was now visible. She became hungrier than usual, craving fresh meat. Guilt gnawed at Sir Rowan. He insisted that she take his meager food portion, a thin strip of salted meat. "It's on the verge of spoiling anyway. I'll bring you fresh meat, as soon as I can," he promised her. She felt guilty for worrying him.

The clan lit a fire. After days of wet weather, it took the work of many. Men gathered firewood and children found dry tinder. A few women set up a frame to hold up a blanket as a rain and wind shelter. Others took turns building and fanning the fire. It took all afternoon, but they had a big, warm bonfire.

Luko, one of the clansmen, eyed Isodore as he worked on the fire. He often kept an eye on them, but he wasn't hostile. Sir Rowan considered him a new friend and on occasions, received furtive donations of food from Luko. Luko called on them to join the clan at the bonfire. Sir Rowan declined, but Isodore told him to go. She knew that he would stay with her any time she wished, but she also knew that the company of cheery people invigorated him.

"Go, Sir Rowan. You're only keeping me from sleep and yourself from good company."

He carried her tired body in his arms to a protected overhang that was vacated by the exodus to the fire. He laid her down, unwrapped the deerskin cloak she was using to keep rain off her, draped his thick robe over her, then placed the cloak on top of that.

"I'm not cold."

"You will be by morning."

"It's not raining on me. At least take the cloak if you're going to the fire. I command you."

He kissed her forehead, tucked her into the cloak, and left. She threw it off and watched the group around the big fire for a while. The men gathered in a cluster on one side, and the women and children filled the remaining space. Their faces glowed warmly in the firelight. Unusually, Sir Rowan was listening instead of talking, probably asking for hunting wisdom again.

Despite the hunger, everyone at the fire was in good spirits. She supposed clan folk were used to cycles of feast and hunger. She had endured hungrier times before, but her pregnancy made it difficult to cope. How long could she starve before it killed the child in her womb?

Hunger accompanied her to sleep, and into her dream. Pyramine carried her down to the foothills, but not over Galt's party. They went a different route, meandering in the sky, lifted by one invisible updraft to glide to the next. She scanned the meadows and rivers below, in search of food. They skimmed the treetops toward a river, then dropped suddenly down to the bank, where a fawn was drinking. The startled animal jumped. But it wasn't fast enough. She reached down and snatched it.

SHE WOKE WITH Sir Rowan next to her, both of them wrapped in the deerskin cloak. It was hard to tell how late it was, for thick, low clouds kept the sky dark, even at midday. A heavy mist raced through the forest on a stiff, bone-chilling wind. Sir Rowan sat with her, watching the clan start their day, while a gale howled and ravaged the treetops.

Matriarchs parceled out minuscule meals to their respective clans. Sir Rowan and Isodore had nothing left, so they sat listening to their stomachs growl. Her mouth watered. He scanned the sky. Wind-driven rain came and went, and came and went, with little break. Thunder rolled through the region. Sir Rowan stood.

"I can't stand this," he declared to whomever would listen. "I'm leaving to hunt."

"You'll find nothing," said Moru, one of the patriarchs and the clan's leader. "You'll only get hungrier. Save your strength until the storms end. They're not forever. It'll be very easy when the rain stops. The animals will be hungry. They'll be up, searching for food." The clan folk nodded.

"Only dragons hunt in this weather, Rowan," Luko said. Nevertheless, he joined Sir Rowan, the only clan member to do so.

Trying to conserve her energy, Isodore fell in and out of sleep. She finally found herself flying with Pyramine over that very forest in search of food. They went along the river, looking for the fawn drinking at the banks. When they found it, he turned away to take an approach over the trees, to muffle the sound of his wings. Then he dove down and she snatched the young creature. They headed back to Dragon's Ridge.

Something struck her. She fell. She held tight to the fawn, but something else wrenched it away.

She heard shouting, angry and threatening. She struggled to get up. A mob of people had her surrounded. The clan. She could understand only parts of what they shouted.

"How dare you?" a woman said.

"We treated you as friends," said another, pushing her down.

"Kick her out!" said a third. "I knew we shouldn't have trusted her."

They were slapping her.

"Stand back! Get away from her!" roared a familiar voice.

Sir Rowan burst through the circle and yanked her up by the arm. But he was angry too, more than any of them. "What were you doing?" he demanded, his breath in her face.

Confused, she answered as well as she could understand it. "I was . . . I was just hungry."

The woodlanders erupted.

Sir Rowan gave her arm a shake. "What?" He was incredulous. His grip tightened.

"You're hurting me!"

"That is a child!"

She looked where he pointed. A matronly woman had her arms wrapped around a crying toddler. By the faces around her, full of anger and disbelief, she must have done something terrible.

"I'm sorry. I thought I was . . . I was dreaming!"

"I won't tolerate this, Rowan," said Moru. "We've welcomed you and helped you. She betrayed us."

"No. She wasn't herself. She was dreaming."

"She said she was hungry. We're all hungry. But we don't take one another's children. What kind of person does that?"

The clan chimed in agreement, their voices still pitched with anger.

"She's confused. Can't you see?" Sir Rowan held her close.

Moru looked at the three other patriarchs, all shaking their heads. "No. She must go. You can stay, but she must go."

Sir Rowan looked at the crowd. He didn't look ready to give in, but Isodore didn't want him to try any further. "I want to go, Sir Rowan."

He looked at her, shaking. He released her and put his arm around her waist, a gesture to assure her and everyone else that she was still under his protection. "Very well," he told Moru. "We will go. We'll gather our belongings and go. She'll be right with me until then. No one lays a hand on her."

"No, you go now!" said one of the patriarchs, and the group affirmed his sentiment. "She tried to take my grandchild," he said to Moru. "We will take their bow and arrows as a price."

Moru gave Sir Rowan a grim look. He was the clan's chief, but it was run by consensus.

"She was only dreaming. She has never hurt a child and she never will. She's sorry, can't you tell? Look at her." He gave them a moment to consider. A figure from the back of the crowd dashed away.

"Just let us get our belongings and we'll never return again." Sir Rowan said. He had his sword, but they were surrounded by a dozen angry men.

Isodore didn't want a fight. "Let's go."

"Look, Moru," Sir Rowan explained. "She was dreaming and confused. She wasn't trying to hide. We all stopped her. No harm was— Do not draw that weapon! I don't want bloodshed." Sir Rowan held a finger up in the direction of a man working his way through the second row of the crowd. The man slowly took his hand off his dagger. He wasn't the only clan member armed.

Sir Rowan tried to reason with Moru, but the crowd had made up its mind. The clan's men shifted to block Sir Rowan's path back to the shelter. Isodore squeezed his arm tight.

"All right, all right. We'll go. We won't make trouble. Give us room, and no one will get hurt."

"Give them room," ordered Moru.

Sir Rowan backed away, guiding Isodore along as he kept himself between her and the mob. With distance and more trees between them and the angry clan, Isodore felt safer but guilty over what she had caused.

Sir Rowan watched their backs, until they could no longer see the clan through the trees. "I'll go back for our belongings tonight," he whispered as they continued weaving through the forest. Isodore protested, but he dismissed her. "You'll have to stay in hiding."

"How will you know where they keep our belongings? They'll hide everything, expecting you to try."

"I'll find it somehow. I might have to take one of them hostage."

That was not reassuring. "Do you have the silver?"

He tapped the bag around his belt. "I never take it off."

"We'll find a town and purchase another bow."

"We don't have time. You're hungry and weak. You need food. Your child needs food!"

He was right, and his tone left no room for argument. They were many days from the frontier, and anyone with a bow to sell might be able to recognize her.

Sir Rowan moved closer to her and nudged her behind a tree. "Hide. We're being followed."

She flattened her back against the tree. He crawled away in the undergrowth and had a look back, slowly drawing out his sword. "He has our bow," he whispered to her. "And our bag."

Sir Rowan peered through the gaps of the thicket. Slowly, a smile appeared on his face, and he stood, shaking his head in disbelief. He sheathed the sword. It was Luko, and he had their quiver of arrows as well. Sir Rowan awaited Luko's approach with a longing smile and eyes that teared up. The two men greeted each other with a long embrace.

When they separated, Luko acknowledged Isodore with a friendly nod. She got the feeling that Luko knew she wasn't Sir Rowan's wife. "It's difficult enough for you already without these," he said, dropping the bag and quiver. Then he took the bow and heavy cloak off his shoulders to hand over.

"We're grateful for this, Luko." Sir Rowan said.

"Yes, very much," Isodore agreed. "I'm so sorry for causing trouble. I truly didn't know what I was doing. I was dreaming."

Luko waved it off. "That was my nephew you took. He'll be fine. It was our shouting that frightened him, more than what you did. I thought you were playing a game with him."

Isodore breathed more easily.

"Your clan will be angry with you for helping us. Let us repay you." She glanced at Sir Rowan, who opened his robe to undo the coin pouch.

Luko put a hand on Sir Rowan's. "No, my friend. You owe me nothing. It was a simple mistake, and they tried to take advantage of it. I'm only righting a wrong." With his hand still on Sir Rowan's, Luko turned to Isodore and awaited her response. She nodded. Sir Rowan wound the pouch back around his belt.

Luko smiled. "They won't be angry at me for long. They need me."

Isodore noticed his eyes which, she realized, looked very much like Sir Rowan's.

"I'm sorry we have to part," said Sir Rowan.

"I know. I wish you a safe journey, wherever it leads. The clan will forget eventually. Perhaps we'll meet again. I shall welcome the sight of you, should that day come."

The two men looked at each other, and Isodore saw why their eyes looked so alike. They sparkled. She suddenly felt like an intruder on something private, and turned away. She unfurled the cloak, refolded it neatly, opened the sack of their worldly possession, added the cloak and closed it. When she finished, Luko was backing away, bidding both of them farewell.

She and her knight were on their own again. Her heart felt oddly glad and empty at the same time.

49

Between Man and Beast

Rain and wind persisted through the day and into night. Sir Rowan shook water off pine boughs to make their bedding on the soaked earth. He slung the deerskin cloak over a rope pulled taut between two trees, and crawled in with Isodore. The two squeezed together, breathing each other's scent mixed with the musty, rain-soaked soil. Barrages of raindrops drowned out the rumblings from their stomachs.

In her dream, it was summer and dry, a beautiful evening under a star-sprinkled, indigo sky. A breeze swept up from the valley, teasing her hair and fluttering her clothing, caressing her neck. She stepped to the precipice and dove, pushing off with her toes. She plunged toward the graveyard of discarded bones. Wind rushed up to her. Faster and faster she went. This time, Pyramine's claws carry her away. Instead, she skimmed down the rampart on her wide-stretched forelimbs. She sped over familiar boulders as easily as she would lean against a post, making use of the extra lift the ground offered, knowing that the stiff cushion of air between it and her wings would never let her crash.

With enough speed, she lifted clear of the terrain, swooped up and began driving forward with unhurried, efficient wing beats. Dusk turned into day. Familiar hunger pangs led her to meadows, lakes, and streams in her territory. Then, she wandered toward the territory of men.

Below, two riders, a boy and a man, disappeared into the woods in the direction of a minor, marshy, pine-enclosed lake. She waited, loitering low and downwind, where the sound of her wing wouldn't carry to them. Then she rose just enough to see them letting their horses drink at the lake. She dropped to the treetops and glided in. She came at them from behind, along the shoreline.

The man was too big, and he wore a heavy mail coat. As she came in, he turned, but too late to save the boy, who she snatched off the saddle. With incredible reflex, the man grabbed her ankle. Attached to his horse by the stirrups, he jerked her backward. The horse lost balance and fell as its rider was pulled away, but the damage was done. She had lost critical speed and couldn't ascend. She dropped the boy to save herself. The man held on, screaming a curse. Still unable to halt her descent, she tried to land on the shore, but when his dangling body struck the water, the lake tugged them both down. She crashed into the shallows. Water flew up in drops and sheets. Her wings sliced under the lake's surface.

Freed from his grip, she got her legs under herself in the waist-high water. Her wing membranes felt heavy as she dragged them back to her side. She heard him splashing behind her, and looked, just as he stabbed her back. He leaned over into his sword, pushing with a two-handed grip, his teeth clenched and eyes truculent. She disregarded the pain to shake him off, suffering more as he wrenched the weapon sideways out of her. She sent flames and spit over her back at him. Already soaked, he didn't burn. He dropped into the water to douse the spit. When he rose, she thrashed her tail to knock him back down. He fled.

As soon as she got her wings and folded her weight onto her knuckles, she turned and launched herself into the pursuit. Water drops flew off her wings. Anger and vengeance masked her pain. The man was strong, moving fast with heavy armor and his legs in the water. He could have escaped, had he not gone to retrieve the boy from the lake. They were splashing across the soggy shore when she raced toward them. She could reach them in time but would immediately crash into the trees. She had to pounce instead of snatch. She folded her wings and slammed feet first into him as he shoved the boy aside. She crushed the man under her, then skidded to a stop between two trees.

A pain ripped through her core. She pushed herself off him and looked down at her belly. Sticking out of it was the hilt of his sword, its pommel broken.

The boy, wet, bleeding, and frightened but safely out of her reach, called out, but the only responses from the twisted body were moans and spasms. She had her revenge and gave the man his. Shaking, she backed up and saw a face she would never forget. The warrior who nearly killed her stared back. He had an olive complexion, a swirling mane of black hair, and twilight blue eyes. Pyramine.

His face startled her awake.

She lifted herself up to her elbows. That was as high as she could rise before hitting the cloak. Rain drops plopped loudly. The sky was low and misty. A touch of dawn showed through the leaves above. She wished she had not awoken, because she was still hungry.

She looked down at the man lying unconscious next to her. He had thick wavy hair too. A big man. With some asterium, he could keep her fed for much of winter. She could save the child in her womb.

She studied the scars on his face. When she recognized the man beneath them, something gripped her deep inside, tightening until she retched. She retched over and over but produced only a cruel reminder that she had nothing in her belly.

A cold fear washed over her as she realized: this had happened before. She had snatched that woodlander child, thinking he was a fawn. And now, Sir Rowan, not a man or a friend, but sustenance.

She suppressed her cry with a hand over her mouth. She was turning into a dragon. That was what the dreams foretold!

Her heart raced. Frightened and lonely, she searched for what to do. There was no point in praying. She had to get away from him before it happened again. The next time she woke, it could be his blood on her chin and his flesh in her throat.

She turned onto her hands and knees and backed out of the shelter. She took the bow and arrows, leaving Sir Rowan with everything else. She didn't know where to go or what to do, but she knew she could no longer be with men, whether friend or foe. With a second for a mute farewell, she turned and walked into the mist.

THE WOODS WERE dark and unfamiliar. Dense canopy and low wintry sky allowed little light onto the forest floor. It was so dull, gray, and uniform all around that midday passed without her knowing. She couldn't tell north from south, but something compelled her toward one direction.

She wandered forth, despite the gloom around her, despite the weather. Her wet tunic clung tight. Its heavy skirt dragged through the continuous fern undergrowth. At times, she thought someone was following her. She would run when she was afraid, and walk when she was tired. Her heart pounded in her chest. Her hair matted against her head and back. Steam blew from her mouth with every breath and rose from her clothing. She had long stopped sweeping the rivulets of rain from her face, letting the world do what it would with her, and spare her further encounters with men.

The air was still. For the first time in weeks, wind ceased before nightfall. The animals should be out while there was light enough to hunt. She nocked an arrow and walked slowly, searching.

Forest fauna was active, but she had trouble getting close to any creature before it saw her and bounded off, took flight or scurried out of sight. Late in the day, she spotted several deer through the trees at a distance. She raised the bow and approached as slowly as patience allowed her, looking for a line through the trees, taking care not to move when her prey looked up. Before she was close enough, several wolves stalked in. The deer bounded away. She loosed the arrow, but its flimsy flight ended nowhere near the target.

From the undergrowth ahead of the deer, a circle of wolves appeared and closed in. One of the oncoming wolves knocked a doe to the ground. She pushed herself back up, but too late. The attackers were upon her, each taking a leg in its jaws. As the wolves worked on the doe, those who flushed her into the trap trotted in to share in the bounty.

Isodore watched the doe's legs, kicking up through the converged mob of attackers. Soon, the hoofed leg was lifeless, moving only to the tugs of savage teeth.

She approached the pack with another arrow nocked, hungry enough to steal. She pulled on the bowstring as hard as she could, to give the arrow deadly speed, but could only draw it part way before her trembling hand prevented a good aim. She was too weak. She'd have to get closer.

"Let me," said a low voice behind her.

Sir Rowan lowered the bag of their worldly possessions and held out his hands. Without thinking, she gave him her weapon. His familiar face melted away the dreary, gray forest. He took the quiver belt from her, buckled it around his waist and gave her his sword. "Stay by me. If they come, let them taste steel."

She took her place by his side, gripping the sword in both hands. She would eat at last or become a meal herself. They advanced, step by soft step, toward the frenzied pack. In the mad rush to feed, the pack ignored the approaching thieves. At fifteen paces, Sir Rowan drew the string smoothly to his ear. His arrow plunged into a wolf's shoulder. It yelped and fell back, limping in a circular path before cowering away. The others stopped, and before they could discern where the attack came from, another arrow struck another wolf, sending it whimpering away. Sir Rowan nocked another. "You'd better run!" he shouted to them.

The pack backed away and spread out, facing the spoilers of their feast. Muzzles drew into menacing snarls as the wolves encircled the humans. Some threatened to charge Sir Rowan while others tested Isodore. She jumped when they began their strange barks. The fright put strength back in her arms, reminding her what she must do, should they come close. Sir Rowan continued toward the carcass, and she followed. He made threatening roars and put his next arrow into the boldest wolf. On Isodore's side, one wolf danced close to her. She swung. The animal caught the blade in its mouth, with a crack of steel on teeth. The wolf turned and squealed. She swung at the next wolf, but it had already started its retreat. The line of wolves loosened.

Sir Rowan became noisy, yelling and stomping his feet, waving the bow in the air. The pack's tails lowered. The wolves' lips came down over their teeth.

Sir Rowan and Isodore made it to the carcass. The next arrow planted itself in the ground, next to one lucky creature. The wolves eyed it and sniffed at it. They seemed to understand. They continued to harass, but from a safe distance.

"Can you butcher it?" Sir Rowan asked, keeping the arrow trained on the pack.

"Yes."

"Take the dagger. Cut off a hind leg. That's all we'll take. Leave the rest."

The wolves had started the job for her. She sawed through hide and muscle and hacked through cartilage and ligaments, and pried apart the hip and leg. Blood coated her hands and wrists. When the deer leg was hers, she and Sir Rowan backed away. "Thank you," he nodded ironically to the pack. "We shall be on our way." The wolves reconstituted the feeding mob. They were as hungry as the humans and deer.

Isodore waited for Sir Rowan to set wet wood alight, then for the meat to cook, the smell of roasting deer intensifying her hunger. She would have taken a bite of the raw meat were it not for Pyramine's unpleasant experience. It was nearly dark when some meat was ready. They ate, respecting the mutual silence between them. Enough food remained to keep them fed until they could kill again, providing a sense of security after weeks of hunger.

They rinsed their hands and he warmed his over the flames.

"How did you find me?"

"Find you? Hah! I never lost you. Don't you remember my time in England?"

She nodded.

"I didn't evade William's men by sleeping through movements in the night. And you are far easier to track than the animals. Now, tell me. Why did you leave?"

She didn't know how to explain. She fell into a daze thinking about what was happening to her.

He added, "I let you go so I could see what you'd do. Your behavior has been . . . unusual."

"I woke up," she began, unsure what she would say. "I was hungry. I . . . was so hungry, I thought I would kill you. And eat you."

He raised an eyebrow but didn't laugh. "Well. My apology for failing to provide for you. But I assure you, you will be better fed with me alive than dead." He motioned to what was left of the meat. "Luko told me of a village. It's long abandoned, of course, but there are orchards and gardens that still produce in the fall. With our strength back, we can reach it in a day or two."

"You don't understand."

"I understand that there's more to your troubles than hunger."

"I'm going mad."

"I've been mad. What better way is there to understand madness?"

"I . . . I think I'm becoming a dragon." The tears that gathered behind her eyes spilled out. She held her face in her hands.

"How can that be?"

She recounted the events on Dragon's Ridge. From Pyramine's wish to have a mate to her plan to betray him once he became a man, and in that, the spell to create a man from a dragon. She told him of the spellbook, of the choices she faced, and her ultimate decisions.

"Something went wrong with that spell, horribly wrong. He became a man, but not fully a man. He didn't know how. In his mind, he was still a dragon. Perhaps he could have learned to be a man, but there was something else. He was strong. He tore a wolf in two. He took a sword in his belly, and out his back, but he still fought. He fended off a dozen dragonslayers and killed some before the regiment knights cut him down. It took three knights! He suffered wounds up and down his body, but he kept fighting. It was because of how the spell worked. One part was supposed to break down the dragon, and another healed him into a human form. I'm not certain I did the first part well, but I may have left part of the dragon in him.

I made some changes, too. I gave him my blood, because I didn't want him to kill another man. I think, because of that, my blood was in him when he became a man. I don't know if that was proper for the spell. I couldn't read the Latin in the spellbook. I used the Gascon translation some people had added, but it was incomplete. What if there were warnings I didn't heed because they were in the Latin instructions? What if I unwittingly changed the spell?"

Sir Rowan frowned deeply. "Even if you did, how could that turn you into a dragon?"

"Do you know who the father of my child is?"

"The man who had been your captor. The dragon."

"The man who was not quite a man. He was still part dragon because of my incompetence."

"And lying with such a man could turn you into a dragon?"

"That isn't all. After giving him my blood, I cast a healing spell on myself. I believe that my blood came back to me in his seed, tainted by his dragon-ness, and was healed back into me. The healing spell continues for months after it's cast. That's why your scars are still fading."

Sir Rowan thought in silence.

"I've been dreaming that I'm a dragon. It happens more and more. Almost every night. Then I wake up believing I am one. Last night, I dreamed I was Pyramine, the dragon who captured me. I killed a knight. But I hadn't yet eaten him. When I woke with you next to me, I thought you were that knight. I thought I could feed on you for the winter. Feed on you!" She covered her face in her hands, unable to do anything else with an idea that was simultaneously laughable and terrifying.

Sir Rowan considered her for a moment then shook his head. "I don't think you are quite that mad."

"The woodlanders do. And they're right. I abducted that child because I thought he was a fawn. You can't trust me when you're sleeping. Even you can't stop a beast who lies next to you."

They studied each other for a sober moment. Isodore tried to think of reasons to remain with him, but she kept seeing the human leg Pyramine once offered her.

"It's an omen. I will become a dragon. I am already . . . not entirely a woman."

"That makes no sense."

"It's sorcery."

Sir Rowan drew his sword and gave her the handle. "Take it." When she didn't move, he repeated forcefully. She did. He rested the point in the notch at the base of his throat. "There. Can you truly do it?" He closed his eyes, spread out his arms and turned his face to the sky.

"This is ridiculous," said Isodore and dropped the sword into his lap.

"Exactly. You can't—"

"Because I've been fed! If I should go hungry again—"

"Then I shall have to make certain you stay well fed."

"A task you have failed at for weeks." She didn't mean to chastise him, only to remind him how close she had come to killing him. His overconfidence was irritating.

He returned the sword to its scabbard. "I am a warrior, my dear lass. And a warrior must expect death, should he fail in his task. Sometimes, even if he doesn't fail. I accepted that long ago. The only thing that has changed is I am now bound to protect you, to die for you, if need be. My life is yours. If you must kill me in order to survive," he looked into her eyes with his characteristic smirk, "then that is exactly what I want you to do."

"Your death would be futile. I couldn't go on knowing I'd taken your life."

He laughed. "You're making my work difficult."

"Then don't do it! Stop being my knight. I relieve you of your duty."

"Isodore—"

"No! Don't talk to me that way. This is not a laughing matter. I don't want the taste of your blood in my mouth. You've no idea what's happening to me. I am not human!" She bit her lip and looked around, but there was no help or comfort. She felt the end was near and had no wish to prolong it.

"I'm leaving," she said in tears. "And don't follow me. You're no longer my knight. I don't want you."

"Isodore, please."

He took a step toward her, and she ran.

He yelled after her. "If you release me from my vows, then I'm no longer bound to do what you command. I will follow you!"

She stopped and looked back. He hadn't moved, but there was no doubt he would do what he said. She cried out, "Why?"

He looked so alone. "If you leave, I fear I will go mad again."

She frowned. "Mad? You're no longer mad. The spell cured you.""No. It wasn't the spell. It was you."

She studied him to be certain he wasn't jesting. Everything from the look in his eyes to his posture told her he was dead serious, frightfully serious. He appeared lost and afraid, though he tried to remain composed. His hands shook and his lips quivered.

"I wanted the spell to cure me, of course, but I could still feel it. It has been with me since I was a boy, a seed that would grow into an unholy lust and drive me eventually to madness. For the past seven years, I've tried to kill it, but the best that I could do was destroy myself so it couldn't have me.

"Your spell made me strong again, in mind and body. It undid the poison I had drunk and restored me to the way I was." He lowered and shook his head. "It didn't change me. I still desire men. I will not try to change. That was my vow to you. But even after the spell, I desperately wanted to. It wasn't until I traveled with you that I truly felt the burden lift."

"How could that be? For me to do what the spell failed to?"

"That was what I've been trying to understand. I saw it when we met Luko. He was like me, but not a fugitive, not a wretch. He wasn't despised by his people, or by himself. He didn't believe he was flawed. The children loved him. His family loved him. He was important to them and to his clan. He had a purpose. I realized then why my burden had lifted. It was because I gave myself the responsibility for your well-being. You are my family and my purpose, Isodore. You accepted me and said I wasn't flawed.

"For years, I was consumed with changing myself, righting myself, preparing myself for God's judgment. I cared about no one but me, as you saw when I showed myself to you and Sir Galt. Though I'd heard what you had gone through, it didn't occur to me to help you. I thought only of what you could do for me. It was shameful. Yet when Sir Galt demanded to know what I was doing to you in the forest, you protected me. You hid my shame. I am forever in your debt for showing me compassion when I least deserved it."

Isodore had not known her words had affected him so much, words she had all but forgotten she'd spoken.

"I'm no longer so blind, Isodore. In the past two months, I have felt more alive than I had anytime in my years as a fugitive. Looking after you has been the most honorable thing I have done with my life. I can face God's judgment, instead of hide from Him. I want nothing more than to serve you. Since you were a girl, you have loved me, even though I hated what I was. You have given me a second chance. As long as I remain your knight, I am ready to give you everything I have. Everything, gladly."

Isodore took a moment to understand all that he said. She supposed he, too, was contemplating it. She didn't know what to do.

"I ask much of you, Isodore. No less than my life and my sanity. I am not afraid to die. We both know how that is, don't we? There are things worse than death. Should I die at your hands, I will have died for something worthwhile. Let me have that. Then I can face God. If I die a wretch, I will be unredeemable."

How could she refuse? What choice was there for either of them? "I suppose," she thought aloud, "we shall live or die together."

He came to her and put his hand on her shoulder. "We shall live, Isodore," he said with a determination that gave her much needed comfort in spite of herself.

HE PROTECTED HER from man, beast, and as the weeks wore on, herself. The dragon dreams took over her nights and spilled into her days. She sometimes wandered aimlessly, not knowing what was real and what was a dream, unsure of who or what she was, something between man and beast. The clan folk they encountered glared at her when she looked at them. She found them fascinating, but her attention was returned with suspicion, and eventually anger. Sir Rowan explained and apologized and stood between her and agitated woodlanders. Afterwards, he thought it best that the two of them be on their own. They never approached another clan.

With her sanity lost in unaccountable visions, she would cry herself to sleep and wake up, wrapped in his arms. He asked about the dreams. She told him of flying over Dragon's Ridge, Gascony and al-Andalus, fighting with other dragons, killing deer, boars, wolves, bears, and men. "I see a woman standing by a fire in the night or on Dragon's Ridge, and I know that's me. When I push off the cliff, I don't do it with my legs. I use my arms, the way dragons do."

"I don't know what it means," he said, "but I can tell you, you appear no more a dragon now than you did when you were twelve."

"You can't see it, because I'm changing inside. We've passed into winter, and I have yet to feel cold."

He nodded, and they shared a look acknowledging that he had been sleeping closer to her since the weather had turned. There was no mistaking that action for desire, but it had created a bond somewhere between the avuncular one of her youth and the false marriage they had presented to those they met.

Looking into her eyes, he said, "I will remain with you, even if you wake up covered in scales."

The idea of a man traveling with a dragon reminded her of a hope she once had, one that had died as savagely as Pyramine had.

"When I was a captive, I thought I could be an emissary between dragons and men, because I understood both sides. Since then, I've seen how much Galt hated dragons. If a good man can hate so much, I don't know if men and dragons can ever get along."

"You would have said the same of the Normans, two hundred years ago. The English have been warring with them for so long, they can't remember not being enemies. The Franks suffered their raids too. Everyone hated the Normans. But now, Auch has Norman knights fighting dragons for Gascony. Anything can happen."

She wished she had his optimism, but he had enough for them both.

While Sir Rowan hunted, Isodore searched the forest's

undergrowth. Edible berries had been picked clean, but she was after something far more valuable. Asterium. She searched near meadows and river banks, where her parents often searched. Staying too long as the faint sounds of wings rose, thinking she was a dragon and had nothing to fear, she was nearly taken by another beast. When she told Sir Rowan, he made her promise not to go to the edge of the woods without him.

She turned her search to gaps in the forest canopy created by the death of a tree, knowing the elusive flora could be right before her, for, when they mature, they took the form of plants surrounding them, gathering all their preternatural botany into seeds for the next generation. One day she moved aside fern leaves to see a single homely stalk. She dug it up, ducked back into the forest, and sat down to rest, relieved to have it in hand. It provided her with some assurance, should her pregnancy, labor, or birth go awry out here in the damp woods of winter without the help of a midwife.

She cleaned it, stashed it in her clothing, and awaited Sir Rowan's return.

She dozed off and woke recalling a dream in which she had found an asterium stalk in that very forest. She immediately searched herself and was relieved that the plant she had found was real. She held it tightly and leaned back, gazing at the column of hazy light dropping through the forest canopy. How did she know to look for the asterium around the penumbra of this gap? This wasn't the kind of place her parents had taught her to look. And when had she learned that asterium changed upon reaching maturity?

Her memory was vivid but confused, like when she looked into the distance and saw two images that didn't quite line up. In one, it was her hand moving aside the fern leaves. In the other, it was a single black wing claw.

It was Pyramine in her dream, searching for the asterium. It had been him all along. It was he who looked at her by the fire and he who saw her on the ledge. He who showed her, from beyond, where to look for asterium. She wasn't turning into a dragon. The dragon was in her!

When Sir Rowan returned with an adolescent boar, she

gleefully told him, "I am not turning into a dragon! I have Pyramine's memories."

"Woodness! What do you mean?"

"He told me that a dragon's offspring inherits the memories of its parents. I'm carrying his offspring, and somehow, the memories are coming to me. Perhaps it was my blood. Or how I improvised the spell. Something did change, but perhaps not as I had thought."

"Well! This makes me very happy," he said, though perhaps he was referring to her mood rather than her form.

Isodore began piecing together the memories seeping into her mind, trying to make sense of them. She could discover them the same way she found her lost memories, tugging on some present strand until something new popped into her mind. It didn't always work, but the last two months of Pyramine's life were the easiest to find. The day he fled back to Dragon's Ridge with her, he was tight with rage and fear, angry for having been so easily downed and nearly breaking a wing in a nest of men, fighting the urge to kill her for the trick of the apron. He wanted her alive to confirm his suspicion that she had used sorcery against him, for it was rare to find a sorcerer. But she was too heavy for the long flight, and he struggled to stay aloft. It took a monumental effort not to drop her and save himself. When he finally landed in the meadow, he was too tired for an interrogation. As his suspicion grew over the coming days, so did his admiration for her spirit.

In the inherited memories, she was Pyramine, his parents, grandparents, and an ancestry that fanned into the past and stopped in multiple lives. They all merged, so it was hard to know who was who, but she recalled the memories as if she had been there. She flew high over men sent to kill her, banking away from their arrow volleys before bombarding them with fireballs. She narrowly dodged a giant spear launched at her as she subdued a horse, forewarned by the noise of the hidden ballista. She looked down on a blue dragon whose wings strained against tethers while dragonslayers ran lances into his chest. She ripped to pieces men of the Deleret Expedition as they screamed for their God. She passed over al-Andalus, eyeing men who dared her to descend. Rode to the heavens on winds of thunderstorms. Struggled against a ferocious brown bear. Dropped down on wolves. Killed countless deer. Watched a dragonet hatch. And in the farthest reaches of the newfound memories, she made love by the light of a hearth and the scent of thyme, in a humble cottage.

Pyramine became a part of her. She knew, more intimately than she thought possible, the creature who had robbed her of her future. She could probe his darkest secrets, his shame, whether he wanted her to know or not. That would be just revenge for the pain he had caused.

He had his fears and regrets, his envy toward stronger kin and a hatred for lazy dragons that rivaled his hatred for men. He had experienced contentment and bliss indistinguishable from her own. But she found no lies to rival the deception she had practiced on him. Nothing to diminish the guilt of her betrayal. Indeed, there was but one startling secret spilled from the vault of his memories: his plan for her, had she refused to be his mate. It was a memory she wished she could forget, for it brought her too much pain.

The memories dribbled forth. Sometimes, they flowed. They occupied her mind like novel knowledge tended to, crowding out other needs. She often felt the dragon's desires as her own. Some days, she was so much a dragon that she forgot about her companion.

When she no longer wished to go to the Duchy of Bordeaux, he asked why. Receiving no answer, he dutifully followed, saying only, "You know, you're heading southeast."

Each time the clouds cleared, the sky seemed brighter than the previous. Snow receded from Dragon's Ridge. Lofty winter cloaks melted into rushing rapids. The whites of heaven gave way to darker tones of earth.

She entered Dragon's Ridge through the long valley where she had first come as a captive. She had no trouble finding her way under the forest canopy, using the mountains occasionally visible along the way. She turned into the narrower and steeper valley and ascended. The route, etched into Pyramine's memory from generations of residence, felt like a well-worn path to her, her journey like a homecoming. She crossed the stream where she had once washed the puncture wound in her chest. Rushing snowmelt soaked her and knocked her off balance, but she still felt no cold.

Out of the thin forest at the tree line, an unobstructed view of the high ridges filled her eyes and heart as though they were her own garden. A feral desire to rejoin the jagged peaks quickened in her. She didn't understand until that moment that although she couldn't return to Savelle, Dorune, or even the roads of her runaway years, she was not without a home. The dragon within was a child of this wilderness, for whom those peaks were home. She didn't come here only to avoid men. She came to Dragon's Ridge to nest.

"This is dragon territory, Isodore," said her companion. "Are you certain you wish to leave the woods?" She continued without a word. He glanced toward the heavens, whispered a prayer, and followed.

Though her womb and breasts were full, they urged her on rather than holding her back. Unladen, Isodore didn't slow down over the rugged terrain. Sir Rowan had a sword and a quiver swinging from his belts, the bow across his back, their worldly belongings over one shoulder, full water skins and the hindquarter of a deer over the other. At times, she left him in the distance.

She climbed out of the three-sided chasm and over the ridge at the notch. At the base of the ramparts lay the remains of the beast who had tried to steal her, a dry, skeletal carcass blackening a crater gouged out by a dragon's remnant heat as it slowly turned into ash.

"Isodore!" called her companion. "Dragon above!" He dropped the bag from his shoulder and was shedding other items while scrambling over the boulders. Overhead, a pair of dark leathery wings glided down toward her.

It wasn't one of the oversized and lazy lowland dragons. She recognized the red dragon, her old neighbor. She hailed him, trusting that he had not come to attack her. He circled, studying her.

Her companion rushed forward, sword in hand, screaming shrill human sounds. The red dragon banked toward him.

"No!" shouted Isodore. "He's mine!"

The red dragon landed on the ridge, between Sir Rowan and herself. Sharp teeth bared a greedy smile.

"He is mine, Rogadin! He serves me. Do not take what is mine!"

Rogadin bent his neck and examined her. "The sorceress. Pyramine's sorceress."

"No. I am Pyramine. I am a dragon." She slammed a fist into her chest. "I saved your life. True dragons do not steal, Rogadin. Do not dishonor yourself now."

"You are . . . the sorceress."

"I am Pyramine. The sorceress and I are one."

Sir Rowan came, panting, and stood between her and the red dragon, brandishing his sword.

Rogadin disregarded him and studied Isodore with a sinister look. "How did you save my life?"

"I attacked the men with wing rippers. I broke their circle to let you escape."

Sir Rowan watched in disbelief as Isodore talked to the red dragon. Rogadin bared his teeth at him. He swung his weapon. The dragon pulled back his head just beyond the sword's reach, then returned it, daring him to try again. Isodore recognized Rogadin's smirk.

"You will not harm him. He protects me from men."

"He is a man. Shall I throw him off the cliff? He will make you a good meal."

"Leave us."

Rogadin eyed her belly and sneered. "You, Pyramine, are with child. I warned you not to play with sorcery." He leaped into the air and departed with a lingering look back.

Sir Rowan turned to her. "What was that?"

"A neighbor."

"Why didn't it attack?"

"I told him you were mine."

"Indeed. But in what language?"

They stared at each other, while she recalled the words she'd just spoken and recognized the dragon tongue.

They continued on, though there was no way to reach the nest

from below or come in from the sides, as she knew well. She
followed the narrow spine that ran above the nest until she reached
Pyramine's old perch. She looked down to the ledge, the precipice,
and the valley so far below that it might as well not be there. The
fear of airy heights was a vague memory. Wind tossed her hair and
ruffled her clothing. She closed her eyes and lifted her chin, feeling
light despite the state of her womb.

Her companion had lagged behind again, slowed whenever he
had to haul up their sack of worldly possessions by the rope, for he
couldn't climb with his hands full. Without waiting for him, Isodore
lowered herself down the steep wall until she hung against it by her
fingers. Her feet dangled where her head once had been when she
stood at the apex of the slab trying to climb to freedom. Just as her
companion called out, "Isodore, no!" she let go and slid down, her
hands cradling her belly. She landed on the apex.

Her companion called frantically, slamming his fist into the
rocks, but she ignored him and scrambled down the slab to the
ledge. Snowmelt had left a puddle where there once was mud.

Inside the familiar cave, under a pile of rocks that she had built
at the end of summer, she found a morsel of meat and a few figs, still
moist and fresh, preserved by a spell she had learned with nothing
more than the writings in a book. Smiling, she picked up a fig and
took a bite. It had been so long since she'd had fresh fruit. Her
companion peered in as she savored her last bite of the months-old
food. She smiled at the visitor to her home.

The nesting instinct that had never found her when she was in
the forest at last swept into her. She rearranged the firewood that
she had stashed in the cave to keep out of the rain. He wedged their
worldly belongings by the little hole at the end of the cave to reduce
the wind. They saved the wood for cooking and in case a healing
spell was needed. Her body heat and the deerskin cloak were
enough to keep them warm at night.

While her companion paced and kept watch for dragons, she
gazed out over the mountains and Gascony, lost in recollection and
contemplation. At night, she guarded the rocky peaks and
wandered through memories of stormy skies, gliding across blazing

sunsets on wings of bliss.

Though it had been many months, the tortured scars had not all disappeared for Sir Rowan as they had for Galt and herself. Perhaps her parents could have explained why, but Isodore didn't know. An orphan lost so much more than the protection of her parents. She missed the wisdom they could have imparted to her and the assurance that she deserved to live. It had taken her so long to learn.

Sir Rowan didn't mind the remaining scars. "A man should never forget the mistakes he's made," he said.

She cherished moments with him. When she felt like a dragon, she needed no one. But when she felt like a woman, his companionship and his sheltering embrace made all the difference. He was all she had.

A spring blizzard blew in and covered the mountainside, but she remained warm and kept Sir Rowan warm, the two of them wrapped together in his robe and deerskin cloak. Cramps came and went. They brought her to her feet, pacing, then to her knees, on all fours, then back again to her feet. Over the course of a day, they grew more intense, painful, and frequent. She prepared the asterium, in case something went badly. Sir Rowan kept a small fire burning by the cave entrance and he knew what he had to do if a healing spell was needed.

When the surging cramps told her the child's arrival was imminent, she knelt down on the folded cloak. She thought she was going to die, torn open by her own child. The cramps' discomfort was now something to long for, as she shook in agony. She had heard women speak of childbirth's excruciating pain, but those same women also laughed about it. She couldn't see herself ever laughing again. She was afraid for her life.

Sir Rowan knew nothing about bringing life into the world, but he was endlessly tolerant of her. She gave up being a proper lass. Warm fluid leaked continually down her legs, tinged with blood. Pushing the baby out of her, she grunted and screamed and clawed at his robe.

She was on one knee, bracing against the mountainside to stay upright, in agony and pushing, when she felt the child pass through her. The pain, which had mounted seemingly without end, suddenly dropped, the pressure and strain on her body relieved. She collapsed against the wall, then onto the cloak.

She caught her breath, staring up at the dim cave. There was no other sound. No cry of a newborn. She held her breath, listening. Sir Rowan had his back turned to her, folding his robe around a bundle.

"Show me the child," she said.

"Lie still. You need rest."

"I can rest with my child."

She sat up and pulled on his shirt. He turned, showing her a scarred face devoid of color. She took the bundle from his hands and opened it. Then she screamed and, at last, felt the cold of the blizzard.

50

The Secret of Dragon's Ridge

Long after the dragonslayers killed their last beast and disbanded, the warm skulls in the halls of the duke and the archbishop turned to ash, then to legend. Stories were told and reshaped by successive generations, until no one knew for sure from whence the dragons had come, or if they had ever been.

A millennium since Isodore's scream pierced the air around the nest, Dragon's Ridge, its name forgotten, once again lay asleep under winter's white cloak. A young mountaineer picked his way along a sharp spine atop two steep mountainsides, leaving deep footprints in the snow. Flurry-laced breezes predicted by the day's forecast turned stormy by afternoon. Snow blew sideways, wind howled and gusts threatened to lift him off his feet and toss him off the route. The ridge before him began to disappear into a thickening blizzard.

He scanned the mountainside for options. There was a ledge with a sizable snowbank some thirty feet below the ridge he just passed. He backtracked and pulled a rope from his pack. He cleared snow around a rock firm enough to anchor the rope. He radioed his change of plans, then rappelled down blind. On the ledge, in the relentless wind, he assembled his avalanche shovel and dug a low tunnel into the snowbank for shelter. As he finished, the shovel suddenly broke through, and the mountaineer found himself staring into a narrow, tomb-like space.

He crawled inside, removed his sunglasses, and waited for his eyes to adjust to the darkness. Hoarfrost coated the walls. Snow piled at the entrance and tapered toward the far end of the tall, narrow chamber. He cleared room for a place to sit and found the bones of a deer's leg, frozen stiff. Someone had occupied that cave before. He dug around to see what else was there.

Buried in the snow was an oblong object tucked against the inward-leaning wall. He freed it from the grip of a frozen puddle and brushed away the snow. It was gray and soot-stained, leathery but seamless, firm but not hard. Some kind of casing. He wondered who left it behind, and why. As he examined the oblong object in his hands, its frosty shell melted. It was emitting heat. He held it close to fend off the cold and became attached to its warmth and mystery.

Unable to part with the strange object, he took it with him when he left. Months later, the casing cracked. A trembling creature in midnight-blue scales pushed its way out to stretch open a pair of wet membranous wings. It upended his life, as children often do.

WHEN SHE WAS little, Anna Suzanne rode to school on the back of her dad's motorcycle. At night, she dreamed she was a dragon.

She had a small frame, black hair, an olive complexion, and hazel eyes like a forest on fire. It wasn't just their color but the way they looked out at the world, holding it in wonder and disbelief, then retreating—the way one might look at a scary, alien world.

She slept on a mattress of ballistic fabric shell that her grandmother had sewn around a thick sheet of fiberglass insulation. Her room had a tile floor, an old steel folding chair and a salvaged, indestructible steel desk. Aluminum flashing covered the walls, ceiling, window and doors. Fire extinguishers hung on the walls and corners. The smoke alarm was disabled but there was an array of ceiling vents to draw out smoke.

The arrangement was necessitated by the little blue dragonet whom Anna Suzanne had never met but who sometimes visited while she slept. Over the years, the walls became discolored in places by excessive heat, torn by claws and patched over with more flashing. The ballistic fabric bore a few accidental punctures and melted in places but remained functional. As Anna grew, so did the tears in the aluminum sheets.

DESMOND SAT ON the floor, against the wall, next to his daughter, recalling the years when she fit into his arms. These days, she could race him up a mountain trail. He gently soothed the warm, fading scales on her back. The scales sank away, leaving a pattern of dark blue lines etched into her skin. Before the lines faded, her skin peeled off in a single sheet that wrapped around her little body from shoulders to knees. He continued soothing her through the gown of dragon molting.

Curled up next to Desmond, Anna Suzanne frowned and sniffed the charred air. She lifted her head to scan the floor, then squeezed her eyes shut. "Not again."

"Everything's fine." Desmond patted her. "Just a bit of a rough night. That's all."

She pushed herself up and sat against the wall, taking in the carnage, grim though unfazed. Her backpack, just weeks old, lay ripped and spilling papers and books, covered in the fire extinguisher's white powder. Her dad had dry clothes on, but his discarded jeans and T-shirt lay soaked on the floor, like her mattress. The folding chair was tipped over, lying next to an empty fire extinguisher. New rips gaped open in the aluminum siding. A torn, scorched and soggy jacket. A punctured, melted cell phone. A study lamp hanging upside down from the desk. A burned wall calendar under soot-stained flashing, coated in white foam.

"She bit my phone," observed Anna.

"It fell down and rebooted. I think the sound bothered her."

"That set her off?"

"No. A couple of motorcycles, real loud. Then she skulked around and knocked the phone off the desk."

Anna sighed and rested her chin on her knees. "She's quick to anger these days, isn't she?"

"She does act out a lot. I wonder sometimes if I can still calm her down. What would I do if she won't calm down?"

"She'll calm down eventually. She gets tired. She needs to sleep. And she won't attack you. Even when she's upset."

Upset. An intelligent girl, his daughter had always been precise with language. He was relieved that she didn't use the word he would have used: angry. She had always maintained that Annasuka, whose dragon-tongue name meant "Spirit of Anna Suzanne," would not intentionally hurt a family member.

The tense, eighty-pound Annasuka was far from the vulnerable creature who emerged from the egg fourteen years before. She was wild in most ways and human in some. Her eyes often showed understanding when she looked at him. Her growls came close to words at times. Desmond had learned to trust his daughter. Anna had rarely been wrong about the dragon who shared her body.

"What do you think is bothering her? What's new?"

Anna closed her eyes and thought for a long, long time. Her dad waited. The dragon's visits left traces, like dreams, but recalling dreams took patience. Finally she nodded. "I think she's lonely. No, not lonely. Homesick."

"We've been pretty consistent with taking her to the mountains. The next new moon is a week and a half away."

"Mountains are better than this room, but she's old enough now to know the difference between our mountains and hers. She's looked for places she remembers, and she can't find them. She knows she's not home. Not her ancestral home."

"You think she might want to see Dragon's Ridge?"

Anna perked up. "Yes. Me, as well!"

"Just for a visit. I can't leave you there."

"I thought we couldn't go far at all, because of her."

Desmond sighed. "Well, maybe it's time to try. She's obviously unhappy and it's not right to do that to her. Do you think you can make her aware that we really need her to keep away while we're traveling? Or at least stay to calm when she visits?"

"I can try."

Desmond took his daughter by both shoulders. "Annasuka will

not survive if she's discovered. She can't be on her own. She needs to know that, or I'll lose both of you. But if she can just calm down, give us a chance, I'll take her there. I have to figure out how to do it, but I will take her there."

It worked.

THE FOLLOWING SUMMER, Desmond and Anna Suzanne traveled to Gascony. He wanted first to reacquaint her with the land in her memory. But the towns, vineyards, orchards and fields, which he found charmingly old world, all looked disappointingly modern to her. The endless forests were gone. Only the jagged ridge to the south remained unchanged. When she looked at it, her hazel eyes didn't retreat. He tried to warn her that what she found on this pilgrimage might not be exactly what she hoped to find.

"Okay," was all she said.

At a road's end, father and daughter hoisted their backpacks under the morning sky. She led the way up the mountain, guided by thousand-year-old memories. She followed Pyramine's worn flight path while searching for Isodore and Sir Rowan's route back to the nest. They rose higher and higher, out of the trees and into the barren realm. When they crossed the notch on the ridge that came down from above the nest, she peered into the next valley and squeezed her dad's arm. She pointed to an indistinct spot in the ramparts below. "That's where the striped-green dragoness died."

She scrambled ahead. "I know which way they went!"

Desmond knew, too, for it was the way he had come down years ago, the only feasible route to the ledge where he'd sought shelter. But this was her homecoming, so he followed. The air was fresh, and a breeze cooled their hardworking bodies. They scrambled along the ridge's precarious spine to a point above Pyramine's nest. While he anchored a rope, Anna laid out their climbing harnesses. Thirty feet below was Pyramine's ledge. They rappelled down the sheer wall.

On firm ground, Anna at last allowed herself to be swept away by the view that she could vividly recall long before she knew the place was real. Scattered clouds drifted in the distance under the blue sky. She looked around the valley before them, from the jagged granite rim to the sweeping sides and grassy floor, from heaven to earth. Too distracted for anything else, she held on to Desmond for balance while he helped her out of the harness. A breeze from below teased her hair. Her eyes teared up when she gazed northward, through a narrow window showing the distant lowland. "She used to look there and think of Galt and her orphans."

Anna sat and rested against the slab. Desmond sat beside her, watching waves of memories rise and subside in her eyes. She went through bursts of storytelling as she recalled one thing after another. It was mostly about Pyramine, because he'd spent his life there. "I think this helps me understand Pyramine as an individual," she said. She had never felt as connected with that side of her heritage as she did to her human side. Most of her recollection of her father came through Annasuka.

Gradually, she turned gloomy. Desmond recognized the familiar tears building inside his daughter. He was prepared for it, but there was nothing he could do. Anna had often wondered why her mother had abandoned her. Her memory didn't include Isodore's labor. Perhaps Isodore hadn't survived childbirth; so many women didn't back then. Perhaps another dragon came and snatched her. Perhaps her carelessness toward the dangers of Dragon's Ridge turned suicidal. Perhaps she simply didn't want a beast for a child.

Anna always defended rather than blamed her mother, at least outwardly. After telling her dad of Isodore's encounters with dragons, she had said, "She was terrified of dragons. They're terrible creatures. Imagine your own child turning on you, or using your knowledge to kill your friends."

Desmond had reassured her that he loved the little blue dragonet the moment it pushed out of the egg, and he loved her from the first time she woke in the dragonet's place. But his love and assurance could never replace the mother whom she simultaneously admired, worried over, and resented.

Anna was afraid of what they might find in the cave, so he

entered first. It looked different from how it had that stormy winter's day. No longer covered in snow and frost, the rocky floor showed soot stains where the egg had lain. A film of soot darkened the slanted wall over the site. The bones of the deer leg remained exactly where he had left them. It was still fresh.

"Oh," said Anna. "That was their food supply when they left the forest. She used a preservation spell to keep it from spoiling." Then she added, "That's how the egg lasted so long. If you hadn't come, I'd still be here all these years."

He checked an impulse to take her into his arms. She was tough. Isodore would not be disappointed in her offspring.

Anna examined the bones. "It's picked clean. Could be they ran out of food and starved to death."

She'd always talked of Isodore's fate with detachment, the fate of a distant ancestor, but Desmond knew better. If Isodore had died in the cave, Anna would have forgiven her. But for years, uncertainty had denied the girl that closure.

Anna fished a flat stone out of her backpack. The size of her hand, it was rounded and smooth from years at the bottom of a mountain stream that Annasuka was partial to. One side of the stone had a crude portrait of a girl and her mother, holding hands. On the other, the words "Happy Mother's Day," in the unsteady brushstrokes of a second grader. She leaned the stone against the soot-stained wall.

In the portrait, Isodore had wavy black hair, wore a tunic, and didn't smile. Anna knew her mother's appearance only from memories Pyramine passed down. It was more than Isodore had known of her own appearance. Anna could recall what it was like to be Isodore, to think and feel like Isodore, but not how it felt to sit with her and breathe her scent, to look into her eyes, hold her hand, and feel her warmth. Anna knew Isodore's love for the child growing in her womb. It frustrated her that she didn't know what Isodore was thinking, leaving that child alone on a mountain. Or rather, she didn't like the obvious reason her mother did it.

Anna dropped to the floor, folded her arms over her knees, and cried. Desmond sat and wrapped an arm around her.

"So she didn't die in childbirth," Anna said, wiping away tears with a sleeve. "She lived long enough to cast the spell on the egg. She didn't want to kill me, but she didn't want me to hatch either."

Desmond wished there was more he could do. They had dinner out on the ledge, in silence, with the panoramic view. He knew his daughter would grow past the disappointment that the person she admired so much had abandoned her. She was strong. She had little appetite, but she ate a big meal so that Annasuka would have no desire to hunt that night.

She broke the meditative silence to ask, "Do you ever wonder what your life would be like if you hadn't lost your parents?"

Desmond gave her a warm smile, sensing her desire to talk. "A little. It's more that they may wonder how I turned out, had they lived. Sometimes I imagine them talking with your grandma and exchanging stories. I think I'd like to meet Isodore."

"Me too." Her eyes welled up and overflowed. She bit her lip, looking out over the dimming valley.

"You're mad at her, aren't you? It's understandable, you know."

"I'm angry, but I think that's probably not fair to her."

"I think you have a choice: go crazy trying to figure out why she left you, or believe she did the best she could in a tough spot, and cried her heart out because she couldn't do better. I can't imagine that she took what she did lightly. Why not give her the benefit of the doubt? The worst that can happen is that you won't know if you're right."

Anna nodded and sat with her thoughts. Desmond tried to reconstruct what Isodore did after birthing the egg, but came up empty. "What do you think your life would've been like with her?"

"I don't think she or Sir Rowan could have handled Annasuka like you can. And they were in no position to do it."

Desmond agreed.

"Do you think it was just a coincidence that you found me?"

"Do you mean, was it fate?"

"Maybe she cast a spell to bring you to the cave."

"It would be a pretty picky spell, waiting a thousand years to snag someone."

"Maybe she wanted an orphan. She was an orphan. I'm an orphan. You're one. Maybe she wanted to keep me in a clan of orphans so I'd be accepted."

"Does she know of such a spell?"

"No, but . . . maybe her ghost brought that storm down, right as you came by." She acknowledged the wishful thinking with a shy smile.

"Hmm. I'm pretty sure it was a spell."

"Really?"

"Definitely. I know of no spell greater than the love of a child."

Anna finished her meal with that smile. After dinner, she brushed her teeth and went into the cave to set up their bedding. Desmond cleaned up in the last light of day.

Out of the cave came a trembling voice. "Dad, there's something here."

He rushed in. Anna Suzanne was kneeling by the soot stain, hunched low on his sleeping pad. She had changed into her dragon-skin gown and removed her watch and hair tie. Two tattered army blankets wrapped around her shoulders. She had her headlamp in hand, moving its light across the film on the leaning slab. "There's something here!" She brought the headlamp to the wall. Its tight illumination was almost blinding, but it brought out the marks: faint lines in the time-worn soot, dull and faded, barely discernible in the granite texture. Some straight and some curved.

Letters. Words.

"What language is that?" he whispered, not wanting to break the spell of her discovery.

"Gascon," she whispered back. "Old Gascon."

"Can you read it?"

"Yes," she replied with fierce pride. "My mother was literate. And so am I."

Her light moved across the writing. She whispered each syllable, each word, each phrase. Over and over she struggled. Her little body shook. But her determination didn't flag. She closed her eyes to help the recall. He gave her his hand to hold, and she squeezed it hard. Tears rolled down her cheeks. She put the headlamp down, covered her mouth and collapsed into his arms, crying. He held her and stroked her hair until she lifted her head from his chest.

"It's a message from my mother." Anna wiped away her tears. She shined the light back on the writing to read aloud. "It says, 'My child. I am sorry I must leave you. I cannot bear to bring a dragon into this world to kill men or be slaughtered by them. When dragons and men can exist in peace, I shall come for you. Please forgive me.'"

Desmond apologized for taking so long to bring her here, but Anna was too elated to hear him. "She planned to come back for me! And if she had a plan, it meant that she intended to live! It meant that she looked to a future."

A future that included her child.

Whatever the reason Isodore had for not coming back, her daughter was satisfied. Curious, but no longer resentful. Perhaps the dragons hadn't died out during Isodore's lifetime. Perhaps she and Sir Rowan were killed during their escape. What mattered was that the woman Anna understood intimately and admired deeply hadn't abandoned her. She shook, unable to contain her joy. She held on to her dad and brought the light back onto the writing, looking at it like it was the most beautiful thing she'd ever seen.

Prospects for the past changed irrevocably. Father and daughter stayed up devising ways for Isodore and Sir Rowan to escape the ledge and avoid the dragons. They dreamed up long happy lives for the two misfits. They filled the dreams with fine details until Anna Suzanne lay down with a contented smile and drifted to sleep.

Desmond lay awake, waiting for Annasuka. When the girl and the dragon momentarily occupied the same body, Annasuka would know about the message that took a thousand years to be received. He had a message in response. He shined his lamp at the thin film of soot above his head and ran his fingers over the words, searching for the spirit of the woman who had made them. He whispered to Isodore. "I will take care of her. Don't you worry. No harm will come to her. Let your spirit rest."

Anna Suzanne's blankets rose between Desmond and the tall,

triangular cave entrance. He reached over and pulled it off. A ragged silhouette remained. It swept its neck over the wall, examining the cave, then bent toward the doorway. Under a moonless sky, a dragon emerged on Dragon's Ridge for the first time in an eon.

Desmond followed, wrapped in warm clothes. He left his headlamp off to avoid attracting attention from the hut across the valley.

Annasuka stretched out a twenty-foot wingspan in the night breeze, then put her knuckles down. She gazed north, where, in a narrow window between two peaks, Gascony's sparse lights twinkled. She scanned the starlit crags and cast her eyes toward the heavens. She looked up at the man standing by her side, and he knew that Anna had passed on the news.

He knelt down next to the dragon. "Don't go into the lowlands. And stay away from the lights . . . as always." Annasuka didn't need the advice, but he couldn't send his child into the night without some words to remind her that he cared.

The dragon crouched to the precipice, leaned out and pushed off as she fell, disappearing into the void below. Desmond held his breath, dreading the sound of a sickening crash. The long whoosh of wind stretched on, fading toward the center of the valley. Faint wing beats circled back along the valley's rim, louder and louder. Annasuka hailed him with a rumbling breath. A veil of blue flames engulfed her head, streaking orange fringe along the glossy scales of her neck. She banked and swept across the ledge, touching him with a swirl of wind from her wing tip. Then the Spirit of Anna Suzanne turned and spun into the starry sky.

Author's Notes

Dragon's Ridge is a fantasy story set in historical Gascony, France. Some call this historical fantasy. While the medieval world and the Pyrénées are real, and dragons and sorcery are clearly fantasy, other elements may not be so obvious. I would like to clarify which elements are real and which are fictional.

In developing the setting for this book, I relied on the work of historians and medieval scholars, in forms accessible to the general public. With a broad understanding based on these reliable sources, I searched for further details on the Web. I judged unverified information by how well it fit the information I had from the reliable sources. Where there are gaps in historical knowledge, or in my own knowledge, I used my rational imagination. I take full responsibility for any errors.

The Middle Ages are sometimes called the Dark Ages partly because of the scarcity of surviving historical records. While the missing information was problematic, it gave me some room to make up details that fit my story. The fictional history in chapter 2, Marauders, was that Gascony responded to attacks from the Franks, Asturians, and Muslims by expanding south. While the conflicts did occur, I imagined Gascony's response.

Was there room to the south? It wasn't clear to me how much of Gascony had been settled under Roman rule, how much was abandoned upon the collapse of the Western Roman Empire, and how much of it was resettled. What seemed clear was that enough wild woodland remained in the medieval world to support an eleventh-century population boom. Therefore, it seems reasonable to assume that there was unsettled arable land three centuries earlier, when Gascony expanded southward.

The small villages, towns, and domains in this story are fictitious, as are their religious and feudal leaders, but the culture and larger setting are authentic to the best of my knowledge. All of the major historical events in the story actually happened, except for those linked to dragons. Auch was the seat of an archdiocese.

The archbishops and dukes I named were real people, but I took creative license with their characters so that they fit into the story. Specific interactions between these leaders are fictional, but they fit a common pattern. Religious and feudal leaders relied on each other to support and validate their authorities while competing with each other for the greater power.

The woodlanders are a product of my imagination. While there may have been people who preferred nomadic forest life over feudal governance, I know of no evidence of their existence.

Acknowledgments

Writing is a solo endeavor, but a book project requires many hands, eyes, and minds. I would like to acknowledge these individuals for their encouragement, assistance, and contributions to Dragon's Ridge.

Long before I put the first word down on paper, my children, Annam and Trian, listened to this story on a walk to the farmers' market, back when the story less dark and tragic. Encouraging words from Ariadne Moisiades, the manuscript's first reader, gave me the confidence to think I could write a novel others might want to read. My Tri-Valley Writers Club (TVWC) critique group members Patricia Boyle, Stephanie Bolanos, Elena Manzo, and Keith Ahrbeck gave tons of feedback and encouragement and accompanied me on the long journey through the first two drafts. Nadine Horner gave me the brilliant idea that evolved to define the character of Lord Corvin. JoDee Hunt educated me on horses. TVWC beta readers Lani Longshore and Jordan Bernal gave invaluable feedback. Cheryl Magellan created the cover art from little more than my sterile descriptions and amateur sketches, a process that required a lot of patience. My wife, Lynn Gunney, tolerated my absence from the family as I retreated to my desk to write, took time away from her usual books to read and edit an earlier version of the manuscript, allowed me to interrupt her countless times with questions about grammar, and told me to rewrite the last chapter yet again. Some critiques I was most resistant to turned out to be among the best. For these, I humbly thank Lani Longshore and Lynn Gunney.

My editors Kelly Urgan and Siobhan Gallagher were terrific to work with, educating me on the confusing rules of English grammar as they suggested changes. Their kind words relieved the nagging fears of this first-time author. One of the most pleasant surprises in this endeavor was working with such wonderful, patient professionals. Paula Chinick of Russian Hill Press guided me through the self-publishing process, and I would have been lost without her help.

Though I've received great advice in the writing of this book, the final decisions were all mine. Any errors are mine alone.

About the Author

Brian Thao Nguyen Gunney was born in Vietnam and escaped to the U.S. as a refugee in 1975. After briefly considering a creative writing major, he earned a Ph.D. in aerospace engineering and scientific computing from the University of Michigan. He works in scientific computer simulations. He drew on his scientific training, outdoor experience, and interest in history to bring dragons into the real world in his first novel, *Dragon's Ridge.* Brian writes, hikes, runs, and bikes in Northern California, where he lives with his wife and two teenage children.

CPSIA information can be obtained
at www.ICGtesting.com
Printed in the USA
BVHW032147221121
622316BV00005B/150

9 781735 176390